His Chosen Bride

"Why did you marry me? Why not declare the contract broken?"

"Because I wanted ye."

The words were simple enough, but made absolutely no sense to Annabel. He'd wanted her? Why? She was untrained and unskilled. Why on earth would he want her to be his wife?

"Why?" Without her meaning to, the word slipped from her lips, sounding as bewildered as she felt. Much to her amazement his chest vibrated against her back with amusement, then his hands slid up from her waist, and Annabel glanced down with shock as his large, rough fingers slid over and cupped her breasts through the cloth covering them.

"Because I wanted ye," he repeated by her ear.

By Lynsay Sands

LYNSAY SANDS

AN
English Bride
IN
Scotland

AVON

An Imprint of HarperCollinsPublishers

This is a work of fiction. Names, characters, places, and incidents are products of the author's imagination or are used fictitiously and are not to be construed as real. Any resemblance to actual events, locales, organizations, or persons, living or dead, is entirely coincidental.

AVON BOOKS
An Imprint of HarperCollins*Publishers*
10 East 53rd Street
New York, New York 10022–5299

Copyright © 2013 by Lynsay Sands
Excerpt from *One Lucky Vampire* copyright © 2013 by Lynsay Sands
ISBN 978-0-06-196311-7
www.avonromance.com

First Avon Books mass market printing: July 2013

Avon Trademark Reg. U.S. Pat. Off. and in Other Countries, Marca Registrada, Hecho en U.S.A.
HarperCollins® is a registered trademark of HarperCollins Publishers.

Printed in the U.S.A.

10 9 8 7 6 5 4 3 2 1

AN
English Bride
IN
Scotland

Chapter 1

"*A*NNABEL? ANNABEL?"

Annabel sighed sleepily and rolled away from the persistent voice interrupting her exhausted slumber.

"Annabel, wake up," the voice said more insistently.

"Sister Clara and I were up all night with a foaling mare," Annabel mumbled wearily, recognizing Sister Maud's voice. "The abbess said we could sleep in today."

"Aye. Well, now she wants you up. Your mother is here."

Annabel rolled abruptly onto her back in the small cot and blinked her eyes open to peer at Maud with amazement. "What?"

"Your mother is here and the abbess sent for you," Maud repeated patiently. She then moved away to collect the gown Annabel had stripped out of and left on the floor when she'd reached her room.

Annabel sighed when she saw the disapproving expression on Maud's face as she shook out the wrinkled gown. She had no doubt the woman would tattle to the abbess about the ill treatment of her clothing. The thought made her wish she'd taken the time to fold it neatly and set it on the chest at the foot of her bed, but it had been near dawn when she'd stumbled to her room. She'd been so exhausted she'd simply dropped it and tumbled into bed to fall into a dead sleep. That error would see her doing penance rather than going back to sleep after she saw her mother, she was sure.

Recalled to the fact that her mother was there, Annabel sat up on the side of the small hard bed in her hair shirt and chemise, and wiped the sleep from her eyes as Maud turned back.

"Why is my mother here?" she asked, standing to take the gown the woman held out.

"I would not know. She was taken to the abbess the moment she arrived and they have been sequestered in her office since," Maud said stiffly, her gaze sliding over the hair shirt visible beneath Annabel's chemise.

The hair shirt was to remind Annabel not to rush about in an undignified manner. She was always to walk slowly with poise as a bride of God should. Since she was already wearing it for one offense, her punishment for the discarded gown would probably be a whipping, Annabel knew, and had no doubt Maud was enjoying the prospect. The woman had always disliked her for some reason.

Annabel tugged her gown on over her head. She was waking up quickly, now, worry rushing the

process along. Her mother's being here couldn't be
a good thing. After all, the woman hadn't been to
see her since delivering her to the abbey fourteen
years before. It had to be something important that
brought her now. Had her father died? Her sister?
Had Waverly Castle been taken by marauders? The
possibilities were endless and none of them were
good. Good news would hardly bring her mother
with the dawn. She must have ridden through the
night to arrive that early.

"How long were they sequestered in the abbess's office?" Annabel asked with a frown, doing
up her stays.

"How should I know? I have better things to
do than stand about keeping track of your visitors," Maud said primly, watching Annabel grab
her brush and begin dragging it quickly through
her hair, ripping viciously through any knots encountered. "Does the abbess know you have not
yet shorn your hair?"

Annabel stiffened at the question. The abbess
had ordered it several weeks ago, but Annabel
simply hadn't been able to bring herself to do it.
She was not yet a nun, so hadn't felt she needed to
perform the mutilation yet and had kept it a secret
with her wimples.

Rather than admit as much, Annabel set down
the brush, donned her wimple and headed for the
door with a rushed, "Thank you for waking me,
Maud."

She could feel the woman's eyes burning into
her back as she hurried out of her room and took
a moment to worry over whether the nun would
search her cell for other infractions to tattle on

her for. But there was nothing she could do about that so Annabel turned her attention to why her mother was there instead.

She started out nearly running in an effort to get to the abbess quickly, but a scowl of displeasure from the prioress as she passed her made Annabel slow to a fast walk . . . until she turned the corner and the prioress could no longer see her. She then broke into a run again and didn't slow until she turned into the hall where the abbess had her rooms and office.

Annabel spotted the two women talking outside the abbess's door at once, but knew her mother only because she wasn't the abbess. Annabel had been sent to the abbey at the tender age of seven and hadn't seen her since. This woman looked nothing like the mother of her memory. Her mother had been a fair-haired beauty with sparkling eyes and color in her cheeks. She'd always been smiling or laughing. This woman was pale, her hair more gray than blond, her eyes alive with worry rather than joy. She wasn't smiling. Her mouth was tightly compressed, anxiety showing there as well as in the way she was wringing her hands.

"Ah, Annabel," the abbess, said as she spotted her. The good woman then turned to Annabel's mother and offered a reassuring smile as she patted her hand. "Here she is. You can be on your way now. All will be well."

"Thank you," Lady Withram whispered, staring at Annabel with fierce concentration as she approached.

Actually, the way she was looking at her was

rather disconcerting, Annabel decided. If her mother was not quite what she recalled, she herself apparently was nothing like what her mother had expected . . . or perhaps hoped for. Annabel was sure it was disappointment she saw flash across the woman's face before her expression closed up tight.

Annabel was still only halfway up the hall when the abbess turned and strode into her office, leaving Lady Withram to rush forward to greet her. Although *greet* would be something of a misnomer. She didn't even slow, let alone stop, but hurried forward, catching Annabel's arm and whirling her back the way she'd come, saying, "We must hurry!"

Eyes wide, Annabel allowed herself to be dragged along to the front doors. Frowning slightly then, she asked, "Where are we going?"

"Home," was her mother's surprising answer.

"Home?" she asked with bewilderment. "But I thought this was to be my home. What—?"

"Are the horses ready?" her mother interrupted her and for a moment, Annabel thought she was asking her the question, but they had just stepped out of the abbey doors and a burly old man waiting by a carriage answered.

"Aye, my lady. The abbess sent the prioress out to ensure we got two of the finest beasts they have here in trade for our own. They're well rested and fit. They'll get us back easily as quickly as ours got us here."

The answer drew Annabel's gaze to the horses in question. She recognized both of them and they were indeed the best the abbey had to offer. Annabel had no doubt the horses being left behind were of equal or better quality though. The abbess would accept nothing less. Annabel glanced forward again at a tug on her arm. Her mother still held her tightly and now dragged her toward the waiting carriage.

"Thank you, Aelric." Lady Withram climbed grimly up into the carriage with his help, and dragged Annabel behind her by the arm she still clasped. Really, the woman had her in a death grip, as if she feared she might break free and flee at any moment. Her nails were actually digging into Annabel's flesh, so it was something of a relief when her mother pulled her down to sit beside her in the carriage and finally released her hold.

Annabel took a moment to rub her arm as Aelric closed the door and sent the carriage rocking as he climbed up onto his bench. But once they started to move, she glanced to her mother a little warily and asked, "Where are we going?"

She thought she was being rather forbearing. After all, she'd just been dragged from her bed and out of the only home she'd known for the last fourteen years with nary a word of explanation. However, her mother looked vastly annoyed at the question.

"I told you. Home."

"Elstow Abbey is my home," Annabel said quietly.

"It *was* your home," she agreed and then added firmly, "But no more. Waverly is."

This news was quite unsettling. She was being taken away from the only home she really knew. Young as Annabel had been when she'd left, her memories of Waverly were faint at best. So she was relieved when her mother added, "At least for the next day or two."

So, she was only being taken home for a short visit, she thought, and then felt foolish for thinking otherwise. After all, she hadn't even been allowed to pack a bag or bring anything with her. That now made her frown, because she would be without anything but the clothes on her back until she returned. The fact that her mother had rushed her out without such a consideration told her the situation was a dire one.

"Is it Father?" she asked sympathetically. The idea that her father may have died and she was being brought home for the funeral made sense to her. It also raised a surprising bit of sadness in her. Surprising, because her memories of the man who had sired her were faded at best, but she recalled a tall, bluff, handsome man with a beard that had tickled when he'd hugged her good-bye. As she recalled, he had often been away fighting this war or that battle for their king.

"Is what Father?" her mother asked and Annabel peered at her more closely as she noted the exhaustion in the woman's voice. One glance at her weary, bloodshot eyes told Annabel that the woman must have been up all night during the ride from Waverly, but then it would be hard to sleep while being jostled about so, she supposed. She hadn't ridden in a wagon since being delivered to the abbey and didn't recall it being this bumpy, but then they appeared to be traveling more quickly than one would normally dare with a wagon.

Realizing that her mother was still awaiting an answer, she said, "Has something happened to Father? Is that why you are bringing me home for a visit?"

Lady Withram opened her mouth, hesitated, and then sighed and said, "Nay. Your father is well. Your sister is the reason I came for you."

"Kate?" Annabel asked with surprise and dismay. Of everyone at Waverly, she remembered her elder sister, Kate, the best. They were only a year apart by birth and had been fast friends as children. Kate was the one she had missed most when she'd first landed at the abbey. Annabel had wept for her every night for the first year, but eventually, as time had passed, even Kate had faded somewhat in her memory. "What happened? Is she—?"

"Not now, Annabel," her mother said wearily, closing her eyes. "There is time enough to explain things, but for now I am exhausted from riding in this ridiculous wagon and need to close my eyes for a bit."

Annabel hesitated, but then said, "I am surprised you did not come on horseback."

It was really a question. Her mother had loved to ride as she recalled and few would choose to ride in the back of a wagon. It was not exactly a comfortable journey and much slower than horseback.

"Your father did not think you would be able to ride alone," was the abrupt answer. "There would be no need for you to know how to ride at the abbey."

Annabel didn't comment. There *was* no reason to ride at the abbey and most of the women there rarely or never did. However, Annabel spent half her time working with the abbey animals and rode them often. Although she had to do it at night when everyone was sleeping so that she wouldn't get caught, and then rode bareback. She'd never even bothered to try one of the saddles or side-saddles hanging from the stable walls.

Annabel considered asking again about her sister despite her mother's request that she wait, but then caught herself. Lady Withram really did look exhausted. A state she could sympathize with since she herself hadn't slept more than a matter of moments before being woken that morning. She could wait to find out what ailment or accident had taken Kate. Truthfully, Annabel would rather sleep a bit before she heard the sad story anyway. As exhausted as she was, she feared she might turn into a sobbing Sally did she hear the tale now.

That thought uppermost in her mind, Annabel leaned into the corner of the carriage and tried to make herself comfortable enough to sleep, but suspected it would be a difficult task with the carriage bumping and thumping about as it was.

"How the devil did you end up betrothed to an English lass of all things?"

Ross smiled faintly at Marach's question. The man, one of his finest warriors and about his own age, sounded horrified. But then most of his men were probably horrified at the prospect of having an Englishwoman for their lady. Ross opened his mouth to answer, but had hesitated too long. Gilly beat him to it.

"The Waverly lord saved Ross'd da' while they were on crusade some twenty years ago," the older warrior explained. He then added sorrowfully, "And Ross is paying fer it by being shackled to the English lord's daughter for the rest o' his days."

Ross barely refrained from smiling at the claim. Gilly was his first. He'd also been Ross's father's first before that. While his age usually meant Ross could count on the man for wise counsel, it also meant he had a long memory of what the English had done to the Scots. That fact alone had almost made Ross decide not to bring the man along on this journey, but there was no one he trusted more to watch his back than the two warriors riding on either side of him: Gilly and Marach. They were both excellent in battle as well as good friends to him. He'd trust either of them with his life anywhere, anytime.

"Is that true?" Marach asked with a frown as they rode out of the trees and started up the hill to Waverly Castle.

"Aye, Waverly saved me father," Ross rumbled, and added, "But the two men became friends afterward and decided to seal the friendship by marrying the two houses. I was seven and Waverly's wife had given birth to a girl the year before, so a contract was struck."

Gilly shook his head woefully at this news. "While I am glad yer father lived, 'tis a terrible price ye're expected to pay fer it." He tilted his head and added slyly, "And well ye ken it, else ye would no' ha'e waited so long to collect her. I suppose ye were hoping the lass would fall down a well or something and save ye having to marry her?"

"Nay," Ross denied the accusation on a chuckle and then said more seriously, "Ye ken I intended to collect her four years ago, but Father's death interfered."

"Oh, aye." Gilly nodded solemnly.

Ross fell silent at the memory. The death of his father, Ranson, had been hard enough to bear. The MacKay clan chief had been a good man, and a good father, but what had followed his death had made it all that much harder. His cousin, Derek, had taken the opportunity to try to wrest the title of laird from Ross, claiming that at twenty-three he was too young for the task. The moment Derek had done that, others had stepped forward wanting to claim the title. The clan had split into several factions, each backing another male member of the family. Ross had spent the last three years fighting off the claims and proving himself, but it had taken his defeating his cousin, Derek, in battle the year before for the clan to settle down and accept Ross as clan chief.

He'd waited this last year to make sure that peace and acceptance remained before risking leaving MacKay to collect his bride . . . and he had no doubt she would not be pleased at having been left on the vine so long.

"An English lass," Marach muttered, joining the conversation with a sorrowful shake of the head.

Ross chuckled, but shrugged mildly as they approached the gates of Waverly. "A lass is a lass."

"And an English lass is an English lass," Gilly

said grimly as they rode over the bridge across the moat. "I've yet to meet an English lass who did no' look down her nose at us 'heathen Scots.' They're all spoiled rotten."

"Hmm," Ross said with a sigh. "Well, we shall ha'e to hope this one is no' spoiled."

"Hope away, me friend," Gilly said with a grimace. "But prepare yerself for a fishwife o' a bride who'll make yer life a nightmare."

Ross started to laugh at that prediction, but nearly choked on the sound when a sudden shriek rended the air. They were crossing the Waverly bailey, heading for the stables. Ross reined in and glanced wildly about, seeking the source. It was Marach who pointed toward a tower window.

"It came from there," he commented as a dark-haired woman moved past the unshuttered window.

"Aye," Gilly agreed, eyes narrowed on the window as the woman appeared again. "And I'm thinking that's yer bride. A fishwife," he added knowingly and then shook his head sadly. "We're all in fer it now."

Marach, Gilly and the three other men traveling with them headed their mounts toward the stables, leaving Ross alone to stare up at the now empty window with dismay.

"ANNABEL, KEEP YOUR VOICE DOWN. SOMEONE will hear you," Lady Withram admonished with displeasure.

The directive made her gape briefly. Annabel could hardly believe that was all her mother had to say. She couldn't believe anything that was happening and would have feared her exhaustion was muddying her thinking, but Annabel had managed to drift off in the uncomfortable wagon and had actually slept through the almost day-long journey to Waverly. She'd slept fitfully, awaking only when the carriage stopped. She'd still been wiping the sleep from her eyes when the keep door had opened and an old man had rushed out to the wagon to peer anxiously at first her mother and then herself.

The sudden relief that had slumped the man's shoulders had made Annabel curious, but before she could consider it much, her mother was poking and prodding her out of the wagon, asking, "Is he here yet?"

"Nay. Thank God," the man said with some feeling. "But the men on the wall just announced that they saw a small riding party entering the other side of the woods. Six men on horseback and I am thinking it is him. You had best get her above stairs and get her ready."

"Aye," her mother had agreed grimly and caught Annabel by the arm to drag her into the castle.

Annabel hadn't resisted, but had allowed herself to be dragged along, her head turned the whole time and eyes wide on the man who she had come to realize was her father. Her mother wasn't the only one who had aged these past fourteen years. Her father was no longer the strong handsome man she recalled from her youth. His muscular chest had fallen, it seemed, down to where his flat stomach used to be, only it was muscle no more. And he had somehow grown shorter, or perhaps he had only seemed taller back then because she had been a small child.

As for his once handsome face, it was now covered with graying facial hair that appeared to have grown in as wildly as untended weeds in a garden. She could hardly fathom that this was the father of her memories. So startled by this transformation was she, that Annabel hadn't really taken note of what had been said, so was completely taken aback when they'd entered a bedchamber in the upper tower and her mother had made her announcement. While her initial response had been a squawk of pure protest, she was now trying to understand the information just imparted, but her brain couldn't seem to absorb it.

Annabel took a deep breath and gave her head a shake. A couple more deep breaths and she felt calm enough to ask, "Pray, I do not think I heard you correctly, my lady. Did you just say—?"

"You are marrying the MacKay in your sister's place," her mother repeated firmly. Oddly enough the firm tone she used did not make the words any more comprehensible.

"How can that be?" she asked with confusion. "I am an oblate. I am to take the veil." She paused briefly, but when her mother didn't comment, Annabel thought perhaps she wasn't grasping the situation, and added, "I am becoming a nun. I am marrying Jesus."

"Not anymore," her mother assured her. "You have not yet taken the veil, and are free to marry. The contract states that Ross MacKay is to marry the eldest surviving daughter of William Withram. With your sister gone, that is you now. You have to marry him or we forfeit the dower as well as a great deal of coin. It would ruin us. You *will* marry him."

Annabel stared at her silently and then asked, "What happened to Kate? How did she die?"

Lady Waverly released a snort of disgust and walked over to sink wearily onto the end of the bed. "Would that she were dead rather than having caused the shame she has brought upon us."

Annabel's eyes widened and she rushed forward as hope clutched at her briefly. "If she is not dead—"

"She ran off with the stable master's son," Lady Waverly interrupted harshly. "Your father has disowned and disinherited her. For all intents and purposes, she is dead. You are the eldest daughter now and you *will* marry Ross MacKay."

Annabel sank onto the end of the bed next to her mother, her legs suddenly too weak to hold her weight. Her voice was equally weak when she said, "But I do not know how to be a wife. I was always going to become a nun. All my training has been toward that end. I do not know the first thing about running a household, or—or anything," she added helplessly.

When her mother patted her hand, she glanced to her in the hopes of some encouragement and received, "Aye. 'Twill most likely be a mess. Howbeit, at least your father and I will not be ruined."

"Aye, there is that," Annabel agreed dryly.

Lady Waverly nodded, apparently entirely missing her sarcasm. That was probably a good thing, she acknowledged. The abbess would have frowned on the comment and punished her accordingly. The abbess had punished her a good deal over the years. In truth, Annabel supposed she would not have made a very good nun anyway. Certainly she hadn't made a very good novice. Or a good postulant for that matter. She'd been a postulant for years before the abbess had put her forward to be a novice, and Annabel suspected the woman had done so out of sheer pity.

Annabel wasn't sure what was wrong with her exactly. She had expected to be a nun and had made a real effort to fit into the fold, but despite her best efforts, her tongue did run away with her at times. Her tongue, her temper, her appetite—

Grimacing, Annabel cut off the litany in her head. She was well aware of her shortcomings as a nun. The abbess and prioress had both pointed them out often enough. Still, as bad as she might have been at it, being a nun was the only thing she knew and if she could not manage that after years working toward it, how on earth would she get along as a wife and lady, for which she had absolutely no training?

Annabel sighed miserably and her mother popped up off the bed as if it were some sort of cue.

"Well, I had best go see where the maids are so we can get you dressed," she announced briskly, heading for the door.

"Dressed?" Annabel asked uncertainly, standing as well.

"Well you can*not* meet your betrothed in a wimple," her mother said as if that should be obvious.

"But—is he here now?" she asked with new alarm.

"Nay, but he will be soon and I'm sure it will take forever to make you acceptable. Wait here; I will return directly."

"Mother?" Annabel said suddenly as the woman started out of the room.

Lady Waverly paused in the door to peer back impatiently. "What?"

She hesitated, but then raised her head and asked the question she'd wondered since being taken away from her home as a young child. "Why was I sent to Elstow as a child?"

Her mother's eyebrows rose slightly. "Well, you would have been sent there anyway eventually."

"I would have?" Annabel asked with a frown.

"Aye, and Kate would have too had I born a son after you. But as it happens, while I was with child several times afterward, none survived to birth."

Annabel couldn't tell if it was relief on her mother's face or regret . . . perhaps a combination of the two. She suspected the woman would have been pleased to have born one son for her husband, and that was it. Being hampered with baby girls had not been convenient from what she could tell.

"So," her mother continued with a shrug. "Kate, as the eldest and heir, had to stay here to learn how to run Waverly so that after your father and I died, she would know how to run it when it passed to her and her husband. But there was no reason to keep you here."

"You never considered the possibility of my

marrying instead?" Annabel asked quietly, even though she was quite sure she knew the answer.

Lady Waverly grimaced and shook her head at the very suggestion. "Kate was always the one with the fine looks. You were always a chubby little thing. To find a suitable lord, willing to marry you, would have taken more coin than we were willing to invest. Fortunately, the abbey took you for half the dower it would have cost us to marry you off, and they took you young, so we didn't have to feed, clothe, or bother with training you all those years either. And, of course, it's always good to have a family member in the church praying for your soul as we knew the abbess would make you do." Her eyes narrowed. "She *did* make you pray for us, didn't she?"

"Aye," Annabel said at once.

"Good." Lady Waverly relaxed, but then raked her with a displeased glance. "Now, 'tis going to take a great deal of work to make you presentable. I need to get the servants so they can start on it straightaway."

"Of course," Annabel murmured, and then watched the door close. While her mother had made it obvious she was a disappointment, Annabel was used to that. No matter how hard she had tried, she'd always seemed to disappoint the abbess too . . . and no doubt would be a disappointment to her husband as well.

Pushing the depressing knowledge away, Annabel peered around the room she was in. She was quite sure it was the room she'd shared with Kate as a child, though the bedding and drapes around the bed were different now. It made her recall nights long ago when she and Kate had lain abed giggling about some joke or other. That in turn made her wonder about her sister.

"She ran off with the stable master's son," her mother had said.

The idea was rather shocking to Annabel. A sense of duty was pounded into postulants and novices at the abbey. All she could think was that Kate must have truly loved the stable master's son to go against their parents so. She would have to ask her mother about it when she returned, Annabel decided as she removed her wimple.

"Thank God I did not cut my hair," she muttered as she ran a hand through the long strands. Annabel was quite sure having a shorn head would not have helped matters here.

Chapter 2

"Sɪᴛ, sɪᴛ."

Ross tore his gaze away from the woman rushing down the stairs at Lord Withram's words and moved to settle at the table.

"You must be thirsty after your journey. I shall see about refreshments," the man said and hurried away.

"He seems a touch anxious about something," Gilly commented as they watched the lord of Waverly scurry, not to the kitchens, but to the woman who had just come downstairs. Grimacing, he then added, "But then, so was the stable master. Wringing his hands and avoiding our eyes in the stables."

Ross had noticed that. He'd also noted that everyone they'd passed or encountered so far had smiled nervously and then rushed away as if afraid they may be asked a question they didn't want to answer. It was enough to make a lesser man nervous, but Ross wasn't the sort to worry about things before they happened. He was content to wait and see, so he merely grunted in

response to Gilly's words and watched Lord Withram converse briefly with the lady before the two
hurried off to the kitchens together.

"Where do ye think yer bride is?" Gilly asked.

Ross shrugged, his gaze moving around the
oddly empty great hall. The great hall at MacKay
was rarely empty. There was always someone
coming or going and he would have expected that
to be the case here too, so the complete absence of
people was a bit curious.

His gaze slid to the door he presumed led to the
kitchens as the lady rushed out, followed by several servants carrying a bath and pails of water,
some of them steaming.

"It's looking to me like it will be a while ere ye
see yer bride," Gilly said dryly, his narrowed eyes
following the servants up the stairs.

"Aye," Ross agreed on a sigh. He'd hoped to get
this business over with and head back to MacKay
at once. This being the first time he'd left the castle
since the trouble after his father's death, he was a
bit anxious to get back and assure himself that all
was well. It was looking like he wouldn't be leaving as soon as he'd hoped.

"Will you tell me about Kate?" Annabel
asked as she paused beside the bath the servants
had prepared for her.

"What is there to tell?" Lady Withram said bitterly. "She ran off with that stupid boy."

"She must love him very much," Annabel murmured as she began to remove her gown. "And he
must love her too, to risk Father's wrath this way."

"Oh, aye. She loves him and he loves her," Lady

Waverly said with disgust and then added, "He loves her in her fine expensive gowns and with her hair shiny and gleaming and done up on top of her head by her maid." She shook her head. "The little fool did not consider what would happen to all those fine feelings when the gown is but rags on her back and she is pale and dull-looking from lack of food. As for he, I'm sure he looks just fine to her working here, but they'll be without now. The love will not last long, and then what will she do?" she asked harshly. "Most-like run back here with a bastard in her belly, tears in her eyes, and a plea on her lips for us to take her in."

"Will you?" Annabel asked quietly.

Lady Withram shook her head and muttered, "She is dead to your father."

"And to you?" Annabel asked.

"I am not the lord of this manor. I am but a woman," she said quietly and then with some venom, she added, "But, nay, I would not take her back either. She did not think one wit about us or how this would affect us when she made her choice." Lady Waverly's mouth twisted bitterly. "Well, she has made her bed and must now lie in it."

Annabel thought that was rather harsh, but didn't comment. Setting her gown across the chair by the fire, she removed her chemise and then reached for the laces of the shirt she wore beneath it.

"What the devil is that?" her mother asked, drawing nearer.

"A cilice," Annabel mumbled with embarrassment.

"Is that goat hair?" Lady Waverly felt the hem and grimaced. "'Tis course. It must be fair uncomfortable. Why the devil would you be wearing a hair shirt?"

Annabel sighed unhappily and let the shirt drop to the floor as she undid the last lacing. She stepped into the steaming bathwater before admitting, "The abbess ordered me to wear it."

"Why?" her mother asked at once.

"'Tis a punishment at the abbey," Annabel muttered.

"These marks on your back are not from the shirt," her mother said, running a finger lightly over the welts on her back.

"No," Annabel agreed. "Those are from a whip."

"They whipped you at the abbey?" her mother asked with amazement.

"Nay. I did."

"Why on earth would you do a thing like that?" she asked with dismay.

"Because the abbess ordered me to," Annabel admitted quietly.

"The abbess . . . ?" She stared at her aghast and then asked sharply, "What the devil have you been up to at that abbey?" Her tone suggested she didn't really want to know and Annabel supposed she was now thinking both of her daughters were a great disappointment.

Sadly, Annabel guessed that was true. Kate hadn't been a very dutiful daughter, and she herself hadn't been a very good oblate. She'd tried. Annabel had tried very hard to be a good novice, but she was forever late, or unkempt, or staining, or damaging her clothing, or ruining her slippers, or tracking mud about. The list of her mistakes was endless. She ate too much, talked too much, moved too fast and just generally wasn't a suitable, shy, retiring, dignified, serene nun. That was why the abbess hadn't let her take the veil yet and hadn't raised her to nun status. It was why she was still available for her parents to force into marriage.

Annabel didn't point that out to her mother, but she was very aware of it herself. If she'd just tried a little harder and been a little better, perhaps she'd now be a nun and not facing the horrifying future her parents had arranged for her. And it was horrifying to Annabel. She didn't know a thing about anything to do with marriage, running a castle, or . . . well . . . anything really. She was stumbling blind into an alien situation . . . or being pushed into it . . . and she was terrified.

"Surely Kate and her stable boy cannot have married without Father's permission," Annabel said now, desperation goading her on. "Perhaps if we found her—"

"They may not be married, but do you really think he has not bedded her yet?" her mother asked harshly. "We have learned since her leaving that Kathryn used to slip from the castle at night to meet the boy and often did not return until just before dawn. There are witnesses who were too afraid to say anything at the time, but came forth in droves once they went missing," she added bitterly.

"Well she may not be an innocent anymore, but perhaps she's come to her senses and—"

"And what?" Lady Withram snapped. "What would we do with her? The Scot would kill us in our beds for handing him a sullied bride, and he'd have every right to."

Annabel's eyes widened with dismay. "But—"

"No more buts, Annabel," her mother said sounding suddenly weary again. "This is what must be done. You will marry the Scot. 'Tis better than withering away in an abbey full of women anyway."

Annabel frowned at this comment. She distinctly recalled her mother telling her that becoming a nun was better than being under the thumb of some horrid man all the days of her life when she'd delivered her to the abbey. She'd made it sound preferable to marriage and children. So which was true? It seemed *that* depended on what her parents wanted her to do.

Unfortunately, no matter what was true, she simply didn't have any choice in the matter. Her parents had decided on her future. She didn't have a stable boy to run off with, and certainly the abbess wouldn't take her back after releasing her into her mother's care. That lady was probably relieved to be free of her clumsiness and ineptitude.

With nothing else to do, Annabel began to soap herself. It seemed she would marry, be a wife to this unknown Scot, the mother of his children, and lady of his people . . . Lord save them all.

Ross NODDED POLITELY WHEN LORD WITHRAM excused himself to go check on how the ladies were coming. It was the third time he'd done so since their arrival. It seemed his betrothed, or

her mother, had decided a bath was in order and
was now "prettifying herself for him," as Lord
Withram had put it. Apparently, it was a lengthy
ordeal. He had arrived two long hours ago and
still hadn't seen hide nor hair of the woman he
was supposed to marry.

Hoping that wasn't a sign that his betrothed
was too terribly unattractive, Ross glanced to the
side when Marach appeared there, tapping him
on the shoulder.

"What is it?" he asked, and listened curiously
as Marach bent to murmur by his ear.

"I went to check on our mounts, to make sure
they were bedded down all proper."

"Aye," Ross murmured.

"When I got there I overheard the stable master
and another man talking on how the stable master's boy had landed him in hot water with Lord
Withram by running off with his lady daughter
just two days before she was to marry "the Scot.""

Ross straightened abruptly at this news and
eyed him in question. "Are you sure ye heard it
right?"

Marach nodded solemnly. "I heard them talking as I approached and paused to listen. They
went on about it for a bit. How the stable master'd
like to whip his boy fer being so stupid, especially
for a spoiled light-skirt like the eldest Withram
lass. He went on about how the two don't have
enough sense to come in from the rain, and'll
most like end up dead by the side of the road
somewhere. And if ye refused the second daughter they're replacing her with—and for some
reason they seemed to think ye would," he added

significantly, before continuing, "if ye refuse her, the stable master is thinking he'll most like end up homeless and dead right next to 'em."

Ross relaxed back on the bench with a frown. What was wrong with the second daughter that the men would be so sure he'd refuse her?

"Bloody English," Gilly muttered, having overheard Marach's words. "He could ha'e told ye the situation when we arrived. Instead, he's trying to pass off a sow's ear as a silk purse, he is. Pawning off the second daughter on ye like that. And she must be fair ugly for the men to think ye'd refuse her. Surely his trying to trick ye like this and no' being aboveboard on the matter is grounds to refuse the wedding?" he asked, and then added with sudden cheer, "If so, we can head home and find ye a fine Scottish lass to wed and bed."

"I'm thinking better the second daughter than the first after the stable boy's had her," Marach pointed out.

"So long as someone else hasn't had the second daughter," Gilly said dryly and then pointed out, "The apple doesn't fall far from the tree and usually lands right next to the other apples."

Ross frowned at this suggestion and shook his head. "If honor ran in families, Derek would have been more like me. Just because the elder sister was faithless does not mean the second daughter is as well."

"True enough," Gilly acknowledged. "But consider this, if she is no' a light-skirt like her sister, why do they worry ye may no' accept her?" He waited a moment, but when Ross did not respond, he answered himself. "If she's no' a light-skirt, then she must be ugly as sin, or a sour-faced prude of a fishwife. Or both," he ended grimly.

Ross merely stared at the man, his mind whirling. Dear God, was nothing ever going to be easy in his life? First his mother died, and then his father followed a year later, then he wasn't even allowed time to grieve over the man and take up his duties as clan chief with the support of his people, but had to fight for the right. Now, he finally gets that matter mostly settled and comes to claim his betrothed and start a family of his own, only to find out his original intended has run off—with a stable boy of all things—and he was expected to marry her sister who was either a light-skirt like her sister, or some sour-faced prude of a fishwife.

Life was so unfair sometimes. All the times really, Ross added bitterly. He couldn't think of much that had gone right or easy in his life lately and frankly he was growing weary of constantly battling to get by.

Gilly was right, he thought. The easiest thing to do was to get up, walk out, head home and marry a nice Scottish lass of his choosing. Surely he had that right? He wasn't legally bound to marry the second daughter, was he? Could Withram legally disown his eldest daughter? Had he been able to manage it in so short a time? Frankly, Ross didn't care. He was done with struggling through life. He was going home.

Gilly and Marach had been nattering on about the situation as he pondered, but both fell silent when Ross stood abruptly. He saw the question in their eyes and said, "We are leav—"

"Here she is at last."

Ross snapped his mouth closed and turned slowly at that almost desperately gay announcement from Lord Withram. The man was rushing toward the table from the stairs, two women trailing at a more sedate pace.

"You know how women can be," Withram went on, sounding extremely anxious. "Our Annabel wanted to look perfect for her first meeting with you."

Ross didn't respond. He didn't even acknowledge the words with a look. His gaze was locked on the young woman approaching beside Lady Withram. Short, no more than five feet, with a pretty face, shiny, long, wavy midnight hair and more curves than his shield. He noted all that in an instant, his eyes traveling with appreciation over each asset before settling on her eyes. They were a color he'd never seen before in eyes, a combination of pale blue and green, almost teal with a darker rim circling the unusual irises. They were absolutely beautiful . . . and presently brimming with anxiety and fear.

Before he'd even realized he was going to do it, Ross found himself moving around the table to approach the girl. Taking her hand in his, he placed it on his arm and peered solemnly down into her unusual eyes before announcing, "Well worth the wait."

He was pleased to see some of her fear dissipate. Just a little, but it was something. She blushed too, ducking her head as if unused to and embarrassed by such a compliment . . . and her fingers were trembling where they rested on his arm. She did not strike him as a light-skirt, nor was she sour faced or ugly, but she had the finest eyes he'd ever seen, and he wanted to see more of them, so Ross turned and escorted her to the table.

He didn't miss the audible sighs of relief from her parents at their backs. Nor did he miss Gilly's muttered, "Bloody hell. He's done fer now."

Judging by the slight jerk of Annabel's head first one way and then the other, she didn't miss any of it either, but neither of them commented.

"WELL, NOW YOU'VE MET THERE IS NO NEED FOR delay." Annabel's father paused at her side and urged her to her feet. "Father Athol and the villagers are waiting outside the church."

Annabel stared from her father to her mother with amazement. Ross had literally just settled her at the table. She was positive her behind hadn't sat on the bench for more than the count of four before her father was ushering her up. She understood that her parents were afraid that something else would go awry and land them in ruin after all, so were eager to get this over with, but this rush just seemed a bit unseemly to her. So she was surprised when the Scot stood with a nod of acceptance and once again took her arm.

"Come along, lass," he said solemnly. "Once done, 'tis over."

True enough, Annabel thought dazedly, doing her best not to look at the man. She had been avoiding looking at him since getting her first glimpse. Annabel had spent her life from seven on in the company of women. The only male she had seen was Father Gerder, who had performed mass at the abbey. He was a tall, slender, elderly man with white hair and an emaciated body. On her arrival here, Annabel had thought how shrunken and small her father had grown and that despite his pronounced stomach, he reminded her of Father Gerder.

Ross in no way reminded her of her father or Father Gerder. Nor did he remind her of the women who had raised her. There was nothing soft or serene about his appearance, nothing small and dainty. Ross was huge and rough-looking, a walking wall of muscle-rippling, spicy-smelling, rumbling-voiced man.

He was just so overwhelming that it left Annabel dry-mouthed, nervous and oddly discombobulated. She was quite set aflutter by it all. At least that was what she was blaming for the fine trembling that started in her when he took her hand to place it on his arm. Mind you, she'd reacted much the same way the first time he'd done so to lead her to the table. The sensation had passed to make way for relief when he'd released her. However, there would be no quick respite for her this time. He wasn't walking her a mere few feet to the table.

Ross walked her to the door and out, and across the bailey toward the chapel, and with every step, Annabel's quivering increased until she was sure he must notice.

"Deep breath."

Annabel blinked at those rumbled words from the Scot. Glancing at him uncertainly, she asked, "I beg your pardon?"

"Take deep breaths," he said quietly enough that only she could hear, and then he added gently, " 'Twill help with yer nerves."

"Oh." She managed a smile, but was aware she was blushing brightly. He had noticed. Clearing her throat, she offered in a pained tone, "I apologize for my parents' unseemly rush. They mean well."

Ross shrugged. " There is nothing to apologize for. This suits me well enough. 'Tis best to get unpleasant tasks done quickly, do ye no' think?"

Annabel was so shocked by the words she nearly tripped over her own feet. While she herself had been set aback by the news that she was to marry, it had nothing to do with her groom. She hadn't even considered him in all of this. All of her upset had been due to the abrupt change in her life and circumstances. After all, right up until a few hours ago she had thought she was to be a nun.

Ross, however, had ridden here specifically with the intent to marry. There was no nasty surprise for him . . . except possibly for meeting his bride for the first time. Which suggested that marrying her, specifically, was the unpleasant task of which he spoke. And that was damned insulting. It also didn't bode well for her future. This was the man she was to spend the rest of her life with, after all. If he was displeased after just seeing her, how unhappy would he be once he realized how useless she was going to be as a wife? And she very much feared she was going to be useless.

But there wasn't a darned thing she could do to prevent what was coming. They were at the chapel and pausing before the priest. Her future was set firmly on this course now.

Ross WATCHED HIS NEW FATHER-IN-LAW PULL the door closed behind the departing group with more than a little relief. He'd found the whole bedding ceremony somewhat exasperating; a dozen drunken Englishmen along with his own drunk men had surrounded and jostled him upstairs and then proceeded to tug and pull at his clothes until he was naked. Then they'd shoved him into the bed beside his waiting, and equally naked, bride who was hidden under the linens.

Ross supposed he wouldn't have minded so much if he had been drunk himself. However, he hadn't wanted to start his marriage by being either in a drunken stupor or unintentionally rough with Annabel due to drink, so had abstained after the one goblet of wine used to toast their wedding. He had suffered the men's rough attention sober.

A sudden rustle and movement in the bed beside him drew Ross's attention to the fact that his bride was out of bed. He opened his mouth to ask what she was about, but the question never made it past his lips. She was naked from the top of her head to the tips of her toes . . . and absolutely beautiful. His bride was a fine figure of a woman, all soft and round. Just the way he liked his women, and his mouth watered at the sight. But it was a very brief view he got before she tugged a long shirt on and let it drop to curtain all that loveliness.

"What the bloody hell is that?" As the first real words he'd said since marrying the woman, Ross supposed they left much to be desired. But he was just so shocked at the sight of the ugly shirt covering all that beauty, he couldn't help himself.

" 'Tis a chemise carouse," Annabel explained, looking suddenly uncertain. She hesitated, her tongue poking out quickly to lick her lips, and then gave a pained smile, and added, "Father Athol thought we might like to use it, but I forgot about it until now."

"Use it for what?" he asked nonplussed.

"For the bedding," she explained, blushing brightly.

His gaze slid over her body in the contraption. It was quite simply a long shirt that appeared to be made of a very heavy material, and it covered every inch of her body. "How the devil am I to bed ye in that?"

"Oh, there is a hole," she said quickly and pulled the cloth around her hips tight, only to quickly let it go as she realized what she was revealing. Still, she'd held it long enough for him to see that there was indeed a hole several inches below the apex of her thighs . . . which he presumed he was to use for entry.

Shaking his head, he let his gaze slide over her again. The shirt had obviously been made for a much larger woman, that or someone had overestimated Annabel's size. He turned his eyes back to her face to see that she was blushing brightly and avoiding his gaze. Ross simply stared at her for several minutes, unsure how to react in this situation.

He had heard of the chemise carouse. It was intended to ensure that there was no pleasure accidentally found in the marriage bed. Because, of course, the church frowned on pleasure of any kind, but most specifically, sexual pleasure. Ross, himself, felt sex was healthy and natural and meant to be enjoyed, but he knew not everyone was that enlightened. It seemed his bride had been raised differently.

This was not a problem he had considered encountering, and frankly, he didn't have a clue what to do about it. There was no way on God's green earth that he intended to roll her over onto her back and simply thrust himself into her completely unprepared body. He would not do that to the wife of his worst enemy, let alone his own. They had to spend the rest of their lives together.

Besides, he enjoyed the pleasures of the flesh, and he liked for his partners to experience pleasure as well. He enjoyed hearing them gasp, and moan and groan. He liked to make them shake and tremble with it until they were pleading with need.

When Ross simply continued to stare at her, his wee bride shifted uncomfortably and then climbed back into bed next to him. She settled on her back without pulling the linen and furs up to cover the shirt, closed her eyes, and said stoically, "I am ready."

Ross surveyed her briefly, then shook his head and shoved aside the linens and furs covering him. Grabbing his plaid up off the floor, he wrapped it loosely around his waist and held it in place as he strode out of the room.

ANNABEL BLINKED HER EYES OPEN WITH SURPRISE at the sound of the door closing and frowned at the sight of the empty room. Ross had left. She supposed she should have been distressed, but she was mostly relieved. Annabel had heard the rustling and felt the shifting of the bed and had braced herself for her husband to mount her, but she hadn't exactly looked forward to it.

There had been half a dozen oblates like herself at the abbey, and a few novices, and perhaps not surprisingly the topic of sex had come up on occasion. As they'd scrubbed the stone floors, or cleaned the stables, they'd whispered about how lucky they were to avoid men, marriage and the marriage bed, for all knew it was a terrible trial for those unfortunate enough to land in it. The tearing of the veil of innocence was said to be a painful and bloody endeavor. One girl, much younger than her siblings, had been present at her sister's wedding and claimed that even the sounds of the revelry of the wedding feast hadn't completely covered the screams coming from her sister's room during the consummation that had followed the bedding ceremony.

They had all shuddered at this news, and agreed they were lucky to avoid that. Annabel had never imagined back then that she would be lying abed in a chemise carouse preparing to scream and bleed herself.

Grimacing, she tugged the linens and furs up to cover herself and then simply lay there fretting. Annabel had no idea where her husband had gone—probably to rejoin the revelry—but he would no doubt return. Perhaps he had gone below to find himself a drink or two to shore up his courage for what was coming, for surely if 'twas that unpleasant for the woman, it could not be much better for the man? That seemed a logical conclusion, but another one of the girls had claimed that if her father and brothers were anything to go by, men loved the carnal act, for they were forever chasing maids and cornering them to get under their skirts.

Annabel sighed at that memory. The unfairness of it all was rather depressing. Not only did men get to enjoy sex, which from all accounts was painful for the woman, but they didn't have to suffer monthly bleeding, or push huge babies out into the world from their own bodies, which was not only painful but often killed the woman. Truly, it did seem to her that women often got the short end of the stick in life.

The opening of the door drew her startled gaze and she watched wide-eyed as her husband returned with two goblets in one hand and two pitchers in the other. His plaid was now tied at his waist to allow it.

Annabel automatically started to get out of bed to help him, but a terse, "Stay," made her pause. She simply sat and stared at his very wide, very naked chest as he kicked the door closed and then carried the pitchers and goblets around the bed to her side. Ross set the pitchers and one goblet on the bedside table, and then poured liquid from one of the pitchers into the other goblet before holding it out to her.

"Drink," he ordered.

Annabel tore her gaze from his rippling chest to see that the goblet was full to the brim with honeyed mead.

"Thank you, but I am not really very thirsty, my—"

"Drink," Ross repeated firmly.

She frowned at the terse order, but accepted the goblet and raised it to her mouth for a sip.

"Down it, lass. 'Twill help with the bedding."

Annabel felt herself relax a bit at the added words. He was trying to be kind, anesthetizing her with the liquor before performing the painful and bloody deed. It was really very thoughtful of him, she decided, and swallowed down the liquid as quickly as she could, managing it in three large gulps. Annabel then set the goblet on the bedside table, only to watch wide-eyed as he immediately poured more from one of the pitchers.

"Are you not going to have some?" she asked self-consciously as she accepted the goblet he then offered her.

"Drink," was his only answer.

Annabel drank. She drank five goblets of the honeyed mead in a row, one after the other, but when he tried to give her a sixth, she shook her head, wondering why the room appeared to shake with the action.

"I really pobrably should not have more. Any more," Annabel corrected herself, frowning as she noted that her words were slightly slurred . . . and *pobrably* didn't sound quite right. She was pretty sure she'd got *pobrably* wrong.

"One more," Ross coaxed, pressing the goblet into her hand.

Annabel grimaced, but took the goblet and gulped some down. She'd made quick work of the first couple of goblets, but the more she drank, the slower she got at the chore. She simply wasn't thirsty. In fact, Annabel was the opposite of thirsty, she was beyond sated . . . to the point that she was beginning to have a terrible need to relieve herself of some of the liquid she'd taken in. She was actually growing rather desperate to visit the garderobe, but she was also embarrassed to name that need to the stranger standing half-naked before her.

Annabel's eyes slipped to his chest again, but she forced them away. They did seem to like to look at his chest and just kept doing so without permission. Certainly, if asked, she wouldn't have allowed them to wander all over that wide, naked expanse and follow the thickening hair down to where it disappeared under the plaid around his waist. Certainly not!

"Drink," he urged.

Annabel heaved out a breath and took another gulp. Honestly, she was beginning to wish he'd just get the bedding done with. Not that she was all that sotted. True, she was slurring her words a bit, but she wasn't feeling anything besides that . . . Well, other than the room's tendency to want to wobble around them, she supposed. But that was an issue with the room, not her.

A hiccup slipped from between her lips, and Annabel quickly covered her mouth, just in time to stifle an embarrassed giggle. Oh dear, she really had to pee. Would it be rude to simply announce that? Or should she just excuse herself and slip from the room? Certainly they didn't mention anything as crass as bodily functions at the abbey, but perhaps it was allowed outside the abbey. And what if she excused herself and he asked where she was going?

"Wife?"

Annabel glanced around the room before turning back to him and saying with surprise, "Oh, you mean me."

For some reason that seemed funny to her and she found herself giggling again.

"How do you feel?" he asked, eyeing her closely.

"Like I have to pee," she answered, and then slapped a hand over her mouth with dismay, only to tear it away and mutter, "Damn, I said it," which was followed quickly by an alarmed, "Oh damn, I said damn." Swearing was definitely not allowed at the abbey.

For some reason her words seemed to amuse the man. She could tell by the way his lovely dark eyes crinkled and his terribly stern mouth turned up. He had lovely eyes.

"Thank ye," Ross rumbled. "So do you."

"So do I, what?" she asked with confusion.

"Have lovely eyes," he explained.

"I didn't tell you, you have lovely eyes. Did I?" she asked with a frown. Annabel was sure she'd only thought that.

Still smiling, he shook his head slightly, but apparently decided not to trouble himself answering, because he didn't and simply bent to tug the furs and linens away from her, saying, "Come, I'll walk ye to the garderobe."

"Oh no," she said at once, scrambling to get out of bed. "That is not necessary, my lord. I know where it is. I used to live—Oh," Annabel gasped with surprise when she stood up and the room swung wildly.

Ross immediately reached out to steady her, and she leaned against his chest and closed her eyes briefly in the hopes that the room would settle when she opened them again. After a moment, she cautiously eased them open and tipped her head back to peer up at the man holding her. He had a very nice face. She hadn't seen enough men to decide whether he was handsome compared to others, and so far his face seemed a touch stern most of the time. But filled with concern as it presently was, it was nice, she decided . . . and then had to wonder why it was growing in size. His lips were nearly touching hers before she was able to sort out that it was growing larger because it was drawing nearer.

The first touch of his lips on hers was petal soft and for some reason that surprised her. Annabel supposed that she had expected his kisses to be as rough and aggressive as his outward appearance suggested. When he applied more pressure, she smiled against his mouth, although she couldn't have said why. And when she felt his tongue slip out to run across her lips, she opened her mouth in surprise, intending to ask if that was a normal part of kissing and if she should do it in return, only to gasp in amazement when his tongue took advantage of the move and slid inside her mouth.

Truly, while she knew mouths weren't made to hold two tongues, it was quite nice to have his in there. The feel of it rubbing along hers and filling her mouth was surprisingly exciting and Annabel instinctively opened her mouth wider, her hands slipping up his arms to wrap themselves around his neck.

Ross responded by catching the back of her head in one large hand, and tilting it slightly to a better angle. He then dropped both hands to clasp her behind and raised her as he straightened. Annabel assumed it was so he wouldn't have to bend over, but the action made their bodies rub against each other in the most interesting way.

When she felt him catch her under the thighs and pull her legs around his hips, Annabel went with it willingly, even eagerly. But then he broke their kiss and let her slide down a bit as he turned toward the bed and an alien hardness rubbed against her core. The action sent an unaccustomed excitement rocketing through her that made Annabel clutch at his shoulders even as she threw her head back on a gasp for air she couldn't seem to find. The head tossing probably wasn't a good idea, it made her feel like she was falling, and Annabel opened her eyes to find the world melting around them into blackness.

ROSS CAUGHT ANNABEL TO HIS CHEST WHEN HE realized she was falling backward, and then simply stared down with disbelief at her head lolling over his arm. She'd passed out he realized with consternation and scowled at her for it. But after a moment, he sighed and lowered her to the bed, acknowledging that she wasn't likely to awaken anytime soon . . . and that it was all his own fault. He was the one who had insisted she drink, and Annabel had obediently done so.

He'd intended to get her properly soused and then seduce her out of her chemise carouse. His hope had been that with enough liquor he would have been able to make her forget the church's ruling and relax enough to enjoy the bedding. And his plan had nearly worked. Certainly she had seemed to enjoy their kiss with uninhibited pleasure, and he suspected she would have enjoyed much more had she remained conscious. Unfortunately, it appeared he'd overdone it on the amount of liquor she could handle. In his own defense, she'd seemed to be handling it extremely well . . . right up until she'd passed out.

Ross bent and quickly slipped the chemise carouse off of her. Still holding her upright with one hand, he used the other to toss the offensive article across the room, assuring himself he'd burn the damn thing ere morning. He then turned back to his bride and paused as he noted the welts on her back. Ross recognized them as whip marks at once and it made him stiffen with rage at the thought of anyone touching her so in violence. He hadn't cared much for her parents; their demeanor was cool and uncaring toward their daughter. He hadn't seen a single sign of affection for her, but this pushed his feelings for them from indifferent to active dislike.

Mouth tight, Ross eased Annabel gently down into bed, taking the trouble to turn her on her side so that her welts didn't pain her in sleep. Then he tugged up the linens and furs over her. Straightening, he then stared down at her for a moment, his tight-lipped expression easing and twitching with amusement when she began to snore lightly. She was just so damned cute.

Shaking his head at himself, Ross glanced around to see where his *sgian dubh* had landed when the bedding party had stripped him. Unable to find it, he settled for his sword instead and moved around the bed to grab it up. Sitting on the side of the bed, Ross tugged the top linens and furs out of the way, then sliced his palm lightly and rubbed the blood that oozed out onto the bottom linen next to her hip. It would save explanations in the morning when her parents and the priest came to collect the linens as proof that the marriage had been consummated. Besides, the marriage would have been consummated had she not passed out, and he wouldn't see her humiliated for his own actions in pouring too much mead down her throat.

After setting his sword back on the floor, Ross removed the plaid he'd tied around his waist and dropped that on it. He then spotted the chemise carouse lying where he'd tossed it earlier and quickly retrieved and threw it in the fire before returning to the bed to settle in it next to his bride.

Ross closed his eyes and tried to sleep, but sleep wouldn't come and after a moment he opened them again and turned his head to peer at Annabel. He'd set her on her side facing him, and her mouth now hung open, a small string of drool slipping from it. For some reason the sight made warmth rattle through his chest and brought a smile to his lips. She was just so damned adorable to him.

The thought made him smile wryly. He'd been all set to order his men to the horses and ride out of here rather than marry the lass who was the Withram's second daughter, and then he'd spotted her and something about her had made him change his mind immediately. But he really couldn't say what that something was. She was bonnie enough, Ross supposed, but he'd seen bonnier. And she hadn't said more than a few words to him all night, so it wasn't that she had a shiny wit and charm, at least not that he yet knew of. Perhaps it had been the fear and anxiety in her eyes. Her expression had been calm and even pleasant, but her eyes had been awash with uncertainty and terror. He'd immediately wanted to reassure, soothe and protect her.

Following his instincts in this matter may have been an error, Ross acknowledged. After all, he didn't know the woman at all. But his instincts had never let him down before and he was content to trust in them now. However, he was also determined to get her away from Waverly first thing on the morrow. He didn't like Lord and Lady Waverly. He didn't like the sly way they'd passed off their second daughter as their first without even mentioning the matter to him. Nor had he been pleased by their obvious relief once the ceremony was over and they thought they'd got away with the switch. But even more, he didn't like how they treated Annabel.

Her parents spoke to her with an offhand lack of concern or care. They had treated her with the polite indifference of strangers during the marriage feast. The mother had even sent her off alone with servants when it had come time to see her above stairs, stripped and put abed. In fact, the woman hadn't come up at all, but had sat at the table drinking as the men, led by Lord Waverly, had carted Ross upstairs to join his bride. It was as if, once she was married, the woman had washed her hands of the girl. However, the welts on her back had been the final straw.

Aye, they would leave for MacKay first thing tomorrow morning, Ross determined. He would take her home, where they could consummate their marriage in the bed where she would one day give birth to their children. Annabel's life here was done. She was his now. He just wished he could claim her as his physically.

Ross's eyes slid over her naked shoulders where they peeked out from under the furs. They were round and creamy white. As was the rest of her, he recalled from his earlier view of her. Soft, round white breasts with dusky rose-colored nipples; soft, round white hips . . .

This was his wedding night, Ross reminded himself, licking his lips. When he was supposed to be consummating their marriage . . . and really, it might be a kindness to get the breaching of her innocence over with while she was too sotted to suffer from it. It would clear the way for her to feel nothing but pleasure their first time together that she was conscious.

Realizing where his thoughts were leading, Ross turned his head to stare at the ceiling rather than the temptation lying beside him. Damn, he couldn't believe he was even considering mounting the woman while she was unconscious. But all he'd been thinking since she'd come below that afternoon was that in a matter of hours he'd be able to sink his hard prick into her warm, soft body and . . .

Sitting up abruptly, Ross nearly threw himself from the bed. Grabbing up his plaid as he went, he strode to the door, but then paused. He couldn't go below. He was supposed to be up here doing exactly what he wanted to be doing.

Grimacing, he turned reluctantly from the door and eyed the bed, and then his gaze caught on the pitcher of honeyed mead on the bedside table. He preferred ale or scotch to the sweet drink, but honeyed mead would do. And he could always go below and fetch some ale if he finished off the mead and was still thirsty. By then enough time should have passed that they would assume he'd bedded his bride and was just giving her a rest before going again, did he bring the ale back up with him.

Nodding, he strode around the bed to collect the pitcher and second goblet. As he carried them to one of the chairs by the fire, Ross couldn't help thinking that this was not how he'd expected to spend his wedding night.

Chapter 3

$\mathcal{A}$ LOUD HAMMERING ROUSED ROSS FROM sleep. Rolling his head toward the door, he groaned at the pain the action sent shooting through his poor abused brain, and stared at the wooden panel through bleary eyes. A second knock was followed by a sleepy sigh and rustling on his other side, so he rolled his head that way to see how his poor wife fared that morning. He had no doubt her head would be as sore as his, if not worse, so was surprised when she popped up in bed and peered around with wide clear eyes.

"Oh! They'll be wanting the sheets!" she exclaimed and glanced to him with alarm.

"They can have them," he growled, forcing himself upright and tossing the top linen and furs away to reveal the bloodstain between them on the bottom linen.

"Oh." Annabel stared at the dried stain with wide eyes, peered down at her lap, then to his own and paused briefly, eyes widening even further if that were possible at the sight of his nakedness.

"Oh," she repeated weakly, then dragged her eyes away from his morning erection, gave her head a shake, and tossed the bit of linen and furs still covering her aside to leap from bed.

"Well, that's fine," she said cheerfully, seeming suddenly wide awake and perky as hell as she hopped out of bed. She began to scramble into a chemise, chattering away the whole while. "Goodness, I did not even feel the breaching, or at least if I did, I do not recall it. And I do not appear to be suffering any soreness or ill effects." Finished with the chemise, Annabel cast him a pleased smile and bent to grab up her gown from the day before, adding, " 'Twas kind of you to spare me that way, my lord. I am a very fortunate woman to have a husband as considerate as you."

Ross watched her drag the gown over her head with a nonplussed expression. She thought they'd actually . . . that he'd . . . and she was bloody grateful for it! He could have . . . Damn, he thought, with dismay. He'd been the gentleman and drunk himself to a sore head to avoid touching her, and all for nothing. Bloody hell!

Another knock sounded, making Ross grimace. Did they have to pound so bloody loud? he wondered with disgust and stood up as his bride rushed around the bed. Tying her stays as she went, Annabel called out a happy, "Coming!" as she went, and Ross winced as the cheery sound hit his ears and stabbed into his brain. She obviously wasn't suffering any ill effects from the drink either, he decided with disgust. While his head was pounding something fierce, she was chipper as hell. Life was so unfair sometimes. Although, Ross supposed, to be fair, since he'd urged the drink on her, she shouldn't have to suffer a sore head. Still—

His thoughts died as his wife pulled the door open, beamed at the people in the hall and started to usher them in, only to freeze when she saw that he was simply standing there nude. Flushing, she turned abruptly back, blocking the entrance. "Just a moment, please. My husband is not yet—"

"'Tis fine," Ross growled, stifling a groan as he bent to swipe up his linen shirt and plaid. He didn't care if all and sundry saw him nude, but his wife obviously did, so he left the shirt off for now and simply wrapped the plaid around his waist and then gave her a nod.

Smiling uncertainly, Annabel stepped aside to let the priest lead Lord and Lady Waverly into the room. The trio inspected the bedsheet with silent nods, and then as Lady Waverly began to strip it from the bed, Lord Waverly turned to Ross with a forced smile and said, "That's fine, fine. 'Tis all done and dusted then. When do you plan to leave?"

Ross stiffened. While he had already decided to leave first thing this morning, the man's making it so obvious that he would like to see the backs of them was more than a bit insulting. To both of them, he thought grimly and wondered what kind of life his poor bride had endured as the daughter of two such uncaring individuals. He himself had been gifted with loving and caring parents who had never made him feel unwelcome or unimportant. It seemed obvious Annabel had not enjoyed the same.

He would make that up to her. She would never feel unwelcome or uncared for again, he determined, and announced succinctly, "Now."

"Now?" Annabel turned to him with surprise.

"Aye." Ross removed his plaid to lay it out on the floor, quickly donned his shirt and then knelt to fold pleats into his plaid as he added, "So gather what ye can in the few minutes ye have ere I finish dressing and we'll be on our way."

"But—" Annabel began with dismay, only to fall silent as her mother spoke louder.

" 'Tis fine, Annabel. Come."

"But," Annabel began again. Ross didn't hear anymore and glanced up to see that her mother had dragged her from the room and was pulling her out of sight up the hall.

"Well," Lord Waverly said bluffly, clapping his hands and sidling toward the door, the priest following. "This all worked out nicely then. The two of you have fulfilled the contract and all is set. I guess I shall go see to hanging the linen so everyone can see 'tis done."

Ross simply turned back to his work without comment. He didn't like the sly man, and didn't much care what he did. He was now wholly focused on getting himself, his men and his new bride the hell out of there.

"Never countermand your husband's orders. You must be dutiful and obedient at all times."

Annabel bit her lip at her mother's sharp words as she was dragged away from the room where she and Ross had slept. But after a moment she simply couldn't keep from saying, "Aye, but surely we cannot leave right away? 'Tis a long journey to Scotland. Surely there is much to do to prepare for it?"

"What is there to do, Annabel?" her mother asked pointedly.

"Well . . . pack?" she suggested uncertainly. Never having traveled before other than the trip to the abbey and then the wagon journey back, Annabel had no idea what one did to prepare for a journey like this, but surely packing was—

"You have nothing to pack," Lady Waverly said in leaden tones. "So 'tis good he is not giving you time to pack. You can blame your lack on his rush to leave."

Annabel frowned. "Well, surely Kate did not take all of her gowns with her? Perhaps I could—"

"Your father was so furious he had all your sister's gowns burned when he disowned her," her mother interrupted, and then added, "And do not even suggest I give you some of mine. You are far too large to wear them."

Annabel stared at her blankly. She had always been on the heavy side compared to the other women at the abbey. The abbess was quite firm in stating that pleasures of the flesh were to be avoided, and food was one of those as far as she was concerned, and of course she was right, gluttony was a sin. Most women in the abbey ate little more than enough to keep a bird alive to please the abbess, but Annabel hadn't been able to do that. Working in the stables took energy and she had needed to eat to do the work properly. It had been an issue of conflict between she and the abbess and she had been punished for it repeatedly. However, her mother was not a thin, pallid woman like the nuns Annabel had grown up with. If anything, she was actually larger than Annabel, but she didn't point this out. It seemed obvious her mother didn't wish to give up even one of her gowns, so she would go without.

Which meant she had nothing. Annabel hadn't even been allowed to pack the few things from her room at the abbey before leaving there. Not that she'd had much; a dried and pressed flower from the day she and the other girls had been sent out to find rushes and had laughed and chatted more than worked. That had been a fine day and she'd plucked the flower and pressed it between the stone floor of her room and a large rock until it dried out so that she could preserve it. Other than that all she possessed was a well worn and frayed gown, an old brush, and a scrap of cloth left over from making the gown she'd put on to meet her mother . . . That thought made hope rise in her and she said, "I have the gown I came here in."

"I had it burned," Lady Waverly said at once. When Annabel stared at her with dismay, she pointed out impatiently, "You could hardly have taken it with you. It was made of the cheapest cloth and obviously a noviate's. Your husband does not know you were in a nunnery." She hesitated and then added, "Do not be foolish enough to tell him. He will feel cheated that he did not get a properly trained bride, and while there is nothing he can do to us over it now the marriage is done and consummated, he could take it out on you with his fists."

Annabel swallowed at these words, surprised by the concern that showed briefly in her mother's face before she hid it. They had been like strangers since her mother had arrived at the abbey. This was the first sign of anything even approaching maternal concern from her. Annabel didn't get to contemplate that much however, she was more concerned by what her mother had said. It had never occurred to her that her husband would be angry at her upbringing, but she supposed it should have. Annabel was more than aware that she was not prepared to run his home or be a wife. He was not. Yet. He would learn soon enough, however . . . and may very well be angry as her mother suggested. No man wanted a wife who did not know the first thing about running a household.

"Teach me," she blurted desperately.

Lady Waverly peered at her blankly for a moment and then asked with bewilderment, "Teach you what?"

"Teach me to be a proper wife to Ross, to run his home and rule his people and—"

"Annabel," her mother interrupted with disgust. "I can not possibly teach you all you need to know in the short time we have before you leave."

"No, of course you cannot," Annabel agreed unhappily, her eyes dropping to the hall floor as she considered her future. She glanced up, however, when her mother patted her shoulder.

"You shall just have to do your best and hope it is well enough," Lady Waverly murmured, and then turned to peer up the hall with obvious relief when Ross stepped out of the room where they'd slept and peered around. "Ah there you are. Time to go, I suppose. Come along, Annabel, do not keep your husband waiting."

With nothing else to do, Annabel simply nodded and followed her mother to her new husband. She had no idea why she had been so desperate to delay their leave-taking. While her husband was a virtual stranger, so were her parents, and frankly, he had shown her more kindness in the last twenty-four hours since she'd left the abbey than her own parents had. The thought should have been encouraging, so she had no idea why it depressed her so.

"OH LOOK! ISN'T IT PRETTY? WHAT IS IT?"

"A goldcrest," Ross answered, just refraining from grabbing Annabel's arm to keep her from toppling out of her saddle as she craned about to follow the flying bird's path. The woman had been twisting about, pointing to nearly everything they passed, and asking what it was since they'd left Waverly that morning . . . and despite his worries, she hadn't once fallen out of her saddle. Although, he didn't know how she kept her seat. Honestly, his new bride was the most atrocious rider he'd ever seen. Rather than ride with the animal, she bounced about on her mount's back like a sack of turnips. If he didn't know she was a lady, and therefore must have ridden before, Ross would have sworn she'd never been on a horse in her life. It had forced him to set a much more sedate pace for the journey home than he'd planned for fear she might bounce right off the mare he'd taken to Waverly with him as her wedding gift.

Ross smiled. While he was annoyed at the pace they had to keep, he had to admit her response to his gift had pleased him mightily. When he'd led her out of the keep, Gilly had led the horse up to them and Ross had announced that the mare was her wedding gift.

Annabel had gasped with surprise and then thrown herself at him, hugging him tightly as she cried, "Thank you, thank you, thank you." Before he could gather himself sufficiently to close his arms around her in response, she'd pulled away to rush over and coo and croon to the mare. Ross had watched her with a small smile until he'd noticed the expressions on her parents' faces. They had obviously been both startled and disapproving of Annabel's making such a fuss over the gift, and he hadn't appreciated their reaction.

Mouth tightening, Ross had walked over, caught his bride about the waist and lifted her up onto the side saddle he'd also got for her. He'd then mounted his own horse and led the way out of the bailey, aware without looking that the men would ensure Annabel followed directly behind him, while they surrounded and backed her with their own mounts.

At least that was how it started, but her questions had begun almost the moment they'd passed out of the bailey. While the men had answered her questions at first, Ross had found himself growing a bit jealous of all the chatter and laughter Annabel was sharing with his men. He'd finally dropped back to ride beside her, leaving Gilly to take the lead. And he had been in a state of high anxiety ever since.

"Ooooh, look at that one! What is it?"

Ross glanced to his bride and followed her pointing finger to the blue-and-yellow bird that had caught her eye. "A blue tit."

" 'Tis lovely," she said on a sigh, bouncing away on the horse.

Ross frowned. She'd been bouncing about like that all day without complaint, but must be sore. They'd even eaten in the saddle rather than stop at the nooning, and now the sun was sinking in the sky. The woman hadn't even asked to stop so that she might relieve herself. Speaking of which, he had a sharp need to do so himself now that he thought about it. They may as well stop for the night, he decided, and whistled to get Gilly's attention.

The man immediately slowed and urged his horse to the side of the trail so that Ross could ride up beside him, then fell into step next to him. Moments later they were halting their horses in a clearing along a small stream. It was a beautiful spot, and Ross considered slipping away into the woods to consummate his marriage, but only briefly. Annabel's first time shouldn't be in the woods where anyone might come upon them. Besides, the way she rode, he had no doubt she would be sore as the devil and not exactly in the mood. On top of that, he wouldn't want to add to that soreness, so he put the thought away and resigned himself to another night without. But he couldn't help grimacing over the lack as he dismounted and walked over to lift Annabel off her mare.

"Oh!" she gasped with surprise as her legs

went out under her. She would have fallen had he released her when he set her on the ground, but Ross had expected this and held her up. After a moment, she smiled at him with chagrin. "My apologies, my lord. I fear I have never ridden this long before."

"Have ye never traveled with yer parents to court or to visit others?" he asked with surprise.

Annabel shook her head, and then looked uncomfortable and lowered her head. "Nay. The longest journey I have taken was little more than a half day ride and that was in a carriage."

"But ye have ridden before?" he asked, leaning a bit to the side in an effort to see her face.

"Of course," she assured him, glancing up again. Annabel seemed to want to add something else, but then just smiled and asked, "Are we stopping for the night?"

"Aye."

Annabel had stopped leaning into him and appeared to have recovered, so Ross released his hold on her. He remained ready to grab her again should the need arise, but it didn't. She was able to stand alone now.

She had recovered quickly, Ross acknowledged and that along with her lack of complaining today impressed him. His bride was no weak English miss, he thought with satisfaction, and took her arm to guide her toward the edge of the clearing. "Ye probably wish to refresh yerself."

"Aye," she murmured and he glanced at her sharply. Her tone was uncertain, even anxious and he wasn't sure what that was about, but let it go.

Ross led her to a spot a good distance away from the men and around a bend and then released her, saying he'd wait just the other side of the bend. The relief on her face explained her earlier anxiety. He suspected she'd wondered how to tell him she needed a moment alone to relieve herself. She was still shy around him, of course, and no doubt would be until they really did consummate the marriage.

Ross quickly pushed that thought out of his mind. It wasn't smart to start thinking on touching and kissing her and sinking himself into her warm depths. That was a temptation he had already decided to avoid until they reached MacKay, but damned if just holding her upright beside her horse hadn't stirred his manhood.

Shaking his head at his own body, Ross paused beside a bush, lifted his plaid, took hold of the still half erect member in question and released a little sigh as he watered the greenery. Sometimes, it just felt so damned good to empty the snake, he thought and then jerked around midstream and broke into a run at a sudden scream from Annabel.

He hadn't moved far away, just enough to give her privacy, so it only took him a dozen steps to reach her side. When he did, he found her staring wide-eyed into the bushes opposite the direction he'd come from.

"What is it?" he asked at once, though his mind was half on wondering whether he hadn't just pissed all over his plaid and when he'd get to finish what he'd started. Damn, she'd scared the life out of him and he'd dropped his plaid and whipped about so quick—

"There was someone in those bushes," Annabel whispered, pointing a shaky finger.

Ross frowned when he saw that the greenery was still quivering. That was enough to drive the question of his lower member's activities from his mind. Pulling his sword from the sheath at his waist, he strode forward at once, ordering, "Wait here."

Ross followed the very obvious trail for a good twenty feet before pausing. He didn't want to move any further while Annabel was left alone behind him. If whoever she'd seen circled around and went back to her she would be defenseless. That thought was enough to have him quickly returning the way he'd come.

Much to his relief, Annabel was still waiting where he'd left her. She looked unharmed but anxious, and he couldn't help noting that for all she was stalwart about not complaining and so on, she did seem overly nervous a lot of the time. On the other hand, Ross supposed the possibility of having your maidenhood breached and someone coming up on you while you were relieving yourself were worthy of anxiety.

Taking her arm, he started to urge her back the way they'd come, but she dug her feet in.

"Oh, but I still have to—" She cut herself off and blushed.

"Aye. Ye will. I just want to fetch the men," he assured her, trying to get her moving again.

"The men?" Annabel squawked with dismay, digging in her heels.

"Aye. We can stand around ye and be sure no one creeps up on ye again," Ross explained. It seemed perfectly reasonable to him. But judging by the horror that covered her face at the suggestion, she didn't agree.

"My lord, surely you do not expect me to . . . with men standing around me?" she asked as if he'd suggested she do it in the village square for all to see . . . and naked.

"Well, they won't be able to see anything," he assured her with amusement. Damned if he'd let his men look on her cute little derriere as she knelt in the bushes. "They'll be on the other side of the bushes, but there to stop anyone else approaching."

Annabel was shaking her head before he'd finished. "I cannot possibly—not while I know your men are all standing around listening to me . . . I just cannot," she said helplessly.

"It's pissen, lass," he said helpfully since she seemed unable to voice the word herself. "It's a pissen yer needing. Ye can say the word. I'll no think less o' ye fer it."

Annabel opened her mouth, closed it, and then simply shook her head again.

Ross sighed. If she couldn't even say the damned word, there was no way she was going to do it with guards standing but feet away. He glanced around, considering what to do, then nodded. "Right. Then come here."

"Where are we—?" Her question died as he led her to a bush at the stream's edge and paused.

"Ye do it here," he said releasing her arm and moving three or four feet away to turn his back to her. "And I'll stand guard here. That way yer front and back are safe and we can both keep an eye on the sides."

Ross waited for either agreement or the rustle of her adjusting her clothes, but neither sounded. Resisting the urge to look back and see what she was doing, he asked, "Yer no' doing it, are ye?"

"Umm . . . nay, not yet," she muttered, then paused, cleared her throat, and asked, "Do you think you could whistle, my lord?"

"Whistle?" He did glance around then. She was standing where he'd left her, looking uncomfortable, but still upright, not down on her haunches with her skirt hiked up around her waist.

Annabel grimaced apologetically. "It would help if you did."

Sighing, Ross shook his head, but turned away and began to whistle. He was wishing though, that she'd just hurry up and get it done. He still had some pissen of his own to do. So, he was more than a little relieved when she cleared her throat a moment later and murmured, "We can return to the clearing."

Ross walked her back to where the men were setting up camp, had a word with Gilly and Marach, telling them both what had happened. He then ordered them to keep on eye on Annabel, and ordered the other men to search the area to be sure whoever had come up on his wife had left.

Ross suspected it had been another traveler, on foot, or camped nearby looking for their own spot to take care of private matters, but neither he nor any of his men came across anyone. He found the trail again that he'd been following earlier, but it continued only for another ten feet before disappearing at the water's edge. There was no sign of a boat having come aground there. He doubted the stream was even deep enough for a boat, though, so either they'd crossed the stream, or they'd walked through it for a while before coming back out. That didn't change his mind about it all being an accidental encounter though. They were in England. What Englishman wouldn't use the stream to cover his trail when an angry Scot was after him, ready to trounce him for coming upon his wife like that?

Satisfied that all was well, Ross called off the search and left the men to hunt up dinner while he returned to the campsite and his bride.

Chapter 4

$\mathcal{A}$NNABEL ROLLED ONTO HER BACK AND OPENED her eyes with a happy, sleepy little sigh, then blinked in surprise when she found herself staring at a ceiling overhead rather than open air. Sitting up abruptly, she peered around, eyes wide as she took in the room she was in. It was a large one with a table and chairs in the far right corner, two chairs and a small table before a fire directly across from her, and a stand for a washbasin between two windows to the left of her . . . and then of course there was the bed she was in, quite the largest bed she'd ever seen, and so soft and comfy. It felt like it was stuffed with feathers rather than straw. It was at least five times bigger than the hard, narrow cot she'd slept in for the last fourteen years at the abbey, and almost twice the size of the bed she and Ross had slept in at Waverly. It was also definitely more comfortable than that bed had been. Annabel was quite sure even the king couldn't have a nicer bed when it came to comfort.

The problem was, she had no idea whose bed it was, or where she was. The last thing Annabel remembered was riding her mare on the third day of their interminable journey to her new home. They had stopped the first two days when the sun had begun to set, but on the third night they'd continued on well past sunset. Annabel had wondered about that, thinking perhaps they were near MacKay, but hadn't asked and had simply continued forward.

Annabel supposed she'd fallen asleep in the saddle and was rather surprised she hadn't toppled right off her horse. Really, that silly side-saddle was an atrocious invention. People weren't meant to ride with their legs to the side, she was sure, and while she'd never ridden astride on a saddle, she was positive it must be much more comfortable. Certainly, it had to be easier to direct the horse with a squeeze of legs instead of counting wholly on the reins.

The opening of the bedchamber door drew Annabel from her thoughts and she tensed and glanced to it, relaxing a bit when an older woman stuck her head in. The stranger then beamed when she saw Annabel upright in bed.

"Ah, good! Yer awake, ye are." She opened the door wide then and bustled in, leading a parade of servants carrying various items.

Annabel drew the furs up to her chin and stared wide-eyed as a tub was carted in by two men and set in the large space remaining in the far left corner of the room. It was followed by four men, each carrying a bucket of water in each hand; some of those buckets were steaming, others were not. The men were followed by women carrying soaps, linens, and one a tray with food on it. The last to enter the room were two more men carrying a chest between them.

It was quite crowded in the room for a moment, but cleared out quickly as each person set down their burden and hurried out with a quick curious glance, a bobbing curtsy, or a smile in her direction. Annabel smiled anxiously back, nodding at each person as they passed until just the first woman who had entered was left.

"There we are!" she said cheerfully, closing the door behind the last departing servant. "We're all set then I think."

"Erm," Annabel murmured, still clutching the furs to her chin. She wasn't quite sure what they were set for. She wasn't even sure where she was, though she was beginning to suspect she'd slept through their arrival at MacKay. Someone had obviously carried her up here to bed . . . and stripped her, she realized with dismay as she noted that she was completely and utterly naked under the linens and furs.

"Now ye just break yer fast while I prepare yer bath fer ye." The words were accompanied by the tray of food being plunked on her lap in bed.

The tray held bread, cheese, two fluffy-looking pastries and some sort of beverage. Judging by the scent of the steam wafting from it, warmed cider. Annabel simply stared at the fare, the woman's words winding through her thoughts: *"Now ye just break yer fast while I prepare yer bath fer ye."*

The bath was for her? And the food? Annabel

was not used to being waited on. At the abbey, there had been one standard bath time for everyone at the abbess's discretion. She announced it was bath day, a large tub was readied in the kitchens and the women took turns using it. As one of the younger residents of the abbey, Annabel had always been one of the last to bathe and the water had always been tepid and dirty by the time she got to it.

Annabel had suffered through it because she had to, but she had never felt clean afterward and had often slipped away to bathe in the stream as soon as she could. Actually, she had often slipped away to the stream between bath times too. Annabel had spent half her time at the abbey working with the animals in the stables and half her time illuminating texts. Her work with the texts was no problem, but working in the stables was a dirty job, and the abbess didn't order baths as often as Annabel would have liked, so Annabel had regularly slipped away to the stream.

Unfortunately, the abbess had discovered her little trips and had not been pleased. To her mind, it was vanity that made Annabel want to be clean. The welts Annabel presently bore on her back were her punishment. The abbess never struck the women under her care, but she did make them do it themselves, and if you didn't bring on marks, she threatened a worse punishment. There were many worse punishments at the abbey. The abbess could be very creative when it came to punishing those under her charge.

"Do ye no' like pastries?"

Annabel glanced up from the tray to see that

the older woman had paused in emptying a bucket into the tub to eye her with concern.

"Oh, aye," she said quickly, picking up one of the flaky pastries. Annabel had no idea if she liked pastries. She'd never had one before. The cook at the abbey wasn't a very good one. The best she could manage was stews or other easy and plain fare. Not that the abbess would have encouraged cook to make such things anyway. She did have issues around gluttony and the women daring to enjoy their food. Annabel personally felt there was something a bit unnatural about the abbess's obsession with the matter, but had just accepted it as a part of her life.

Now, she took a tentative bite and then simply held it in her mouth, her eyes slowly growing wide. She had never in her life tasted anything as lovely as that flaky pastry with the burst of sweet fruit in the center. While the cook at Waverly may have presented something as good at her wedding feast, Annabel had been too nervous to eat and had simply sat sipping at the honeyed mead that had been placed before her. But this . . . this was nirvana.

A clanging sound drew her gaze to the maid dumping water into the tub, and Annabel popped the rest of the pastry into her mouth, and chewed on it as she looked around for her gown. She spotted it lying across the foot of the bed. Swallowing the pastry, she set the tray aside and leaned forward to grab the gown. Annabel quickly tugged it on over her head and then crawled out of bed, letting the gown drop down past her waist as she hurried over to help with the water.

"What are ye doing lass?" the old woman asked with amazement when Annabel picked up a bucket and dumped it in.

"Helping?" Annabel said uncertainly, a little set aback by the woman's shocked expression.

"Helping?" the woman said slowly, and then shook her head. "Well, stop it and get yerself back to the bed to finish breaking yer fast. This is me job, no' yers."

"Oh." Annabel flushed with embarrassment and set the bucket back down. She then scampered back to the bed and sat down to pull the tray closer. She had gobbled down the first pastry to rush over and help with the bath, but took her time and savored the second one. It really was delicious, and she couldn't help thinking it might be a good thing that the abbey cook hadn't made things as lovely as this. Her back would have been crisscrossed with welts and scars for gluttony.

Despite taking her time, Annabel finished the pastry before the old woman had finished filling the tub, so she picked briefly at the cheese and bread. But she was no longer hungry, so set it aside after a couple of bites and simply sipped at the warm apple cider as she waited.

"There we are."

That satisfied comment from the older woman drew Annabel's attention to the fact that she was finished filling the bath and was now eyeing Annabel.

Setting the cider back on the tray, Annabel pushed herself up from the bed and hurried over to the tub.

"The laird said he didn't arrange to bring yer lady's maid, so ye'll have to pick one from the women here. In the meantime, ye'll have to make do with me," the woman announced, reaching out to help her take off the dress.

Annabel was not used to the assistance of a lady's maid. That simply didn't happen at the abbey. At least it hadn't happened for her and as far as she knew the other women didn't have maids to dress or undress them. Well, except for the abbess. Perhaps that was why having this nice older lady trying to undress her left Annabel feeling terribly uncomfortable.

Biting back the protest that she wasn't a child and could manage herself, Annabel suffered her help, but it was a relief when the dress was off and she could hop into the water. However, once there, the woman didn't let her be, but picked up a scrap of linen and soap. Rather than hand it to her, as Annabel expected, she dipped the cloth in the water, applied some soap and began to work it into a lather. Even then she didn't hand it over to Annabel, but swept her hair to the side over her shoulder so that it was out of the way and began to wash her back.

Annabel sat completely still for several minutes, and then cleared her throat and asked, "What is your name?"

"Oh," the maid chuckled softly, her back scrubbing stopping briefly as she then said, "I am sorry, me lady. I did no' even think to tell ye, did I? I'm Seonag."

"Seonag," Annabel murmured, pronouncing it *Shaw-nack*, as she had. She then twisted in the tub to peer at her and offer a smile. " 'Tis a pleasure to meet you, Seonag."

"Oh." The woman looked surprised, and then smiled back widely. "Well, I'm sure 'tis a pleasure to meet ye too, me lady."

Nodding, Annabel turned forward again. Seonag immediately began to scrub her back again and after a moment, Annabel asked, "This is MacKay, then?"

Seonag stopped scrubbing briefly, and then straightened and moved to stand at the side of the tub where she could see her face. Her mouth was wide open when she first got there, but she snapped it closed and then said with exasperation, "And well surely ye do no' ken, do ye? Ye were sleeping when the laird carried ye in. Goodness, ye must ha'e been sitting there wondering who the devil we all were when we came barging in." She shook her head and then said, "Aye, m'lady. This is MacKay."

Annabel nodded. She'd assumed as much, but it was good to be sure. "And where is my . . . husband?" It felt odd calling Ross that. Annabel supposed it was because it was all so new.

"Oh, he's off talking with Liam," she said as if that was to be expected. Annabel had no idea who Liam was and supposed her expression was blank at this news, because Seonag explained, "Liam is his second. He'll be filling the laird in on what happened while he was away."

"Oh, aye, of course." Annabel nodded.

Smiling, Seonag shifted behind the tub again, but this time to rinse away the soap she'd applied. As she finished, she said, "I'll wash yer hair now and then leave ye to finish while I sort through the gowns. There must be one or two we can make do with until the merchant comes around with cloth we can buy to make ye a wardrobe."

"Gowns?" Annabel asked with interest, glancing around. Her gaze landed on the chest that had been carried in last.

"Aye. The laird said as how he didn't even give ye time to pack a chest to bring with ye and ye'd need new gowns so I had the boys bring in Lady Magaidh's chest."

Annabel bit her lip, but was saved from having to comment when Seonag had her lean back so that she could dampen her hair. She was very aware, though, that there had been nothing to pack. The gown she'd worn to Waverly had been burned. She wasn't even sure whose gown she'd worn to be married in. In all the panic of the situation, she hadn't thought to ask. She assumed, though, that it had been the wedding gown made for Kate to wear to marry Ross. It certainly hadn't been made for her. Her mother's servants had needed to add panels to the sides to make it large enough to fit her and had worked feverishly to get that done while Annabel had been bathed and prepared. Fortunately, Kate was apparently taller as well as thinner, and the three inches that had been cut from the hem of the skirt so that she didn't tread on it had been long enough to make two panels, one for each side.

"Who is Lady Magaidh?" Annabel asked curiously as Seonag soaped her hair.

"The laird's mother," Seonag answered, and explained, "She passed five years ago, so the gowns aren't new, but surely there will be something that will do."

Annabel nodded silently.

"The two o' ye are of a size too, so there shouldn't be much need for alterations except to modernize them a bit," Seonag added cheerfully. "And that is grand."

"Aye," Annabel agreed as Seonag began to rinse the soap from her hair. But she couldn't help thinking this was the first time anyone had thought her over-generous curves were a good thing. Her mother had made several disappointed comments as they'd prepared her for the wedding, obviously wishing she'd been tall and slender like her sister, Kate, had apparently grown to be. Certainly the abbess had done nothing but criticize her for the gluttony she felt Annabel's size revealed.

"There ye go. All done," Seonag said lightly, urging her to sit up in the tub again. "Ye finish up and I'll go start sorting through the gowns."

Annabel accepted the cloth she was offered and began to run the soapy swath of linen over her arms and chest, but her gaze was on Seonag as she bustled over to the chest and opened it to reveal a collection of colorful material. She watched her lift out the first gown, a deep red creation that she examined briefly before laying it across the foot of the bed. It was followed by a dark forest green gown before a burnished orange one with a large stain on it was dropped to the floor.

Several more gowns were laid across the bed before Annabel finished her bath, but the moment she began to wring out the cloth she'd been using to wash with and started to stand up, Seonag dropped what she was doing and rushed to grab a large dry linen to wrap around her.

"Thank you," Annabel said with a crooked smile. She simply wasn't used to being tended to like this and was uncomfortable with it. But she didn't admit as much. The woman would probably wonder what was wrong with her. Annabel supposed this was how ladies were treated . . . when they weren't oblates in a nunnery.

"Here now, come sit by the hearth and I'll brush yer hair," Seonag said, taking her arm as Annabel stepped out of the tub.

Annabel allowed her to lead her to one of the chairs by the fireplace. There was no fire, but it was summer, and one wasn't really necessary. She was silent at first as Seonag pulled a brush through her hair, but then began to ask questions. Annabel knew nothing about her new husband, her new home, or the people in it, and it did seem that arming herself with information was a good idea, so she asked, "Was my husband close to his mother?"

"Oh, aye. He worshipped his mother," Seonag assured her. "Lady Magaidh was a very special lady. Everyone loved her. She knew everyone's name from the cook down to the lowliest servant. And she ran this keep like a dream." Seonag sighed wistfully. " 'Twas a sad day indeed when she died."

Annabel frowned. She had no doubt that she would not gain such lauding from anyone on her running of the keep. She didn't even know what was involved. What was she expected to do, exactly? Sighing, she let that go for now, and asked, "How did she die?"

"A chest complaint. At first she just seemed breathless on occasion, but then she seemed to gasp for air and cough a lot. Then she couldn't even get enough breath to walk about. She had to run the keep from a chair in the great hall and then from bed, and then she just . . ." Seonag shrugged helplessly and finished, "withered away."

Annabel murmured in sympathy and let a moment pass in silence before asking, "And my husband's father?"

"Oh, aye, the old laird." Seonag sighed sadly, the brush slowing in Annabel's hair. "He died from a sliver."

Annabel blinked and turned to stare at her. "A sliver?"

"Hmm." Seonag nodded and urged her back around so she could continue brushing her hair. "It got infected. I fussed at him over it, but he waved me away and wouldn't listen. The truth is I think his heart was so broken from losing Lady Magaidh that he just did no' care to live," she added with another sigh. "When a black line started up his arm I knew he was as good as done fer."

"Oh dear," Annabel murmured. Death by sliver. She supposed she shouldn't be surprised. It was not all that rare, really. At least, not from what she'd been told. Sister Clara, who had worked with her in the stables, had once said that it was often the small wounds that were ignored and left to fester while larger ones claimed all the attention. Sister Clara had not been an oblate. She'd lived a normal life, growing up with her family before marrying and having children. It was only after her children had been married off and her husband had died that she had found her way to the abbey and taken vows. She'd said that life hadn't been the same without her husband, and she was content to serve God for the rest of her days.

Sister Clara had taught Annabel a lot. She had been one of a very few bright spots in her life at the abbey. She would miss her ... and hadn't even got to say good-bye. The thought made her frown. She hadn't been allowed to collect anything, and hadn't been given the chance to say good-bye to anyone ... Could they not have spared just a couple of moments to do both?

"Ahhh, that looks lovely."

Annabel blinked as Seonag suddenly thrust a hand mirror with a cloudy, slightly warped surface before her. Then she simply stared. Mirrors had not been allowed at the abbey. The abbess said vanity was a sin, and mirrors were a toy of the devil. Whether there was a mirror at Waverly, Annabel couldn't say. Certainly her mother hadn't offered her one once she was prepared for her wedding and she hadn't thought to ask. The only time she'd seen herself ere this was in the surface of the stream she had swum in at the abbey, which reflected a wavy image at best.

"Do you like it?" Seonag asked, smiling.

Annabel reached up and touched her hair. Seonag had brushed it dry. It was a shiny, black mass in the reflection and flowed around a pale oval face with rosy cheeks. The maid had pulled back and braided a few small strands on either side of Annabel's face, clasping them behind her head somehow. It made her eyes look huge. That or she had huge eyes, Annabel supposed.

"I look beautiful," she said with wonder and for some reason the words made laughter burst from Seonag.

"Lovey, ye *are* beautiful," Seonag said with amusement, and then more gently, "Surely yer parents told ye that?"

Her mother had done nothing but mutter with distress over how large she was, and moan over how shameful it was that the abbess had allowed her to get to this size. Annabel suspected that Lady Waverly would not agree that she was beautiful. She was saved from having to say so, however, by the opening of the bedchamber door. Both she and Seonag glanced to it with surprise, but Annabel had to lean to the side to peer past Seonag to see that it was her husband.

"Ah, good. Yer ready," Ross said with approval when he spotted her.

"Well, that depends on what ye want her ready fer," Seonag said with amusement, stepping aside to reveal that Annabel was still garbed in only the linen wrapped around her.

"Oh." Ross stared briefly, his eyes slipping over her so that Annabel didn't feel covered at all. After his gaze had devoured every inch of her, he growled one word. "Seonag."

The woman released an amused chuckle and bustled toward the door, detouring briefly to collect the gowns from the bed along the way. "I'll just take these below and see what I can do to repair and prepare them while ye have a word with yer bride."

Ross grunted a sound of approval and tugged the door open for her. The moment the servant was through it, he closed the door and stalked across the room toward Annabel.

"Oh," she said faintly as he approached. His eyes were fixed on her like those of a wolf on a wee, defenseless rabbit and she rather felt like a rabbit in that moment. There was something in his eyes that was making her extremely nervous. He looked hungry, and not for food. For some reason it made her think perhaps he wanted to consummate their marriage again. Although she supposed you couldn't consummate it more than once, though she was certainly no expert in the matter. In fact, she didn't even recall the first consummation, so she was as ignorant as could be on the subject, but she was pretty sure he was having some rather carnal thoughts.

When his gaze settled in the area of her breasts through the damp cloth and he licked his lips, Annabel stood abruptly, her hand tightening on the linen she was holding around her shoulders. She managed a smile, but her feet were carrying her backward away from him as she said, "I am sorry for sleeping so late, my lord."

"It was a long journey and ye did no' sleep well during it. I told the servants to let ye sleep in," Ross said, following her backward progress.

"Oh. Well, that was . . . er . . . that was sweet," Annabel stammered as she felt the top of the mantelpiece bump against the back of her neck. Unable to move back anymore, she started shifting sideways instead and said, "Thank you."

"Yer welcome," he responded. As he stalked

her, his eyes dropped to slide over the linen covering her as if he could see right through it. That fact made her glance down to see that he could indeed see through it. At least he could in the places where the linen was damp . . . which seemed to be over all the more important bits, she noted with alarm and recalled Father Gerder's lectures on the evils of women and the temptation they offered. Dear God, it seemed she was doing just that without even meaning to, tempting her husband with the pleasures of the flesh . . . and on a Wednesday, one of the days the church had outlawed carnal pleasures.

Annabel bumped unexpectedly into the second chair by the fire and came to an abrupt halt. Her husband, however, did not, at least not until he was a bare inch away. Crowding her against the chair, Ross reached for her waist and drew her forward until their bodies pressed against each other.

Annabel gazed up at him wide-eyed as his face descended toward hers and then blurted, "'Tis a fine Wednesday morning, is it not?"

"Aye," he agreed, his mouth aiming for hers. She was quite sure he would have kissed her had she not turned her head away.

When his lips instead sought her neck and began to nibble there, doing the oddest things to her equilibrium, Annabel clasped his upper arms to keep her balance and said desperately, "Aye, a fine *Wednesday* morning." When he still didn't seem to grasp the significance of that, but allowed his lips to trail down to her collarbone, she added desperately, "I wonder why the church deems

Wednesdays an unsuitable day for couples to in-dulge in the bedding?"

Ross stiffened at her words, and stood com-pletely still for a moment, but then he straight-ened slowly. His expression was not happy as he eyed her. "It does, doesn't it?"

Annabel nodded apologetically and was almost sorry she had mentioned it to him. Part of her regretted having to remind him and prevent his gaining what he wished. However, another part was rather relieved. While she appreciated his consideration in getting her sotted for the con-summation of their marriage so she hadn't had to suffer through it . . . well, really, since she couldn't recall it, she was as ignorant and nervous of the act as she had been on her wedding night. And it was her opinion that it was always better to get unpleasant matters done and out of the way.

Darn Father Gerder for harping on the matter of marital relations and when they were and weren't acceptable, Annabel thought with irritation. Had he not done that, in five minutes or so she would probably be crawling out of bed a wiser woman, because surely it didn't take long?

Truthfully, Annabel had no idea why the priest had bothered lecturing on it to a bunch of nuns, but then there were many things he'd lectured on that had not seemed relevant for the inhabit-ants of an abbey. The man just seemed to get in these moods where he would rant and rave about the evils of the world. It was usually about such things as the marital bed and sins of the flesh. Really, the man was as obsessed with the subject as the abbess.

Sighing, Ross straightened and released her. He then gave her a solemn nod and turned to leave the room without another word.

Annabel stared at the closed door and bit her lip. She knew she had done the right thing. The church had outlawed the bedding on Sundays, Wednesdays and Fridays. Still, she felt like she had failed her husband somehow. Annabel suspected that was a sensation she should get used to. She had no doubt at all that she was going to disappoint him often as she proved how ignorant and untrained a bride he had gained himself.

Grimacing, Annabel pushed that thought away and glanced around the room until she spotted her gown lying over a nearby chair where Seonag had apparently laid it after helping her to undress. Walking over, she picked it up and immediately grimaced at the stench of it. Annabel had worn it for four days straight, which was not unusual, but three of those days had been during the journey here and it now smelled of horse, grass and sweat. Funny how she hadn't noticed before bathing, and it did seem a shame to pull that on after having a bath.

Turning, Annabel considered the gowns Seonag had left scattered around the chest. They had been the rejects, set aside because of some fault or other, but there might be one in good-enough shape to wear, or at least to make it preferable to her sullied gown.

After a quick examination, Annabel settled on a pale pink gown with a small stain on the décolletage. The stain was really quite small, barely noticeable she was sure, so she donned the dress and then peered down at herself. It seemed Seonag had been wrong; she and Ross's mother were not exactly of a size after all. At least not in the bust-line. The rest of the gown fit perfectly, but Lady MacKay definitely had not been quite as well en-dowed as she.

Annabel pushed at her breasts, trying to tuck them inside the gown as much as possible, but they still appeared to be trying to crawl out. Sigh-ing, she dug through the chest until she found a bit of fine white cloth. She placed that in the neckline to make it more decent, and then think-ing she had done the best she could, she headed for the door, intending to go in search of Seonag. However, she had just reached for the door when a clatter and shriek from the window behind her made her pause.

Frowning, she turned and moved back across the room. There were shutters that were presently wide open. She supposed Ross had opened them on rising that morning to allow light in to help him dress. That or they had been open all night. Whatever the case, they were wide open now and Annabel leaned out the window to peer down into the bailey. At first, she couldn't tell what had happened, but then she saw a small group of people gathered around an overturned wagon. When one of the people shifted, she caught a glimpse of a man on the ground and blood and it was enough to have her straightening and rush-ing for the door.

"Oh, m'lady, I was just coming to—" Seonag began when Annabel passed her as she rushed down the stairs from the upper floor. If the maid finished what she was saying, Annabel didn't hear it. She hadn't even slowed for the woman, but flew past to race down the rest of the stairs, across the busy great hall, and out into the bailey on feet that seemed almost winged, she was moving so swiftly.

Annabel had to pause on the stairs once she pushed through the doors and out into the bailey so that she could orient herself, but it was the briefest of pauses before she spotted the growing crowd around the overturned wagon and hurried that way. Murmuring apologies and "Excuse mes," she made her way through the crowd to the center and the injured man, and immediately dropped to kneel beside him, her eyes taking in the situation.

"What happened?" Annabel asked as she shifted her attention and hands to the man's bloodied leg and began to feel along its length, checking for broken bones. Silence met her question and Annabel glanced up with a frown to see that everyone, including the man she knelt over was staring at her with wide-eyed amazement and uncertainty.

"Well answer yer lady, ye dolts!"

Recognizing Seonag's voice, Annabel glanced over her shoulder to see that the maid had followed her out of the keep and now stood at her back. She offered the servant a grateful smile and turned back to the injured man as several people began to speak at once in a confusing cacophony of voices.

"One at a time," Seonag barked as Annabel ran her hands down the man's leg again. She hadn't felt anything that suggested a break, but it was best to be sure before moving him too much.

"That damned dog startled my horse. The beast reared and took off and his halter snapped, but not before my cart overturned, throwing myself and my goods to the ground," the injured man explained through gritted teeth. His accent was English rather than Scottish and had Annabel not already guessed he was a visiting merchant, his mention of goods would have. However, she had no idea what he meant by "that damned dog," but that didn't matter at the moment anyway.

"I need a knife," she announced, glancing around at the faces in the crowd.

"What do ye need a knife for? You don't need a knife," the injured man assured her, his voice suddenly several octaves higher.

"Here. Will me *sgian dubh* do, m'lady?"

"Thank you." Annabel smiled absently at the man who offered her a small knife and then turned back to the merchant, who was staring wide-eyed at the small sharp blade.

"What the devil do you think you'll be doing with that?" he asked with alarm.

"Hush. I shall not hurt you," Annabel said reassuringly and quickly slit a line up the length of his braies from the bottom to several inches above the wound on his thigh just above his knee. The action sent an immediate rush of whispers through the crowd, but Annabel ignored it and tugged the cloth aside to get a better look at his wound.

"You've ruined my drawers!" the tradesman squawked with dismay.

"Yer drawers were ruined by the accident," Seonag pointed out dryly. "If ye were a Scot and wearing a plaid, her ladyship would no' ha'e had to cut that away."

There were several murmurs of agreement to that, but Annabel ignored them all as she examined his wound. She had no idea what he'd cut his leg on. It was deep, straight and clean, almost like a sword wound. Not what she would expect from an accident involving an overturned wagon, and then she noted the tip of a bloody blade sticking out under his other leg and she reached over to tug it free. She examined the blood on the blade and then glanced at him in question.

"I was eating an apple," he admitted reluctantly. "I had the blade in my hand. Must have cut myself when I went ass over heel off the wagon. Begging your pardon," he added quickly as he realized what he'd said.

Annabel's lips twitched with amusement at his apology. She didn't hold his words against him. The man was no doubt in shock. He was also losing a lot of blood, she noted, and was about to rip a strip off the hem of the gown she was wearing to bind it up, but then recalled the cloth at her throat, and tugged that off instead to wrap around his leg.

The merchant sucked in a sharp breath as she tightened the makeshift bandage and Annabel glanced up to offer him an apologetic smile, only to pause when she saw that his wide eyes were fixed on her bosom. Glancing down at the expanse of creamy flesh trying to work its way out of the gown, Annabel sighed and straightened.

"He shall have to be brought into the keep. I need to sew him up," she announced.

Seonag nodded and opened her mouth, no doubt to order a couple of men to cart him inside, but she didn't have to. Several men were already lifting the fellow off the ground. More men than were really necessary, truth be told . . . and every one of them seemed to be staring at Annabel's bosom rather than the man they were lifting.

"I'm thinkin' we'll be havin' to let out the bosom o' Lady Magaidh's gowns," Seonag commented, falling into step next to Annabel as she led the way to the keep doors.

"Aye," she agreed quietly, resisting the urge to try to push her breasts back down again. It would just draw more attention to them. Besides, it didn't really do much anyway. They just bounced back up. Driving that issue from her mind for now, she said, "I'll need a needle and thread."

"I shall fetch it fer ye as soon as we're inside," Seonag assured her.

"And salve and whiskey," Annabel added.

"Whiskey?" Seonag asked with interest.

"To clean the needle and thread as well as the wound," she explained. Annabel was more used to working with animals than people, but there had been the occasional injury among the women at the abbey and Sister Clara was the most knowledgeable of the nuns when it came to injuries and illness whether it was animals or people. Annabel had always helped her in such cases. However, she'd rarely had to actually tend the wound herself. She'd usually just assisted; handing her what she needed when she needed it and soothing the animal or person being tended. This would be her first time doing the actual sewing of the wound. Oddly enough, she was nervous.

"Where do ye want him? On the table?" Seonag suggested as they entered the keep.

Annabel glanced at the trestle tables, and then back to the crowd following them . . . and it was a crowd. It wasn't just the men carrying the merchant who had trailed her and Seonag into the keep—every single person who had gathered around the accident appeared to be following them inside.

Apparently, she would have an audience while she tended the man. Brilliant, Annabel thought, but nodded in response to Seonag's question. "The table will do."

Chapter 5

Ross DROVE GILLY TO HIS KNEES WITH THE last blow to his shield, and then lowered his sword and stepped back. This was obviously not a good time to practice warfare, he acknowledged with a grimace. He was likely to kill one of his men if he continued in this mood.

"Is everything all right?" Gilly asked, eyeing him warily as he lowered his shield and got to his feet.

"Aye," Ross muttered, but shook his head when Gilly reluctantly raised his sword and shield again. "Enough for now."

Gilly didn't bother hiding his relief as he relaxed. When Ross turned and started to cross the bailey, Gilly fell into step beside him and commented, "Yer in a fou' mood for someone newly married to the sweet young lass ye've just brought home."

The words startled a wry laugh from Ross. "Sweet young lass? I thought her being English convinced ye she was Devil's spawn," he pointed out dryly and reminded him, "Ye were the one saying I should no' marry her because she was the second daughter."

"Aye, well I did no' ken her then, did I?" Gilly said with a faint smile. "But by the second day o' the journey home I kenned I was wrong about all that. She's a good lass. Smart, and curious and . . ."

"Sweet?" Ross suggested dryly.

"Aye." He nodded.

Ross sighed. It had not gone without his notice that his wee bride had quickly wrapped his tough-as-rocks, battle-hardened warriors around her little finger during the journey home. Annabel had chattered away like a magpie for the majority of the journey, asking what this or that was, and telling this or that tale. Most of her stories, he'd noted, had to do with animals or women . . . to the point that he'd actually wondered at one point if her father had not kept her completely segregated from his soldiers and male villagers. Even her father did not feature in any of her stories. Nor had her mother. Though she'd mentioned her sister often enough. "Sister did this" and "sister did that."

Ross shook his head as he recalled it, and how every tale had held his men enthralled. She had a way of telling a story that made even the most boring event seem an adventure and his men had sat astride their horses or around the fire, watching her with an incredulous fascination that would have made most think these men had never seen a female before.

But he supposed the truth was none of them had ever encountered a female quite like Annabel before. There was an innocence and naivety to her that seemed to ooze from her skin and she was always so bloody cheerful. Even after a day trudging through rain on horseback, and with an undoubtedly sore backside from bouncing about in the saddle, she could still see the bright side of things and manage a smile and story that cheered them. And Annabel hadn't once acted the lady of the manor on their journey, demanding special treatment. Instead she'd insisted on helping out when they'd made camp each night. The truth was, she'd got in the way more than anything else. If he hadn't guessed it from her atrocious riding skills, her lack of knowledge when it came to camping would have told them that she'd never been on a proper journey in her life. But she'd tried and that was worth more than gold to his mind, and obviously it had impressed his men as well.

Truthfully, while Ross could claim no responsibility for her disposition, he'd been proud as hell at how she'd conducted herself during the journey. She hadn't once complained at the discomfort, or the fact that she hadn't been allowed to pack and bring even one extra gown let alone her lady's maid and such. She'd simply made the best of everything. She hadn't even commented on the lack of a tent and the fact that they'd had to bed down around the fire each night with his men. She'd simply snuggled up to him when he'd spooned up behind her and she'd instantly dropped off to sleep as only the innocent and just could.

It was Ross who had lain awake each night, listening to her breathe and wishing he'd brought a tent for them to have some privacy. Idiot that he was, he'd lain there each night, imagining what he could have done had they a tent available to them. He'd imagined stripping her naked, rolling her on her back and finding all those secret places that made women such a joy to be with. He'd imagined making her moan and then weep with pleasure, and then sinking his body into hers and finding his own. These imaginings had not helped him sleep. Only the promise that when they reached MacKay he would get to do all those lovely things to her had eased the ache enough to allow him to eventually find sleep.

However, it had been after midnight when they'd arrived at MacKay. He'd been exhausted, and Annabel even more so. She'd actually dozed off in the saddle hours before that and he'd taken her on his horse so she wouldn't topple out of her own. By the time they'd arrived, it had been all Ross could do to carry his sleeping bride inside and upstairs to their room. There he'd stripped and set her abed, and then tugged off his plaid and dropped into bed beside her, falling immediately into an exhausted sleep.

Despite that, Ross had woken before her this morning. Annabel had been burrowed under the furs, sleeping so peacefully he hadn't had the heart to disturb her. So he'd gone in search of his second to get his report on events during his absence. However, he'd had one hell of a time concentrating on the man's words. His mind had kept wandering upstairs to his sleeping bride until he'd finally excused himself to go up and find her . . . only to have her remind him that it was Wednesday.

He should have known that a bride who wore a

chemise carouse on her wedding night would definitely balk at consummating on a Wednesday. The
church frowned on anyone, even married couples,
indulging in carnal acts on Sundays, Wednesdays, and Fridays. In fact, he'd heard it had been
made a law. That wouldn't have stopped him. As
far as he was concerned, such laws were ridiculous and made up by bitter men who were jealous
of what others could have and they couldn't. The
rest of God's creatures did not refrain from pro-
creating on certain days. He doubted God cared
when people did either. However, if his bride was
upset and anxious about the church decrees and
breaking them, he wouldn't force her. That would
hardly encourage her to enjoy the bedding and he
did want her to enjoy it.

"So with such a sweet wife, why are ye so
miserable?" Gilly asked, drawing him from his
thoughts.

Ross sighed. " 'Tis Wednesday."

Gilly looked briefly mystified and then his eyes
widened. "Ohhhh."

"Aye," Ross said dryly.

Gilly nodded sympathetically. "That's a
damned shame. Especially after ye could no' in-
dulge these last three nights on the journey."

"Aye," Ross agreed miserably.

"Hmmm." Gilly shook his head and then
brightened and pointed out, "Well, as I recall our
priest always calls it bedding when he's going on
about that decree."

"So?" Ross asked with bewilderment.

"The priest at Waverly probably calls it the
same thing," he pointed out.

"So?" Ross repeated.

"Well, is it still bedding if yer no' in a bed?" Gilly asked.

Ross blinked at the question and then considered it, a slow smile claiming his lips.

"Ahhh, see," Gilly grinned. "Yer getting me thinking now."

"Aye," Ross agreed.

"And here's another thought fer ye," Gilly said. "As I recall, she vowed to obey ye in that wedding ceremony, did she no'?"

"Aye," Ross said, wondering what he was getting at.

"Well then, even does she argue that if yer no' in a bed 'tis still bedding, ye can order her to allow it. After all, she vowed before God, the priest and her family to obey ye."

Ross frowned at that. He would not order her to allow it. He'd rather try seduction and convincing. He wanted a true partnership with his bride as his own parents had enjoyed, not a bitter resentful wife who lived under his thumb. He didn't say as much though, but simply turned away and headed for the keep. As he went, his mind was planning how to handle the matter. He would take her on a picnic in the woods outside the wall and seduce her on a blanket under the trees, Ross decided. And if she had the presence of mind to protest before he kissed her silly, he'd point out that there was no bed about, so technically it was not bedding.

Nodding to himself, Ross pulled open the keep doors, stepped inside and paused abruptly as he noted the noise and activity around the trestle tables. A large crowd had gathered and was protesting loudly over something.

Curious, Ross approached the table as someone said, "What are ye thinking? Ye can no' waste good *uisge beatha* like that."

The crowd immediately murmured in agreement.

"I told you. The whiskey will clean the wound and help prevent infection." Annabel's voice was clear as a bell and obviously exasperated as Ross reached the edge of the group and peered over the heads before him to where his wife presently knelt over a man on the trestle table. She was scowling at the cook, Angus, and as he watched, she held out her hand, a determined expression on her face. "Now give it over, Angus. I am your lady, and I order it. I need to stitch his wound ere he bleeds to death on me."

The surly old cook tsked with disgust, but handed her a goblet apparently filled with whiskey, muttering, "Aye fine, clean his wound then. But next ye'll be cleaning the great hall floor with it."

"I will not," Annabel assured him dryly, and then glanced down with a start as the man lying on the table suddenly sat up, snatched the goblet from her and gulped down the liquid. Eyes wide with amazement, she snatched the goblet away, peered into what Ross guessed was the empty container and then scowled at the man and asked, "Why the devil did you do that? Now I need more whiskey."

"I thought I was supposed to drink it to clean

my wound," the man spoke the obvious lie with a straight face. His accent, Ross noted, was English.

"Drinking it will not clean your wound, and well you know it," Annabel said on a sigh, and then glanced to Angus and held out the goblet. "I need more."

Angus crossed his arms, eyes narrowing, and lips pursing and Ross could see he was about to rebel. Scowling, he started to move through the crowd, intending to set the man straight on the matter of obeying or disobeying his lady, but he needn't have bothered. His sweet, chatty magpie of a wife, Annabel, suddenly leaned across the man to snatch the cook by the front of his apron and dragged him closer to the table as she hissed, "I am your lady, Angus. Fetch me the bloody whiskey or you shall be searching for a new position elsewhere. I will not let this man die because you are a stubborn cuss too used to having your own way. Understood?"

Angus nodded wildly. "Aye, m'lady. At once, m'lady."

Annabel nodded and released him, and then watched the man hurry away with a sigh and an expression that suggested to Ross that she regretted what she'd had to do to get the man to obey her.

Movement under his wife drew Ross's gaze from Annabel to the man she was leaning over and his surprise turned to a scowl of displeasure as he noted that her position had placed her chest over the injured man's face, and apparently his injury was not so bad that he was not enjoying the view. Seeing how grand the view was did not improve his disposition any and Ross continued through the crowd, traveling much more swiftly than he had the first time.

"Oh, husband," Annabel gasped with surprise and apparent embarrassment when he caught her attention by grasping her arm and dragging her upright where she knelt on the table. "I was just—Cook—I—"

Her stammered effort to explain what he had just witnessed died when he suddenly put his hands to her breasts. He had meant to fan them over the expanse of creamy flesh bulging out of the tight neckline, but somehow his hands got the message mixed up and simply latched on to each generous globe through the cloth. That brought a choking sound from Annabel that was accompanied by a blush so bright red he wondered there was any blood left in her body. It appeared to have all risen to her face and neck. Muttering under his breath, he shifted his hands to do what he had meant to do all along and said, "Ye need to change."

When Annabel's mouth worked without anything coming out, Seonag stepped up beside them and reminded him, "She has nothing to wear but the gown ye brought her in and yer mother's gowns. Yer mother was no' quite as large in the upper area as your lady wife is. Lady Annabel did have a kerchief there, but—" Seonag turned and gestured to the man on the table and he saw the blood-soaked cloth tied around his wound.

Ross frowned as he realized that his wife's present situation was all his fault for not letting her pack a chest to bring with her. He had been so damned eager to get her away from her parents

. . . Ross sighed and then glanced to the interested crowd around them and said succinctly, "Out."

The word was sharp enough, or perhaps his expression was unpleasant enough, that every single person turned and headed at once for the doors. Satisfied, Ross let his hands drop from Annabel's chest and relaxed a little.

Annabel hesitated, but then cleared her throat and said, "I know I was overstepping when I threatened Angus. But I need the whiskey to clean the needle and the wound or this man could lose his leg."

"Lose my leg?" The man on the table squawked with horror.

"If it is not cleaned properly before I sew it up, yes," Annabel admitted and then patted his arm and assured him, "But I will not let that happen. I was trained by the best. You will be fine."

Recalling the way the man had been ogling his wife's chest as it had hovered over his face, Ross scowled at him. His scowl only deepened when he realized he didn't recognize him. "Who the devil are you?"

"The spice merchant," Seonag answered for him. "He was injured when Jasper startled his horse and the beast overset his wagon."

Ross cursed under his breath.

"Jasper?" Annabel queried curiously.

"He was my father's animal," Ross admitted. "A damned fine hunting dog and companion until father died. He's been uncontrollable ever since."

Annabel nodded solemnly, and glanced around as the cook hurried out of the kitchens and rushed across the room with another goblet of whiskey.

She murmured "thank you," as she took the liquid, her earlier anger with the man nowhere in evidence.

Angus nodded, his anxious gaze sliding from her to Ross and back, and then he turned and hurried away, back to the safety of his kitchens.

"How are you going to—Yowww!" The merchant broke off and howled when Annabel undid the cloth she'd tied around his leg and quickly poured a good portion of the liquid over the open wound. The merchant also sat abruptly upright, reaching for Annabel. No doubt, wanting to throttle her for causing him such pain, but Ross caught him by the shoulders and forced him down flat again.

His wife did not even seem to notice the man's action. She simply held the half-empty goblet out to Seonag and said, "Please soak the needle and thread in this for a few minutes."

Seonag nodded and moved at once to do as asked while Annabel bent to inspect the wound she'd just soaked. Ross held the merchant down and watched silently as his wife carefully cleaned the wound, applied some sort of salve Seonag provided, and then sewed it closed.

The merchant passed out near the end of the ordeal. Whether from pain or blood loss Ross didn't know. He was just glad the man was silent. He'd howled and moaned throughout the exercise. Even so, he didn't stop holding the man until Annabel finally straightened from her chore, her hand going to the small of her back as if it pained her.

"Yer well skilled at tending the injured," Ross

complimented, and it was no more than the truth. She'd worked with care and precision and her stitches had been small and straight. He had no doubt the merchant would get away with a nice scar and a story to tell. That didn't always happen. He could just as easily have lost the leg to infection, or could even have died from the wound in time, but Ross was pretty sure Annabel's efforts had just prevented either outcome from occurring.

"Thank you." Annabel stopped rubbing the center of her lower back and ducked her head to hide the blush his words had brought on. It made Ross want to kiss her.

Reminded of his plan, he turned abruptly and headed for the door to the kitchens. He stuck his head into the room just long enough to bark orders at the cook, then headed for the keep doors and stepped out to survey the people close enough to be hailed. Spying Gilly and Liam approaching, he waited patiently until they were close enough to hear without shouting, and then gave them instructions on moving the merchant before leading them inside.

Annabel and Seonag were both still by the man on the table, debating what to do with him, he realized when he got close enough to hear.

"Liam and Gilly are going to move him to a room upstairs," he announced, interrupting their discussion. " 'Twill make it easier fer ye to check on him. 'Sides, if Jasper caused this, 'tis the least we can do."

"Aye," Seonag agreed on a sigh. "It might mollify him enough that he does no' warn all the other merchants away from us."

"Oh, surely he would not do that?" Annabel protested and then asked worriedly, "Would he?"

"It's been known to happen at other keeps with lesser incidents," Ross admitted with an unhappy expression. If the man warned off the other merchants, Annabel would be forced to wear his mother's gowns indefinitely. His gaze slid to her over-exposed chest and he frowned. He was enjoying the view, but didn't want everyone enjoying it.

"I'll sit with him and make a fuss over him," Seonag said reassuringly.

Ross nodded as he watched Liam and Gilly pick up the man and start toward the stairs with him. Seonag immediately followed.

"I had better watch over him too," Annabel decided.

She turned to leave then, but he caught her hand to stop her.

"Nay, I—" He released her and glanced around when the door to the kitchens opened. Angus was rushing toward them with a sack in hand.

"Here ye are, me laird. I put it together meself. The best of everything," the cook assured him.

Ross nodded and murmured a "thank you" as he took the bag. Catching Annabel's arm in his free hand, he urged her toward the keep doors. "Come with me."

"Where are we going?" Annabel asked.

Ross didn't answer. He wanted to surprise her.

"A PICNIC," ANNABEL SAID WITH WONDER AS she bounced along on her mare beside her mounted husband. "I have never been on a picnic before."

"I thought it would give you an opportunity to see some of our land," Ross commented. " 'Tis your home now."

Our land . . . and home, Annabel thought and felt her face stretch as her smile widened. She had lived at Waverly her first seven years and at the abbey these last fourteen, but if she had ever thought of Waverly as her home, she couldn't recall. She had definitely never thought of the abbey that way. For the first few years she'd simply been waiting for her parents to come collect her again. She had been sure the abbess was wrong when she said that would not happen. And even when years passed and she'd given up that dream and acknowledged that she would never leave the abbey it had not felt a home. She had never quite fit in there, never felt like she belonged or was accepted. Annabel simply did not have the dignity to be a nun.

"But somehow," the abbess had said with long suffering, "I must teach you to be one."

And she certainly had tried. She had made Annabel's life a misery with her attempts to teach her. And Annabel had done her best to learn. Truly, she had. But no matter how hard she tried it had simply not been enough.

The thought made her consider her present situation, and her worries that she simply would not be enough here either. MacKay might not be her home for long if that were the case. Her husband might set her aside, or banish her, or . . . well, she didn't know what he could do, but she was quite sure she wouldn't enjoy it.

These unpleasant thoughts slid away as she noted that her husband had stopped his mount.

Bringing her mare to a halt, Annabel glanced around curiously. They had crossed the treeless valley that surrounded the keep and entered the forest beyond some time ago. Now they were in a clearing beside a river—not a stream, but a full and proper river, she saw. When her husband dismounted, she released her reins and started to slide off her mare. It was as far as she got before Ross reached her side and caught her by the waist to lift her down.

Her gaze shot to his when he let her body brush against his as he lowered her. The action sent a riot of feelings through her that Annabel was unprepared for. They left her breathless, but then she seemed to be breathless around the man a lot. It was as if he had some secret spell that stole the air from her body.

"Thank you," she murmured, ducking her head and then easing away from him once her feet were on the ground.

"Ye're welcome." His voice was a deep growl that seemed to say much more than the words he'd spoken. Moving back to his horse, he retrieved a fur and handed it to Annabel. "Here, lay this out where ye think we should eat while I untie the bag with our food."

Annabel nodded and accepted the fur. She scanned the clearing, and quickly settled on a patch of grass next to the water's edge. She laid the fur out and then glanced around just as Ross approached with the small sack the cook had given him.

"Settle yerself," Ross said, and then waited for

her to choose a spot on the fur to sit before settling down next to her. He set the sack on the fur before him and opened it to peer inside. Grunting, he pulled out a skin of wine. It was followed by a roasted chicken wrapped in cloth, bread, fruit, cheese and finally several pastries also wrapped in cloth.

Annabel found herself licking her lips as she surveyed the offerings. They all looked positively delicious. She did wonder though if the chicken had been one of many meant for that night's supper. If so, she supposed there was time to roast another to replace it.

"'Tis a feast," Annabel pronounced with a smile.

Ross smiled faintly and nodded. "Cook is obviously trying to make up fer his earlier bad behavior."

"He *was* difficult about the whiskey, but I should not have lost my temper," Annabel said quietly.

"That was you losing yer temper?" he asked with amusement. "Me mother would have had him whipped fer no' obeying at once in a crisis like that."

Annabel blinked at this news. She had expected at least a dressing-down for her behavior. Certainly, had the abbess witnessed it, she would have ordered Annabel to give herself at least a dozen lashes from the whip. Thank goodness she was no longer at the abbey, she thought. Annabel was not a great fan of pain and had detested every blow.

"Tell me about MacKay," Annabel said as Ross

removed two trenchers from the sack and they began to fill them with the chicken and other offerings.

"What do you wish to know?" he asked.

"Everything," she admitted with a grin, and for some reason that made him chuckle. Annabel picked a piece of chicken from her trencher and ate it, but when his laughter slowed, she asked, "Have you no brothers or sisters?"

"I had a younger brother," Ross admitted, surprising her. Lifting a chicken leg, he took a bite, chewed and swallowed and then added, "He died when we were still but boys."

"How?" she asked with a frown, a piece of cheese forgotten in her hand.

"He was gored by a boar on his first hunt," Ross said quietly.

"I am sorry," Annabel said solemnly.

" 'Twas a long time ago," Ross said with a shrug, and then added, "I have a younger sister too and she survived our childhood."

"Really?" she asked with interest.

"Aye. Giorsal. She is married to our neighbor, Bean."

"Bean?" Annabel echoed the short form uncertainly.

" 'Tis short for Beatham," he explained. "The MacDonald laird. They visit often. No doubt ye'll meet them soon as she hears I've returned with me bride. Which ought to be by the morrow at the latest," he added dryly.

Annabel smiled faintly and nodded as she watched him pop cheese and bread into his mouth, but his words made her think of her own

sister, and wonder how she faired. She hoped
Kate was happy with her stable boy and that their
mother's predictions had been wrong. Annabel
had always looked up to and adored Kate.

"Giorsal and Bean have a bairn. Young Bryson,"
Ross informed her and Annabel glanced to him
with surprise.

"Then you are an uncle?"

He nodded. "And ye're an aunt."

Annabel blinked several times as she realized he was right. They were married now and
his nephew was her nephew. Shaking her head,
she swallowed a bit of cheese and thought how
amazing it was that her life could change so much
with just one action. The size of her family had
increased more than twofold with one marriage
vow.

"Ye had no brothers?"

Annabel glanced up at that question and then
shook her head quickly. "Nay."

"But ye have a sister."

That comment made her suck in a breath. Annabel knew her parents had not brought up the
subject of their offspring to him, hoping to pass
her off as the eldest, but she supposed it was too
much to hope that he would not know they had
more than one child.

"Aye. I have a sister. Kathryn," she added quietly.

"Who is the eldest?"

Annabel had bowed her head and now closed
her eyes. She knew without a doubt that her
mother would have advised her to lie to him and
claim that she was the eldest. She also knew that

telling him the truth might make him very angry, but she simply could not lie.

Her appetite suddenly gone, Annabel set her food down and stood to move to the river to wash the chicken juices from her hands. She had not donned her shoes that morning, something she had often got into trouble for at the abbey, but her husband hadn't seemed to mind. Or perhaps he simply had not noticed it when he'd put her on her horse, she acknowledged. Running about barefoot had often gotten her into trouble with the abbess, but it came in handy now as she merely had to tug her skirts up and wade into the stream and then bend to wash her hands.

Most convenient, Annabel decided as she finished and straightened. Staring out over the water then, she took her courage in hand and admitted, "I am the younger sister. Kate was my parent's firstborn."

She sensed Ross approaching behind her and added quickly, "However, she was disowned and so I am now their eldest daughter."

Annabel could feel him at her back and wondered that he'd removed his boots so quickly. When his hands settled on her shoulders, she bit her lip and simply waited.

"I already kenned that," he admitted, his hands sliding around her waist.

Annabel instinctively tried to turn then, but his hold on her prevented it, so she merely glanced over her shoulder to ask, "You already knew what?"

"That you were not the eldest."

She frowned. "Then why ask?"

"To see if ye would tell the truth," he admitted.

"Oh." Annabel turned forward again with a little sigh, glad she had opted for the truth. But then she frowned and glanced around again to ask, "How did you know?"

"People talk," he said simply.

"Did you know when you married me?" she asked, sure he hadn't.

But he nodded solemnly.

Annabel turned forward again, uncertain as to what she should make of that. Finally, she asked, "Then why did you marry me? Why not declare the contract broken?"

"Because I wanted ye."

The words were simple enough, but made absolutely no sense to Annabel. He'd wanted her? Why? She was overlarge, untrained and unskilled. Why on earth would he want her to wife?

"Why?" The word slipped from her lips, sounding as bewildered as she felt. Much to her amazement the chest at her back vibrated against her with his amusement, and then his hands slid up from her waist and Annabel glanced down with shock as his large, rough hands slid over and cupped her breasts through the cloth covering them.

"Because I wanted ye," Ross repeated by her ear as his hands began to knead the soft flesh. To add to her confusion, he also began to do something to her ear, nibbling and sucking at it in a way that was as exciting as what he was doing to her breasts. The combination of the two caused a strange fluttering in her stomach and lower.

"Husband?" Annabel said uncertainly, and

then gasped when one of his hands dropped down to slide between her legs through her gown. He cupped her there and used his hold to lift her out of the water and back against him so that Annabel could feel a hardness pressing against her bottom.

Releasing his hold on her other breast, Ross then urged her head back and around to claim her lips in a kiss that was nothing like that first one they'd shared on their wedding night. Their first kiss, the one after the wedding ceremony, had started softly and built in intensity. This one was a deep ravaging from the start that had her grabbing for whatever she could get her hands on to help her remain grounded and upright. She ended up covering one of his hands with her own, and reaching back with her other to clutch at the plaid at his hip as his tongue delved into her mouth.

Annabel did not notice the hand he had used to turn her face to meet his dropping away until she felt cold air on her breasts and realized that he had used it to tug the ill-fitting neckline down. Breaking the kiss, she glanced down to see that her breasts had spilled eagerly out and he was now catching one in his hand and squeezing it eagerly.

"But 'tis Wednesday," she moaned as Ross tweaked one nipple, sending shafts of excitement shooting down to where his hand still cupped her between the legs. " 'Tis against the law to commit the bedding on a Wednesday."

Annabel was very sorry to have to say that, for truly she was enjoying what he was doing.

"There is no bed here," Ross pointed out by the

ear he'd returned to nibbling when she'd broken their kiss, and then he set her back on her feet in the water so that he could shift the hand between her legs. He did not take it away as she'd first expected, but used it to quickly tug her skirt up with a couple of jerks so that his hand could snake beneath it and slide between her legs without the gown in the way.

It was a most effective maneuver, Annabel acknowledged, pressing back into him with a moan as his fingers danced over flesh that had never been touched before, even by herself. Perhaps that was why her skin reacted so wantonly, swelling eagerly beneath the caress and nearly dancing to his touch.

"Husband?" she gasped uncertainly, unable to prevent her hips from shifting into his touch as excitement built in her.

"Aye?" He left off caressing the breast he'd been attending and shifted his attention to the other breast, squeezing and kneading that eager flesh now and Annabel moaned and then turned her head in search of his lips again. It was a great relief when his mouth covered hers, and she opened wide for him, welcoming his tongue's thrusts. Her own tongue did battle with his briefly, and then she settled for simply sucking on it as the kiss continued.

Annabel was clutching at the arm of the hand between her legs now, urging him on as he drove her to a frenzy with his caresses, but she was completely unprepared for the sudden insertion of what she thought must be a finger down there. It startled a cry from her as the excitement in her ratcheted up another unbearable degree. Annabel had to tear her mouth from his to prevent biting his tongue and once she had she simply twisted her head against his chest, breathless, nonsensical pleas spilling from her lips as she rode his hand, and then the building tension between her legs suddenly exploded through her body, tearing a scream of pleasure from her lips as she convulsed with it.

Chapter 6

ANNABEL'S BODY WAS STILL PULSING WITH HER release when Ross suddenly scooped her up and carried her out of the stream. The hem of her skirt slapped wetly against her legs, but Annabel didn't care. She was too stunned by what had just taken place.

In all the lectures from the abbess and Father Gerder, as well as all the whispered conversations with the other oblates, not once had anyone mentioned that what she had just experienced could take place. And that was just shocking, she decided. Many women would go to their marriage bed with less fear and outright terror did they know it could be like that. In fact, she was now feeling a bit cheated that Ross had got her sotted so that she did not recall their first time together.

Her thoughts scattered when Ross knelt on the furs to lay her on them and then began working on the ties of her gown. Flushing, she grabbed for his hands to stop him, suddenly shy at the thought of his seeing her unclothed. Which was ridiculous, she supposed, when she realized that her breasts were already out and that her skirt was tangled around her hips.

Noting the question on Ross's face, and unwilling to admit her foolish feelings about being completely nude in front of him, Annabel did the only thing she could think to do, and the one thing she truly wanted to do . . . she kissed him. Annabel pressed her mouth to his and, much to her relief, he responded at once, taking over and urging her lips open for a full kiss.

Sighing her relief into his mouth, Annabel slid her arms around his neck and held on tight as he eased her back onto the furs, his body coming down on top of hers. He still wore his plaid, so it was something of a surprise when she felt his hardness between her legs. Having experienced the pleasure of his caressing fingers down there, Annabel was not worried and eased her legs apart, moaning when his shaft immediately slid across her damp flesh, reigniting her earlier excitement so freshly sated.

The sound seemed to encourage him, and her husband did that again, and then a third time.

"Please," she groaned, her legs shifting restlessly before wrapping instinctively around his hips. Annabel could not have said what she was actually pleading for, but her husband gave it to her anyway and her eyes shot open with shock as she discovered just what everyone was talking about when it came to the pain of the breaching. Dear God, it felt as if he'd slid his sword into her, and Annabel became aware that she was making little gasping grunts of pain and cut them off at once as Ross halted, still planted inside her and lifted himself up enough to look at her face.

"Are ye all right?" he asked with concern.

Annabel bit her lip. She wanted to shriek, "No!" but nodded instead and tried for a smile that she suspected failed miserably.

"Should I stop?" Ross asked with a pained expression that suggested to her he did not want to.

She hesitated, but then asked, "Is it done?"

Annabel was very disappointed when he shook his head. She closed her eyes briefly, buying a moment to let the worst of the pain ease, and then shook her head. "Nay. Then go ahead."

He did. Ross slid his body slowly from hers, no doubt in an effort to go gently, and then he slid back in and she had to grit her teeth to keep from whimpering in pain. By the third thrust she was quite sure she would never want to do this again, but then Ross reached between them and began to caress her again.

Annabel almost told him not to bother, sure it would make no difference. Her earlier pleasure was a dead and done thing, but then a remaining ember sparked and her earlier excitement began to stretch and yawn inside her. Annabel held her breath as it began to grow and the pain began to diminish in comparison and then Ross paused in his thrusting to claim her mouth with his.

She kissed him back, her hips beginning to shift into his caress and unintentionally dancing on the shaft presently buried in her.

Ross groaned into her mouth, and then broke their kiss to straighten and concentrate on caressing her. He had stopped moving now, all of his attention on driving her crazy with his touch, but it didn't matter. Annabel was now shifting her hips against him, riding his erection as she'd ridden his hand. As the tension built in her again, she grabbed desperately for the fur on either side of her and thrust harder into his touch, and unintentionally into his erection. Just as the tension inside her exploded again, Ross stopped caressing her and grabbed her hips as he thrust into her one final time with a shout that startled the birds from the nearby trees.

ANNABEL LEANED HER ELBOW ON HER RAISED knees, her chin on her palm and stared at her husband.

After collapsing next to her on the fur and dragging her to lie half on his chest, Ross had fallen asleep. Annabel had tried to sleep with him, but found she wasn't tired. So after lying there restlessly for several minutes, she'd eased out of his embrace and sat up. Now she found herself simply staring at him with fascination.

The man had always fallen asleep last and woken first since their wedding night. This was the first time she had ever seen him while asleep and it was an interesting experience. In sleep, Ross's face was unguarded, his expression soft. It made him appear much younger. He also snored loud enough to wake the dead. It made her think it would be a good thing did she fall asleep first every night for the rest of their marriage.

Annabel smiled faintly at that thought, but her smile faded as she recalled his admission that he had known she was the second daughter when he'd married her. The knowledge was something of a relief. At least he was not angry about that. However, it didn't ease all her worries when it came to their marriage. He still had no idea that she was going to be useless as a wife because she'd grown up at the abbey.

Sighing, Annabel shifted to her feet, grimacing when she saw that the skirt of her gown had dried and was now wrinkled beyond repair. She tugged at the neckline, trying to coax her breasts back into it. But it seemed an impossible feat without undoing the lacing and doing it up again.

Shrugging, she quickly undid the laces, but then, feeling liquid sliding down the inside of her thighs, she decided to take a quick dip in the river to clean off and simply let the gown drop onto the fur. Annabel felt very brazen and brave for a moment, but the possibility of Ross's waking while she was in the river and her having to cross to the furs naked to retrieve her gown with him watching was enough to make her bend and grab the gown to carry it to the river's edge with her.

There she laid it over a boulder almost big enough to keep the hem of the gown off the grass and then stepped tentatively into the water. It must have come down from the mountains, because the water was extremely cold, clear and soft. It was also moving surprisingly fast and Annabel decided she would have to be cautious lest the current carry her feet out from under her.

With that thought in mind, she eased slowly out into the water until it reached her waist, which didn't take long at all. The bank dropped off swiftly, and the current also grew stronger with each step so she didn't risk moving further out, but paused there and quickly cleaned up before turning to head back to shore.

Annabel retreated from the water much more swiftly than she'd entered, the cold did not encourage lingering. Once on shore, rather than wait for the soft breeze to dry her, she immediately tried to put on her gown to cover her chilled skin. That was a mistake, she was forced to acknowledge minutes later, as she struggled to don the gown. She'd pulled it on over her head, which had been relatively easy that morning when her skin was dry. It wasn't so easy now. The waist had caught and tangled around her shoulders and breasts, leaving her hands caught in the sleeves and the bodice covering her head.

Muttering under her breath, Annabel struggled to at least get the sleeves tugged down her arms to free her hands so that she could either remove the gown, or pull the bodice down around her neck and free her face, but the sound of branches snapping made her suddenly pause. Turning her head in the cloth, she listened blindly for a moment and then a rustle and another snapping branch made her heart stop.

"Ross?" she whispered uncertainly. He had stopped snoring and if he was awake and up . . . well, that would be embarrassing. But if it was someone else who had not yet entered the clearing and spotted them, she hardly wanted to draw their attention.

Biting her lip, she listened to the answering silence with a sinking heart. Surely Ross would have answered? Well, unless he'd died laughing on spotting her predicament, she supposed, but Annabel was sure she would have heard that. Besides, the sudden silence was not a good sign. Either the sounds she'd heard were from someone who had heard her whisper and was now listening for another call to see where it had come from, which she definitely did not want. Annabel did not want her husband to see her like this let alone a stranger.

Or the alternative was that the sounds were from someone who was trying to sneak up on them in the clearing, and who had paused cautiously at her call to convince her that there was no one there. However, the goose bumps now covering her arms and chest were telling her that there was definitely someone nearby.

Taking a deep breath, Annabel tipped her head back and found she was able to see out the top of the gown's neckline. She'd barely made the discovery when a rustling sound caught her ear. It was closer than the other sounds had been. Whoever it was, was nearly upon her. Turning abruptly in the direction of the sound, she bent sharply at the waist while keeping her head at the same angle and tried to spot the source of the sound.

When Annabel caught a glimpse of a large figure moving toward her, she didn't stop for a better look, but shrieked, straightened and turned to run blindly in the opposite direction at once.

Ross was woken by a high-pitched squeal. Blinking his eyes open, he sat up at once, but was slow to orient himself to where he was. Then he recalled the clearing, his wife and that his marriage was finally consummated. The knowledge was trying to pull a smile across his face when a second squeal caught his attention and drew his gaze to the side. What he saw then left him poleaxed. Someone, his wife he presumed, since it looked like her dress tangled around her head and shoulders, was charging blindly about the clearing with the skirt of her gown barely covering her private bits and leaving her legs naked. He was so startled by the sight of her like that, that it took Ross a moment to notice that someone was chasing her. A man. A big bloody man too. Dressed in a plaid and a white cotton shirt, the fellow was rushing after his wife, arms outstretched.

A thud drew his gaze back to his wife in time to see her bounce off a tree trunk and flop backward onto the forest floor. Ross was on his feet in an instant, a battle roar on his lips. The sound brought the head of his wife's pursuer around just as he reached Annabel. When he saw Ross charging, he did what any smart man would do . . . he left Annabel where she was and ran like hell in the opposite direction.

Ross watched him disappear into the woods as he rushed to his wife's side, but did not pursue him. He was too concerned about Annabel. She had hit the tree hard and there was already blood staining the gown where he thought her head must be. She was also lying unmoving. All of that was enough to decide for him that she took precedence.

"Annabel?" he said with concern, kneeling beside her in the grass.

Relief poured through him when she moaned in response. She was alive at least, Ross reassured himself, and began the struggle to get the gown off of her so he could see how bad her injury was. In the end, the tangle she'd got herself into defeated him and Ross had to find his *sgian dubh* and cut her out of the tenacious material.

A curse slid from his lips when he saw her head wound. A large knot was already rising in the center of Annabel's forehead and coloring an ugly mottled black and blue with a red gash in the center that was oozing blood. Scooping her up, Ross carried her to the horse, but then paused and peered from her to the fur where his plaid and sword were. Cursing again, he carried her to the fur and laid her on it while he grabbed up his shirt and plaid. Ross pulled on his shirt, but he didn't bother folding pleats into his plaid. He simply tied the material around his waist. He then grabbed his sword, and crossed the clearing to the horses to slide the weapon into a loop on his saddle before returning to collect his wife.

The sight of Annabel lying there half naked with the ruined gown beneath her made him gather her up, fur and all. Tugging it around her as if it were swaddling around a baby, he carried her to the horses and then came to a halt again. He could not mount with her in his arms like that. Muttering an apology despite the fact that she was unconscious, Ross tossed her atop his horse on her stomach, grabbed the reins of her mare and then mounted behind Annabel.

Once in the saddle, he quickly shifted her to rest in his arms again. Ross then urged his horse out of the clearing and into a run for home. He had to get Annabel to Seonag. She would know what to do.

ANNABEL'S HEAD WAS POUNDING WHEN SHE woke up. That pounding only got worse when she tried to open her eyes and light crowded in, so she closed them again quickly with a moan and reached for her head, only to have her hands caught halfway there and held firmly.

"Now, lass. Ye won't want to be doing that. 'Tis no doubt tender at the moment and ye'll just cause yerself more pain."

"Seonag?" Annabel said uncertainly, unwilling to open her eyes again just now, but sure she'd recognized the older woman's voice.

"Aye. 'Tis me, and yer safely home now," the woman said soothingly.

"Home," Annabel echoed the word softly, confusion filling her. "What happened? Why does my head hurt so much?"

"Do ye no' remember?" Seonag asked.

Annabel heard what she felt sure was concern in her voice and frowned, trying to recall. After a moment she said slowly, "Ross took me on a picnic."

"Aye," Seonag said with a tinge of relief.

"And we . . . er . . . picnicked," she finished lamely, not willing to say what else they'd done. That being the case, she glossed over the next bit quickly. "Ross fell asleep."

"Men often do after a picnic."

Annabel was quite sure there was amusement in the woman's voice as she said the word *picnic*, and suspected the maid knew that more than pic-nicking had gone on, but continued, "And I went for a swim in the river."

"In the river?" Seonag squawked with alarm. "Bloody hell. Yer lucky the currents did no' carry ye away. Don't be doing that again, lass."

"I will not," Annabel assured her and knew it was true, but it wasn't Seonag's warning that would prevent it. It was how cold the water had been, and what she was now recalling had happened after her dip in the river that would prevent her doing that again. "I tried to don my gown, but I was wet and got tangled up in it."

"Ah," Seonag said as if that explanation clarified something she hadn't understood.

"And then I heard snapping branches and rustling as if someone was approaching," Annabel continued slowly as the recollection flowed over her. "I could just see out of the neck of the gown if I tipped my head back and looked through it, so I bent in the direction the sound was coming from."

"Did ye see him?" Seonag asked.

"Just enough to know someone was approaching," Annabel said with a grimace. In her memory all she'd glimpsed was a band of plaid moving toward her.

"And was it an Englishman or someone in a plaid?" Seonag asked with a frown.

"A plaid," Annabel answered.

"Ah." Seonag paused briefly and Annabel guessed she was nodding when she added, "Aye, 'tis what the laird said. A man in a plaid."

"He saw him?" Annabel asked with surprise,

blinking her eyes open briefly, only to close them again as pain once more stabbed through them into her head along with the light.

"Aye. He said he saw you first." There was a brief pause and then she said tentatively, "He said ye were racing about the clearing like a chicken with its head cut off, yer gown around yer head and blind from it."

"Oh." Annabel breathed the word out on a sigh. The picture Seonag's words painted was not a grand one. No doubt she had looked a complete fool.

"He said as how ye ran into a tree like that?" Seonag prompted, obviously wondering if she recalled that part of her adventure.

"Was it a tree?" Annabel asked weakly. "All I remember is hitting something hard and pain exploding in my head."

"Hmmm. Yer memory's still all there then," Seonag said, sounding relieved.

Annabel didn't comment, but merely asked, "Did my husband catch the man?"

"Nay," Seonag answered. "The laird didn't give chase. He was more concerned with getting ye home to tend yer wound. He's out there now with the men though, beating the bushes and searching for him."

"Oh," Annabel murmured, oddly disappointed that he'd simply dumped her there in Seonag's care and rushed off rather than stay to see her wake up and reassure himself that she was all right. She supposed it was silly, but after what they'd done in the woods she'd thought—

"He wanted to stay," Seonag added. "But he was driving me wild pacing about like a caged animal and hovering over me shoulder while I tried to clean yer wound, so I ordered him from the room. Told him did he no' leave and go find the man responsible, I'd stop what I was doing and leave Cook to tend ye. Cook is no' very good with wounds, so he left," she added.

"Oh," Annabel murmured, feeling a little better about being abandoned. Although, she would have felt better still to hear that he'd left the room only to hover anxiously in the hall, haunting the door like a ghost in his worry. That, she supposed, was silly too, but she couldn't help what she wished for.

"Can ye open yer eyes now?" Seonag asked suddenly.

Annabel hesitated, but then eased her eyes open, and again closed them. "Nay."

"Try more slowly," Seonag suggested. "Open them just a wee bit, then a bit more."

She grimaced, but cracked her eyes open just a sliver. It caused pain, but wasn't as bad as when she'd opened them wide, so Annabel eased them open just a crack more. It took a couple of moments, but in the end she was able to open her eyes all the way without too much discomfort.

"Good," Seonag praised her, and then picked up a goblet on the bedside table and asked, "Do ye think ye can drink this?"

"What is it?" Annabel asked.

"A white-willow-bark tincture," Seonag said. " 'Twill help with the pain."

"Aye," Annabel murmured. She knew about white willow bark from her work with Sister Clara. The good sister had often used it to ease pain or reduce a fever.

Seonag helped her sit up and Annabel drank the liquid when she pressed the goblet to her lips.

"There," Seonag said, easing her back onto the bed when she was done. "Why do ye no' rest a bit now until that takes affect?"

"Aye," Annabel murmured. Her head hurt enough that sleep sounded like a good escape, but she doubted she'd manage it with her head pounding as it was. Still, she closed her eyes and tried to relax.

"NOTHING?" ROSS ASKED WITH A FROWN WHEN Gilly rode into the clearing and dismounted. He had returned only moments ago himself after searching the area. He had found several trails, but hadn't even caught a glimpse of the man who had been chasing his wife.

Gilly shook his head, his expression grim. "I found the remains o' a campsite though. It was probably someone just passing through. He spotted yer pretty little wife, thought she was alone and—" He shrugged, and then suggested, "Or mayhap he was trying to help her with her dress. Ye did say she was in a might tangle with it."

Ross frowned at both suggestions and shook his head. "Either option is possible, I suppose," he admitted reluctantly, and then added dryly, "The first option is more likely than the second."

"Aye." Gilly nodded, and then raised his eyebrows and asked, "But?"

Ross hesitated, but then admitted, "That was the decision I came to when we couldn't find the man who came upon Annabel that first night on the journey here."

"I'd forgotten about that," Gilly admitted with a frown.

"I hadn't," Ross said quietly and then added, "A fellow traveler stumbling upon her by accident once was one thing, but twice?"

"Hmmm." Gilly considered that, but then pointed out, "Still, ye said the first man was wearin' English garb."

"I didn't see him—just his trail. It was Annabel who later said he was in braies," Ross reminded him. He'd questioned her further on what she'd seen as they'd sat around the fire that night and Annabel had been quite clear that the man she'd seen had been dressed in English garb, a dirty white shirt and braies.

"Oh, aye." Gilly nodded. "And ye say this one was wearing the plaid?"

"Aye," Ross agreed, and reluctantly admitted, "I suppose they have to be two unrelated occurrences."

"Probably," Gilly agreed, but *he* now sounded doubtful.

Ross stared at him briefly, but then shook his head and headed for his horse. They were not going to find anything out here and he wanted to check on Annabel. He had only left because Seonag wouldn't allow him to stay in the room while she was tending her and he had felt useless pacing the great hall. Searching for the man who had chased his wife into the tree had seemed a better expenditure of time than pacing about wringing his hands like an old man. But he'd searched, found nothing, and now wanted to see his wife . . . whether Seonag liked it or not.

Chapter 7

$\mathcal{A}$NNABEL SIGHED SLEEPILY AND OPENED HER eyes before she was awake enough to remember the pain that action had caused her the first time she'd woken. Fortunately, it did not cause pain now. In fact, other than a dull throb in her head, like a far-away voice barely heard, she felt fine.

"How do ye feel?"

She glanced to the side with surprise when she heard that question in a deep rumbling voice and stared blankly at her husband. Ross was leaning forward anxiously in a chair beside the bed, eyeing her with concern.

"Good, my lord," Annabel admitted, and then grimaced and added, "And a little foolish."

His eyebrows rose in surprise. "Why?"

"Well, I knocked myself out," she pointed out dryly, and recalling Seonag's recital of his description of her ordeal, added, "And in a most undignified fashion."

Ross sat completely still for a moment, his lips

twitching, and then he turned and coughed into his hand.

The action made Annabel's eyes narrow. The cough had sounded suspiciously like an attempt to cover a laugh. Surely he wasn't laughing at her suffering? She scowled at the idea, but then shook her head and closed her eyes, amusement curving her own lips as she imagined the picture she must have made running blindly about with the gown over her head. It had not seemed funny when she was fleeing the unknown figure in the clearing, but Annabel had to admit that it now might be . . . a little.

"We searched fer yer attacker," Ross said after a moment, which she supposed he needed to compose himself.

Her eyes flickered open and she turned to peer at him again, this time frowning. "I was attacked? I thought I just ran into a tree."

"Aye, ye did," he acknowledged. "But when yer squawking woke me up, someone was chasing ye."

"Squawking?" she asked with affront. "I do not squawk, husband."

His mouth worked briefly and he turned away for another pseudo cough, but then nodded solemnly. "I meant scream. When yer screaming woke me up."

"Hmmm," Annabel said, only slightly mollified, and then asked curiously, "Who was he and what was he doing there?"

All traces of amusement fled from his face then and Ross looked grim when he admitted, "I don't ken. It looked like he was chasing ye, but he might ha'e been trying to stop ye from running into the tree. Whatever the case, he got away," he admitted unhappily, and then added, "We searched the area after I brought ye back to the keep fer Seonag to tend, but found only his campsite. He'd fled the area."

"Oh," she murmured, and then asked, "But he *did* give chase?"

"Aye." Ross tilted his head, and asked. "What happened ere I awoke? Did he attack ye? Is that why ye were running from him?"

"Nay," Annabel assured him quickly, lest he think something untoward had happened. She wouldn't have him thinking she'd been sullied by his touch. "I took a dip in the river after ye fell asleep and—"

"The river?" Ross interrupted sharply, and then said firmly, "Never swim in the river, Annabel. I should ha'e warned ye of that. 'Tis no' safe."

"Aye, Seonag told me," she said soothingly. "I will not do so again. And I did not go in far. I did notice the current was strong."

Sighing, he rubbed one hand over his face and sat back with a nod for her to continue.

"At any rate, I should have waited to be dry before trying to don my dress. However, I did not and it got caught and all bunched up around my head and shoulders." She noted the amusement on his face and suspected he was recalling her in that state, but ignored it and continued, "I heard branches snapping and thought mayhap you'd awakened and were approaching, but you did not answer my call, so I bent over to look out the top of the dress and caught a glimpse of a large, plaided figure and—" She grimaced. "Well, I just panicked. I shrieked and started to run away."

He knew what had happened after that so she didn't bother to continue.

Ross was silent for a moment and then asked, "So ye did no' see who it was?"

"Nay. Just that he was big and wore a plaid."

Ross nodded and asked, "And he did no' touch ye?"

Annabel shook her head solemnly and realized it was true. She'd heard a sound, seen a figure and run away in a panic, knocking herself out. Whoever it was hadn't harmed her at all . . . and may not have meant to, she acknowledged. It didn't seem very bright to attack her with Ross lying but feet away. If his intentions had been nefarious, surely the man would have approached Ross first and knocked him out or even killed him. She wouldn't have known, as blind as she'd been at that point.

" 'Twas probably nothing," Annabel said on a sigh. "I was half dressed, in a tangle, and blind and may have overreacted. I probably scared the poor man as much as he scared me."

Ross was frowning now, not looking convinced, but frankly, Annabel simply wanted to forget the whole matter. She'd made a fool of herself. That image of her running around with her gown tangled around her head would no doubt reside in her husband's head for the rest of his days. It was not the image she wanted there when he thought of her.

Annabel started to toss the linens and furs aside, and then quickly dragged them back up as she saw she was naked. Sighing, she asked, "Where is my gown?"

"I had to cut it off ye," Ross admitted apologetically.

"Oh," Annabel said weakly, and then asked, "I do not suppose Seonag set aside something for me to wear when I woke, did she? I should like to go below."

"Why?" he asked rather than answer her question.

"I wish to get up," she said simply, and then added, "My head no longer hurts and I feel fine. Besides everyone is probably gathering at the trestle tables for the sup by now."

"Nay," Ross said with a shake of the head. "'They'll no' be gathering at the tables. 'Tis no' time for sup."

"Is it not?" Annabel asked with disappointment. She was hungry, although she supposed she shouldn't be. It seemed like all she'd done that day was eat. She'd broken her fast with pastries before her bath, helped the merchant, picnicked in the clearing with Ross, been tupped there by him, and then knocked herself out. And now she wanted to eat again. She couldn't help it. She was hungry. Although her husband probably thought her as gluttonous as the abbess had always accused her of being.

"Nay, 'tis well past that time," Ross announced interrupting her thoughts. "Everyone ate hours ago."

"Oh." Annabel was so relieved to know she had a reason to be hungry that she beamed at him. "Well then I should like to go below and find something to eat. But I need to find a gown first and—"

"No need," Ross announced, and then scooped her up out of the bed, linens, furs and all.

While her front was covered by the linens and furs, Annabel was very aware that his hands were on her bare back and bottom. Biting her lip and trying not to blush, she clutched at his shoulders as he carried her toward the table and chairs in the corner to the right of the fireplace.

"Seonag thought ye might be hungry when ye woke and brought up some food fer ye," Ross announced as he set her in a chair at the table. When he straightened from putting her down, she was able to see that there was a trencher of stew, crusty rolls, cheese and a goblet of cider there, awaiting her.

"Oh," Annabel breathed, surveying the food. It looked delicious and she was hungry, but she glanced up to Ross with a frown when he continued to stand at her side. "There is plenty here. Are you hungry?"

"No' fer food," he said wryly, and then added, "I'll quench me thirst after yer done."

Annabel supposed that meant he would be leaving her to go below and join the men in drinking once she'd finished eating and was safely back in bed. The thought depressed her for some reason. It was not that she expected him to spend all his time with her, and really, perhaps his preferring his men's company to her own was normal—she had no idea. Perhaps all husbands spent their evenings laughing and talking over an ale with the men rather than sitting by the fire with their wives, but she would have liked to spend time with him.

With those thoughts marching around inside her head, Annabel found her appetite quickly waning. It did not help that the stew was cold, and the cheese hard from sitting in the open air so long. She'd barely touched her food before she was pushing it away and letting the fur slip to the floor so that she could draw the linen around herself in the roman style and stand.

"I thought ye were hungry?" Ross said, stepping closer and scooping her up when she stepped from between the table and chair.

"So did I," Annabel admitted quietly, slipping her arms around his neck as he carried her back across the room.

Her words made him stop at the foot of the bed and he eyed her with concern. "Is yer head aching again? Seonag said it was pounding something fierce when ye woke up the first time, but that she'd given ye something fer it."

"She did, and 'tis fine. I am just not hungry anymore," Annabel said with a shrug.

"But ye feel all right?" he persisted.

"Aye. You may go quench your thirst without worrying about me," she assured him.

Ross grunted with satisfaction at this news and promptly set her to sit on the foot of the bed. That startled her a bit. He could have at least carried her to her side of the bed, she thought with irritation. But it seemed now she'd given him leave to go play with the men, he couldn't be bothered . . .

The thought trailed off with confusion when Annabel realized he wasn't heading for the door, but had removed the pin from his plaid and was letting it drop to the floor. She stared at him wide-eyed, but when he then kicked off his boots and tugged off his shirt to let it fall to the floor too, leaving him completely naked before her, Annabel murmured, "Er . . . husband . . . what—?"

The question died when he knelt on the plaid before her and leaned forward to cover her mouth with his.

Annabel quickly realized that the hunger he'd been speaking of hadn't been for ale, and he had no intention of leaving her alone to join his men. The idea made her smile against his mouth, until she recalled that it was Wednesday and there was most definitely a bed present this time so he couldn't argue it wasn't bedding.

It took some effort, but Annabel managed to tear her mouth from his to murmur, "Husband?"

"Hmm?" Ross mumbled, his mouth trailing down her throat and toward her breasts even as his hands tugged the soft linen from her fingers to bare them.

" 'Tis—Oh!" she gasped as his mouth closed over one nipple, and then desperate to stop him while she still had the strength to do so, Annabel blurted, " 'Tis Wednesday!"

Pausing, Ross raised his head and thoroughly confused her by grinning. Cupping her face in his hands, he said, "Nay. 'Tis well past midnight. 'Tis Thursday now."

"Oh," Annabel breathed just before his mouth covered hers again. This time she couldn't have broken the kiss had she wished. Ross held the back of her head firmly with one hand as he devoured her with his lips and tongue.

Annabel was breathing heavily and released a long, disappointed moan when he broke the kiss. She opened her eyes, surprised to find she was now lying on her back on the end of the bed. Lifting her head, Annabel peered at the top of Ross's head as his lips glided over her chest, pausing to suckle briefly at first one nipple and then the other, before continuing down across her stomach. She gasped and released a small giggle when he paused at her belly button, his tongue tickling her there briefly before his head shifted to the side to find and nibble at her hip bone. The sensation *that* caused killed any amusement and Annabel sucked in a breath and held it at the tingling running through her as Ross followed the bone toward the apex of her thighs.

When his head ducked between her legs and Annabel felt the first lash of his tongue there, she cried out and half sat up in shock, her hands instinctively reaching for his head to push him away. It was like trying to move a castle. The man had planted himself there and was not moving. When she tried to squeeze her legs closed around him, Ross forced them open again with his hands and continued his efforts with an enthusiasm that tore her breath from her.

Annabel was now tugging at his hair rather than trying to push his head away. Suddenly aware of that and afraid she'd hurt him, she forced herself to release her hold on the long, dark strands and grabbed for the linen beneath her instead as he did things Annabel was sure she would be doing unending penance for when she confessed them to the priest. She didn't care though; if one could be killed by pleasure, Ross was dangerously close to murdering her . . . and she never wanted it to end. Not that she was disappointed when it did. When Annabel found herself teetering on the edge of that point of exploding, she cried out and threw herself over the cliff with wholehearted enthusiasm, embracing the convulsions and shudders that accompanied it as her body was racked with pleasure.

She was still humming with it when her husband straightened, caught her by the knees and drew her bottom to the edge of the bed so that he could thrust his hardness into her. Her body welcomed him, stretching to make way and then clasping at him when he almost immediately withdrew partway.

Wrapping her legs around him, Annabel sat up and then wrapped her arms around him as a new excitement grew to replace the one that had just passed. This time when the tension Ross was stirring exploded within her, he joined her, thrusting into her one last time with a triumphant shout and holding her tight as he poured his seed into her . . . and all Annabel could think was, "Thank God it is Thursday."

ANNABEL SHIFTED RESTLESSLY AND PEERED AT the man asleep beside her. He was snoring fit to raise the roof, while she was lying there wide awake . . . not because of his snoring. That didn't bother her. She quite simply wasn't tired. She'd been sleeping all afternoon and evening thanks to the tincture Seonag had given her and now she couldn't sleep . . . and was hungry.

Imagining the abbess's disapproval at the admission, Annabel wrinkled her nose. That good woman would probably lecture her on gluttony about now, she supposed. She also supposed she'd deserve every word of it, for there was no other word for what she was feeling, but gluttonous . . . and not just for food. She would bypass food in favor of waking Ross for another tupping. However, he hadn't slept all day and was tired.

"So it's food," she mumbled, sliding out of bed and peering around in the light from the dying fire for something to wear. She had no idea who had built and started the fire. Seonag or Ross, she supposed. Annabel wasn't sure if there had been a fire the first time she'd woken up, but it had been burning merrily away when she'd woken up the second time. It was mostly embers now, with a few small flames, but it was enough for her to see by. Sadly, she wasn't seeing a single dress. Not even the one she'd been wearing that Ross claimed he'd had to cut away.

Perhaps she'd just have to crawl back into bed and wait for morning to break her fast, Annabel thought, only to have her stomach rumble in protest. It reminded her that aside from the fact that she'd barely touched the food when Ross had set her at the table earlier, she'd really only picked at the lovely picnic Angus had prepared for them that afternoon.

Annabel glanced toward the table and then went over to survey the food there. Sadly, a quick sampling proved that the stew was even colder and less appetizing now than it had been earlier, and the cheese had just grown harder.

Tsking under her breath, Annabel turned back toward the bed, pausing when she spotted her husband's shirt and plaid. In the next moment, she'd crossed to snatch both up. Annabel dragged the shirt on first. It was overlarge, nearly a tent on her smaller frame, but it covered everything more decently than Lady Magaidh's dress had, so she quickly folded the plaid in half and wrapped it around her waist as a makeshift skirt. A quick search revealed the pin Ross used to secure his plaid half buried in the rushes on the floor. Bending to collect it, Annabel used it to fasten the skirt in place, and then peered down at herself.

The skirt she'd fashioned reached to the tops of her bare feet. It would do, she decided.

The hall was dark when Annabel opened the bedchamber door and stepped out, dark enough that she didn't see the shape lying in her path and stumbled over it. Catching at the door frame, she managed to save herself from a nasty fall, and then squinted at the black mass on the ground at her feet. It was the low growling that gave away what she couldn't see very well. A dog. More specifically, Ross's father's dog, Jasper, she guessed, recalling the name Seonag had mentioned. No doubt this room had belonged to Ross's father while he'd lived and the dog was here, waiting for his master to return, not understanding that he never would.

Annabel contemplated the dark shape, wondering just how wild he'd gone since the old laird's passing and whether he was dangerous. But then she decided that Ross would hardly let him run wild if he was dangerous, so she ignored his growls and said softly, "What is it, Jasper? Missing your master, are you?"

The growling paused and Annabel heard a thump that she guessed was his tail hitting the floor. She didn't reach out to pet him then, she'd worked around animals in the stables and knew enough not to try to move too quickly, so Annabel turned her side to him and calmly pulled the bedchamber door closed. Her eyes had adjusted enough that she could make out shapes and shadows in the hall now by the faint light coming from a fire in the great hall below. Turning toward the stairs, she headed that way, saying softly, "You may come with me if you like, Jasper. I would appreciate the company."

Annabel didn't think for a moment that the dog understood what she'd said other than to know that she'd used his name, but that was enough for him to get to his feet and follow her curiously at a safe distance. He was perhaps four steps behind her as she descended the stairs, but moved a little closer once she reached the great hall floor and began to make her way through the bodies sleeping there.

Annabel peered curiously at the sleeping faces she passed. She had been at MacKay for twenty-four hours by her guess, but other than the cook and the handful of people who had been present when she'd tended the wounded merchant, she hadn't met many of the people she was now lady over. Actually, she hadn't even met the people who had attended while she'd cared for the merchant. She'd simply been in their presence. Goodness, Annabel realized suddenly, she hadn't even yet eaten a meal with anyone but her husband. It made her wonder what the people of MacKay must be thinking. She hoped they did not think that she thought herself too good to sit at a table with them. Of course, they would know she'd been wounded today, but did they understand that she was not the one who had chosen not to break her fast or eat her nooning meal with them? That those decisions had been made for her?

Grimacing, Annabel decided she was most definitely going to break her fast in the great hall come morning. She might be unskilled at the job that had been thrust on her with this marriage, but she would at least be present and make an effort at being a proper lady to the people of MacKay.

Jasper was still keeping a two-foot space between them when Annabel reached the doors to the kitchens. Not wishing to crowd him, she passed through the door and then stepped to the side and held the door for him to follow. Once he had entered and moved out of the way, she let the door slide closed and then peered around the kitchens. The light here was much better than in the great hall. It was also a lot warmer. Uncomfortably so, and Annabel understood why when she noted that a fire was still burning with some enthusiasm under a pot across the room.

Curious, she walked to it and peered at the contents. It appeared to be a soup of some kind bubbling away. It smelled delicious and Annabel briefly considered finding a trencher and serving herself, but she didn't see any handy trenchers lying about for her to use. Deciding she'd probably spill it on her way back through the great hall and burn some poor unsuspecting sleeper anyway, she gave up on the idea and made a quick search for something else.

Moments later Annabel had found a pantry and loaded herself up with cheese, fruit and a crusty roll, and was leading Jasper out of the kitchens and back across the great hall. The dog followed her much more closely on the return journey. Much to her amusement, he was nearly treading on her heels in his eagerness not to be left behind. Annabel had dropped him a couple of pieces of cheese as she'd cut it and thought wryly that it was amazing what a little culinary bribery could do. The dog had gobbled up the offerings as if starving and had stuck close to her ever since.

Jasper stopped in the hall and sat down to watch silently as Annabel shifted her booty and opened the bedchamber door. When she stepped inside and then glanced back to whisper, "Come," he stood up eagerly and rushed into the room.

Smiling faintly at this sign of good training, Annabel closed the door and then led him to the chairs by the fire. When she sat in one of the chairs, he settled at her feet and steadfastly refused to look at the food she held. He'd been trained not to beg, she noted with satisfaction and rewarded him with a bit of cheese and then some fruit as well. Jasper was careful not to nip her as he took the offerings and then gobbled both up eagerly before laying his head on her knee. Taking that for the invitation it was, Annabel gave him a pat and told him he was a good boy, then caressed his head and stared into the fire for a bit, marveling over how her life had changed and wondering when she would wake up from this dream she was surely having.

"WIFE."

Annabel stirred sleepily, and then sighed as a warm hand slid down her side and over her hip under the linens and furs. When that hand then made the return journey, she rolled back until her husband's chest pressed against her back, and was rewarded by that hand detouring to find one breast and caress it.

"Mmm," Annabel murmured as heat began to seep through her. "Good morning, husband."

"Good morning," Ross said softly, and kissed her ear before asking, "Why is there a dog in our bed?"

Annabel's eyes popped open and she lifted her head to look around until she spotted Jasper lying at the bottom corner of the bed. When the dog raised his head to meet her gaze and began to wag his tail, she had to bite her lip to keep from laughing at the doggy grin he was giving her.

"Your father must have let him sleep there," she said apologetically. Jasper had lain down on the floor beside the bed when she'd finally decided she might sleep and had rejoined Ross. Apparently, the dog had joined them in it after she'd dozed off, because she hadn't felt him climbing onto the bed.

"How did he get into the room?" Ross asked next.

"Ah." Annabel grimaced, and then admitted, "I let him in."

When silence met this admission, she added, "He misses your father, husband."

"He is a dog, wife," Ross said dryly.

Annabel turned over in bed so she could see his face and said, "Aye, but dogs are not solitary creatures, husband. They are used to a pack. Your father was Jasper's pack. Now he is gone and Jasper has none. 'Tis why he has been difficult. He just needs to feel part of a pack again."

Silence crowded in again when she stopped talking and Annabel was trying to think of something else to say, when Ross asked curiously, "Did ye have dogs growing up?"

"Nay," she admitted reluctantly. She had wanted one, but of course the abbess would never have allowed it.

"Then how do ye ken so much about them?" he asked.

Annabel sighed and then admitted, "Sister Clara was very knowledgeable about them. She raised them when she was married and used to tell me about her dogs and their behaviors and such."

"I thought yer sister's name was Kate," Ross said with a frown, and then glanced to the door when a knock sounded. Annabel quickly tugged the furs up to her chin as he called, "Come in."

Gilly immediately stuck his head into the room. He paused long enough to smile and wish Annabel good morning, and then turned his attention to Ross and announced, "A messenger just arrived from yer lady sister. She and her husband'll be here by noon."

Ross nodded and murmured his thanks, then turned back to her as Gilly pulled his head back and closed the door, but Annabel was already throwing the linens and furs aside and leaping from bed.

"What are ye doing?" he asked, a frown in his voice. "Come back to bed."

"What?" Annabel asked, glancing at him with amazement, and then she shook her head and turned away to grab up his plaid and wrap it around herself in the roman style, saying, "Nay. Your sister is coming. We have to get ready."

"She will not be here fer hours," Ross protested on a laugh. "Come back to bed. 'Tis Thursday."

Annabel glanced at him in confusion, not knowing what it being Thursday had to do with anything, and then hurried to the door, clutching his plaid closed above her chest. "I have to get a dress ready. I will not be bursting out of the neckline when I meet your sister."

"That's—" Ross paused when she tugged the door open and they both saw Seonag on the threshold, hand raised to knock.

The woman only paused a beat before bustling into the room, several gowns over one arm. "I brought the best of the gowns I found yesterday, but they all need work. I never got to repairing them yesterday what with running between ye and the merchant," she added apologetically.

"No, of course you did not," Annabel said with understanding as she pushed the door closed.

" 'Tis all right. Surely we can get one ready by noon?"

"Aye," Seonag agreed, sounding relieved that she wasn't angry.

A sigh from the bed made them both glance that way as Ross tossed the furs and linens aside to get up.

"I suppose there is no reason fer me to stay abed then," he said dryly, bending to pick up his shirt. He tugged it on and then walked to Annabel and gave her a slow, hungry kiss that had her releasing his plaid to reach for him. The moment she did, he broke the kiss and stepped back taking the plaid with him.

"I'll need this. Besides, I like ye better that way," he said with a grin as Annabel gasped in surprise at being left naked.

"WELL?" ANNABEL ASKED ANXIOUSLY WHEN Seonag remained silent too long.

" 'Tis perfect," Seonag pronounced at last. "Ye can no' even tell it has been let out in the bust."

Annabel sagged with relief, but glanced down at the deep red gown she wore and asked worriedly, "Is the color all right on me? I have never worn anything so bold before."

"Well, ye should," the maid said firmly. "The color suits ye. The pink ye wore yesterday was too pale fer yer coloring."

Annabel smiled wryly at that. Pale and drab fabrics had always been favored at the abbey. No one would have dared to wear this color for fear of displeasing the abbess.

Fortunately, she did not have to deal with the woman's likes or dislikes anymore, Annabel reminded herself firmly, and turned her mind to what else had to be done to prepare for Giorsal's visit. The problem was, she didn't have a clue what that list included.

She was ready in the gown she and Seonag had prepared. The maid had even done her hair again for her. But what else should she do?

Food, she thought and asked, "Has someone informed Angus that we are to have company?"

"Aye. Gilly told both Cook and I ere coming upstairs in search of the laird," she assured her. "Angus was planning what he would serve as I left."

"Good," Annabel murmured, but wondered if she was expected to check with the cook about what he was preparing. Or would that be considered insulting? She decided not to check with him. Whether Angus was aware of it or not, he knew better what was expected in this situation than she did.

Grimacing over that, Annabel hurried to help gather the remaining gowns when Seonag began to collect them.

"I can manage, m'lady," Seonag said at once, but Annabel shook her head.

"I can help. I am going below anyway, and I would not want you tripping over the material on your way down the stairs."

Seonag had commented earlier that she would store away the gowns that still needed mending in a sewing basket by the fire in the great hall so that they could work on them as they had time.

Annabel had wondered that they would all fit in the basket mentioned, but she needn't have worried. The basket in question was huge. Lady Magaidh must have done a great deal of mending over the years, she decided. Fortunately, that was something Annabel could manage. She had made her own dresses and mended any tears and such for years now. Annabel knew she was not quick at the task; working with Seonag had proven that, but she could sew a straight line.

"There," Seonag said as they straightened from packing away the gowns. She glanced at Annabel and then said, "Ye should break yer fast now, m'lady. I should ha'e thought to bring ye up something when I headed to yer room. Ye must be hungry."

"I am fine," Annabel assured her as they headed toward the trestle tables. "I ate late last night. But a warmed cider would be nice about now. I—what is that smell?" She interrupted herself to ask, her nose working as a most unpleasant odor reached it.

"It's that damned dog."

Annabel turned at that announcement from Angus. The cook stood between the tables and the door to the kitchens, a cleaver grasped in his hand and a scowl on his face as he eyed Jasper. The dog was hunched over in a corner, proving that he was the source of the smell by creating more of it.

"The bloody beast was in the kitchen doing his business and stinking it up and I chased him out, not thinking he wasn't done and would continue out here." Cook turned to her, his anger giving way to despair as he cried, "This stink will ruin the lovely squab I am preparing for the nooning."

"Oh dear," Annabel muttered, eyeing Jasper unhappily. The poor beast appeared to be suffering a digestive ailment of some sort at the moment, and while she had all the sympathy in the world for him, she wished he could have waited until tomorrow to have it.

"The poor bugger has no' smelled that bad since that time the Gordons were visiting and their boy fed him some cheese," Seonag commented with a frown.

Annabel stiffened guiltily. "What? Cheese?"

"Aye. It seems he does no' like cheese. Or his stomach does no' like it anyway. It always affects him badly for days afterward. 'Tis why the old laird ordered that no one feed him but hisself. He's a delicate stomach, does Jasper."

Annabel closed her eyes briefly at this news. She had done it to the poor dog herself by feeding him cheese last night. Dear God!

"What are we going to do?" Cook asked miserably. "He shall ruin everything."

Annabel rubbed her suddenly aching forehead, careful to avoid the gash there and then sighed and let her hands drop away. "We shall have to put him out in the bailey and clean up this mess."

ROSS WAS TALKING TO GILLY AND MARACH as they watched the men practice at battle. They were discussing their strengths and weaknesses and deciding how best to improve on their skills, when the stable master came rushing up. The man was red faced and out of breath, but it didn't stop him blurting, "She's gone!" the moment he reached them.

"Who's gone?" Ross asked with a frown, but the man had used the last of his breath on the announcement and merely shook his head, then bent over, resting his hands on his knees as he panted for breath.

"Speak, man," Gilly snapped, never having been very patient.

The stable master raised a hand, silently begging a moment, but then straightened and looked to Ross as he managed to get out, "Yer bride."

"What?" he barked, stiffening. "What the hell are ye talking about? Where has Annabel gone?"

"Back to England?" Gilly asked and Ross glared at the man. Annabel better not have headed back to England. He'd wring her bloody neck if she had. She was his. And why the hell would she go there anyway? Surely life with him was better than life with those two coldhearted English—

"Nay. To fetch flowers," the stable master said, sounding a little less breathless.

Ross turned an uncomprehending glance his way and asked with bewilderment, "Flowers?"

"Aye. Jasper has the flux. He's stunk up the great hall with it. They cleaned up the mess, but the smell just will no' leave, and yer sister is comin', so yer lady went to . . ." His words trailed away. Ross was no longer listening. He'd turned on his heel with a curse and was running for the stables. Gilly and Marach were hard on his heels.

"HONESTLY, JASPER, WHY ON EARTH DID YOU EAT the cheese if it affects you so?" Annabel asked with exasperation from beneath the hand covering her nose and mouth. Her head was turned away from what the dog was doing so she didn't have to see it, but there was no escaping the smell.

Jasper had been waiting on the steps when she'd come out of the keep and had promptly fallen into step beside her as she'd headed to the stables. That being the case, she had not been surprised when he'd trotted out of the bailey right behind her mare. She should have ordered him to stay behind though. The poor beast was suffering. This was the third time he'd had to hunch over and vacate himself since they'd left.

Annabel let her hand drop with a sigh and urged her mare to move again when Jasper finished his business and moved into view. Truthfully, judging by the way he was still prancing about, he wasn't suffering all that much. Everyone else was though. The smell in the keep was enough to bring tears to the eyes, even after a thorough cleaning, and all Annabel had been able to think to do was to find flowers to add to the rushes and cover the smell. However with the servants spread so thin giving the great hall floor another good wash, dusting and polishing, and bustling about in the kitchen to help Cook with this unexpected meal, there had been no one to send on the task . . . And since she was the one responsible for this mess, Annabel had decided she would fetch the flowers she hoped would help mask the matter.

Afraid Seonag would try to stop her, Annabel had not told her what she planned to do. Unfortunately, she hadn't been able to slip out of the stables with her mare undetected, despite not bothering to saddle the beast, and she'd ended up telling the stable master where she was going. He, of course, had protested vehemently that he was quite sure his laird would not be pleased, and Annabel, of course, had simply shrugged helplessly and gone ahead and done as she wished. Though she'd had to remind the man that she was his lady and to be obeyed when he placed himself physically in front of her mare in an attempt to stop her.

The old man's face had turned red then and he'd suddenly whirled and raced off, no doubt to tell on her.

By now, Annabel suspected Ross would be pacing angrily about, deciding what to do with her when she got back. She just hoped it wasn't anything too bad. She was very aware that husbands were allowed to beat their wives.

"Now where are those bluebells?" Annabel muttered to herself as she surveyed the area. She and Ross had ridden through a veritable field of bluebells on their way to the clearing where they'd picnicked. The smell had been intoxicating. With enough of that strewn among the rushes, she was sure they could hide the stench Jasper had caused in the keep. And they were pretty too, she thought.

Annabel smelled the flowers almost at the same moment as she spotted them ahead. As she eyed the rash of flowers that had sprung up under the trees, Annabel supposed *field* was not quite the right word, though there were so many of them they could have made a field. But bluebells didn't like strong sunlight and preferred more shaded areas where the sun could only reach her fingers through the branches overhead to sprinkle them with her light.

Releasing a sigh, Annabel reined in her mare and slid off her bare back to the forest floor, then untied the bag she'd brought with her from her waist. She'd had the forethought to bring a knife in case the stalks were tough in Scotland, and a large sack to put them in for the ride home. Leaving Jasper to wander as he wished, she began her work, quickly gathering an armful of the fragrant flowers and stowing them in her bag before continuing on.

Annabel was placing the third and last armful of flowers she could fit in the now bulging bag when she spotted movement out of the corner of her eye and glanced that way. She was expecting it to be Jasper. The dog had wandered off almost the moment she'd dismounted and she'd kept an eye out for his return. Annabel was hoping he'd come back on his own and save her having to call for him.

But it wasn't Jasper. It was a large man in a plaid, and Annabel stared at him nonplussed for a moment as she recognized him as the man who had come upon her in the clearing the first night they'd made camp on the journey here. But that had been in England. And he'd been wearing English clothes then. And this couldn't be an accidental encounter.

Straightening, she dropped her bag, but kept her hold on her knife as she began to back away, and asked, "Who are you?"

"It'll go easier on ye do ye just come quietly, lass," the man said, his words so soft-spoken she almost missed the threat until he added, "I don't want to have to hurt ye."

Those words though decided her course and Annabel stopped backing away and turned to make a break for her mare. She nearly reached her too, and was only a couple steps away when he tackled her from behind. Annabel went down with a cry, pulling the hand with the knife back toward herself to avoid stabbing her mare as she tumbled to the ground at the horse's hooves. Of course, the commotion frightened the poor mare, making her scream and rear. All Annabel could do was cover her head and pray she wasn't stomped on.

She should have been praying the horse stomped on the man on top of her though, Annabel decided a moment later when her mare backed away, still making distressed sounds and she heard a tearing as she was dragged over onto her back. All she could think as her back slammed into the dirt was that she didn't have anything else to wear to meet her new sister-in-law and this man was ruining the one presentable dress she did have.

With that thought, Annabel swung furiously at his head, not recalling the knife held in it until it slammed into the arm he lifted to block her blow. Annabel froze then, eyes going wide, and she almost blurted an apology. Before she could do something as ridiculous as that, though, he slammed the fist of his uninjured arm into her head, briefly stunning her.

It was a deep growl and bark that brought her eyes open again, but Annabel had trouble focusing on the blur that was Jasper as he charged toward them at full tilt. The man leapt to his feet and took off at a dead run. He never would have outrun the dog, but she wouldn't risk his harming the beast with a kick to the head or something and immediately shouted, "Jasper!" when he charged past her after her attacker.

The dog responded at once, nearly doing a somersault in his effort to stop. He then stood there for a moment, looking to her and back to the man twice before turning and trotting to her side.

"Good boy," Annabel breathed, hugging him when he sat down beside her. She had meant it only to be a brief hug to reward him for obeying despite his instinct to give chase, but ended up holding on to the animal to stay upright as a wave of exhaustion rolled over her.

That exhaustion disappeared though, as her ear caught the sound of approaching riders. Her husband and his men, no doubt, Annabel thought and forced herself to gain her feet to face his anger. Only it wasn't her husband and his men. She didn't recognize a single man in the approaching party, and Annabel instinctively tightened her fingers around . . . nothing. She no longer had the knife she'd borrowed from the kitchen for this excursion. It was still in the arm of the man who had attacked her. The only weapon she had now was the dog at her feet.

Mouth tightening at this realization, Annabel raised her chin and watched as the party of about six riders drew to a halt before her. Silence filled the glade as the men eyed her. It went on long enough that she began to grow uncomfortable, so Annabel finally said, "Good morning."

For some reason her polite greeting drew a chuckle from several of the men. The only one who did not laugh, that she could see, was the one in the lead. Her words brought a frown to his face and he said, "English."

"Aye," Annabel said warily, raising her chin a little more.

The other men had stopped laughing abruptly at the word *English* and were now eyeing her with a speculation she did not understand until he asked, "Ye'd no' be Ross MacKay's new bride, would ye?"

Annabel stiffened, suspicion beginning to creep up within her. That suspicion exploded into full-blown realization when a woman on horseback charged out of the trees with a mounted man hot on her horse's tail.

"Dammit, Giorsal, I told ye to wait," the leader barked as she reined in next to him. Truthfully, he sounded more exasperated than surprised. At least, he did until his gaze shifted to the man drawing to a halt behind her. Then his voice was short with anger as he said, "Ye were to keep her where she was safe until we'd scouted out the situation."

"Don't fash at Brody, husband," the woman said with a laugh. "Ye ken he did his best. But I wanted to know what was happening and why the lass screamed."

Annabel listened to this exchange, her heart sinking as her fear was proved true. When everyone then turned back to her in question, she instinctively raised a hand to push the hair back from her face, only to pause as she spotted the blood covering it and glistening on the sleeve of her gown.

Frowning, Annabel peered down at herself then and could have shrieked with frustration when she saw that her gown was torn and covered with blood and grass stains. Really, it was enough to weep over. This was not how she'd planned to meet her husband's sister.

Chapter 8

"THIS ISNA' GOOD."

Ross's mouth tightened, but he didn't respond to Gilly's comment as he watched Marach run his hands over his wife's saddleless mare in search of wounds, and then checked her hooves to see where she'd been.

Annabel had disappeared into the woods by the time he'd led Marach and Gilly out of the bailey. They'd crossed the narrow barren land that surrounded the castle and then had begun to search the area just across from the drawbridge, thinking the woman didn't know the area so wouldn't have strayed far. But when that had turned up nothing, they'd begun to discuss splitting up and searching further afield, only to pause when her mare came charging through the woods toward them. The horse had been in a panic. On spotting them, she'd turned sharply and tried to avoid them, but the men had given chase and caught her.

"Anything?" Ross asked as Marach finished his examination and straightened.

"No injuries, but something spooked her," he said, running a soothing hand down her back. "She has black dirt ground deep into her hooves."

"Hmm," Ross muttered, considering the different areas nearby with black dirt. There were a lot of them. Stomach clenching with frustration and worry, he ordered, "Marach, take the mare back to MacKay, and round up some men to help search. Gilly and I will split up and head the way the horse came. If we find Annabel—" He paused and jerked around in his saddle as a tinkle of laughter reached his ears.

"It sounds like more than one woman," Marach said as a second burst of female laughter joined the first.

"Seonag?" Gilly suggested uncertainly.

Ross considered that, but said, "The stable master did no' mention anyone accompanying me wife."

"Nay, he didn't," Marach agreed, and then as the riding party came into view through the trees, he added, "And that's definitely no' just a couple o' women."

"Nay," Ross growled, squinting to get a better look at the group. Another moment hadn't passed, though, before he recognized them as MacDonalds.

"Ah, Giorsal's come for a visit," Gilly said, apparently recognizing the group as well. "And it appears she and yer wife are getting along like a hut on fire."

"Then why isn't she riding with her?" Ross asked testily as he noted his wife's wee figure seated before his brother-in-law on his mount.

She threw her head back on another laugh then, her dark hair flying back and splashing over Bean's cream shirt and dark green plaid, and Ross growled deep in his throat, his fingers tightening on his reins.

"On the bright side, she looks unharmed and well from here," Gilly pointed out, sounding amused for some reason.

Ross merely grunted and urged his horse forward to meet the party.

Bean spotted him first, and the MacDonald laird gave him a solemn nod over Annabel's head. Giorsal, who had been grinning as she listened to something Annabel was saying, saw her husband's action and turned to look Ross's way. A wide smile immediately claimed her lips and she cried, "Brother!" and urged her mount eagerly forward. The silly chit damned near knocked him off his horse when she threw herself off her mare and at him. Fortunately, Ross knew his sister well and had braced himself the moment she urged her mount forward. He was prepared for the impact and quick enough to catch her to his chest so she didn't tumble to the ground.

"I like your new bride," Giorsal laughed, hugging him so tightly she near choked him. Then she sat back in his lap and said seriously, "But ye'd best find out who it is that keeps attacking her. Next time she may no' be so lucky."

Stiffening, Ross shifted Giorsal to the side so that he could get a better look at his wife. Bean had continued forward at a sedate pace, a long-suffering expression on his face as he watched his hooligan of a wife greet her brother. Even so, he had nearly reached them and Ross could now see that his wife wasn't as well as he'd first thought. Her hair was a little wild around her head, a dark bruise was coloring her left temple, looking almost a match to the one in the center of her forehead from the day before, and her gown was torn, the neckline hanging askew and almost indecent.

"The blood's not hers," Giorsal said reassuringly and Ross suddenly noted that her red gown was a little darker red in places; her right sleeve, neckline and bodice. Drying blood. Her gown hid it well.

"Her attacker?" he asked, eyes narrowing and rage rising up within him at the thought of his wee bride alone and fighting for her life against some faceless bastard like the big behemoth he'd seen chasing her in the clearing the day before.

"Aye. She stabbed him in the arm, and then Jasper scared him off," Giorsal announced and he now noticed Jasper trotting along beside Bean's horse. The dog kept tipping his head up to Annabel, and then to the path ahead, and then back to Annabel again. It was how he used to follow his father, Ross recalled, and suspected his wife had been adopted by the beast in his father's place.

He was distracted from this thought when Giorsal added, "We heard her scream and came to investigate, but he was gone ere we got there. The men were going to search for him, but she said no' to bother, that you and the men have searched each time he has appeared and the man seems to disappear into the wind."

Ross frowned. Annabel had claimed not to see the man who had chased her in the clearing the day before, and the only other event had been the man who had walked up on her while she was trying to relieve herself on the journey here. Both times the man had seemed to disappear into thin air, but surely she wasn't suggesting all three incidents involved the same man? It had been an Englishman in England, and a Scot yesterday. Or, at least, the man had been wearing English clothes in England by Annabel's account; he had not seen him. He had, however, seen the man the day before and had noted he wore a plaid.

"May I have my wife back?"

Ross blinked his thoughts away to peer at his brother-in-law at that question. A frown claimed his face when he saw that Annabel was no longer seated before the man. Ross looked around, his expression turning grimmer when he saw her presently pulling herself up onto her mare's bare back with a leg up from Marach. A bulging bag that no doubt contained flowers hung from her one hand. Ross immediately scooped up his sister and tossed her the couple of feet to her husband. He barely waited to ensure Bean caught her before turning his horse to urge it up next to his wife's. Ross plucked her up just as she settled on the animal's bare back with a little satisfied huff at the successful effort.

"Husband," she protested. "I can ride. I am not hurt."

"Yer gown is torn and bloodied and ye've added yet another bruise to yer pretty face. Do no' tell me yer no' hurt," he said grimly, shifting her about before him until she was pressed snugly up against his groin. Satisfied with her position, he then gestured for the others to follow, and turned his horse toward the castle. He rode fast at first and let a moment pass to get ahead of the others, before saying, "Ye told me ye had no' seen the man in the clearing yesterday."

"I did not," Annabel assured him, swiveling to look at him with a bit of excitement as she was recalled to the day's events. "But I saw his plaid and the man today was wearing the same color plaid. He was big too. And, he was the same man as the one who startled me in England on our journey here, so I am beginning to think it was the same man all three times."

"Ye're sure it was the same man as in England?" he asked, not happy at the thought.

"Aye. I only caught a glimpse that first time, but he is hard to mistake," she assured him. "He is very large and has a pretty face."

That brought a scowl to Ross's lips. He didn't at all like her finding someone else attractive, which was silly, he supposed. It wasn't like she was going to run off with her attacker. According to Giorsal, she'd stabbed him. Besides, he himself wouldn't have been flattered to be called pretty.

"Ye mean handsome, do ye no'?" he suggested.

"Nay. *You* are handsome, husband. *He* is pretty," she said in a tone of voice that suggested that should clear the matter up. It didn't.

"Is there a difference?" Ross asked cautiously.

"Aye," Annabel said as if that should be obvious. "Handsome is rugged and manly and . . . well . . . *handsome*," she finished helplessly, and then added, "Pretty is big eyes, sculpted jaw and hair that flops across the eyes." She paused briefly before continuing with some consideration, "He would make a lovely girl were he not so muscular across the shoulders and chest."

"Ah," Ross said, unable to repress a grin. Whether she realized it or not, his wife was saying she thought he was a sexy beast, while the pretty boy was . . . pretty, but not in a way she found especially attractive. He liked that.

His smile didn't last long though. Now that he'd got past the bit about her attacker being pretty, he was considering that her description fit the man he'd seen chasing her through the clearing yesterday. It would seem that he was the fellow from all three incidents, after all. "Did he speak?"

"Aye," she answered and then recalled, "He had a Scottish accent."

Ross let his breath out on a disappointed sigh. He'd rather been hoping it was an Englishman trying not to draw attention up here, rather than a Scot who had taken on English garb that first time, no doubt in an effort to try to fool them into thinking he was English. If it was a Scot, though, it meant these events likely had more to do with him than with his bride. Someone was trying to get to him through her.

"He said it would go easier did I not fight," Annabel added suddenly. "That he did not wish to harm me, but would. So I guess it was my fault he punched me in the head."

"I am going to hurt him when I find him," Ross said grimly.

"I already did," Annabel admitted on a sigh. "I fear I stabbed him in the arm."

Ross tightened his hold on her. She sounded

almost apologetic when she admitted it, but he was proud of her. She was a fighter, his wife.

"I did not mean to," she admitted. "I had forgotten I had the knife in my hand . . . and I was aiming for his head." She grimaced, and then added, "I am glad he raised his arm. Knifing him in the head would have been disgusting."

"Aye," Ross agreed. He'd done it in battle on more than one occasion, but on purpose. A good jab in the ear, in the eye, or up under the jaw was always a battle stopper. Removing the knife afterward was the disgusting bit. The suctioning sound that accompanied the chore was rather gruesome, and sometimes the eye might come out with the blade if you stabbed them there, and then you had to remove that . . . also gruesome.

"Could it be the old trouble?" Gilly asked.

Ross glanced to the side and back at that question to see that he hadn't left everyone behind after all. Gilly and Marach had kept apace, and had apparently heard all. Ross turned forward again, a grim expression on his face at Gilly's words. He was suggesting that the battle for clan chief was not yet over and someone was trying to use Annabel to force him to give up the title. But, if that were the case, the attacker would be his uncle or Fingal, and he'd seen the man in the clearing and—"I did no' recognize him. He's no' a clan member."

"He could ha'e been hired to do the chore for another," Gilly pointed out quietly.

That was a very real possibility and one Ross wished he didn't have to consider, but he did. He'd hoped killing Derek had put an end to it all, and certainly the other three men who had been vying for the title of clan chief at the time had seemed to back down and fall in line. His cousin, Derek, had been the son of his father's deceased twin brother. He had used age as the excuse for why he would be a better clan chief, but the man had only been four years older. The moment Derek had brought up age as the reason, Ross's two remaining uncles, Ainsley and Eoghann, had each stepped up, pointing out that they had more age and wisdom than either of the two younger men and therefore should be the choice. The final man to try to claim entitlement to the chiefdom was Fingal, the blacksmith in the village, and the bastard son of Ross's grandfather. As such, he too felt he had every right to go after the seat.

All three of the older men had backed down after Ross had killed his cousin, Derek, in battle. Derek had lain in wait and ambushed Ross, Gilly and Marach while they were out hunting. The element of surprise had not helped him. Nor had his having a dozen men with him. Ross had ended the battle quickly and decisively, riding furiously through the other men to his cousin, who was staying at the back of the group, allowing his men to fight the battle for him. Ross would never see such a coward rule their people. He'd given Derek a mortal chest wound as the man had tried to turn his horse to flee.

Whether it was shame at their leader's cowardly behavior or simple self-preservation, the moment Derek was dead, the other men had lain down their weapons and sworn fealty.

Fingal and his uncles had done the same on

learning the news. All three claimed they had simply been trying to show Derek that his being four years older did not give him a claim to the title, and that leadership skills and courage were what mattered, not age.

Ross's uncle Ainsley had since passed away when his heart seized up the past winter, but Eoghann and Fingal still lived. Eoghann had a little farm outside the village, and Fingal still worked as a blacksmith in the village. The question now became, was one of them still interested in the title clan chief, and if one of them was, how was he planning to use Annabel to gain it?

"Thank you," Annabel murmured when Ross helped her down from his horse. Reaching down to give Jasper an absent pat when he rushed up, she glanced the way they'd come and saw that the others were just crossing the drawbridge. She only had moments before they would reach the keep. Fingers tightening on the bag in her hand, she whirled and rushed up the stairs to the keep doors, aware that Ross and Jasper were following.

The smell in the great hall was not nearly as bad as it had been, but still hung in the air like a ghost, faint but noticeable and very unpleasant. Grimacing, Annabel glanced over the dozen or so women re-scrubbing the various spots where Jasper had left his gifts earlier. She was looking for Seonag, and spotted her just as the maid glanced up and saw them. The woman glared briefly at Jasper when she saw that he was with them, but then her gaze found the bag Annabel carried and relief replaced the scowl. That relief turned to a pained grimace, however, as she struggled to her feet. Annabel frowned with concern and rushed forward as the woman started to shuffle toward them with a limping gait.

Seonag was too old to be kneeling on the cold stone floor for any length of time. She should have simply directed the women, rather than helping, but before Annabel could say so, Seonag said, "Oh, thank goodness. Ye found the flowers. They'll—" She paused abruptly as she got near enough to see the state Annabel was in and gasped, "What in the bloody blazes happened to ye?"

"She was attacked," Ross answered and didn't sound very happy about it.

"Again?" Seonag asked with dismay.

Impatient at this delay when the MacDonalds were nearly on their doorstep, she waved the question away. "Never mind that now. We must get these bluebells spread about. Ross's sister and her husband are right behind us and shall be coming through the door any moment and it still smells in here."

"Aye. We have scrubbed and scrubbed but the stench remains," Seonag said. Her tone was distracted, however, her attention seeming locked on Annabel's forehead, and she couldn't resist asking, "Did ye run into another tree?"

Annabel gaped at the question and then sighed. She would never live that one down and really wished her husband hadn't felt the need to explain her injury and tell everyone about it. Though to be fair, he'd probably only told Seonag so that she knew what she was dealing with. Annabel didn't doubt that everyone now knew about it, though. It was impossible to keep secrets in castles.

"Me wife was attacked and punched in the head," Ross explained. "And doubtless she has other bruises and wounds from the attack too. Take her above stairs and be sure there is nothing serious. Then see her changed. I'll—"

"There is no time for that now," Annabel protested at once. "We must get these bluebells strewn about. Your sister and her husband—"

"I'll tend the flowers," Ross interrupted. He took the sack from her and then urged her toward the stairs. "Let Seonag examine ye and help ye change . . . else *I'll* do it."

When he paused on the last word and suddenly turned to look down at her, his eyes going smoky, Annabel felt her own eyes widen. She recognized that look and instinctively knew that his examining would be a lot more involved and take much longer than Seonag's. She suspected it would include his getting naked too, and for a moment she was tempted, but then Seonag tsked with exasperation and took her arm to pull her away from Ross.

"There's time enough fer *yer* kind o' examining later, *after* yer guests have left," the maid said to Ross as she urged Annabel up the stairs. Glancing over her shoulder she added, "Now get on with ye and give those flowers to the maids to strew about. Ye don't want yer wife embarrassed by yer home when yer sister enters."

Recalled to the situation, Annabel stopped dragging her heels and hurried up the stairs. When they reached the top and started along the landing, she glanced over the rail to the great hall to see that rather than hand over the bag to one of the maids, her husband had opened and tilted the bag and was walking about shaking out the contents over the rushes.

"It'll do," Seonag assured her.

"Aye," Annabel agreed and led the way into the master bedchamber.

"Bloody dog," Seonag muttered when Jasper rushed past her before she could close the door.

Annabel bit her lip and petted Jasper when he hurried to her side. After a moment, she said, "Do not be too hard on him, Seonag. 'Tis not his fault he had a bad tummy. I did not know it troubled him and fed him cheese." She allowed time for that to sink in and then added, " 'Sides, he saved me in the woods when I was attacked."

Seonag's scowl eased a bit and then she sighed and said, "The water is still in the basin from this morning. 'Twill be cold, but I suppose 'twill have to do. While ye strip and clean up, I'll find ye something to wear. Then I'll check ye over and help ye dress."

Annabel simply stared as those words filled her head. Find her something to wear? All she had were Ross's mother's dresses, which were all far too small in the bust. Unless—

"I do not suppose the gown I traveled here in has been cleaned yet?" she asked hopefully.

"Nay. I'm sorry," Seonag said apologetically.

The woman moved to a large basket beside the bed. Annabel recognized it as the one that had been downstairs by the fire in the great hall, the one that held all the dresses that were repairable.

Annabel hadn't noticed it before, but supposed Seonag had brought it up to work on the gowns while she'd watched over her the day before while she was unconscious.

"I should ha'e done it yesterday. It would be dry now if I had," Seonag said with regret as she began to sort through the remaining gowns in the basket. "But between watching o'er the merchant, and then yerself after yer accident, all I managed was to make the one yer wearing larger in the bosom fer ye."

"And I have gone and ruined it," Annabel said on a sigh, peering down at the now destroyed dress.

"Never mind. We'll find something," Seonag said, and then added with asperity, "And if yer bosoms hang out and Ross does no' like it, 'tis his own fault fer no' giving ye time to pack ere dragging ye here from yer home."

Annabel bit her lip at the irritation in Seonag's voice. She was blaming Ross for all of this, but while it was true he hadn't given her time to pack, she hadn't had anything to pack anyway. She was debating whether to admit all to the woman, when Seonag glanced over and saw her simply standing there.

"Is the water that cold? Should I send fer fresh warm water?" she asked with a frown.

"Nay." Annabel let go of the brief desire to confess all and turned to the basin. She poured the last of the water from the ewer into the cool water from that morning and then quickly stripped out of her gown and set to work at cleaning off the blood that had splashed onto her chest, hands

and arms. Busy with the task, she didn't realize
Seonag had settled on a gown and come to join
her until the other woman spoke.

"Ye've a nasty bruise here," Seonag said with
concern, brushing a finger over the center of her
lower back.

"I must have got it when he knocked me to the
ground," Annabel murmured, craning her head
around to try to see it, but it was impossible.

"Does it pain ye?" Seonag asked.

"Nay," Annabel lied and when Seonag looked
dubious, she admitted, "Well, mayhap a little, but
'twill be fine."

"Hmm." Seonag let it go and peered at her face.
"How is yer head? Is it painin' ye?"

Annabel took in the maid's arched expression
and didn't even bother trying to lie this time.
"Aye. 'Tis pounding a bit."

"I'll make ye some willow-bark tea when we go
below," Seonag decided, and then turned her attention to the dark blue gown she'd selected and
announced, "This one is in the best shape. No
tears, or fraying."

"Let us hope 'tis a little larger in the bosom
than the others then," Annabel muttered.

"So yer wife has been set upon three times
by a lone Scot?"

Ross glanced to his brother-in-law. Bean sat
turning his tankard of ale absently in his hands,
his expression thoughtful.

Once Annabel and Seonag had disappeared
upstairs, he'd spread the bluebells about, then in-
structed one of the maids to go tell Cook to send

out refreshments. His sister and her husband had entered just as he'd finished giving the order. Ross had welcomed them and seen them seated even as servants rushed out to the Great Hall with the requested drinks. Now they were discussing what had happened to his wife.

"Aye," he said finally. "It would seem so."

"The old trouble over the title of clan chief?" Bean asked.

"Gilly suggested as much too," Ross admitted.

"But?" Bean asked, apparently hearing the doubt in his voice.

Ross shrugged and then said, "I can see no way to gain the title using Annabel. I might agree to step down to get her safely back, but then I'd just challenge whoever it was and kill them for daring to touch her."

"Aye." Bean nodded with a grin. "Yer right. It would no' work."

"That does no' mean either Eoghann or Fingal would no' be stupid enough to try it," Giorsal said dryly. "Uncle Eoghann was never very bright. Neither is Fingal for that matter."

Ross smiled faintly at her dry words. "How do ye ken how bright Fingal is or isn't? Have ye even met him?"

"Nay," she acknowledged. "But only an idiot would have tried to take the title from ye."

He grinned at her staunch words, but turned to Bean and said, "If 'tis no' for the title, what else could it be? Has she enemies in Scotland?"

Ross shook his head slowly as he considered the question. "She has no' been here long enough to make enemies."

"From where she came from then?" Bean suggested, and then added, "I know it appears to be a Scot attacking her, but he could ha'e been hired by an Englishman."

"I can no' see that being likely," Ross said dubiously. "She's a kind heart, does Annabel."

"That makes no matter," Bean said dryly. "Ye have a kind heart too, but ye have enemies."

Ross stiffened and scowled at the other man. "Do I insult ye in yer home? Nay," he answered himself. "So do no' insult me in mine, thank ye very much. I am no' kindhearted. I am fair, mayhap, but no kindhearted."

Bean chuckled at his affronted words. "Very well, yer fair, no' kindhearted."

"Hmmm," Ross muttered, only slightly mollified. He couldn't have the man going around suggesting he was kindhearted or such. His people would think he was going soft.

"If no' Annabel, mayhap her father has enemies here," Giorsal suggested. "He visited once or twice when we were younger, ere he and Father's friendship waned. Mayhap he angered someone here in Scotland on one o' those trips."

Ross grunted at the suggestion. Lord Waverly had visited MacKay twice, both times within the first five years after saving his father's life. His father also had stopped in at Waverly for a visit or two in that time as well. However, the distance between the two homes, along with the responsibilities of family and their positions had prevented further visits. Not surprisingly, their friendship had cooled and died a natural death over time.

"The last time Lord Waverly was in Scotland

was more than fifteen years ago, Giorsal," Ross pointed out now. "And while I don't doubt the man makes enemies everywhere he goes, fifteen years is a long time to hold a grudge."

Bean raised an eyebrow. "Ye did no' like her father?"

"I did no' like her father or her mother," Ross admitted grimly.

"Why?" Giorsal asked at once.

Ross frowned, considering everything and then said, "They were cold and uncaring toward her, and insultingly eager to see us gone once they had the linen, and . . ."

"And?" Giorsal prompted when he paused.

He hesitated but then admitted, "On our wedding night there were welts on her back from a recent whipping, and scars from previous ones."

Giorsal sat back, displeasure on her face.

"But," Ross added, "I can't see anyone holding a grudge against him this long and then taking it out on his daughter."

"Then we are back to these attacks having to do with her time here," Bean said reasonably.

"Aye." Ross scowled, not liking that his wife was getting hurt because of him. It seemed ironic that while he wished nothing but to protect her and show her caring, he was the one causing her the hurts she was suffering, if only indirectly. Certainly, if he hadn't taken her to the clearing to consummate their wedding, she never would have been chased into a tree.

His thoughts were distracted by the appearance of Seonag hurrying down the stairs and across the great hall into the kitchens. Ross watched her go, and then glanced toward the stairs. When there was no sign of his wife, he excused himself and stood to stride to the kitchens.

Seonag was at a cauldron of boiling water over the fire, scooping the steaming liquid into a goblet when he entered. Moving to her side, he peered curiously at the drink she was preparing as she set the scoop back in the water and began to stir what looked like bits of bark into the liquid in the goblet.

"What is that?"

"Willow-bark tea fer Annabel's head," Seonag answered, and then added solemnly, "I was going to tell ye on me way back, but she sends her apologies. She'll no' be joining ye at table tonight."

"Why?" Ross asked, and then glanced to the beverage she was making and asked, "Is her head paining her?"

"Aye, but that's not why," the woman said with a sigh, and then shook her head. " 'Tis all my fault. Had I ordered one o' the girls to wash her dress, or worked faster and fixed two dresses to fit her properly instead o' just the one . . ." She shook her head again. "I'd best get this up to her. 'Twill ease the pain. At least I can fix that for now."

Ross took the drink from her and headed for the door. "I'll take it to her."

Chapter 9

ANNABEL ACCIDENTALLY POKED HERSELF WITH the sewing needle, yowled in pain and felt the tears that had been threatening for the last few minutes begin to slide down her cheeks. Even as she popped the abused digit into her mouth, she acknowledged that the tears were owing more to self-pity than the pain from the needle poke.

Really, this was not a good day in her books . . . and the worst part about it was that it was all her own bloody fault. First there had been the issue of Jasper's smelling up the great hall *because she'd fed him cheese*. That had been followed by the attack in the woods, which wouldn't have happened, she was sure, if she'd taken someone along on the excursion with her, and now she could not join the party below because her bosom was too bloody big for the gowns available.

She peered unhappily down at the dark blue gown in her lap. It had looked beautiful once she'd got it on . . . except for the fact that it was so tight it forced her breasts up far enough that her nipples showed. Seonag had selected another gown for her to try after that, a green one that needed a bit of repair in the hem, but it had been just as bad. When the woman had rushed back to select another gown from the collection in the basket, Annabel had told her not to bother. They would all be indecently small in the bosom. She would have to add panels to them all before she wore them in public. She simply could not go below until she did so.

Seonag had reluctantly admitted that she too feared that would be the case. The woman had then announced that she was going below to fetch her some tea for her aching head and would help with the task when she got back. Perhaps with the two of them working, they could manage it quickly, she'd added encouragingly.

Annabel had nodded in agreement, but knew that even with the two of them working it would take them hours to accomplish. The hem had to be cut off, the dress rehemmed all the way around, and then the removed material had to be sewn into panels and inserted in the gown. Seonag was a fast seamstress, but Annabel was not. She was quite sure Giorsal and her husband would be well on their way back home ere they finished the task.

She sniffled miserably at the thought. While Annabel had been nervous of meeting Ross's sister, she'd quickly come to like Giorsal during the short time in the clearing when she'd explained everything to her and Bean, the MacDonald lord. That liking had only grown during the short ride with their party before they'd come upon her husband and his men.

Annabel had never met anyone like Giorsal. The girl was like sunshine, full of happy chatter and loud laughter. The abbess would have hated her for both, Annabel was sure. She was also sure Giorsal would have spent as much time in penance as she had, but that just made her like her all the more. And she really would have enjoyed visiting with the couple below stairs, but instead was stuck upstairs sewing side panels into the blue gown to make it more presentable.

On top of all that, her head was beginning to pound something fierce. She hoped Seonag did not take long with the willow tea.

Annabel barely had the thought when she heard the door opening. Relieved, she glanced around, expecting to see the old woman crossing the room toward her—but instead it was Ross. Eyes widening, she turned her head quickly away and used the material in her hands to mop up the telltale tears from her cheek. Trying for a composed expression, she then turned back to her husband.

"Seonag could have brought that up. You should be down visiting with your sister and Bean," she chided with a forced smile.

"They'll be fine for a moment," he said, his eyes narrowing on her face with concern. "Ye've been crying. Does yer head pain ye so much?"

"'Tis fine. I am sure the willow tea Seonag was making will set it right quick enough. Is that it?" she asked.

"Oh, aye." He handed her the goblet and watched silently as she drank it, then took the empty goblet from her. He didn't leave then, though, but shifted his feet and then asked,

"Seonag said something about yer gowns being the reason why yer no' coming down? Surely it can no' be so bad? We should talk about—"

His words died abruptly when Annabel stood up and let her hands drop to her sides. She'd been holding the panel she was sewing in front of her breasts, but now they were on full display above the green neckline and while Ross's lips were no longer talking, his eyes were. They nearly popped out of his head as he took in the situation.

"Oh, aye, I see. That's . . ." He had raised his hand to her waist as he spoke, but now the hand continued up to run a finger lightly over the top of one nipple where it was visible above the material. "That's . . ."

"Indecent?" she suggested breathlessly as his finger brushed across the nipple again.

"Beautiful," he muttered and bent his head to kiss her.

Annabel sighed into his mouth as it covered hers. She'd needed this, she realized as she leaned into him and let her mouth fall open. His kiss and touch had wiped away all other thoughts and worries from her mind each time he'd graced her with them and she needed that just then. This morning's activities had made her feel such a failure. Annabel had known she would have some difficulties managing his home and people, but she had worked with animals in the stables at the abbey. Jasper was not the first animal she'd encountered who reacted badly to certain foods. She should have stuck with meat for him until asking someone who knew the beast if there was anything it was best not to feed him.

As for the incident in the woods, she should have run for her mare, mounted and ridden off the moment she'd spotted the man rather than waiting. Annabel was sure she would have managed it had she not stood there like a deer rooted to the spot when she'd first seen him.

These errors on top of her other failings made her feel completely useless. But Ross's kisses pushed that from her mind. She didn't feel like a failure with his arms around her and his tongue rasping against her own. She just felt hungry, and without knowing how she'd got there, Annabel was suddenly aware that her arms were around his shoulders and her legs wrapped around his hips so that she was plastered against him.

When Ross broke their kiss briefly to look around, she groaned and kissed, and then sucked at his neck, not stopping until he carried her to the window ledge and set her there. Annabel reached for his head then, drawing his mouth back to hers, moaning into his mouth when he tugged the neckline of her gown down, allowing her breasts to pop out into his hands.

"Oh husband," she gasped when his mouth left hers to suck at the side of her neck briefly as he squeezed and fondled her breasts. She clasped his head eagerly in her hands, fingers tugging at the strands of long hair, and then sucked eagerly at his tongue when he raised his head to kiss her again.

The pressure of his body against hers eased briefly as he kissed her and she felt one hand drop from her breast to slide up her leg, pushing her skirt ahead of it. Annabel squirmed under the touch, her mouth becoming more demanding. But she broke the kiss altogether and threw her head back on a gasping groan when his hand reached the apex of her thighs and set about caressing her there.

"Ross," she pleaded, her hips shifting into the touch as a fire burst to life there.

"How's yer head?" he growled.

"What?" she asked with incomprehension.

Ross chuckled and slid a finger into her and Annabel moaned and forgot about the question as he continued to caress her with his thumb while sliding his finger in and out of her. The sensation was amazing, but she wanted . . .

Reaching down, Annabel touched him tentatively through his plaid, surprised to find him hard and huge against her hand. It was the first time she'd touched him, and she was caught up in the moment until she realized Ross had gone suddenly still. Opening her eyes, she peered at his face uncertainly. His eyes were closed, his expression frozen in a rictus of what might have been pain.

"Should I not—?" Annabel began uncertainly.

"Aye, ye should," he assured her, opening his eyes. Then Ross kissed her again even as his free hand dropped to tug his plaid out of the way, leaving her free to touch him without the obstruction. Annabel hesitated, but then closed her fingers around the hard flesh, marveling at how silky it felt: hard but soft all at once.

"Damn," Ross muttered, breaking their kiss again.

Annabel glanced to him with concern when

he brushed her fingers away, afraid she'd done something wrong, but then he moved closer and glanced down to frown. She glanced down as well, just in time to see that the window ledge was too high for what he'd intended, and then he was scooping her up into his arms and carrying her toward the bed. They were halfway there when a knock sounded at the door.

"Go away Seonag," Ross called out, continuing forward.

" 'Tis no' Seonag, brother."

Ross cursed and paused with indecision.

"I cornered Seonag in the kitchens and she told me of Annabel's wardrobe problems," Giorsal said through the door. "I've come to help. That way you and Bean can discuss how best to keep her safe in future."

Ross bowed his head with a defeated sigh and set Annabel on her feet, muttering apologetically, "I know me sister. She'll no' go away."

Annabel merely nodded and quickly tucked her breasts back in the gown as far as they would go. When she finished and glanced up, he was peering with regret at the orbs swelling over the neckline.

"Are ye going to open the door or shall I just walk in?" Giorsal called out with exasperation.

"I'll get it," Ross said, catching her arm when Annabel started around him. He gave her a quick kiss on the forehead, then used his hold on her arm to urge her in the direction of the chair she'd been seated in when he entered, before heading for the door.

Annabel was seated in her chair, the mending

back in hand and held high to hide her neckline by the time Ross opened the door.

"Well, and sure ye took yer time letting me in," Giorsal said dryly to her brother as she breezed into the room.

"Count yerself lucky I opened it at all," Ross muttered with irritation, stepping out into the hall in her place.

"Ah, but then ye had no choice, did ye?" Giorsal asked with a grin. "Ye ken I'd just ha'e come in anyway."

"Aye, I ken," Ross said dryly, glanced past her to nod at Annabel. He then pulled the door closed, leaving them alone.

"Well," Giorsal said gaily, crossing the room to Annabel. "Let us see this wardrobe tragedy that has ye stuck up here."

Annabel hesitated, but then lowered the mending in her hand.

Giorsal's eyes widened and she nodded. "Aye. I can see the problem." She grinned suddenly and added, "Though I somehow do no' think the men would think it so much a tragedy as good fortune sent their way."

Annabel blushed at the words and felt her mouth crack into a smile.

"And it explains me brother's misshapened plaid when he opened the door," Giorsal teased as she dropped into the chair across from her. "I gather I interrupted his efforts to soothe ye? No doubt yer grateful I saved ye from the big brute."

Annabel's eyes widened at the suggestion and she said earnestly, "Nay, he is a kind and gentle husband. I—"

"Whist, Annie, I'm teasin' ye," Giorsal interrupted with amusement. "Ye ha'e to laugh at life's trials. It makes them lighter to carry."

"I suppose," Annabel said, relaxing, but then thought that might be true. Life's trials had weighed heavily at the abbey, where laughter had been frowned on. The abbess had seemed to disapprove of anything enjoyable, as if she thought that serving God meant you should be miserable. Annabel didn't think that was the case. Surely God had not made man to suffer and be miserable? Surely, he would want his children happy, just as mortal parents wanted happiness for their own offspring?

Well, most mortal parents, she corrected herself, thinking of her own. Her mother had seemed more concerned with avoiding scandal than Annabel's happiness. She had certainly been more resentful of what Kate's choice had meant to her and father than whether Kate was all right.

"So, what are we doing?" Giorsal said, interrupting her thoughts. "Are we making panels for the gown so it better covers yer breasts?"

"Aye," Annabel said dragging her thoughts back to the matter at hand. "The gown was too long, so Seonag and I cut the hem off. We are making panels with that and then must insert them and rehem the gown at the new length."

"Well, with the three of us working we can have it done in no time," Giorsal said brightly, picking up the other half of the removed hem that was to be used to make the second panel. "Which reminds me, Seonag was going to put together a tray with drinks and pastries for us and then she will join us." Pausing, she wrinkled her nose and admitted, "I do miss Cook's pastries. Honestly, much as I love me husband, does he no' find us a better cook, I think I may have to love him from here."

Annabel chuckled at the claim. She knew the woman didn't mean it, but assured her, "You are welcome here anytime."

"Thank ye. I like ye too," Giorsal said with a grin, and then admitted, "I was no' sure I would, yer being English and all. But I do. Me brother got lucky when our fathers contracted this marriage."

Annabel's smile faded a little at that, and she turned her head down to her work, muttering, "I fear he may not agree with that in time."

"Why?" Giorsal asked with surprise. "Yer pretty and smart and funny."

Annabel smiled wryly and, thinking of the incident where she'd run about blindly in the clearing with her gown tangled around her head, said, "Even when I do not mean to be."

Giorsal smiled faintly, but then said seriously, "Ye seem to lack a wee bit o' confidence though." She tilted her head. "Were yer parents no' encouraging when ye were growing up? Mine were, but I ken Bean's were no' and while he seems to have weathered it well, his little sister suffers some want in the area of confidence."

"Well, since my parents did not raise me after seven, I fear the lack must be my own," Annabel said wryly.

"What do ye mean?" Giorsal asked with surprise. "Who raised ye from seven on?"

Annabel stilled with alarm as she realized what she'd unthinkingly revealed.

"Annie?" Giorsal asked insistently. When Annabel continued to stare blindly at the cloth in her hand, she murmured thoughtfully, "Ross did no' mention yer parents no' raisin' ye. From what he said, they're still living. Though he did no' seem to like them. Did they neglect ye and leave it to the servants to raise ye?"

Annabel frowned at the suggestion and reluctantly raised her head. She didn't want to vilify her parents to save her secret, but . . .

"What is it?" Giorsal asked, noting her expression. "Ye can tell me. I promise I'll no' tell Ross if ye do no' want me to." When Annabel still hesitated, she added, "Ross said there were welts and scars on yer back from whippings. I ken they beat ye."

"Oh, nay," Annabel said with dismay. She had forgotten all about the marks on her back. She was used to the discomfort they caused and hadn't considered that he might have seen them and jumped to the conclusion that her parents had caused them.

"Nay, what?" Giorsal asked.

Annabel sighed and then said, "Those were not from my parents. They never beat or whipped me." She paused briefly, but didn't see any way around telling the truth. "Giorsal, I was sent to the abbey at seven as an oblate and lived there right up until the day I married Ross."

Giorsal stared at her blankly for a moment and then said slowly, "Is an oblate no' a girl meant to become a nun when she's considered old enough to take the vows?"

Annabel nodded and it seemed to confuse Giorsal.

"But how could yer parents send ye there to be a nun when ye were to marry me brother?"

Annabel grimaced. It seemed she had to tell the whole tale.

"So yer thinking to set a guard on her at all times until ye find out if it's your uncle or Fingal behind these attacks?" Bean asked. "Even in the keep?"

"Aye," Ross said firmly. "He may ha'e only attacked when she was outside the walls ere this, but I'll no' take chances with her safety. He might strike within the walls next when he realizes she will no' be out where he can get to her."

"Yer no' going to let her go beyond the bailey?" Bean asked with surprise.

"I'll no' be letting her leave the keep until we settle this thing," Ross announced.

"Hmmm," Bean said dubiously.

"Hmm what?" Ross asked with a frown.

Bean shook his head. "I'm thinking that'll no' go over well at all."

"Why?" he asked with surprise.

"Well, I do no' ken Annabel well, but I ken Giorsal would never put up with a guard on her at all times," Bean said dryly. "Hell, she would no' even put up with it for a day. As for restricting her to the keep . . . I can no' see her liking being a prisoner in her own home."

Ross relaxed and waved that away. "Annabel is no' Giorsal. 'Tis for her safety. She will be fine with it. 'Sides, she will be busy running the keep and my servants. There is no reason fer her to be out in the bailey."

"We will see," Bean said looking amused.

Ross felt doubt claim him briefly, but then scowled and pushed the doubt away. Annabel was a sensible woman, wasn't she? Surely she would see the sense of taking precautions.

"WHAT A HORRID OLD BITCH!"

Annabel gasped at that proclamation from Giorsal and lowered her sewing to glance worriedly to Seonag, only to see the maid nod solemnly.

"Aye. A nasty old bitch," she agreed, continuing to stitch the hem she was working on. "'Tis a wonder ye turned out so sweet tempered after being raised by a nasty old cow like that abbess."

Annabel sat back and peered from one woman to the other with wide eyes. This was not the response she'd expected when she'd confessed that her clumsiness and constant failures at the abbey were the reasons for her whippings. Or that it was also why she had still not been allowed to take the veil, so had been available to marry Ross when Kate had run off with her lover.

"Well, that settles it then," Giorsal said with satisfaction.

Annabel hesitated, but then asked uncertainly, "What does it settle? And what exactly is it that is settling it?"

"Ye were destined to marry Ross," Giorsal said as if that should be plain as day.

"I was?" Annabel asked dubiously, not sure how her being inept would lead to that conclusion.

"Aye. 'Tis why ye never fit in at the abbey," Giorsal explained. "'Twas so ye'd no' take the veil.

Ye were no' meant to be a nun, Annabel. Ye were meant to be Lady MacKay."

"Aye." Seonag nodded as if it were as obvious as could be to her as well.

Annabel simply stared at the two women for a moment, and then shook her head. "But do you not see? I was *not* to marry Ross. *Kate* was. She is the one who was truly contracted to marry him."

Giorsal snorted at that. "Nay, he was to marry you, no' Kate."

"But the contract—"

"Oh, devil take the contract," Giorsal waved it away as unimportant. "Ross is a good man, he deserves a good wife like you, not a light-skirt who runs off with the first cock that crows."

When Annabel made a strangled sound at this description, Giorsal slapped herself in the forehead, and then said quickly. "I'm sorry, I should no' call yer sister a light-skirt. I just mean that—"

"Nay, 'tis all right," Annabel waved away her apology. She understood how Giorsal felt. She loved her brother and wanted the best for him, and the best was not a woman who would ignore a binding contract, go against her parents and run off to live in sin with another man. Annabel also understood that she hadn't meant to offend her with the words. But what Giorsal didn't seem to understand was that she was not a much better prospect, though for different reasons.

Taking a breath, she considered her words and then admitted, "But do you not see? I am not much better. I was not trained to be a wife and lady of a large castle like MacKay while at the abbey. I illuminated texts and worked in the stables."

Giorsal waved that away as unimportant. "Ye can learn all ye need to ken easily enough. In fact, ye're partway there already."

"I do not see how," Annabel admitted, almost afraid to hope the woman was right.

"Well, if ye were illuminating texts at the abbey, ye ken how to read and write," Giorsal pointed out.

"Aye," Annabel acknowledged.

"Then ye can help school the pages," she pointed out.

"What pages?" Annabel asked with confusion.

"Well there are none at MacKay at the moment because there was no lady of the keep to train them. Now there is. You." She smiled brightly. "They need to be trained in music, dancing, riding, hunting, reading and writing and arithmetic. O' course, Ross will take care of the hunting, but ye can manage the rest."

"I fear I have never danced, and I am not trained with any musical instrument," Annabel admitted unhappily.

Giorsal shrugged. "Ye can hire a teacher for those and learn yerself. And ye should be a fair hand at the writing, reading and arithmetic."

"Aye," Annabel agreed, brightening. "And I am a fine rider too."

"Er . . ." Seonag said, and then paused abruptly.

"What?" Annabel asked.

The maid hesitated, but then set down her sewing with a sigh and admitted, "I overheard the men talking on yer riding skills, me lady, and they seemed to think they were no' so fine. They said ye bounced about on the mare's back like a sack o' turnips."

Annabel winced and then explained, "We were not supposed to ride the horses at the abbey. I used to volunteer to walk them out to the far pasture, and as soon as I was out of sight, would mount up and ride them bareback. Sometimes I would slip out at night to ride too, but I couldn't risk anyone hearing so took them bareback then as well. I have never ridden sidesaddle." She pursed her lips and then said, "Those are a horrid contraption."

"Aye," Giorsal agreed with distaste. "I prefer astride too, and bareback is even better."

Annabel grinned, both surprised and pleased to find they had this in common.

"She'll do fine with riding," Giorsal assured Seonag. "We must tell Ross to get rid o' the sidesaddle. He should not fuss too much about it," she added, and grinned at Annabel as she said, "Fortunately, he had me fer a sister and I broke him in on things like that fer ye."

"Aye, that's truth," Seonag announced.

Annabel chuckled along with Giorsal at the dry comment from the maid, but then Annabel's laughter faded. "Aye, but I am sure there is much more to being chatelaine than training pages and I know not what that is."

"The rest is easy enough too," Giorsal assured her. "Ye must oversee the servants; Cook and his staff, the housemaids, spinners, weavers, embroiderers and—" She paused suddenly and glanced to Seonag with a frown. "Speaking o' which, why are we doing this? The embroiderers would have made short work of it." Clucking, she added, "And the weavers would have produced new material for a new gown for Annie rather than her having to wear Mother's old clothes."

Annabel glanced to Seonag, interested in hearing the answer herself. She hadn't realized castles had spinners, weavers and embroiderers. They'd had women at the abbey set to each task, but she had left Waverly as a child and hadn't returned for long enough as an adult to know if they were in Waverly Castle. Certainly, she hadn't seen or heard of them here at MacKay.

"Derek's mother was the head spinner," Seonag said solemnly. "And her sisters and nieces made up the weavers and embroiderers."

"Oh, aye, I forgot," Giorsal said on a sigh, and then explained to Annabel. "Derek was our cousin. When Father died, he rose up and tried to wrest the title of clan chieftain from Ross. He even ambushed him and his men one night, intending to kill him and take the title, but instead, Ross killed him."

"And the women?" Annabel asked with a frown. "Surely Ross did not banish them for what your cousin did?" It would explain why there were no spinners, weavers or embroiderers here, but it also seemed unfair, and not something she hoped her husband would do. Much to her relief Giorsal shook her head vehemently.

"O' course not. Ross would ne'er blame anyone fer someone else's actions. He told them he held no ill will toward them because o' Derek's actions and that they were welcome to stay."

"But Derek's mother, Miriam, hated Ross fer killing her boy," Seonag put in. "She spat in his face, she did. Then she packed her goods and left. The rest followed."

"Ross could ha'e ordered them to stay, as clan chief, but he let them go," Giorsal added.

"Aye, and we've no' seen nor heard from them since."

"Hmmm," Annabel murmured, wondering where they'd gone.

"So, I suppose finding new spinners, weavers and embroiderers falls on yer shoulders now too," Giorsal said apologetically.

"Aye," Annabel muttered, wondering how the devil she was to do that. For that matter, how exactly was she to oversee the others? Did she hover over each servant ensuring they did it right? And if they were doing it wrong, what was she expected to do?

"Seonag and I'll help ye sort it all out," Giorsal said reassuringly. "I shall tell ye what I can now, and visit often to see how ye're getting along, and Seonag's been here a long time. She kens what's what. She can help a great deal when I'm no' here."

"Aye," Seonag agreed at once. "I'll help ye. It'll be fine."

"Thank you," Annabel said sincerely and smiled the first true and relaxed smile she'd enjoyed since reaching MacKay. She no longer felt alone in this. She had allies.

Chapter 10

"THE LAIRD SAID YE WERE TO STAY INDOORS, and indoors is where yer staying."

Annabel scowled at Gilly's stubbornness, but tried to remain patient as she reasoned, "But Jasper needs to get out and run off some of his energy else he shall get destructive out of sheer boredom, and I need to go to the village and speak to a woman who may be able to help us with sewing. Surely with the two of you accompanying me, 'twould be all right?"

"Jasper can go out if he likes, and Seonag can go talk to this woman in the village fer ye, but yer not," Gilly said firmly.

"Sorry." Marach shrugged when she turned to him for help. "The laird was very specific that ye were to stay in the keep."

Annabel wanted to stomp her feet and have a screaming fit. Instead, she turned on her heel and marched across the great hall to the stairs and up. Aware that the men were behind her, she picked up speed as she reached the top and nearly ran to the bedchamber door. She then rushed inside and slammed the door closed, narrowly missing hitting Jasper with it when he raced in on her heels.

"Sorry, Jasper," she murmured, sliding the bolt home to prevent the men from following. She'd barely done so when one of the men tried to open the door.

"Me lady?" Gilly called out. "Open the door. Ye ken we're supposed to stay with ye at all times while the laird is out."

"Nay. I do not know that," Annabel said sweetly. "My husband did not tell me so."

"Aye, but we did," Marach pointed out.

"Hmmm. Aye, you did. But how do I know 'tis true? After all, surely my husband would have mentioned something of such import to me himself?" she pointed out grimly. "Besides, I am sure if he did give such an order, he did not mean you were to enter our private chamber and watch me"—she paused briefly, searching for something he wouldn't want them to witness, and then said—"strip and bathe myself."

There was a brief silence and then Marach cleared his throat and pointed out. "Me lady, ye've no bath in there just now."

"Nay, you are right," Annabel agreed. "So mayhap you would be kind enough to go ask Seonag to have it brought up: the tub, water, soap, linens and so on."

If it would gain her some privacy, she would take a bath despite not really needing one yet. In fact, Annabel suspected if that was what it took to gain some time without tripping over the two men presently outside her door, she would be taking a lot of baths. After just one morning of this non-sense, they were already driving her wild.

Grimacing, she turned and paced to one of the windows to peer down at the busy bailey below. The visit with Ross's sister had gone very well indeed. Rather than go below and join the men once the first gown was done, the three of them had eaten their nooning meal in the bedchamber and mended a second gown as Giorsal and Seonag had given Annabel more advice and information on her duties as chatelaine. They had only gone below when Ross had come up to say that Bean was ready to leave.

Despite the hours together, Annabel had been sorry to see Giorsal go and had gone below to see her off. The two had hugged affectionately and Giorsal had promised to come back soon. Bean and Ross had watched this with raised eyebrows, but had not commented. It wasn't until they'd returned inside that Ross had said anything at all, and then it was a simple, "Ye seem to like me sister."

"Aye. She is lovely," Annabel had responded at once. "I like her a great deal."

Ross had grunted at that, scooped her up in his arms and carried her back up to their room to finish what his sister had interrupted earlier. By the time they'd gone back downstairs the great hall was filling with people claiming seats at the trestle table in preparation of dinner. Afterward, Annabel had sat by the fire with Seonag and continued sewing while Ross, Gilly and Marach had sat at the table discussing some business or other.

Annabel had sewn until Ross had appeared at

her side. He hadn't said a word, simply reached out to take her hand. She'd set her sewing aside and allowed him to walk her up to their room where he'd taken full advantage of it being Thursday. It wasn't until afterward that Annabel even thought to be grateful that he hadn't given her time to pack. She was glad not to have to wear the chemise carouse that had been left behind. She liked it when her husband touched her. On that thought, Annabel had drifted off to sleep with a smile on her face.

She wouldn't have been smiling had she realized what today would hold, Annabel thought grimly. Ross was gone when the watchman on the donjon had blown his bugle to wake the castle. She'd hurried to wash and dress and had stepped out into the hall to find Gilly and Marach waiting there. The two men had been leaning against the wall on either side of the door, but had straightened abruptly at her appearance.

Annabel had murmured a perplexed, "Good morn," and headed for the stairs, aware that they were following. The men had taken up a seat on either side of her as she'd broken her fast, and then had stood on either side of her as she'd attended mass in the chapel.

"Where is my husband?" she'd asked when mass ended without his making an appearance.

"He had some business in the village," Gilly had answered, following her along the hall toward the great hall. While the chapel at Waverly was across the bailey by the gatehouse, at MacKay it was in the keep itself, down a long hall off the great hall.

Annabel hadn't commented, but had allowed the men to escort her back to the great hall. She'd been relieved, however, when they'd both settled at the table and let her continue alone when she'd spotted Seonag and had commented that she would have a word with the woman.

Mostly, Annabel had wanted to ask Seonag what she should be doing that day. She had a general idea, but was feeling uncertain enough to want a suggestion. She'd been glad she had when Seonag had told her that she'd found out that there was a woman in the village said to be handy with a needle. So handy, in fact, that many of the men were going to her when they had items that needed mending. She'd wondered if the woman might be interested in a position at the keep as an embroiderer if the pay was sweet enough.

Excited by the prospect, Annabel had assured Seonag she would speak to the woman and had headed for the keep doors intending to travel down to the village at once. She was vaguely aware of Gilly and Marach standing to follow when she passed the trestle tables. However, she was still stunned when they'd suddenly hurried around to block her way as she reached the keep doors. And she'd been positively shocked when they'd told her that she wasn't allowed to leave the keep until her husband settled this business of the man who had attacked her.

Annabel now propped her elbows on the window ledge and rested her chin in her hands. This business with the attacker was a great nuisance. And restricting her to the keep just seemed silly to her. The man had only ever appeared outside of the castle walls. She was perfectly safe in the bailey. Of course, the village was not within the walls, but she was perfectly happy to allow Gilly and Marach to accompany her there, only they wouldn't allow her to go. How was she to do her job as chatelaine if they would not allow her to do what needed doing?

Sighing, she watched the stable master lift a hand and call out a greeting to someone she couldn't see. Curious, she leaned out to see who he was hailing. She had to lean out quite a ways to see the priest standing in a doorway further along the wall on the ground floor. It was the second door to the chapel, she supposed—one entrance to the keep for the lord and lady to use and one leading out into the bailey for those coming from outside.

Annabel stilled briefly, and then straightened and turned for the door.

Gilly was alone when she stepped into the hall, and Annabel raised an eyebrow as she pulled the door closed behind Jasper. "Where is Marach?"

"He went below to tell Seonag yer wanting a bath."

"Oh aye." She nodded. "I shall take it after confession."

"Confession?" Gilly barked with surprise, and then scrambled after her when she headed for the stairs.

"Aye. I have not confessed since leaving England, and have a confession or two to make," Annabel said mildly.

"Well, that's fine, but it'll ha'e to wait until Marach returns," Gilly said with a frown.

"I do not need Marach for confession," Annabel said with amusement. " 'Tis a priest I need."

"Aye, but—Oh there he is," Gilly said with relief and Annabel glanced ahead to see Marach stepping into the great hall from the kitchens.

She didn't comment and simply continued down the stairs as Marach rushed to meet them.

"I thought ye wanted a bath?" he asked with a frown.

"She's wanting confessing first," Gilly said for her.

"Now?" Marach asked with a frown. "But I've just told the maids to fetch ye a bath."

"Perfect," Annabel said lightly as she headed across the great hall. "First a clean soul and then a clean body. Will that not be nice?"

Marach muttered something under his breath about the vagaries of women, but fell into step beside Gilly at her heels and followed.

"Lady MacKay," the priest greeted her with obvious surprise when Annabel led the men into the chapel moments later. If he was surprised at her returning, she was a little surprised at being called Lady MacKay. It was a new title and he was the first to address her so, but she decided she liked it. "Good morn again, Father . . ." Annabel paused uncertainly, realizing with some shame that she did not even know the priest's name. She hadn't even managed to make it to mass until that morning. The abbess would have fits if she heard about that.

"Gibson," the priest said helpfully.

"Gibson." Annabel smiled widely at the man. "You are English?"

"Aye." He nodded. "Fortunately the MacKays do not hold that against me."

Annabel grinned at the light words, and then said, "I have come for confession."

"Of course," the man said, immediately becoming solemn and serious.

"Thank you," Annabel said and then turned to eye Marach and Gilly with arched eyebrows.

The men hesitated, glanced at each other and then backed away to give her some semblance of privacy, but Annabel simply scowled at them. They moved a couple more feet back, and then all the way to the door when she simply continued to glare at them.

"Can you hear me?" Annabel asked solemnly.

When both men nodded, Annabel turned to Father Gibson and said with regret, "I guess I shall have to bypass confession for now, Father. I apologize. But thank you for—"

"Oh, no, no, no," he interrupted and started toward the men, waving them away. "Come now. Off with you. Lady MacKay deserves some privacy for her confession. You shall have to wait outside."

"But we're no' to leave her alone, Father," Marach protested, even as he backed to the door. "She was attacked yesterday in the woods and we're to—"

"Well, no one is going to attack her here. She is perfectly safe in the chapel. You can wait outside until she comes out," Father Gibson insisted.

"But—" Gilly tried.

"Out," the priest repeated, and the two men backed reluctantly out into the hall.

"We'll be right outside this door," Gilly said.

"Yes, yes," Father Gibson said impatiently and then closed the door in his face. Turning, he smiled at her with satisfaction and walked back, saying, "There. We are all set now. Would you like to—"

"I am sorry, Father, but I really do not have a confession," Annabel interrupted quietly, taking his arm to urge him as far away from the door as she could. Pausing then, she frowned and said, "Although I suppose I should confess that I lied about confessing."

"What?" Father Gibson said with bewilderment.

Annabel patted his arm and explained, "You see, I am chatelaine now."

"Aye, of course you are, my lady," he agreed.

"And part of my responsibilities is to oversee the spinner, weaver and embroiderer here. Only there are none."

"Aye, I know," Father Gibson said sadly, peering down at his somewhat frayed vestments. "'Twas a sad day indeed when we lost Miriam and her brood."

Annabel nodded solemnly, but inside she was smiling. The man had just told her how to get him to agree with her plan. "Well, the good news is that I hope to replace them all, and the better news is that I understand there is a woman in the village who is excellent with a needle."

"Is there?" he asked with interest.

"Aye, and I was hoping to slip down to the village and have a word with her, to convince her to come work in the castle. It would be the first step in setting things to right in the matter of clothing here. The first step toward being able to have you made some fine new vestments."

"Oh, that would be lovely. It has been such a trial this last year."

"Aye," Annabel agreed, and then heaved out a little sigh and said, "Sadly, my husband has told Gilly and Marach not to let me out of the keep because of a couple trifling little incidents the past two days."

"Oh yes, I did hear about the attacks, my lady." Father Gibson patted her arm and shook his head. "I was not prying, of course, but did wonder why you had not yet attended mass since arriving and so I asked around and was most distressed to hear about the attacks on your person."

"Aye, it was most unfortunate that I was forced to miss mass," Annabel murmured, thankful that whoever had told him the tales had somehow made it sound as if she'd missed mass both days because of the attacks when the truth was she'd slept through the first and had been cleaning up dog dung during the second. Neither was a very good excuse to miss mass and she should be ashamed of herself, especially when she'd spent the better part of her life in an abbey where they held seven services a day starting at two o'clock in the morning. Honestly, it had been hard to get anything done when they were constantly forced to stop for this service or that one. Annabel had always been glad to help out in the stables because of that. You simply couldn't leave an ailing animal to attend service and she'd missed several over the years thanks to that excuse.

"Just as distressing is the fact that those attacks have now made my husband overly cautious to the point that it is interfering with my ability to go to the village and convince this woman to come work for us," Annabel said sadly.

"Oh, aye, that is distressing," Father Gibson said unhappily. "Very unfortunate indeed."

"Aye." Annabel nodded. "Then you will help me?"

Father Gibson blinked with confusion, and then frowned. "Help you with what exactly, my lady?"

"Well, nothing really," she said with a smile. "You need only stand here and say nothing while I slip away to the stables, fetch my mare and ride out to the village."

"Oh," he said, still frowning, and then his expression filled with realization. "Oh! You mean to let the men think you are in here confessing and—Oh nay, I could not possibly."

"Oh, but Father, they would never know," Annabel assured him.

"What if something befell you? What if you were attacked again? Nay, I could not possibly be a party to putting you in harm's way." He shook his head firmly.

"I would ride quickly, and Jasper will accompany me," Annabel argued, the words drawing the priest's attention to the dog at her feet.

He scowled as if just having noticed the animal was in his chapel, and then turned his attention to her and said firmly, "My lady, you presently have two very unattractive bruises on your face from your previous encounters with your attacker. I will not risk being responsible for a third. The next one might kill you."

Annabel tapped one foot with exasperation as she thought, and then peered at him consideringly. "What if you only waited until I fetched my mare and started out of the stables with her, and then went to tell Gilly and Marach?" When he started to shake his head, she rushed on, "They would hurry after me and I would be sure to allow them to catch up enough that I was in their line of sight all the way to the village. That way I could speak with the woman and be safe at the same time."

Father Gibson frowned, but at least he was no longer shaking his head.

"Your fine, new, *rich* vestments would be the first thing I ordered done," she wheedled. "Even before I had gowns made for myself and surely you have heard I arrived without anything but the gown on my back."

"Aye. Ross confessed that he was so eager to get you away from your horrid parents that he did not even allow you time to pack your things," Father Gibson murmured.

"Did he?" Annabel asked. She hadn't realized that was the reason he'd rushed her away from Waverly. Giorsal had said Ross had seen her welts and thought her parents beat her. Apparently, that was why he'd rushed her off so abruptly. The man was just such a surprise at times. Truly, he showed her more care and concern than anyone previously in her life. She was so lucky to—

"Very well," Father Gibson said suddenly. "I shall watch you to the stables. But the moment you come out with your horse I am fetching Gilly and

Marach and telling them you slipped out while my back was turned and when I looked about for you, I spotted you on horseback in the bailey."

"Thank you," Annabel said, squeezing his hands.

Father Gibson grunted unhappily, and frowned as he walked her to the chapel door leading into the bailey. He caught her arm there and muttered, "Just promise me you shall wait for the men before riding far."

"I promise," she assured him.

"And keep them within sight all the way there," he added.

"Aye." She squeezed his hands again. " 'Twill be all right. I promise."

"I will pray for you," Father Gibson announced.

Recognizing the doubt entering his expression, Annabel simply nodded and slipped out of the chapel, afraid if she waited any longer or said anything else, he would change his mind. She crossed to the stables at a dead run. She was a bit surprised that she made it without being stopped or hearing shouts or the sound of running feet behind her. Even so, she didn't slow but ran straight to the stall holding her mare before even glancing around to see who was about. She was a bit shocked not to have the stable master rushing her way to try to thwart her plan, but the man was nowhere in evidence. In fact, no one was. The stables were empty.

Glad for this good luck, Annabel quickly opened the stall and led her mare out. She glanced around then, relieved when she spotted a stool near the back of the stables. Leading her horse to it, Annabel used it to mount her mare, then clucked her tongue against her cheek and urged the animal to move.

Annabel glanced toward the chapel door as she rode out of the stables. She was just in time to see Father Gibson whirl away and hurry out of sight. Off to warn Marach and Gilly, she knew, and turned her mare toward the barbican and drawbridge, urging her to a run.

The moment she was across the drawbridge, Annabel brought her mare down to a trot, though, and spent as much time looking behind her as ahead. She would move slowly until she spotted the men coming after her, partially because she'd promised Father Gibson she would and preferred not to break a promise. The other reason, however, was that the man had scared her with his worries for her well-being. He was right. She had been lucky so far . . . and she might not be so lucky the next time. Annabel had no desire to sustain another injury or die just to gain an embroiderer.

"I TOLD YE, LAD, I'VE NO INTEREST IN BEING CLAN chief," Fingal said firmly for the fourth time. "I'm an old man. I'm content with me life as it is now without the stress and troubles of being clan chief."

"Yer age did no' seem to bother ye when ye tried to make a claim fer the title four years ago," Ross reminded him quietly.

"Aye, well four years is a long time at me age," Fingal said dryly. "The clan needs a strong young warrior to lead it, and I'm no' young anymore.

Hell, I wasn't young even four years ago, but every year that passes, me sight wanes a little more and I've more aches and pains to complain about." He shook his head with disgust and then added, " 'Sides, like I told ye after ye killed Derek, I only stepped forward because the whelp was trying to claim ye were too young fer the position." Disgust covered his features. "As if his being four years older made much difference. He may ha'e been four years older in age, but he was still a lad in every other way. Worse yet, he was a coward, ambushin' ye like he did and then sitting back waiting on his supporters to kill ye." He spat on the ground to show his distaste with the tactics, and then continued, "Nay, Ainsley, Eoghann and I had no real interest in the title. We just drank too much one night and decided to muddy the waters by making a claim to it. We were every one o' us happy to step down when ye settled the matter with Derek."

Ross sighed. He believed the blacksmith, but wished he didn't. It would have made things much easier if he were the man behind the attacks on Annabel. He could have resolved the matter right now. However, it looked like he still had work to do.

"Go talk to yer Uncle Eoghann," Fingal suggested. "He'll tell ye the same thing I just did. Too much drink and affront at the whelp's arrogance were the only reasons we stepped up."

Ross nodded and turned to leave the man's hut, but paused abruptly in the doorway when a horse and rider charged past.

"Annabel?" he muttered, staring with amazement and then glancing to the dog that now streaked past after her. Jasper.

"Yer wife, Annabel?" Fingal asked stepping up beside him. Staring after the woman and the horse he commented, "She's a fine rider."

"Nay, she's not," Ross said with a frown. "At least I didn't think she was."

"Well, ye thought wrong, lad," Fingal said with amusement as they watched her jump the mare over a tree stump and bring the beast to a shuddering halt in front of a hut. The stop was so abrupt, the mare reared to achieve it, but Annabel stayed in the saddle. Or not a saddle, Ross realized; she kept her seat on the bare back of the beast.

"Looks like she's going to see Effie," Fingal commented as they watched Annabel slide from the mare's back and hurry to the door of the hut with Jasper on her heels.

Ross grunted and then turned his head to the left as the sound of pounding hooves drew his gaze to Gilly and Marach charging through the village now in hot pursuit. Scowling, he stepped out into the lane and lifted his hand. The two men immediately slowed and had to rein in nearly as sharply as Annabel to avoid running him down. He couldn't help noticing they did it with a little less finesse than his wife, nearly colliding with each other when their horses reared in protest.

"She tricked us," Gilly blurted before he could say anything. The man sounded highly offended. "She said she wanted to confess and then slipped out o' the chapel and snuck off."

"How did she sneak off when ye were no' to leave her side?" Ross asked silkily.

"Well, the priest made us leave the chapel for her confession, didn't he?" Gilly said helplessly. "Made us wait outside the door in the hall, and then she slipped out the door to the bailey."

Ross arched an eyebrow and then turned to Marach to see what he had to say for himself.

The man grimaced and shrugged, his voice admiring when he said, "She's damned clever."

"Aye, she is," Gilly agreed with some admiration of his own. "And she rides a hell of a lot better than we thought too."

Marach nodded. "I do no' think e'en you could ha'e got more speed out o' her horse than she did on the way here, m'laird. And brave?" He shook his head. "She set the mare to jumping over things e'en I would no' have dared to jump did we no' have to do it just to keep her in sight." His gaze slid to the mare now nibbling grass in front of the hut and he shook his head again. "Looks like she's getting to speak to the sewing woman after all."

"The sewing woman?" Ross asked from between gritted teeth. His anger had built with every word out of Gilly and Marach's mouths. He didn't know what angered him more, the fact that his men had failed so spectacularly at keeping Annabel in the keep, the risks she'd taken to get here, or his men's admiration of her for accomplishing it. He wanted to throttle all three of them just then.

"Effie's a damned fine hand with the sewing needle," Fingal murmured helpfully behind him.

"Aye, a sewing woman, that's what she said," Gilly told him, not having heard Fingal, his voice had been so low. "M'lady said as how she wanted to talk to a woman in the village about working at the castle sewing or some such thing," Gilly explained and then added quickly, "We told her right then as to how ye said she wasn't to leave the keep . . . and we were firm on the matter. Weren't we?" he asked, glancing to Marach.

"Firm," Marach agreed, nodding solemnly and then frowned and added. "Then she hurried up to yer bedchamber and locked us out. We told her we were to stay with her at all times, but she said as how she was sure that didn't include while she was bathing."

"Nay, it doesn't," Ross said succinctly.

"I suspected as much," Marach said and Ross was sure he didn't imagine the hint of disappointment in the man's voice at this news. Nor did he imagine the disappointment that flashed across Gilly's face. It seemed his men had gone from moaning over the fact that he was marrying an Englishwoman to admiring her and hoping to get a peek at her in the bath. He didn't really blame them—Annabel was beautiful, but he'd be damned if they were going to see just how beautiful.

"Go back to the castle," Ross said grimly.

The men exchanged a glance and then Gilly asked, "Are ye sure ye don't want us to wait for yer lady wife? We could see her back and—"

"Home!" Ross snapped.

"Aye, m'laird," they murmured together and turned their horses back the way they'd come.

Ross scowled after them until he became aware of Fingal chuckling behind him. Turning, he glowered at the man. "What is so funny?"

"Nothing," Fingal said, shaking his head, but then blurted, "It seems to me I remember a situation not dissimilar to this involving yer sister some time back . . . or mayhap it was yer mother," he added thoughtfully, and then shrugged. "Anyway, one o' them was no' supposed to leave the keep for some reason or other, yet came racing down into the village with MacKay men hot on her trail." He pursed his lips and then commented, "That was a sight to see too."

"Dear God, I've married a lass just like me sister," Ross muttered, closing his eyes at the horror of it all.

"Or yer mother," Fingal offered helpfully and then burst out in a full belly laugh. Ross did not laugh with him.

Chapter 11

"WELL, THAT IS FINE," ANNABEL SAID, beaming with relief at Effie. She could hardly believe it had been so easy. After all the trouble she'd had of late, she'd expected to have to plead and offer the woman the moon and stars to get her to agree to work in the castle. But in the end, Effie had been happy to accept the offer.

"I can start tomorrow, if ye like," Effie said, beaming as well.

"Oh, that would be marvelous," Annabel assured her, getting to her feet and patting her leg for Jasper to follow.

"I'll come up first thing then," Effie announced, sounding happy at the prospect.

"Come in time to break your fast and I shall have Cook save some pastries for you," Annabel said as they walked to the door.

"Oh, that would be lovely," Effie breathed, and then admitted, "While I'm a fair hand with a needle, I can't cook to save me soul. 'Twill be nice to have something other than burnt bread to break me fast with."

"Then I shall have Cook put aside pastries for you every day," Annabel decided. A servant always worked better when they weren't hungry. At least she always had.

"Oh my, yer a wonder," Effie said happily as she opened the door for her. "I hope the laird kens the blessing he has in you."

"The laird kens exactly what he has in his wife."

Annabel's smile froze at that deep voice, and her head swiveled abruptly to take in the man on the doorstep. Eyes widening, she breathed with dismay, "Husband."

"Wife," he said dryly. Ross then turned to Effie and smiled as he caught Annabel by the arm and drew her out of the hut. "I gather by the fact that yer both smiling that ye've agreed to work in the castle, Effie. Thank ye, kindly fer that. Yer well needed."

"Oh, yer welcome, me laird," Effie gushed, a blush brightening her old cheeks. " 'Tis me pleasure."

Ross nodded. "We'll see ye on the morrow then."

"Aye," Effie breathed as he turned Annabel away to lead her to her horse.

Annabel bit her lip and glanced sideways and up at her husband. His face was expressionless now that they'd left Effie, but she was pretty sure he was angry. She just wasn't sure how angry . . . or how he meant to handle it, and that worried her. After all, it was perfectly legal for a husband to beat his wife so long as the rod he used was no bigger around than his thumb.

Annabel glanced down at his hands as he grasped her at the waist and lifted her up onto her mare. She then grimaced. Ross had big thumbs.

"Wife."

Annabel gave a start and shifted her gaze to his face. "Aye?" she asked warily.

"Take the reins," he said quietly.

"Oh, aye," she muttered and reached for them as he released her and moved to his own horse now waiting a few feet away.

They traveled in silence at first, which really wasn't a good thing, Annabel decided. It gave her far too much time to imagine how he would punish her for this flouting of his orders.

By the time they reached the edge of the village Annabel had managed to scare herself silly with the possibilities. It was then she started trying to think of ways to deflect his anger when he let it loose. The only thing she could think might distract him from it was the bedding. But it was Friday now, and the church had decreed no bedding on Fridays, so if he waited until they reached the castle to vent his anger, she would be without what she was sure was likely to be the most successful defense. She needed to bring something about before they reached the keep, Annabel realized and immediately began working on the stays of her gown. She had them undone and was tugging her neckline down to free her breasts when Ross glanced over and drew his mount to an abrupt halt. He then simply stared at her breasts for the longest time before asking with bewilderment, "What the devil are ye doing?"

"I am not sure," Annabel admitted, blushing

furiously. She was so overset, she then blurted, "I just thought—I mean, I understand you are angry at me, and I thought mayhap I could soothe your temper somehow so you would not beat me, and—"

"I shall never beat ye," Ross interrupted solemnly. "No matter what you do, Annabel, I shall never strike you."

"Oh," she breathed with relief.

"Howbeit, I would appreciate it, did ye take yer vows more seriously," he added grimly.

Annabel tilted her head uncertainly. "My vows?"

"Ye did promise to obey me during our wedding," he pointed out dryly.

"Did I?" she asked with surprise. The wedding had all been something of a blur for her. Annabel had been rather distressed at the change in her future at the time.

Noting the way his mouth tightened at her words, she said quickly, "Aye, I must have." But she couldn't help adding, "But to be fair I did not disobey you. You are not the one who told me I could not leave the keep."

"Gilly and Marach told ye me orders," Ross said.

"Aye, but not you, so I disobeyed them," she reasoned and then added a bit testily, "If *you* had told me I could then have explained why I found the order unacceptable and you could have explained your position on it and we could have come to an agreement."

Ross scowled at her briefly, then sighed and reached out to draw her from her horse to his. Once he had her settled before him, he then caught her mare's reins in his hand and urged his mount to move again.

Annabel immediately reached for her stays, intending to do up her gown again, but Ross whispered, "Don't," by her ear.

After the briefest hesitation, she obeyed, left the gown gaping open and let her hands drop to her lap.

Ross murmured something that might have been praise then. Annabel wasn't completely sure, she was a little distracted by his free hand suddenly rising to cup one of her breasts.

"So ye were going to make a grand sacrifice and bed me to soothe me temper?" he murmured, sounding amused.

"A—aye," Annabel admitted breathily as he plucked at her nipple, and then confessed, "But 'twould not have been a sacrifice. I like it when you bed me."

Ross rewarded her honesty by reining in and releasing her breast to urge her face up and around for a kiss.

Annabel relaxed in his arms and opened to him with relief, sure he was no longer angry with her. Much to her surprise, she hadn't liked it when he was angry with her. She liked his kisses though and moaned as his tongue urged her lips apart to gain entrance.

Ross ended the kiss far too soon for Annabel and she blinked her eyes open with disappointment when he did. She peered around with surprise when he suddenly turned them back the way they'd come. "Where are we going?"

"Back through the village," he answered, and

then gave her breasts another caress each before saying, "Do up yer gown."

Annabel did up her stays and then simply peered ahead, wondering back through the village to where. She didn't ask again, though. He obviously wanted to surprise her or he would have answered fully the first time.

They did head back toward the village, but not before weaving around a bit in what she began to realize were large circles. It took Annabel several such detours before she realized that Ross was making sure they weren't being followed. Just as she did, he stopped his evasive tactics and steered the horses through the village.

"We have lost Jasper," Annabel said with concern as she saw him charge off after a cat that had been sunning itself in front of the cottage next to Effie's.

"He'll catch up," Ross said with a shrug. "And if he doesn't he'll show up back at the castle once the cat either evades him or gives him a good swat."

Annabel frowned, but then noted they were leaving the village. They did not seem to travel long after that ere Ross was reining in by a good-sized cottage and barn.

"Are we visiting someone?" Annabel asked uncertainly as she peered at the shuttered windows on the cottage.

"Nay. This is Carney's cottage and he's no' home. I sent him on a task the day we got home," he assured her, dismounting.

"Oh." Her gaze slid to the barn again and she said, "This Carney must be very wealthy to have such a big barn."

"It's no' really his," Ross said, glancing toward the structure as he moved up beside her mare. "It's only called Carney's barn because his home is so close, but everyone helped build it and everyone stores their goods here."

"Oh," Annabel said, and then as he reached up to lift her off her mare, she asked, "Why are we here?"

"Because I happen to ken that Carney's barn has a nice big stack o' hay in it at the moment."

Annabel stared at him blankly as he set her down. "Hay?" she asked as she watched him tie their mounts to a pole. She didn't understand the relevance.

" 'Tis Friday so we can no' go back to the keep," he pointed out, finishing his task. Scooping her into his arms, he then strode toward the barn as he added, "I'll no' risk ye out in the open again, but in a nice cozy barn with a stack o' hay . . ."

"Oh," Annabel said with understanding and smiled. "Hay is a lovely not-bed."

"Exactly," Ross said with a grin.

She fell silent as they entered the barn. It was a large structure, with stone walls and a slate roof that left the interior dark and a bit chilly. Peering over his shoulder, she saw through the dim light that there were several different crops in the building; wheat, oats, peas, beans and barley to name a few.

She didn't see the hay until her husband suddenly opened his arms and let her drop. Annabel released a surprised squawk that turned into an "oomph" as she landed. She sank down into it a bit and had to climb back out.

Ross chuckled, unbuckling and setting aside
his sword as he watched her struggle to her knees
in the pile. Annabel had just managed the feat
when he then tugged at his plaid and sent it float-
ing to the floor around his feet. Smiling at her expression and the way she stopped to stare, he then
quickly pulled his shirt off over his head to stand
naked before her in naught but his boots. And he
was a sight to see. She would never have thought
a man could be described as beautiful, and she
would not have said that about Ross's face, which
was handsome, strong, rugged and manly. But
while his body was strong and manly too, it was
also breathtakingly beautiful to behold.

Ross let her look her fill for a moment in the
dim light, and then held out a hand. "Come. If
ye'll stop playing in the hay, I'll lay me plaid out
on it to make it a more comfortable not-bed."

Since she was presently being poked in several places by the hay, Annabel took his hand and
crawled forward on her knees. But stopped when
she found her face a mere inch from his manhood.
It had been stirring as she'd stared at him, but
now with her face so close that her breath was no
doubt rippling across it, his manhood hardened
and rose to its full glorious state.

For some reason that recalled her to their first
time in the woods when he had pleasured her
with his mouth, and Annabel suddenly leaned
forward to lick it, giving it one long swipe as if
it were her thumb and the fruit center of a pastry
had squirted out over it. The action brought a
hissing sound from Ross and she peered up to see
that his head had gone back, his teeth clenched

as if in pain. A glance down showed his hands clenched as well.

Recognizing the pose from when she'd touched him for the first time, Annabel suspected he liked that and did it again, this time ending by closing her mouth over the tip and sucking as she drew her mouth away, as she would if she were trying to get absolutely every last drop of fruit center from her thumb.

"Wife," he growled and suddenly plucked her up under the arms to lift her to her feet. Meeting her gaze then, he warned, "Yer playing with fire."

"Mayhap I like fire," she said with a smile and then added more seriously, "Certainly I like the way ye make me burn."

Eyes widening, Ross tugged her up against his chest and kissed her. Annabel immediately slipped her arms around his shoulders and kissed him eagerly back. Feeling his hardness pressing against her stomach through her skirts, she then shifted her lower body from one side to the other, using her body to caress that hardness.

His response to that was to use both hands to quickly drag her skirts up the back of her legs until he could clasp her bare bottom. Cupping her cheeks, he then lifted and pressed her more intimately against himself. Annabel moaned but more with frustration than anything: her gown was still between them. She was no more pleased, however, when he broke their kiss and set her back on her feet.

"I must make our not-bed," he reminded her, stepping away and bending to collect his plaid from the ground. Annabel grimaced when she saw the bits of hay clinging to the material. As he shook it out, she glanced around in search of somewhere to place her gown that would not result in it ending up the same way as his plaid. Spotting two posts with a rail between them, she moved over to it and quickly undid her lacings and lifted the gown off over her head rather than drag it across the ground. She was laying it over the post when she felt hands at her waist. Annabel jumped in surprise and glanced over her shoulder, smiling wryly at her husband.

"You startled me," she admitted with a crooked smile as he pulled her back against his chest. She peered down at his hands as they slid up to cup her breasts, fascinated by the sight of his tanned hands enclosing her creamy skin. When he caught each nipple between thumb and finger and rolled, then pinched them lightly, Annabel moaned. Her back arched, pushing her breasts into the caress, and her neck stretched as she twisted her head sideways against his chest.

When Ross bent to kiss her forehead, Annabel tipped her head back to offer him her lips. He accepted the invitation, claiming her mouth in a kiss that was almost violent. Annabel responded in kind, nipping at his lips with her teeth before he thrust his tongue into her mouth. She was aware when one of his hands slid from a breast to drop down, gliding over her stomach as it sought out places further south. Moaning, she pressed her bottom back into him and then shifted her stance a bit to allow him better access as his lovely fingers slid between her legs.

"Husband," she gasped, breaking their kiss and

clutching at his upper arms as his caresses made her legs go weak. He gave up caressing her other breast then, and wrapped that arm under her breasts to help hold her up as he drove her crazy. Annabel's world tilted, all sensation narrowing to that point between her legs that his fingers were dancing over and she unthinkingly turned her head and bit into his arm to ground herself, easing her jaw when he grunted. She had just enough sense left in her poor passion-muddled head to feel guilty for unintentionally hurting him, and reached back with her hand, seeking to make up for it by distracting him.

Annabel found his manhood and closed her fingers eagerly around it to slide gently up and down. She stopped that though and squeezed when he suddenly thrust a finger into her. They both groaned then and Annabel felt his shaft jump in her hand.

In the next moment, Ross bent her forward. Annabel grabbed at the post in front of her with her free hand and gasped in surprise when he pulled his manhood free of her other hand and thrust it into her from behind. She was a good deal shorter than him, and his legs were on either side of hers, bent to lower him enough to do that. Annabel had the momentary thought that the position could not be comfortable for him, but then he withdrew and thrust back into her even as the hand still between her legs began caressing her again and she forgot the worry. Still, she wasn't surprised when he suddenly stopped, withdrew, and scooped her up to carry her to his plaid in the hay.

He dropped to his knees with her once there,

then laid her on his plaid and shifted over her. Annabel reached for him, but he caught her hands at once and pressed them down on either side of her head, holding them there as he bent to nip at her lips and then claim them. Annabel moaned into his mouth as she felt his manhood slide across her slick skin, she then spread her legs and arched and shifted in an effort to help him enter her. But it seems he didn't want to enter her yet for he was enjoying tormenting her by rubbing his hardness against her again and again without actually joining with her.

Annabel suffered it for a time, enjoying the excitement he was continuing to build in her, but then frustration rose up. She wanted him inside of her, she wanted . . .

Twisting her mouth away from his, she gasped, "Dammit husband. Please!"

For some reason that made Ross chuckle, and then he released her wrists and rose up on his knees between her spread legs. Grasping her hips, he raised her bottom off the hay and thrust into her.

"Oh God, yes," Annabel groaned with relief. He then simply held her there, joined with him with one hand at her hip while his other moved between them to caress the bud weeping for him. Annabel groaned again, her heels digging into the hay so that she could shift herself against his hard, still shaft, dancing to the tune his lovely fingers played on her flesh.

Panting with excitement and exertion, Annabel opened her eyes and found that he was watching her. Suddenly self-conscious, she stopped.

Ross removed himself and lowered her to the hay, then turned her onto her stomach and pressed down on her to kiss the side of her neck before murmuring, "Ye shouldn't ha'e stopped. I liked watchin' ye take yer pleasure on me."

Annabel's eyes widened as she realized that was exactly what she'd been doing, and then she gasped as he suddenly rose up off her, lifting her to her knees with him so that he could plunge into her from behind again. Using her hands to brace herself the best she could in the hay, she gasped and moaned as he drove into her over and over again. But Annabel wasn't sure she liked this position as much since she couldn't kiss or touch him like this, and then she stiffened and gasped out a breath when he reached around to touch her again.

In the next moment, they were both crying out in pleasure and collapsing onto the plaid-covered hay. Ross was still on top of her at first, but quickly shifted off and onto his side next to her. He then turned her onto her side as well and wrapped his arm around her waist, cuddling her so that her back was pressed tight to his chest.

She heard Ross's breathing slow and even out and knew he'd fallen asleep. Content where she was, Annabel dozed off as well, but didn't think she'd managed to fall into a proper sleep before a sound stirred her. Opening her eyes, she peered drowsily at the swath of sunlight stretching across the floor from the open barn door behind them. It was long and wide and had a shape in it, Annabel noted, frowning as she tried to sort out what the shadow in the middle of the sunlight was and why it was growing smaller. The answer came when the shape shifted and shrank toward the ground, almost disappearing into the shadow cast by her and Ross's bodies. It all clicked then. The shadow in the light had been a figure approaching, and he was now kneeling behind them.

Annabel lay completely still, ears straining and eyes locked on the swath of light, and then she saw an oddly shaped, thinner shadow rise out of the darkness cast by their bodies. Even as she realized it was an arm with some sort of club in hand, she shrieked and sat up. The thud came as she did and she whirled on the plaid as the man from the previous attacks glanced up from clubbing her husband over the head.

Annabel's eyes shot to Ross. She couldn't see blood yet, but he was unmoving. Rage merging with her terror, she shrieked furiously and glanced wildly around for a weapon. What she spotted was Ross's sword at the edge of the hay on her side. Scrambling to it, she grabbed up the heavy metal and pushed herself to her feet in one stumbling move, then whirled holding the sword out before her, arms shaking with the effort.

"Now, lass, ye don't want to be doing that," he said in a low rumble, casting Ross a wary glance as he straightened to stand behind his prone form.

"I did not wish to stab you in the bluebells, but I did," she pointed out, and then added coldly, "Now you have harmed my husband and I *do* want to hurt you."

"Now, now," he cooed, easing sideways until he could step around Ross's body to move toward her. "I only knocked him out. He'll be fine. Lower yer weapon before ye hurt yerself."

"Go to hell," Annabel growled and swung at him. She didn't know which amazed her more, that she'd cursed him to hell, which was really quite fitting and somewhere she had been warned repeatedly that she would go, or that she actually winged the man, catching the same arm she'd stabbed during their last encounter. She'd caught his lower arm previously, but this time she creased his upper arm with the blade, cutting a nice straight line across it before her momentum and the weight of the sword spun her around so she couldn't see him anymore.

Cursing, she started to turn to face him again, and then stumbled forward as she took a blow to the back of the head. Lights flashed briefly behind her eyes, but she remained conscious, on her feet, and even managed to shift the sword out of the way in time to avoid slicing off her own leg.

A hand closed around hers on the sword before she had quite recovered. Annabel struggled briefly to keep her hold on it, but he was crushing her fingers into the metal and she finally let it go with a cry of pain and stumbled away toward the corner of the barn and the shadows offered there.

"There's no sense in trying to run," her attacker said behind her. "We've got yer horses. We'd just ride ye down."

Annabel didn't respond, she simply continued into the shadows, hands outstretched to avoid running into anything as it got darker and darker around her.

"And ye can't hide either. I ken yer here, I'll just find ye," he pointed out.

Her hand bumped against and then closed over

a piece of wood when it started to slide along what she thought must be a wall. At first she snatched at the wood to prevent it crashing to the ground and giving away her location, but as she felt the wide plank and judged the length and strength of it, she picked it up to use as a weapon.

"If ye make things too difficult we might harm yer husband," the man warned now. "And ye wouldn't want that, would ye?"

Annabel didn't think, she simply raised the wooden plank over her head and charged at him, shrieking like a banshee. She must have been something to see—a naked woman, hair wild around her head and mouth open on a mad scream as she raced out of the darkness at him. The man didn't even think to raise the sword until the last moment; he simply stood there gaping until she was almost upon him. Only as she started to swing the plank did he lift his weapon, but before he raised it halfway, she was slamming the wood into his head with all the strength she had.

His head swung on his neck, the skin on his face vibrating with the impact, and then his body seemed to follow his head's turning and he stumbled around and away from her. Annabel waited for him to fall, but he didn't, he took several stumbling steps to the open door of the barn and then sagged against the wooden frame briefly. Mouth tightening, Annabel started forward, prepared to give him another whack, but she'd only taken a couple of steps when he slid off the frame and fell forward, collapsing on his face in the dirt.

She hesitated, still considering another whack, but then glanced to Ross and hurried to his side instead.

"Husband?" Annabel said worriedly, looking him over with concern as she knelt at his side. She carefully felt his head until she found a bump and felt damp blood on her fingertips. His eyes didn't flicker at her touch, not even when she slapped him lightly, "Husband, please wake up."

She tried to rouse him for several minutes, and then glanced toward their attacker, stiffening when she didn't see him lying where she'd left him. Her heart stilled briefly, and then she tightened her grip on the plank, and forced herself to her feet. Annabel took a step, but on the second one stubbed her toe on something. She glanced down blankly at Ross's sword, realizing only then that the man had dropped it. After a hesitation, she bent to pick it up. It was heavy and awkward for her as a weapon, but she didn't want to risk leaving it there for someone else to use, so she held the plank in one hand and dragged the sword with her as well as she moved cautiously to the door to peer out.

Annabel had expected to see the man either stumbling or dragging himself away from the barn, but he was nowhere to be seen and she suddenly recalled the man speaking in the plural, saying, *"We've got yer horses. We'd just ride ye down."* And, *"If ye make things too difficult we might harm yer husband."*

Taking a deep breath to steady herself, she peered toward the trees not far away. Annabel didn't see anything, but suddenly felt as if she were being watched.

After a quick glance to see that, indeed their horses were gone, Annabel backed into the barn several feet, and then whirled and hurried back to Ross.

"Husband, please," she hissed, dropping to her knees beside him and releasing her weapons to shake his shoulders. "You have to wake up. We must get out of here."

Annabel knew even as she did it that he wasn't going to rouse and lead her out of there. She was on her own, and had to save not only herself, but him. Somehow she had to drag her unconscious husband out of the barn and to safety. She didn't dare leave him there.

Grinding her teeth, she glanced around. The afternoon was waning, the sun heading for the horizon to make way for night. Soon it would be dark and she had no intention of being there when that happened. Turning back to Ross, she tucked his sword under his arm where she hoped it would not be found and used against her should their attacker return. Annabel then stood to move to the two posts and board where her gown still hung. She grabbed it up, pausing to unhook it when it caught on a raised nail. Once it was free, she donned it quickly, keeping her eyes locked on the open barn door.

Annabel felt a bit better once she was dressed, but she still watched the door nervously as she began to explore her surroundings. After several minutes of searching, she came up with a second long plank, some rope and little else of use. Annabel carried what she'd found to Ross and tried again to wake him.

When he didn't stir, she glanced nervously toward the door, then sat down cross-legged and set to work tying one corner of the plaid by his head around the end of one plank. She then shifted down to the bottom of the plaid her husband lay on and tied that corner to the far end of the plank before shifting to the other side of the plaid to do the same with the second plank.

Annabel then picked up the rope and stood to consider her next move. She needed to fasten the rope to the top ends of the planks, but in such a way that it wouldn't slide off. After a hesitation, she glanced toward the two posts with the rail across them and then hurried over to examine the nail that had caught on her gown. She tugged on it briefly, but when it wouldn't budge, she rushed back to fetch Ross's sword and used it to pry the nail free, nearly slicing her hand off in the process at one point.

Once Annabel got it loose, she searched for, found, and pulled out three more nails before taking her booty back to her husband. She used the sword hilt as a hammer to drive them into the planks where she needed them. She attached the rope to the planks, tying each end just past the nails at the top of either plank so that it wouldn't slide off.

She then considered her makeshift pallet and her naked husband on it. After a moment, she bent to collect handfuls of hay and dropped it on his groin, hiding his manhood. Satisfied that she had done the best she could, she then reluctantly set her husband's sword on the plaid with him and knelt by his head. Taking up the rope, she wrapped it around her shoulders and upper arms, and then straightened with a grunt.

Her husband was a big man and heavy, and the rope burned as it tightened around her skin, but she set her teeth and began to drag him out of the barn. By the time she reached the door, she was less concerned with their attacker than how far the village was.

Chapter 12

ANNABEL OPENED HER EYES TO FIND SEONAG standing at the foot of the bed. Her hands were on her hips, her head was tilted, and she was eyeing Annabel and Ross with pursed lips. When the maid saw that Annabel was awake, she gave a "hrrumph" and said, "Yer a pair o' bookends ye two are, with yer bruised faces."

Grimacing, Annabel sat up and turned to peer at the man she'd dragged, for what had seemed like miles, to the safety of the village last night. The sun had long set and the cottages were dark, their inhabitants apparently sleeping, when she'd finally arrived. She had stopped at the first cottage, intending to roust the people inside and ask for assistance for their laird, but even as she started to lower to a kneeling position to remove the ropes around her arms and shoulders, the sound of pounding hooves caught her ear. Stilling, she'd stared worriedly toward the opposite side of the quiet village until Gilly and Marach rode into view, leading a party of at least twelve men.

Within moments she'd been surrounded, her burden removed, and Ross, who had long ago lost his covering of hay, raised up to lie on his stomach before Gilly on his horse, while Annabel was lifted up before Marach. It was on the ride back to the castle that she explained what had happened and learned that Jasper had returned to the keep hours earlier. No one had been terribly concerned at first, but when night fell without Annabel and Ross returning, a search party had been organized. Sixty men had been divided into four groups and had ridden out in different directions. Gilly and Marach had headed to the village because that was where they'd last seen their laird and lady.

Annabel now scanned Ross's pale, unmoving face and asked, "Did he wake up at all in the night?"

"Yer asking me?" Seonag asked dryly. "Ye were the one who insisted on watching over him."

"Aye, and I did," she assured her. "The sun was coming up when I finally laid down next to him. I did not intend to sleep. The chair was just so bloody uncomfortable after so long in it . . ." She shrugged unhappily and brushed the hair from Ross's face. "I should not have risked lying down."

" 'Tis just past dawn now," Seonag said soothingly. "Ye've naught to feel guilty for. Why do ye no' go rest a bit? I'll watch over him now."

Annabel hesitated, tempted by the offer, but then shook her head. "Nay. But if you will stay with him for a few minutes, I will go below and break my fast. Perhaps that will wake me enough to keep me up until he wakes."

Seonag opened her mouth in what Annabel suspected would have been another suggestion that she rest, but then closed it again and simply nodded.

"Thank you," Annabel murmured pushing herself from the bed and heading for the door. "I will only be a couple moments."

"Take yer time," Seonag admonished. "I'll call ye does he wake."

Annabel didn't comment. She didn't want to be called when he woke. She wanted to be right there, holding his hand and peering into his eyes. With her luck, however, he'd open his eyes the moment she left the room and think she hadn't cared enough to sit by him while he was injured.

Grimacing at the thought, Annabel pulled the door closed and then stood for a moment, listening. When several minutes passed with no sudden cry of joy or even a wry, "So ye've decided to wake, have ye," from Seonag, Annabel reluctantly turned away and headed for the stairs.

The great hall was full with servants and warriors breaking their fast, and every single one of them seemed to turn to peer at her as she descended the stairs. Questions rode on every face, and Annabel considered whether she shouldn't make some sort of announcement about Ross's state as she walked to the table, but there was really nothing to tell. He hadn't woken yet, and she didn't know if he would.

She sighed at that thought as she settled at the head table, and then sighed again when Gilly and Marach immediately stood and moved to sit on either side of her.

"There is no need to guard me. I promise you I will not be leaving the keep so long as my husband is unconscious," she said with grim dignity.

"So he hasna woken yet," Marach said morosely.

Annabel shook her head and picked up a piece of bread, but only tore at it absently, her gaze drifting back to the stairs.

"Well, that just makes no sense," Gilly burst out after a moment and when Annabel peered at him uncertainly, he added, "He's a big braugh lad, strong and sure and yer a weak, wee woman, yet ye've come around after two blows to the head, but one lays him low?"

"Head wounds are—" Annabel began automatically, only to be interrupted.

"A tricky business. Aye, I ken," Gilly said with disgruntlement. "Still, it makes no sense."

Annabel patted his hand soothingly. "I am sure he will wake up soon. As you say, he's strong. We must just give him time."

"Lady MacKay?"

Annabel was slow to turn at that name, mostly because she was not yet used to hearing it and it took a moment to realize she was being addressed. When she did turn and glance over her shoulder, it was to find Father Gibson standing there.

"Oh, Father," she murmured, getting to her feet.

"I just wanted to say, I understand that after this latest incident, you most likely would prefer to be at your husband's side than at mass."

Annabel winced guiltily, for here she was willing to leave him to break her fast, but he was right and she hadn't intended to attend mass. But mass was soooo long.

"So I thought to offer to give mass in your bedchamber," the priest went on. "That way neither of you will miss it at a time when prayer is surely needed most."

"Er . . ." Annabel said uncertainly, not sure Ross would be pleased to wake up and find everyone gathered around his sickbed for mass.

"A private mass," Father Gibson clarified and Annabel relaxed.

"Thank you," she murmured. "That is very kind."

"Not at all. 'Tis my place to minister to those in need, and the two of you are surely in need what with these continued attacks."

"Aye," she agreed and then agreed again when he suggested he join her and Ross in their room after he'd done the usual mass in the chapel.

Annabel thanked him again, watched him walk away and then dropped onto the bench and said grimly, "We must sort out who is behind these attacks."

Marach and Gilly exchanged a glance, but it was Marach who said, "That is what Ross was doing in the village yesterday when ye tricked us and slipped away on yer horse."

"Was he?" she asked with interest. "What was he doing exactly?"

"Talking to Fingal," Gilly answered. "The blacksmith."

"The illegitimate son of Ross's grandfather who tried to claim a right to the title of clan chief?" she asked, and when both men looked surprised she rolled her eyes. "Giorsal told me all about it."

"Oh, aye," Marach said.

"Did he find out anything?" she asked.

Gilly raised his eyebrows. "Yer asking us? We did no' speak to him after that. He was with you."

"Oh, right," she murmured. Ross hadn't mentioned anything about it. Would he have if he'd suspected the man of anything? She wasn't sure.

"Then I should probably talk to this Fingal myself," she decided.

"Did ye no' just promise us but moments ago that ye'd no' leave the keep while Ross is ill?" Gilly asked with exasperation.

"Aye, but I have changed my mind," she said apologetically.

"Well ye can change yer mind all ye want, but the laird ordered us no' to let ye leave the keep and I fer one intend to follow orders."

Annabel scowled at him. "Gilly, who am I?"

"The laird's lady wife."

"And who is in charge when my husband is unwell or away?"

He cursed under his breath and looked away, refusing to answer, which was answer enough for Annabel. Gilly and Marach, and everyone else, had to obey her orders now.

"I will not leave the keep do I not have to, but I will get to the bottom of this. I want one of you to go down to the village and ask Fingal to come up here so that I can speak to him," she said, and then added, "And the uncle too . . . Eoghann, I think Giorsal said?"

"Aye." Gilly nodded. "Eoghann."

"I want to talk to them at the same time," she decided.

"Why?" Gilly asked. "Ye can no' watch both o' them at the same time and may miss a telling expression from one while looking at the other."

"I might, but not if I have you two there while I talk to them," she said and then pointed out, "They may give away more together than apart. They may exchange a glance at a certain point, or one may show surprise or disbelief if the other lies." She shrugged. "Each of you can watch one of them the whole time and then we can share what we saw."

"That's a good idea," Marach said with admiration.

"Aye," Gilly agreed with a grin. "The lad did well marrying ye."

Annabel smiled faintly at the praise, but then asked, "What is your opinion of Derek's mother?"

"Miriam?" Marach asked with surprise.

Annabel nodded, and then said, "Giorsal said she hated Ross for killing Derek, blamed him for the whole thing."

"Aye, she did, but—"

"Was that hatred enough for her to seek revenge?" she asked.

The two men exchanged a frown, and then Gilly shook his head. "Nay. I mean, aye, she may have. But then she would be attacking Ross, no' you."

"Mayhap," she agreed, "Unless her revenge took the form of taking something or someone from him." When the men stared at her blankly, she sighed and said, "In her mind, Ross took away the son she loved. Is it possible she decided her revenge should be—"

"To take away someone Ross loves from him," Marach finished with understanding.

"Well, mayhap not love," Annabel murmured. She didn't think her husband loved her. At least he had never said anything of the like. He liked her though. She was pretty sure about that. And he seemed to enjoy bedding her, and he was caring and—

"That's clever, that is," Gilly said slowly, considering her suggestion. "And sneaky like a woman."

Annabel scowled at the insult and he grimaced.

"Sorry, I mean sneaky like some women," he muttered.

"Hmmm," she said with displeasure, and then sighed and added, "Ask around and see if you cannot find out where Miriam has got to and if anyone has seen her in the area." She paused briefly and then added unhappily, "Although not seeing her may not mean she is not behind this. After all, 'tis a man doing the attacking. It could be someone she hired. She would not need to be in the area at all if that is the case."

"I heard she went back to her kin," Marach said thoughtfully. "If she did send someone, it's most likely kin. We can ask if anyone has seen members of her family about, or if any of her kin fit the description of the man that chased ye in the clearing," he suggested.

"Aye. Good thinking," Annabel praised, and then stood. "I am going back up to check on my husband."

"But ye've no' broken yer fast," Gilly pointed out with a frown.

Annabel glanced down at the bits of bread littering her spot. She'd torn her bread to shreds but had not eaten a bite. Shrugging, she said, "I am not really hungry anyway."

"I'll ha'e a maid bring ye up some cider and food," Marach said quietly. "Ye must keep yer strength up. Ye may need it in the future."

"Thank you," Annabel murmured and turned for the stairs. But as she walked, it suddenly occurred to her to wonder what he'd meant. Did he mean she needed to keep her strength up in case of another attack, or in case Ross died? Her mind shrank from the second possibility. Annabel simply didn't want to think about that. She liked her husband. Perhaps even was coming to love him. He was caring and concerned in his treatment of her, and he made her blood burn and her body sing. She didn't want to think of never experiencing any of that again.

"LIKE I TOLD THE LAIRD, AINSLEY, EOGHANN and I were drinking the night we decided to put in a claim to the title."

Annabel nodded to encourage the man to continue, and then glanced over her shoulder to be sure Gilly and Marach were each paying attention. A snort from Eoghann brought her gaze back around.

"We weren't just drinking, we were sotted," Ross's uncle put in. "We were supposed to be playing cards, but instead the three of us were yammering on about Derek."

"Aye," Fingal agreed. "We all three were annoyed with the little idiot blathering on about his being four years older, and how it would make him the wiser and better chief than Ross." He scowled. "And some folk were falling for it."

"Can ye imagine?" Eoghann asked with dismay. "After all Ross had done to prove himself, stepping up repeatedly and takin' the reins when his father, God rest his soul, was away or unwell. The lad is a born leader."

"Aye, and what had Derek done?" Fingal asked, and then answered in unison with Eoghann, "Nothing."

They both nodded together, looking like the brothers they were, and then Fingal muttered, "The lad's ridiculous yammering made us fair froth."

"Froth," Eoghann agreed.

"So, we decided if he wanted to play the age card, we could beat him there and we'd all put ourselves forward as runners for the title," Fingal continued. "Give the little bastard a scare."

"Aye," Eoghann agreed, and then added quickly, "But none o' us really wanted it. I'm a farmer at heart. Always ha'e been. Can't be bothered with all that political nonsense. Give me some good, fertile soil and I can feed the village. Give me a sword and I'd most like poke meself by accident," he said with a grimace. "I'd rather slop me pigs than kowtow to the English and our neighbors . . . and our father kenned that. Set me up with a fine bit o' land to till when I was still a boy, and I've made fine work of it. I'm content."

"And I like being blacksmith," Fingal assured her. "Always had a temper, and I can beat that out hammering me metal. I'd forever be at war were I clan chieftain."

"Aye, he would," Eoghann said with a grin.

"And that's no' a good thing," Fingal assured her. "I can hammer a fine sword, the best in the highlands, but wielding it?" He grimaced and shook his head. "I'd get meself stuck through, the first battle."

"Aye," Eoghann agreed. "As would I."

The two men were silent for a moment and then Fingal said, "I ken yer trying to find out who is behind these attacks as Ross was doing ere he was hurt, but if yer looking to us, yer looking in the wrong direction. Ross is a good leader, and bad as I am with a sword, I'd take one up in his defense, but I'd ne'er turn one against him."

Eoghann nodded solemnly and then asked, "How is the lad? Has he stirred at all?"

"Nay," Annabel admitted quietly.

Eoghann sighed, looking suddenly old. He shook his head. "It's no' fair. The lad's had a tough row o' it the last five or six years."

"Aye," Fingal sighed. "And it was just starting to look like he was comin' out o' it. He handled Derek and things were settling here and then he fetched ye back. It seemed things had taken a turn."

Eoghann nodded. "We were expecting the squawl o' bairns soon and a contented laird. A happy laird makes for happy people."

"I am sure he will wake soon," Annabel said soothingly. "He is strong."

"Aye, but head wounds are a tricky business," Eoghann muttered unhappily.

Annabel grimaced at the words. They had been repeated often of late, even by her, and she was sick of them. Tricky or not, Ross had to recover from this head wound.

"Ha'e ye considered Miriam?" Eoghann asked suddenly, and then added, "She did no' take Derek's passing well, and blamed Ross despite her boy starting this whole business."

"Hell, she was probably the one prodding Derek to claim the title," Fingal said with disgust. "That way she would be mother o' the laird and live in the castle."

"That's more than possible," Eoghann decided, and then added with disapproval, "Miriam always aspired to grander things than village life. She wanted to be Lady MacKay as a lass, chased our brother, Ranson, Ross's father, and was furious when the boy's mother won him over instead."

"Really?" Annabel asked with interest.

"Aye. That's a fact," Eoghann assured her. "I wouldn't put it past the woman to try to make trouble for Ross for dashing her last hope o' being the grand lady o' the manor."

"Do you know if she—" Annabel paused and glanced toward the keep doors when they suddenly opened. She recognized the man who entered. He was a MacKay and often guarded the front gate, but she had never been told his name, so she was a little alarmed when he glanced around, spotted her at the trestle tables and headed straight for her.

"Begging yer pardon, me lady," the man murmured with a slight bow as he reached her. "But there's a lady at the gate asking to see ye."

"A lady?" Annabel asked with surprise, searching her mind for what woman in Scotland might want to see her. The only women she knew so far were the servants here and Giorsal, and Giorsal would never be kept waiting at the gate.

"An Englishwoman," the soldier clarified.

Annabel's eyes widened and she stood at once.

"Hold on there," Eoghann said, jumping to his feet and then he eyed the soldier. "Is it Miriam?"

"Miriam?" Annabel asked with surprise. "But she is Scottish . . . isn't she?" she added uncertainly.

Fingal and Eoghann shook their heads as one, but it was Eoghann who said, "Nay. Miriam is English. Our father hired her father on as cook here when she was twelve. Her mother was dead, so he brought her along and they had a little room off the kitchens."

"It's where she got her liking for castle life. Wanted to run the damned place and get out o' the hot kitchens," Fingal added.

"I see," Annabel murmured and then glanced to the soldier. "Is it Miriam?"

"I do no' ken," the man admitted apologetically. "I never met the woman."

"Bearnard is a MacDonald," Marach said quietly behind her. "He married a MacKay lass this past spring and only moved here then."

"Aye." Bearnard nodded. "I ken not what this Miriam looks like. Howbeit, she did no' say she was her."

"Well, I ken what she looks like," Eoghann announced and started around the table, with Fingal on his heels. "We'll accompany ye and be sure if 'tis her, she does ye no harm."

"Oh, that is very kind," Annabel said with surprise. "But I am sure Gilly and Marach will recognize her if 'tis Miriam."

"Gilly and Marach are no' family," Eoghann said grimly as he took her arm, then glanced to the men and added, "No offense, lads. But with Ross down it falls to his family to see his lady's safe. Come on Fingal," he added, and the other man hurried to take her other arm. The two then proceeded to march her toward the keep doors.

Annabel glanced over her shoulder to be sure Gilly and Marach were following and then glanced from Eoghann to Fingal and said, "The two of you seem quite close."

"We're brothers," Eoghann said with a shrug.

"Half brothers," Fingal corrected. "And we were no' always so close. As lads I resented Eoghann, Ainsley and Ranson for having things I did no'. And for being acknowledged as the laird's sons where I was no'."

"What happened to change things?" she asked curiously as Fingal tugged the keep door open and the men ushered her out.

"Ranson," Fingal said solemnly as they crossed the bailey. "When our father died and he became laird, he came down to the village to speak to me. He acknowledged me as his half brother and offered me a position among his warriors." He smiled wryly. "But as I mentioned I was no good with the sword. He offered to train me himself, but I'd been training with the blacksmith since a boy and I liked it, so . . ." He shrugged.

"Ranson was the one who started the weekly game nights with the four of us," Eoghann announced. "Sometimes we took turns at playing Merels, other times we played cards. 'Twas the four o' us then. Derek's father had already passed on."

"Mostly we drank and laughed and just had a good time," Fingal informed her. " 'Twas a sad day indeed when we lost him."

"Aye," Eoghann sighed. "We considered inviting Ross to take his place in the game nights, but then this business with Derek happened and idiots that we were, we did no' explain to him that we did no' really want his title ere naming our claims to it. As ye can imagine, our stepping up did no' please him."

"We did no' think he'd welcome the invitation after that," Fingal added dryly. "So we decided to just let him be for a bit."

"And then Ainsley died," Eoghann said on a sigh.

"Aye." Fingal nodded solemnly and they all fell silent as they crossed the last few feet to the gate.

Ross had given the order that no one was to enter the bailey without good cause after the attack in the field of bluebells here in Scotland. Only villagers or visitors who were expected or had business at MacKay were to be allowed past the drawbridge. All others were to be held there until he, or in this case, Annabel, said it was all right.

Annabel didn't at first see anyone waiting at the gate until she had nearly reached it, and then a woman in tattered clothes, her face and hair dirty, stepped from the shadows near the wall of the barbican and into the light.

"It's no' Miriam," Fingal said with disappointment.

"Nay. Too young and pretty under all that dirt," Eoghann agreed and then informed her, "Miriam was a beauty when she was young, but grew into a bitter old sour-faced crone." Glancing to Annabel he lectured, "That's what greed, envy and bitterness does to a woman. Bear that in mind and keep envy from yer heart, lass, and ye'll be as lovely when yer old as ye are today."

"Thank you, I shall remember that," Annabel murmured, trying to ignore the blush she knew was creeping up her cheeks at the compliment. She was not used to being thought lovely. Ross was the first person who had claimed she was. It seemed the men in his family agreed. All she could think was that liking plump women was a family trait.

"Annabel?"

She turned back just as the woman tried to rush forward only to have the man who had kept her at the gate hold out a hand to stop her. The stranger peered down at the arm in front of her chest and then turned desperate eyes to Annabel.

"Annabel, do you not recognize me?" she asked in an English accent, and sounding close to tears. " 'Tis me. Kate."

"Kate?" Annabel said with amazement, her eyes narrowing on her face. She wanted to recognize her sister, but it had been fourteen years, and they'd both been children when she'd last seen her.

"Belly," she said pleadingly, and Annabel recognized the nickname Kate had called her when they were children.

"Let her in. She is my sister," Annabel said at once.

The moment the guard lowered his arm Kate rushed forward. Annabel started to raise her hands to take hers in greeting, but never got the chance. Kate threw herself at her like a child and burst into loud, heart-wrenching sobs.

Annabel stiffened briefly in surprise, but then patted her back and murmured soothingly. She also tried very hard not to wrinkle her nose or shrink away from the stench coming off of her. Kate needed a bath desperately.

She was not the only one to note this. The men who had surrounded her all the way to the gate, almost crowding her in their determination to keep her safe, had all suddenly taken several quick steps away. Annabel scowled at them for it and then eased the woman to her side. Circling her back with her arm, she then began to urge her toward the keep, murmuring *there, there*'s and *'tis all right now*'s, though she hadn't a clue what she was comforting her over. Had her lover died? Abandoned her? Or perhaps he was abusive and Kate had fled him. Whatever it was, it seemed to have utterly destroyed her sister. And it must have happened soon after she'd left with him. It had only been little more than a week since Kate had run off with her lover. By the looks of her, she hadn't bathed or changed once since then and had been living in rough circumstances.

Annabel knew the men were following them. Despite Kate's continuous and loud sobs, she could just hear their mumbling amongst themselves as they trailed them back across the bailey and into the keep. That didn't surprise her; what did was the fact that they then also trailed them upstairs when Annabel herded Kate that way.

"There, there," Annabel repeated as she ushered Kate into the empty bedchamber next to the master bedchamber. "I shall order you a bath and some food. You shall feel much better after that and we can talk."

"A bath and food?" Eoghann asked with dismay from the door. "But she's English."

Annabel ignored him and urged Kate to the bed. Once she had removed her clinging hands and seated her on the bed, she patted her shoulder and said, "I shall go roust some servants to bring you a bath and food. I'll be right back. You just rest."

Turning then, she started for the door where the four men were huddled watching her.

"Lass, ye can no' waste food and trouble the servants on this," Eoghann told her solemnly. "She's English."

Annabel paused in the door and scowled. "Sir, in case my accent had escaped you, I am English."

"Nay, yer a MacKay," he countered.

"Aye, but I am also English," she insisted with exasperation.

"Nay," he said stubbornly. "Ye were *raised* English, but ye married a MacKay, so now yer a Scot."

Deciding this was a waste of time, Annabel waved the men out of the way with exasperation and moved past them to hurry to the stairs.

"I did no' ken she had a sister," Fingal commented as the men followed her.

"Aye. She ran off with the son o' Waverly's

stable master," Marach said dryly. "Waverly disinherited and disowned her and presented the
laird with Annabel as his eldest by contract."

"Which we're all grateful for. Our lady is a
sweet nun—" Gilly's words died abruptly when
Annabel whirled in horror.

"Giorsal told?"

"Giorsal?" Gilly asked with confusion. "Does
she ken?"

"Nay, m'lady," Marach assured her. "I overheard the Waverly stable master and another man
talking after we arrived there."

"Not that," Annabel waved impatiently. Ross
had already told her about the conversation where
it had been revealed she was the second daughter. "I meant did Giorsal tell you about my being
raised at the abbey, intended to be a nun?"

Dead silence met her question, and then Gilly
cleared his throat, and said, "Actually, I was no'
saying ye were a nun. I was saying ye were a
sweet nun next to yer sister's loose ways," he explained, and then glanced to Marach in question
as he added, "I do no' think any o' us kenned ye
were a nun, did we?"

Marach shook his head silently, his gaze on Annabel with concern.

"I am not a nun," Annabel said quickly, mentally
kicking herself for jumping the gun and revealing
what she hadn't yet told her husband. Sighing, she
admitted reluctantly, "I was an oblate."

There was a moment of silence and then Fingal
asked, "An oblate? Isn't that a fledgling nun?"

"An oblate is a lass raised in the abbey, intended
to be a nun, but without having taken any vows or

signed contracts to that effect," Marach said quietly.

"Aye, a fledgling nun," Eoghann said.

"Well, nun or no', I'm thinkin' Ross got the better sister," Fingal muttered. "The other one is a fair mess."

Reminded of her intended task, Annabel turned away and continued down the stairs, muttering, "She merely needs a bath and change of clothes. By all accounts she is the beautiful one in the family."

Her mother had made that more than clear, and had moaned over Annabel's lack in comparison as she'd prepared her for the wedding.

"Nay," Fingal disagreed and then predicted, "Even cleaned up ye'll outshine her. Her face is too narrow, and her nose big, and she's too skinny. No meat on her bones to hold on to or cushion ye while ye—"

His words stopped abruptly and Annabel glanced over her shoulder just in time to see Eoghann remove his elbow from the man's stomach. Shaking her head, she faced forward again, sure they would change their minds once Kate was cleaned up. None of that really mattered though. Annabel had resigned herself to being the unattractive failure in the family. Besides, Ross seemed to like her just as she was. Although, she did wonder how he would feel when he woke up and met Kate. He may feel he had been cheated in the deal . . . especially once he heard that Annabel was an untrained exoblate. And while it was obvious the men hadn't known that part before, they did now, and she knew they would tell him when he woke. If he woke. Whether she lost him or not, Annabel hoped he would wake. The world would be a much sadder place if he didn't.

Chapter 13

"*I* MADE A TERRIBLE ERROR," KATE SAID WEARILY, wiping tears from her face.

"You were in love," Annabel said sympathetically.

Kate had bathed and looked an entirely different person than the filthy waif she had first appeared at the gate. Her sister's hair was a fine golden color, her face slender, eyes big and wide apart, and nose straight. She was also quite slim. The abbess would have loved her, Annabel thought as she took in the gown Kate now wore. It was a pale yellow gown with white trim that she and Seonag had mended and altered, making the bustline bigger for Annabel. It had fit her like a glove when they'd finished, Annabel recalled unhappily, but it hung on Kate's much smaller frame like a sack.

"Aye, I did love him," Kate said unhappily. "More fool I."

"Oh, Kate, do not say that," Annabel said sadly, patting her hand. They sat on the bed in the room she'd first taken her to, a tray of food between them that neither of them had touched yet.

"But I *am* a fool," Kate cried unhappily. "He was not at all the man I thought he was." She almost moaned the words.

"What happened?" Annabel asked, releasing her hand to pick up her cider and take a sip.

"It was all grand at first," Kate said sadly. "The excitement, the adventure . . . and the bedding too."

Annabel choked on the cider and quickly set the goblet back on the tray as she began to cough.

"Are you all right?" Kate asked, thumping her back.

"I—yes, of course," she gasped, waving away her thumping.

"I am sorry. Should I not have mentioned the bedding?" Kate asked uncertainly. "I thought as you are married I could talk about it to you. But I suppose being raised in the convent, you may be a little more reticent."

"Nay, 'tis fine," Annabel assured her, and then prompted, "So, 'twas all wonderful at first."

"Aye." Kate slumped where she sat. "That first day and night were magical, but things started to go bad the next day. Grant woke up surly and short-tempered. He was hungry, and we had nothing to eat and then it started to rain." She closed her eyes, her expression unhappy at the memory. "We rode all day in a downpour, both of us on my mare." She grimaced and told her, "I wanted to take one of father's horses too when we left, but Grant refused. He said they could hunt us down and kill him for stealing it. But at least with an extra horse we could have sold it for food or something."

Annabel murmured soothingly, unsure what else to do. She thought Grant had been right in refusing to take something that wasn't his.

"Anyway, we found shelter in an old abandoned hut." Kate continued, her mouth tightened. "It was full of spiders and rats, but at least it was out of the rain. We cuddled together to get warm and made love again and it was even better than the first time. But once it was done he rolled away and went to sleep and I was so cold and hungry . . ." She paused on a little sob, and wiped away a tear with her hand. "The next morning Grant was even more surly. He said I was a mess and should clean myself up in the river. But I was not going to bathe out of doors!" she cried, tears forgotten in favor of indignation. "Why, I could have caught my death. Besides, I had bathed just three weeks before we left Waverly."

"Ah," Annabel murmured. She wasn't surprised at these words. While she had got used to bathing in the stream three or more times a week thanks to working in the stables, most of the women at the abbey had bathed much less frequently. However, Grant had worked in the stables and she suspected he'd bathed more often because of it as well.

"And then he started in on my hair being a mess and could I not do something with it?" She snorted. "How, I ask you? I had a brush, but no maid to wield it."

"Hmmm," Annabel murmured, biting her lip. There had been no maid for her at the abbey, she had always managed brushing her own hair.

"And then he caught some fish in the river and

brought them back, expecting *me* to cook them,"
she said with open horror. "I said, do I look like
a servant to you?" Her eyes flashed with remembered fury and then pain flashed across her face
and she added, "And he said, nay, I did not look
like much of anything at the moment, except perhaps a whore who had fallen on bad fortune. And
certainly, that was about all I was good for."

"Oh dear," Annabel breathed.

"How could he say that to me?" Kate cried miserably. "I thought that he loved me. We were supposed to run away and live happily ever after, and
. . . and . . ." Covering her face, she burst into loud
noisy sobs again.

"Oh dear. All right, 'twill be all right," Annabel
said, hugging her and rubbing her back soothingly.

"How can it be all right?" Kate cried miserably, pulling back. "He brought me up here and
dumped me at your gate like waste. He said I was
ugly and as useless as a stone and he knew not
what he had ever seen in me." Wiping her face,
she snapped. "Me. Can you imagine? I am not
ugly. I am the beautiful sister. You were always
the fat, ugly one. And I am not useless. I was born
to rule, not grovel in the dirt like a peasant."

"Ah," Annabel murmured, finding it hard to
think of anything sympathetic to say at that point.
She did not think Kate had meant to hurt her with
her comments. She was simply stating fact when
she said Annabel was the fat, ugly sister. All one
had to do was look at how her gown hung on Kate
to see that, but Annabel was hurt anyway.

Sadly, she also had a bit more sympathy for

Grant. What had Kate expected? That her life would somehow miraculously continue unchanged? That Grant would provide her with fine clothes, a maid and a castle to live in from thin air? He was not even a stable master, but the son of a stable master, who had no doubt helped muck out the stalls. She doubted he had one coin to spend on her sister.

"Everything will work out," Annabel said finally, getting off the bed and bending to collect the tray. Straightening, she added, "I think you should rest for now. Things will look brighter when you wake up."

"I do not see how, but I *am* tired," Kate said on a sigh and stretched out on the bed. "Will you come back and talk to me later? I have so much to tell you. It has been a long time since we have seen each other."

"Aye." Annabel smiled, but more in relief that she wasn't protesting her leaving than anything else. She felt even more relief once she was actually out of the room with the door closed behind her, which made her feel guilty as sin. Her sister had been through a lot. All her hopes and dreams had just collapsed around her. It was uncharitable of her to resent that Kate wanted only to talk about herself and cared not what had gone on in Annabel's life during this "long time" since they'd seen each other.

Releasing a little sigh, Annabel walked up the hall and carried the tray of meat pies and beverages into the master bedchamber. Seonag glanced up at her entrance and set down the sewing she was working on.

"How is yer sister?"

"Tired and disappointed in how things have turned out," Annabel said quietly as she set the tray on the bedside table and turned to peer at Ross. "No change?"

"Not yet," Seonag answered. "But I'm sure he'll be right as rain in no time."

"Aye," Annabel muttered, beginning to fear that may not be true. "Thank you for sitting with him, Seonag, but I shall take over now. 'Tis almost the sup," she added. "You should go below and join the table."

The maid hesitated, but then said, "Only if ye promise to lie down and sleep fer a bit." When Annabel opened her mouth to refuse, Seonag added, "Ye've slept no more than minutes this last night and day since he was injured. Ye'll do the laird no good do ye make yerself sick. He would no' want that."

Annabel let her breath out and slumped in defeat. The truth, was, she was exhausted, and sleep sounded a heavenly idea. Raising her shoulders again, she said, "Very well, but only for a couple of hours. I would appreciate it if you would wake me up after that. I promised Kate I would go speak to her later."

Seonag nodded and stood. "Sleep well. Ye need it. Ye do no' want Ross wakin' up to find ye looking so haggard."

Annabel's eyes widened with alarm at those words as she watched the woman leave the room. No, she certainly did not want to look haggard when Ross woke up. It would just make Kate look even better, which she certainly didn't need. She was already insecure about how he would react when he saw what he had missed out on, and worried that he might set her aside to claim her sister.

She probably wouldn't fret so much about that had her mother not moaned on about how disappointing she was in the area of attractiveness, and how Kate had looked so much prettier in the gown, and how she was sure "the Scot" would refuse the contract the moment he saw her. Truly, after hours of that, Annabel had been amazed when he had been so kind and agreed to marry her. But then he had never seen Kate. He probably thought them similar in looks.

Pushing that worry away as something she could not do anything about anyway, Annabel stripped off her clothes and slid into bed next to her husband. While she only planned to nap, she wanted to be comfortable for it, not tangled up in her skirts.

Breathing out a sleepy little sigh, she cuddled up to her unconscious husband. Resting her head and hand on his chest, Annabel pretended for a moment that he was not unconscious, just sleeping, and that he loved her and thought her more attractive than her sister and wished to keep her to wife for always.

Thanks to her exhaustion, it was a short daydream and she quickly drifted off to sleep.

Ross woke to silence and early morning sunlight creeping through the cracks in the shutters. Despite that, for one moment he felt disoriented and unsure of where he was, but then the woman draped across his chest murmured sleepily, drawing his attention to her presence. He recognized Annabel at once, and then recognized the shapes and shadows of their room in the near darkness.

He was home.

The thought made him smile. MacKay had always been his home, but he had never felt comfortable in this room. This was his father and mother's chamber to his mind, or had been when he'd moved here on taking up the title of clan chief. He'd done it only because it was expected, and because Seonag had ordered the servants to move his things here while he was out in the practice field. But it had never felt quite right . . . until now. At that moment, with Annabel in his arms, and dawn clawing its way through the shutters to touch on this item or that, he felt like he belonged there.

He was also so thirsty he could drink moat water, and hungry enough to eat a raw horse. Grimacing, Ross eased Annabel off his chest and sat up on the side of the bed. He was about to stand up when he spotted the tray on the bedside table holding four small meat pies and two goblets of cider. Stomach rumbling, he reached for a pie and popped it in his mouth. It was good, damned good, and he reached for another even as he quickly chewed and swallowed the first.

Ross ate all four meat pies one after another, and then gulped down both goblets of cider as well. Once finished with his feast, a wave of exhaustion swept over him and he decided a little more time abed wouldn't go amiss. Stifling a yawn, Ross lay back down and tugged the linens and furs back over himself.

Annabel immediately rolled toward him, her head coming to rest on his shoulder and her leg shifting sleepily over his. Ross peered down at the top of her head, then carefully moved his arm out from beneath her and wrapped it around her instead. Annabel shifted sleepily in response, her head moving onto his chest and her hand coming to rest on his stomach.

Ross smiled faintly and slid his right hand along her arm in a gentle caress. He loved touching Annabel. She had such soft skin. Everything about her was soft: her skin, her body, her heart, and he loved that about her. He also lusted over her something fierce, he admitted wryly, letting his left hand slide down under the linens and furs to cup her sweet, round behind.

"Mmmm," Annabel murmured, shifting closer. Her leg slid over him again, this time riding up and nudging his sleeping staff. She may as well have slapped it, Ross thought wryly as his penis woke at the touch and began to harden. Damn, she hadn't even meant to touch him and he was reacting like that.

Following his awakening needs, he eased her off his chest and onto her back, and then drew the linens and furs covering them down to her waist. Annabel hardly stirred at either action, which made him smile. It meant he could wake her in any way he wished. He could kiss her sweet lips to stir her, or suckle at her breasts, or perhaps slide down her body, bury his head between her legs, and bring her awake with the screaming need he was now suffering, thanks to her unintentional nudge.

His eyes settled on her breasts, round and full with pale rose nipples that presently were as asleep as their mistress. He liked them better when her nipples hardened into sweet little buds he could toy with, take between his lips and teeth, and nip lightly as he flicked with his tongue.

That idea was an appetizing one and Ross shifted down the bed a bit until his head was even with her breasts, and then bent to claim one with his mouth. He caught it between his lips first and suckled to draw it to life, but once it hardened in his mouth, he caught it lightly between his teeth and flicked it repeatedly with his tongue until Annabel moaned in sleep.

Out of the corner of his eye, Ross saw her legs shift restlessly and let one hand slide down to caress her thigh. He smiled around her nipple when her body reacted automatically, legs shifting further apart in invitation. How could he resist such a generous offer?

Nipping lightly at her nipple, Ross slid his hand between her legs, not surprised to find her warm and wet for him already. That was something else he loved about his wife. She warmed to him quickly, seeming always ready and happy to welcome his attentions. He knew not all men enjoyed such pleasure with their wives, and he intended to nurture that and do what he could to keep the fire that grew between them alive.

When Annabel released a long groan, her body arching and shifting, Ross raised his head to peer at her face. Her eyes were closed, her mouth hanging open in a way he was sure she would not allow were she awake. The woman was sleeping like the dead while he was wide awake, every inch of him.

It was time to wake her up, Ross decided, and lowered his head to claim her nipple again. He suckled more insistently for a moment, and then let it slip from his mouth and moved further down her body, running his tongue over her creamy flesh as he went. He paused briefly at her hipbone to nibble and lick there, and then continued on to bury his face between her legs.

ANNABEL WOKE GASPING FOR BREATH, HER BODY arching and writhing in the bed. Her groggy mind was slow to understand why her whole body seemed to be on fire with pleasure. Then she became aware that the pleasure was centered between her thighs and she raised her head to look down. The sight of Ross's head buried there, along with the sensations he was causing as he apparently tried to make a meal of her, held her in thrall for a moment and then it struck her . . . Ross was awake.

That realization hit just as her orgasm did, or perhaps the joy that washed over her at the realization helped push her over the edge. Whichever the case, all of it together had Annabel sitting up sharply in bed, screaming his name in a voice that sound racked more with pain than the pleasure she was experiencing.

Fortunately, her convulsive pleasure also had her unable to keep from squeezing her thighs on either side of Ross's head, covering his ears and preventing his eardrums being shattered by the shriek. By the time Ross eased her thighs apart to free himself and then sat up on his knees between her legs, thumping could be heard from outside the bedroom door. It sounded like a stampede of horses.

Annabel didn't bother to turn her gaze from Ross. She didn't care what the sound was, she was just too happy to see her husband awake and well. Chest still heaving, and body still pulsing from her violent release, Annabel opened her mouth to say that, but what came out was, "I love you."

Ross's eyes widened, and then his head shot around to the door as it burst open and what seemed like the whole castle tried to cram their way into the chamber at once. Gilly and Marach were in the lead, uncles Eoghann, Seonag and Fingal right behind them with at least two dozen servants and warriors at their back that she could see, and every single face held a fear and dismay that she didn't understand, until Father Gibson's voice rang out.

"What has happened? Is your laird dead? Is Lady MacKay—my lady?" the holy man ended uncertainly as he reached the front of the crowd and took in the tableau.

Suddenly free of the shock that had held her in place, Annabel glanced around wildly for the linens and furs that were not there, and then simply threw herself off the far side of the bed to use it as cover.

"Lady MacKay? Lord MacKay? 'Tis Sunday. Surely you were not . . ." Father Gibson sounded injured and even a little bewildered at such betrayal. Annabel was not absolutely positive, but suspected that what Ross had been doing was probably right up there with the original sin in the church's eyes. They did lecture on about carnal acts being meant only to procreate and certainly Ross couldn't plant his seed through his tongue.

Would that he could, Annabel thought wryly and then closed her eyes on a sigh. Coward that she was she also stayed right where she was rather than face the priest. Ross did not make a peep either, though that may have been because he didn't get the chance. Uncle Eoghann was pretty quick to say, "Well, surely ye see that Ross is on his knees, do ye no', Father? The man was obviously praying. No doubt he was giving thanks for being alive."

"Aye, and who would no' do that with a wife as sweet as Annabel?" Fingal asked wryly. "Praise the lord, if I had a wife like Annabel, I'd be praying meself at the moment. In thanks," he added, but Annabel could hear the devilment in the man's voice and caught the double meaning when he said praying.

Wicked old man, she thought.

"But Lady MacKay was—*She* was not praying," Father Gibson said firmly. "And that scream. Nay. This was—"

"My wife was asleep until the moment before she screamed," Ross interrupted. "'Tis why she did not leap immediately from the bed when ye entered. I'm sure she would ha'e recovered from her shock at this intrusion more quickly had she been awake more than the moment it took ye all to charge up here."

Hearing movement, Annabel glanced around to see him getting off the bed.

"Now, if ye're all done gawking, I'd appreciate it did ye leave our bedchamber."

"But she screamed," Father Gibson said with suspicion. " 'Tis why we came up here. We feared you had died."

"Obviously she screamed in shock when she woke up to find him awake and well," Uncle Eoghann said, taking the preist's arm and turning him toward the door.

"Aye, and what we mistook for a cry of mourning at finding him dead was actually rapture," Fingal added. "Rapture that he yet lived, I mean."

The wicked old man was going to get them a lifetime of penance did he not stop helping, Annabel thought with dismay.

"I suppose that could be the case." Father Gibson did not sound at all sure that was the case, but it appeared he was willing to let it lie for now, because he allowed the two older men to usher him out of the room. However, Annabel had no doubt he would have some pointed questions for her the next time she went to confession. She decided then that confession could wait a while, and wondered if not confessing a sin for a decade or so was as bad as the sin that had taken place here this morning.

The click of the door closing drew her from these thoughts and Annabel turned to peer over the bed, relieved when she saw that they were alone once again. But then she noted that Ross still faced the door, his hand on it and head bowed slightly as if in deep thought. Or pain, she worried, and forgetting her nudity, stood to move around the bed toward him.

"Husband?" Annabel asked, pausing behind him. "Is your head paining you?"

Ross gave his head a shake and turned to face her, worry evident on his expression. "What happened?"

She stared at him uncertainly. He should know what had happened. He'd made the world shift for her this time with his attentions, and as he'd said, she'd only woken up just a moment before she'd screamed with her pleasure.

"Annabel," he said quietly. "I woke up in bed, but do no' recall how I got there. The last thing I remember is . . ." He paused and frowned, and then said slowly, "I talked to Fingal . . . I think I finished talking to him . . . but . . ." He shook his head.

"Oh," she breathed, beginning to understand. He didn't recall fetching her from Effie's, making love to her in Carney's barn, or the attack. He'd woken up, but without some of his memories. She had heard of that happening before. Sometimes the victim of such a loss regained their memory and sometimes not. But that was a small loss, for he was awake, she reminded herself.

"Come," Annabel said, quietly taking his hand to lead him to the bed. Seating him there, she asked, "How is your head? Does it hurt?"

"Nay. Should it?"

Annabel bit her lip. Her head had hurt when she'd woken up after getting knocked out. But she'd only slept hours. Ross had slept a day and a half, mayhap he'd slept through the pain.

"Annabel?" he prodded when she remained silent. When she focused on him he raised his eyebrows in question and said, "Tell me what happened."

Nodding, Annabel settled beside him on the edge of the bed and announced, "We were attacked. You were knocked out and have been asleep for a little more than two nights and a day."

"What?" Ross turned on her sharply.

Annabel nodded. "We have all been very worried and waiting for you to wake."

Ross considered that briefly and then said, "So when ye screamed, everyone came charging up here because . . . ?"

"Because they feared you had died, I would guess," she admitted solemnly.

"Damn," Ross muttered, and then said, "Tell me everything ye ken from the moment I left Fingal. I did leave Fingal's hut? We were no' attacked there, were we?"

"Aye, we left there, and nay that is not where we were attacked," Annabel assured him and then tried to decide where to start.

Chapter 14

"*W*IFE?"

"Aye?" Annabel glanced up at Ross as they paused at the top of the stairs. She had told him everything that he could not remember about the day he'd taken the blow to the head, not leaving out a single detail even to spare herself. It had been an experience. Ross had got angry all over again at the risks she'd taken in slipping away from her guards. But he'd given a startled laugh when she'd admitted to baring her breasts in a bid to lure him into a "non-bedding" to appease his anger. But the laugh had died quickly and his eyes had begun to glow as she described what had followed. That was where her narrative had fallen apart. Ross had interrupted her telling of the tale to kiss her and relive almost exactly what had happened that day in Carney's barn, but with the bed in place of the hay pile.

Annabel supposed she should have reminded him it was Sunday, but they had already broken that rule once. Besides, really, it had been worth whatever future penance they suffered for it.

Afterward, Annabel had picked up the tale again. He'd listened silently, but she suspected by the expressions that flashed across his face and the way he'd nodded occasionally that her telling had helped pull out some of his own memories.

They had cleaned up and dressed to head downstairs after that, and Annabel had found herself wishing she'd finished telling him about the attack before they'd made love. The mood now was too solemn for her liking, where he had been smiling and much lighter of spirit after their romp.

"Ye neglected to mention why me uncle and Fingal are here in the keep," Ross said, drawing her attention back to the trestle tables below.

She smiled wryly as she noted the two older men talking and laughing with Gilly and Marach at the table. Everyone was finished breaking their fast now and the four men sat alone, no doubt awaiting Ross's arrival, she thought and murmured, "Ah . . . well, you see we tried to get to the bottom of these attacks while you were sleeping. Gilly and Marach said that you had spoken to Fingal and planned to speak to your uncle Eoghann too. We had no idea what had come about from your talking to Fingal, so we decided we should speak to them ourselves, and Gilly went down to the village to ask them to come to the keep so we could speak to them."

"I see," he murmured, and then said, "And?"

Annabel shrugged helplessly. "And once here,

they would not leave. They seemed to think that as you were low and unable to keep me safe, it fell to them as family to ensure nothing befell me until you woke and could take over the task once more."

"Hmm." Ross turned his gaze back to the tableau below as he asked, "And what conclusion did ye come to after speaking to them?"

"They are not behind the attacks," she said with certainty. "They both respect your skills as a laird, and appreciate what you do for your people, and—"

"And?" he prompted when she stopped herself.

Annabel hesitated, but then said, "In truth, I do not think they have a mean bone between them. And while both claim to be useless with a sword, I suspect they would each take an arrow or sword blow for you . . . and mayhap even for me."

Ross studied her for a moment and then the beginnings of a smile curled one side of his mouth and he said, "Ye like them."

Annabel smiled wryly and nodded. "Aye. They are good-hearted men. A little wicked with their sense of humor," she added dryly, "but good men."

"I'm glad," was all he said, and then he took her hand and placed it on his arm to continue down the stairs.

"Ah, good, ye've finally dragged yerselves down to join us," Uncle Eoghann said when he spotted their approach. "What took ye so long? We were beginning to worry ye'd *both* fallen unconscious this time."

"Aye, lad, but we did no' want to check in case ye were prayin' again," Fingal added with a grin and then laughed and added, "Ah, aye, ye were too. I can tell by the pretty blush yer wife just donned."

Annabel grimaced, wishing she could control the telltale color, but since she couldn't she merely shook her head and settled at the table, hoping that if she did not respond he would let the matter go.

She should have known better, Annabel supposed as Fingal continued, "And on a Sunday too. Tsk tsk, yer a naughty little nun."

"Nun?" Ross echoed with confusion.

Annabel's eyes shot wide as she realized there was one thing she had yet to tell her husband.

"Belly? You never returned last night like you promised."

Two things, Annabel corrected herself, stiffening at that complaint from behind her. Turning, she watched Kate approach from the stairs in the borrowed pale yellow-and-white gown that hung so badly on her.

"Wife?" Ross said in question, drawing her attention again.

"Belly," Kate snapped the moment she turned away from her.

Sighing, Annabel rubbed her forehead and forced a smile for her husband. "I shall explain everything, I promise," she assured him, getting to her feet again before adding, "later."

Turning then, she moved the few feet to join her sister and said, "I am sorry, Kate. I did mean to come back. I intended only to take a short nap, but I guess Seonag forgot to wake me as promised. I slept clear through the night."

"Nay," Seonag announced, drawing Annabel's confused gaze as she approached from the general direction of the kitchens. Pausing next to them, she clarified, "I did no' forget. Ye did no' sleep but moments the first night fer watching over the laird. Ye needed yer sleep last night, so I did no' wake ye as ye asked."

"Oh," Annabel said faintly, unsure what to do with that. The woman had been looking out for her well-being. Besides, Annabel wasn't that sorry that she'd missed revisiting with her sister. The first visit had rather put her off. And really, while she'd wanted to be awake for Ross when he first opened his eyes, the way it had turned out . . . well, she could hardly be sorry for the way he'd woken her instead.

Although she could have done without the whole castle bursting in on them, Annabel thought. And the man hadn't said a word about her stupidly babbling that she loved him either. Not that she wanted him to say anything, Annabel assured herself. She wasn't even sure where those words had come from. Certainly she liked her husband, and enjoyed his company and his bedchamber skills. And yes, she respected him. He was a good leader to his people and—

"Belly."

The snapped word drew Annabel from her thoughts to peer at her sister with a bit of irritation. She absolutely hated that nickname, but all she said was, "Aye?"

"You cannot allow such insolence," Kate said grimly. "I wanted to talk to you last night and instead sat about bored and unhappy. She ruined everything by not waking you. Punish the old crone."

Annabel's eyes widened at the demand, and then narrowed. While Seonag's not waking her had not upset her, her sister's words did. Somehow the girl seemed to just get under her skin. She had never met anyone so . . . so . . . *spoiled*.

"I am not punishing her," she finally said, her voice quiet but firm. "And her name is Seonag. Please call her that in future."

Kate's face screwed up with rage at the mild setdown, so it was a relief for Annabel to turn away from her and glance to the table when Ross said, "Wife?"

At least it was until she noted his expression. He did not look happy as he asked, "Who is this woman?"

"Oh!" Kate gasped, and her anger with Annabel apparently forgotten, she pushed past her to rush to Ross. Once she'd reached where he sat on the bench, she gave a sort of exaggerated shiver and gushed, "You must be Ross. It is such a pleasure to meet you *at last*."

Annabel stilled, her eyes narrowing on her sister, but Ross merely arched an eyebrow as he looked Kate over and then asked, "Who are ye? Another new embroiderer?"

Kate's head went back as if he had slapped her, but she recovered quickly and released a tinkling laugh as she said, "Oh, goodness no. Although, in this gown you could be forgiven for confusing me with a new servant." She peered down and held it out to the sides, emphasizing how large it was and somehow making the neckline drop indecently low at the same time. " 'Tis borrowed of course. From Annabel," she added in case he hadn't realized. "But then she is far larger than me. I fancy you could fit two of me in here."

She laughed away at that and glanced over her shoulder as if expecting Annabel to join in laughing at the joke. She didn't.

"No' to worry, lass," Uncle Eoghann said, mildly drawing Kate's attention back to the table. "Ross has the best cook in the highlands working fer him here. He'll soon feed ye up and ha'e ye looking less sickly."

Kate stiffened briefly, but otherwise managed to ignore the comment. Annabel, however, felt better for it and cast the man a grateful smile.

"I still do no' ken who ye are," Ross pointed out quietly.

"What?" Kate asked with surprise. "I should think you could guess by now. Or did Annabel not tell you of my arrival?" Kate asked, sounding amazed, and then she shook her head and settled on the bench next to him, saying, "She probably just worried you would be disappointed at having her foisted on you in my place." Leaning toward him, she ended in a throaty voice, "I am your Kathryn."

"*My* Kathryn?" Ross asked, eyebrows arched.

Reaching out to caress his arm, she said huskily, "Well, I was always meant to be yours."

And apparently had decided she was willing to be his now that her grand romance with the stable master's son had failed so miserably, Annabel thought unhappily, her hands clenching at her sides as she watched the couple worriedly.

"She's yer lady wife's sister, Kate," Fingal announced abruptly, and then, just to be helpful, Annabel was sure, added, "Ye ken . . . the lass who kindly ran off to toss up her skirts with the stable master's son so ye were able to marry our sweet Annabel in her place."

While Kate had managed to ignore Eoghann's earlier comment, this one she couldn't. Turning her head sharply, she stared daggers at Fingal. Honestly, Annabel was surprised not to see blades sticking out of his eyes. Fingal, however, grinned back at her like the cat who ate the cream, and said, "We're forever grateful fer that, lass. Our Annabel is a true lady."

"You nasty old bas—" Kate began, and that was when Annabel stepped forward and caught her sister's arm to urge her off the bench. Kate bit off the rest of what she'd been about to say and turned furiously on Annabel instead. "What are you doing? I am not done here, Belly."

"Aye, you are," Annabel assured her solemnly and dragged her toward the stairs.

She got her halfway there before Kate tugged her arm furiously free and stamped her foot. "I will not be manhandled. I am going to break my fast as I planned."

She whirled away to start back toward the tables. Annabel did not give chase or grab her back, she simply barked, "Kathryn Jane Withram!"

Kate paused and turned reluctantly back, her expression petulant. "What?"

"This is *my* home," Annabel said firmly. "And *I* am lady here. I suggest you take yourself up to your room now, else I shall order the men to drag you there."

Gilly and Marach rose as one at those words, apparently more than happy to do it.

Kate's eyes narrowed and her mouth tightened, but then she shrugged and moved back toward her. "Very well."

Annabel waited until she had passed, offered her husband an apologetic smile and then followed her sister upstairs. Both of them were silent as they mounted the stairs, but the moment they were in the bedchamber and the door was closed, Kate rounded on her.

"How could you let that man speak to me like that? You reprimanded *me* for unintentionally insulting a servant, and then acted as if I was the one in the wrong when that man as good as called me a whore. Me, a lady, and your *sister*." Turning then, she threw herself on the bed and burst into sobs.

Annabel stood by the door, shifting her feet uncertainly and rather confused. She'd followed Kate up here intending to reprimand her again, and more firmly for her behavior below, but instead now felt like the one in the wrong. How had that happened? And was she in the wrong? Fingal hadn't called her a whore . . . exactly. Truthfully, he'd just bluntly stated what Kate had done, though she supposed the way he'd said it could have been more . . . er . . . or well less . . . er . . .

"Oh bullocks," Annabel muttered and then walked to the bed and settled on the side of it to stare at her sobbing sister uncertainly. Finally, she said, "I apologize if Fingal's words offended you. He could have been more diplomatic in his phrasing."

"They did offend me," Kate snapped, crying harder.

"Aye, well, perhaps I should have said something," Annabel muttered. But recalling how Kate had leaned up against Ross, petting his arm, talking all husky, and being all skinny and sexy, she added, "I suppose I was just set aback by the way you were flirting with my husband."

"Flirting?" Kate gasped, rising up and whirling to eye her with outrage. "I was not flirting with him. I would never do that. I am the one who did not want him in the first place. That is why he is your husband. Besides, my heart is broken right now. Grant is all I can think about."

"But you were leaning into him, and—"

"I was being polite to my sister's husband," she said staunchly. "If you thought it was anything else, then perhaps it is because you feel ugly and jealous of me. You always did, Belly."

Annabel blinked in amazement at that. She'd been seven when she was sent to the abbey, too young to know enough to be jealous of anything. And as she recalled, she'd adored her sister. She'd followed her around like a mooning calf, looking up to her and—hell, she'd wept every night in bed for a year after leaving Waverly because Kate wasn't there to laugh and talk with.

Nay, she hadn't been jealous of her then. She might be now though, Annabel admitted fairly. All right, aye, she was. She wished she were as pretty as her sister, wished she'd been trained to be a proper wife to Ross as Kate had no doubt been. Annabel never would have tossed him aside for the stable master's son . . . who she was sure was a lovely man, but, really, he could not be as wonderful as Ross, she thought.

Sitting there, she wondered if perhaps that jealousy had not caused her to read more into Kate's behavior than had really been there. Or perhaps the only way Kate knew how to interact with men was in a flirty manner so didn't see it as flirty. The way she'd acted with Ross may even be how all women acted around men, at least those women who had not been raised in an abbey where the only man in sight was a quaking old priest.

"All right," Annabel said finally. "Perhaps I misread your intentions with Ross."

"Aye, you did," Kate assured her.

"Well, I shall try not to allow my feelings about my lack as a woman and wife affect my judgment in future," she said quietly.

"Good." Kate gave a sharp nod as if to say that was as it should be.

"But in return," Annabel continued, bringing a wary expression to Kate's face, "I would appreciate it if you did not call me 'Belly.'"

"But that's your name," she protested.

"Nay, my name is Annabel."

"But I always called you 'Annabelly' or 'Belly.'"

"And I always hated it," Annabel informed her quietly.

"Nay, you did not," Kate said at once.

"Aye, Kate, I did," Annabel assured her.

"Nay. You liked it," Kate insisted.

"I never liked it, Kate," she said impatiently, finding it ridiculous to have to argue the point. She knew what she liked and did not like. "I hated it from the day you first started using it, and I told you that at the time and you just laughed and danced around me in a circle singing, 'Annabelly has a fat belly. Annabelly has a fat belly.'"

"Oh, God, I did, did I not?" she said with horror. "I am an awful sister!" On that note she threw herself back down on the bed and began to weep copiously again.

Annabel rubbed her forehead with her fingers, wondering how her requesting that Kate not call her what was ultimately a rather offensive name ended with a situation where she felt she had to comfort the girl. At least some part of her was urging her to comfort Kate. Another much larger part of Annabel simply didn't want to.

Frankly, at that moment she didn't even want to deal with her. She wanted to pack her up in a wagon and send her home to their parents and let them deal with the daughter they had raised into the woman she'd become. Unfortunately, her mother had made it clear that Kate was no longer welcome at Waverly. But did that mean that she was stuck with her? She had not even seen her in fourteen years. Really, they were strangers.

But she was her sister, her conscience reminded her, and she had been raised better than that. She had been taught charity and service and suffering and perhaps Kate was just her cross to bear.

And reasoning like that was why Annabel had always disliked life at the abbey. Charity was fine, and service to God, but the suffering bit? She wasn't so sure about. Should you give charity to the point that you hurt yourself? Were you expected to serve with complete and utter self-lessness, even when the people you were serving were selfish as hell? And was she really expected to spend her life suffering in misery so that others were happy? Because she was pretty sure that taking care of Kate was going to be a thankless, miserable experience that made her life a living hell. But by the same token, she couldn't just put her out; Annabel's conscience wouldn't allow that. So it looked like she was stuck with Kate . . . unless she could think of something else to do with her.

Perhaps her parents would take Kate in after all, Annabel thought hopefully. Perhaps their anger had cooled now that there was no more worry about the marriage contract. Maybe they would allow her to return. They could always arrange for her to marry someone else, couldn't they? Kate was their daughter; surely they couldn't just cut her out of their hearts that easily. Of couse they hadn't seemed to care much for Annabel's well-being, but then she was as much a stranger to them as she now found Kate to be to her. But Kate had grown up at Waverly—surely they had some affection for her?

"Are you just going to let me lay here crying?" Kate asked, sitting up to scowl at her. "Are you not going to comfort me?"

Annabel stared at her, wondering why Kate's demanding comfort just made her want even less to offer it.

"I am going to write a letter to Mother," Annabel said, standing up and heading for the door.

"What?" Kate gasped with horror. "Nay!"

Annabel didn't realize she'd rushed after her until she caught her arm as she reached the door, and swung her back around. "Nay. You cannot do that. It would be humiliating and—"

"Kate," Annabel interrupted wearily. "I know this whole thing is humiliating for you. You ignored the contracted marriage Father arranged for you, went against our parents and ran away for love only to have it fail miserably. 'Tis unfortunate, but that is the situation. However, Mother and Father may be able to yet save the situation. They may be able to arrange a marriage with some nice man willing to overlook your transgression."

"Oh, aye," Kate sneered. "You would like that, would you not. Me having to marry some fat doddering old fool and let him touch me. Never!" she snapped. "Besides, I am already married."

"You are?" Annabel asked with a frown.

"Aye. We handfasted before we ever indulged in the bedding. In fact, we handfasted weeks before we ran away," she said triumphantly. "So you see, I cannot be married off to someone else, I already have a husband."

Annabel frowned. She had no idea what handfasting was. She'd never heard of it and supposed the abbess and Father hadn't thought it important for nuns to know about. But Kate seemed to think it meant she was married . . . which was something of a wrinkle, since this husband she had handfasted with now appeared to want nothing to do with her.

"Promise me you will not write Mother and Father," Kate said now.

Annabel hesitated. If she didn't write their parents, she was definitely stuck with her sister.

At least, she was if Ross allowed it and at that moment she didn't know which she hoped for more: that he would be furious and insist Kate be packed off to Waverly, or that he would be understanding and let her stay.

It would be easier in one way if he was furious and sent Kate away. At least she would not have to suffer guilt at sending her away herself. However, she did dislike it when Ross was angry with her and didn't want him to be. But if he let Kate stay, Annabel would be stuck with her, especially if she could not write her mother.

"I will have to think about this . . . and talk to Ross," she added, turning to the door.

"Nay," Kate cried, clawing at her arm. "You have to promise. I will not have you writing them."

"I promise I will tell you before I send a letter if I do, but that is the best I can offer at the moment," Annabel said firmly, tugging her arm free and slipping out of the room before Kate could grab her again. Pulling the door closed, she hurried up the hall to her own chamber, sure with every step she took that Kate would give chase. When she reached the master bedchamber and managed to slip inside unaccosted, Annabel leaned against the door with relief and closed her eyes for a moment.

Her eyes popped open a heartbeat later at a shuffling sound though, and Annabel stared with dismay when she spotted her husband turning from the window to face her. Damn, she thought wearily, it seemed she would now be giving those explanations she'd promised Ross.

Ah well, Annabel thought, pushing herself

away from the door. Better to get it done. At least then she would not have to worry about how he would react to the news that she was an untrained ex-oblate, as well as the presence of her sister in their home.

ROSS WATCHED ANNABEL MOVE AWAY FROM THE door and walk sedately to the chairs by the fire. When she settled in one and glanced to him expectantly, he left his position by the window to join her. He'd barely set his behind in the chair before she blurted her explanations.

"I was sent away to the abbey at seven and raised there. I was trained to take the veil. I illuminated texts, and worked in the stables until the morning my mother arrived to collect me. I had not yet taken the veil so she took me from the abbey to Waverly, where I was married to you. I have no training to run a castle and a passel of servants. I am doing the best I can, but will no doubt make mistakes and please say something for I shall continue to babble until you do and I—"

"Breathe," Ross interrupted quietly.

Annabel paused and stared down at her hands in her lap as she took a deep breath.

Ross considered her silently, her words slipping through his mind. Actually, learning this explained some things. Her discomfort around his men at first, something she still suffered when in the presence of men she hadn't met previously. Her patient acceptance of his sometimes less than considerate behavior, like—

Pausing, he frowned and asked, "If ye lived in the abbey since ye were a child, yer wardrobe—"

"I had none," Annabel interrupted him to confess. "I was not given a chance to pack when my mother collected me from the abbey, so I had only the gown I was wearing and the one they altered to fit me for the wedding and then wore here. You did me no disservice by not giving me time to pack. There was nothing to pack."

Ross nodded at this news. It made him feel a little better. He'd felt guilty on several occasions about that business. Every time he'd found his wife and Seonag sewing diligently away, for instance, and the day Giorsal had visited with her husband and the women had been forced to remain upstairs sewing because Annabel had nothing to wear. It eased his conscience somewhat to know he wasn't entirely at fault for that. He was glad.

"Now explain how yer sister came to be residin' in the bedchamber next to ours," he said and Annabel frowned.

"That is it?" she asked uncertainly. "You are not going to chastise me for your not being told about my lack of training and experience? You are not going to demand the marriage be annulled because you were tricked into marrying someone so inept?"

Ross raised his eyebrows with surprise and then shrugged. "Yer a smart lass, wife. Ye'll learn."

Annabel seemed somewhat stunned by his response and sat back for a moment to simply stare at him as if seeing him for the first time. He let her get away with that for a moment and then reminded her, "Yer sister?"

"Oh," Annabel let her breath out on a weary

sigh. "She just showed up here yesterday while you were sleeping. Apparently, Grant, her stable boy, was not prepared for her to be so . . . er . . ."

"Spoiled?" he suggested dryly.

"Aye, she is spoiled," Annabel admitted with an apologetic grimace.

"And demanding."

"Aye, that too," she agreed unhappily.

"And a bitch."

Annabel gasped at the word, but Ross shrugged.

" 'Tis no use pretending she is no' a bitch. She ordered ye to punish Seonag, and then was doin' her damndest to hurt ye below with her comments about the gown being so big and whatnot."

"I do not think she meant to hurt me exactly," Annabel said without much conviction. "To her it is just fact that she is prettier than me . . . and slimmer."

Ross frowned at her disheartened tone of voice and the way she had slumped in her seat as if trying to make herself look smaller. Sitting forward in his own, he said, "First o' all, she is no' prettier than ye. Her eyes are a mud brown, not the lovely teal blue o' yers. Her hair is a nice gold color, but 'tis lank and just lays on her head like straw, while yers is the color o' midnight and flows in waves from yer head to frame yer lovely face beautifully. And her lips are smaller, thin even, not like yers, which are large and luscious enough to give a man ideas that turn his staff into a sword in search o' a sheath."

Her eyes widened incredulously at this and Ross shook his head.

"Wife, ye should ken by now that I find ye

beautiful, and love yer body. I bed ye at every opportunity."

Annabel flushed at this.

Satisfied that he had made it clear that she had nothing to fear when it came to her looks, Ross sat back and added, " 'Sides, even if she had been fortunate enough to have been born more attractive than ye physically, she's no' a nice person, and that combined with her acting like a light-skirt would counter it quickly enough."

"Light-skirt?" Annabel echoed, feeling as if she should defend her sister . . . whether she wanted to or not. "That seems a bit harsh, husband. She simply fell in love with the wrong man and ran off rather than marry the one she was supposed to."

Ross's eyebrows rose. "So ye saw nothing wrong with the way she was sidling up to me, jiggling her bosoms in me face, and pawing me body right there in front of everyone. And me being yer husband, too." He shook his head with disgust at the memory.

"Ah." Annabel frowned. "So ladies do not act like that?"

Ross felt his eyebrows fly up his forehead, but then asked with concern, "Surely ye jest?"

Annabel bit her lip, but admitted, "Kate insisted she was not flirting with you, that she was just being nice because you were my husband, and that I must be jealous. So I started wondering . . ." She hesitated and then shrugged helplessly and pointed out, "I grew up in an abbey, husband. I do not know what is appropriate behavior outside the abbey walls. Perhaps her flirty attentions were how women interact with men."

"Flirty attentions?" he echoed with amazement. "Is that what ye call her sliding her hand up under me plaid trying to measure me manhood?"

"What?" she gasped with some amazement of her own.

Ross nodded grimly. He'd nearly plowed his fist into the chit's head when she'd tried that. Fortunately, Fingal had distracted her with his less than complimentary comments and then Annabel had dragged the lass off.

"I only saw her rub your arm," she muttered with displeasure and he recalled she had been behind the girl and several feet away. He had no doubt she hadn't been aware of what Kate was doing under cover of the table. That was a relief, for he'd wondered why the devil she wasn't smacking the girl silly herself.

"What are yer plans fer her?" Ross asked finally. Much as he disliked Kate, she was Annabel's sister and if she wished her to stay with them for a while, he would try to be forbearing. Although, frankly he wanted to toss the sneaky wench out of his home and never let her return. Not because she'd tried to feel him up at the table—that had disgusted him—but the thing that had really infuriated him was the way she treated Annabel. She had hurt her several times in just a matter of moments below and he wouldn't have that. No one was going to hurt Annabel . . . and if Kate called Annabel 'Belly' one more time—

"I am going to write to Mother and Father," Annabel announced, interrupting his thoughts and Ross felt his heart sink. They would be stuck with her for a bit then as the letter went south to England, and then longer still as the response traveled back. Damn, he'd be lucky not to kill the woman ere she left.

Chapter 15

ANNABEL WOKE SLOWLY, ROUSED BY THE donjon blowing his bugle. Shifting sleepily, she rolled toward Ross to see if the sound had awakened him, only to find the bed beside her was empty. He'd left early . . . again. Ross had been up and out of the keep well before the morning bugle every day for the last week. The man worked far too hard.

A knock sounded at the door, and Annabel sighed and sat up, tugging the linens and furs to her chin as she called, "Come in."

It was no great surprise when Seonag bustled in, a ewer of warm water in one hand and soap and linen in the other.

"Is the laird gone already again?" Seonag commented dryly as she carried the ewer to the small table against the outer wall where Annabel performed her morning ablutions.

"Aye," she murmured, pushing the linens and furs aside to sit up on the side of the bed as the woman poured the steaming water into the waiting basin. "He left early to ride to MacDonald. There was something he wished to discuss with Giorsal and Bean."

"Ye mean he left early to get out o' the keep ere yer sister goes down to break her fast," Seonag said dryly.

"That too," Annabel murmured unhappily. She understood his desire to avoid Kate. She was most unpleasant to be around now and had been since Annabel had confronted her with what Ross had told her about her slipping her hand up under his plaid. It had been obvious from Kate's expression that she hadn't expected him to tell. Annabel supposed her sister had thought herself so irresistible that he'd keep it to himself and simply arrange some secret assignation with her. Annabel was so very glad he hadn't.

When first confronted, Kate had tried to claim she was just testing Ross, trying to ensure that he would be a faithful husband and could not be lured into straying by a beautiful face. But when Annabel hadn't fallen for that, she'd got nasty . . . with everyone. Her one goal now appeared to be to make everyone's life as miserable as she possibly could.

Annabel couldn't blame Ross for wanting to avoid that. But she did miss cuddling up to him in the morning before they started their day, and chatting with him at the table.

"M'lady?"

Annabel glanced to Seonag in question. The maid had finished filling her basin and had moved to the chest that held all the gowns they'd mended. They'd finished the very last one the afternoon before, and both of them had been greatly relieved to be free of the chore. Now, Seonag was staring down into the open chest with confusion.

"What is it, Seonag?" Annabel asked with a frown.

"Where did ye move yer gowns to?"

Annabel raised her eyebrows in surprise at the question. "Nowhere. They should be there."

"Well, they aren't," the woman assured her, vexation covering her face.

Annabel hurried to her side to peer into the empty chest. Bewilderment was her first reaction. "But they were all there before sup last night when I put the cream-colored gown away."

"Well they're no' there now," Seonag pointed out grimly.

"Aye. I can see that," Annabel murmured, rubbing her forehead. "I just do not see where they could have gone, or who would have moved th—" Pausing abruptly, she glanced to Seonag and the two women said together, "Kate."

Annabel cursed and headed for the door, fury giving her feet wings and making her ignore Seonag's squawked, "Wait!"

She threw the bedchamber door open with a crash and hurried to the next door along the hall, reaching it just as Seonag caught up with her and threw a linen around her shoulders. It was only then Annabel realized she'd charged out of her room naked. Normally, she would have been embarrassed. In that moment, however, she didn't care. She merely drew the linen around her, caught it under her chin with one hand, and threw Kate's bedchamber door open with the other.

"Why sister, do you not look fetching," Kate said with a mean laugh.

Annabel tore her gaze from the bed where she'd instinctively first looked, and glanced to the chair by the fire where her sister's voice had come from. Kate was ensconced there, a rainbow of cloth scraps littering the floor around the chair as she sliced away at Annabel's dark blue gown.

"Actually, I am glad you are here," Kate continued idly. "I could use some help sewing these now I have done all the hard work and cut them down to my size."

Annabel simply stared at her for a moment, and then her gaze shifted to the cloth on the ground and she choked out, "My gowns."

"What?" Kate asked, and then gave a laugh. "Nay, of course not. I got these out of that chest in your room. 'Twas obvious they were old secondhand rags, so I knew you would not mind me cutting them down for myself. I was growing ever so weary of the two you loaned me to wear."

Annabel clenched her fists and turned a fury-filled gaze on her sister. She wanted to kill her in that moment. She wanted to drag her out of that chair by her hair and wring her scrawny little neck and—

" 'Tis all right," Seonag said quickly, scurrying forward to begin collecting the scraps of cloth off the floor. "We can sew these back into the gowns and fix them. No one will ken they were ever cut apart. I can—"

"Oh, those are not the parts I cut off," Kate said. "Those are what is left to make my dresses out of. I threw the extra panels in the fire as I cut each one off. Although," she added pensively, "I suppose that was silly. I could have made at least one other gown from the scraps I removed from each gown since they were so big. Oh well." She shrugged, and then raised her eyebrows. "Are you not going to sit down and help me?"

"Help you?" Annabel hissed with disbelief.

"Aye. After all 'tis apparently your fault the cloth merchant will not come up to the castle. Otherwise I could have just had you buy new cloth for me to make my wardrobe from, rather than having to make do with cast-off cloth from a dead woman's gowns."

"To make your wardrobe from?" Annabel asked, amazed by her gall.

"Well, you do not expect me to have to make do with just one or two gowns, do you?" she asked as if the answer should be obviously no.

"I do not expect to outfit you with a wardrobe at all," Annabel growled, her temper overflowing . . . a temper she had never realized she even had. If she weren't so furious, Annabel would have been shocked by the rage racing through her as she stalked toward her sister.

"Well, of course you should expect to make me a wardrobe. You are my sister and this is my home now. I expect—"

"This is *not* your home. You are a *guest* here, Kate," Annabel interrupted furiously. "And a very unpleasant one at that. Perhaps had you tried to act like a proper sister, I would welcome you here, but as it stands, I do not wish to even see you, let alone house and clothe you." Her mouth tightened and she added grimly, "I have been waiting to hear back from Mother on her willingness to take you in, howbeit I am not willing to wait any longer, and I do not care if she wants to take you in. She shall have to. As soon as Ross returns I am going to ask him to arrange for your return to Waverly. Your lady mother is the one who raised you to be such a selfish, spoiled, spiteful brat, and she can now live with what she has created. I am done."

Kate's eyes widened and then her face crumpled. "How can you say that to me after everything I have suffered!" she said through a sudden storm of tears.

"Because it is true," Annabel answered coldly, unmoved this time by her tears. "You have driven my husband from his home, terrorized the servants and done nothing but bedevil me, and now, *now* you have gone and cut up every gown I own but one."

"Every gown you own?" Kate asked with amazement and immediately shook her head. "Nay. These were secondhand gowns—"

"In *my* chest in *my* bedchamber," Annabel interrupted, growing furious all over again. "You had no business in there! And pray, do not try to tell me you did not know that while they were secondhand gowns, they were all I had to wear."

"Fine, I knew they were your gowns," Kate snapped. "But I only destroyed them so that your husband would be forced to buy you new material for a proper wardrobe as befits a lady."

"Oh, please," Annabel said dryly. "You are the most selfish creature in Scotland and England combined. 'Tis more believable that you did it to ensure I would buy new cloth and *you* could get new material for a proper wardrobe of your own. Besides, you already said the merchant will not come here so you know that is not—" Annabel stopped abruptly, her head coming up. "The cloth merchant will not come here? Why would the cloth merchant not come here?"

She turned to Seonag in question, but Kate answered.

"Because your dog attacked the spice merchant, and—"

"Jasper did not attack the merchant," Annabel snapped in the dog's defense.

"I am just telling you what I was told," Kate said with a shrug. "Whatever the case, apparently the merchant stormed out of here yesterday morning. He was ranting about being dumped in a room and left to starve, and he would see you sorry for it. He was going to stay at the inn in the village until his wound healed, and then he would tell all the other merchants not to come here if they cared for their hide."

Annabel stared at Kate, absently noting what she was sure was glee in her sister's eyes as she revealed this information. It was as if she was enjoying her misfortune. But Annabel couldn't be bothered worrying about that now. Her mind was taken up with the enormity of what she'd just learned. No more spice, no more cloth, no more trinkets or pots.

Most of what they needed to survive could be produced here at MacKay. They would not go hungry. What they counted on merchants for were the items that they couldn't provide or make for themselves, like silks and spices from Asia, fur from Russia, salt and wine from France, cloth and tapestries from Flanders, and so on. They were luxuries really, not necessary really, but once used to those luxuries . . . Annabel couldn't imagine months or years without being able to buy spices to aid Angus in his efforts. This was horrible.

She turned to Seonag with dismay. "Is this true?"

Seonag looked at a loss for a minute and then shook her head and admitted unhappily. "I'm sorry m'lady. I . . ." She let her breath out on a sigh and admitted, "After the last attack and your sister's arrival I—" She grimaced and confessed, "I just plain forgot all about the man."

Kate made a snorting sound and arched her eyebrows at Annabel as if to say, Will you let her get away with this? Annabel ignored her. She was going to let Seonag get away with it, because she too had forgotten about the man. How could she punish Seonag for something she too had done?

Annabel turned abruptly and swept from the room, uncaring that the linen she wore billowed out around her like a cape. Her mind was racing. What was she to do? She could not allow MacKay to be banned by the merchants. Dear God, Ross would be so disappointed in her.

"I'll help ye kill her," Seonag announced, following her into the master bedchamber and closing the door.

The words made her pause and blink. It actually took Annabel a moment to understand who the maid was talking about, which was surprising since moments ago she would have enjoyed choking the life out of her trying older sister. Truly, Kate had unintentionally given Annabel everything she hadn't known she desired with that one act of running off with her lover. Yet now she seemed bent on ruining and destroying everything Annabel had gained.

However, the news about the merchant had driven her worries about Kate from her mind. The truth was, she only had to put up with her sister until she grew tired of taking her nonsense and her conscience could withstand kicking her out and sending her elsewhere. Had Kate even tried a bit to be a good person, just a bit, if she were just a little less selfish, a little less unpleasant . . . Well, Annabel would have put up with her and given her a home for life. But Kate was a stranger who seemed to love to touch and rub up on her husband, abuse the servants and torment Annabel. The voice of her conscience was quickly growing faint in her ears. To the point where choking the life out of her sister with her bare hands and being dragged to hell by the abbess was beginning to look attractive.

"We'll tell everyone her stable boy returned for her and then bury the body in Angus's herb garden," Seonag continued, and then pursed her lips and said, "He may even help with the task. She has complained and insulted his cooking so much he is ready to take a cleaver to her anyway—"

"Seonag," Annabel said wearily. "Kate is the least of our worries right now."

The maid goggled at her. "Are ye mad? She ruined yer gowns, is driving the laird out of his marriage bed, and—"

"Aye, but Kate will be gone as soon as our mother agrees to take her in. But—"

"Well and surely she's takin' her time about that," Seonag interrupted with disgust. "She probably no more wants her than we do and will no' answer at all rather than say so."

Annabel felt her heart lurch at the suggestion, but simply said, "The point is that Kate is a temporary problem, whereas do we lose the merchants, they could be gone for years, even decades. And then when they do return they will charge even more exorbitant prices than they already do because they will know we are desperate."

"Aye, but what if yer mother does no' agree to take Kate?" Seonag asked, apparently more concerned with that than anything else.

Annabel rubbed her forehead with frustration and then shook her head, and teased, "Well, then you can offer to help kill her again and then I may accept."

"Right." Seonag relaxed, a good deal of her anger slipping away. Expression solemn, she then asked, "What shall we do about the merchant?"

"I am going to have to go down to the inn and bribe him," Annabel said grimly.

"Bribe him with what?" Seonag asked with concern.

"What does a merchant like best?" she asked dryly, and answered, "Coin."

Seonag frowned. "Will the laird allow it?"

"My husband gave me the chatelaine keys and free rein to do as I saw fit," Annabel murmured, remembering when he'd done it, and thanking God he had. "He also gave me the coins that were part of my dower and said to use it to buy a new wardrobe. And he gave me the freedom to see to Kate as I saw fit. I shall use part of it to bribe the merchant if necessary."

Seonag nodded, relaxing a bit, but not completely, and then she said thoughtfully, "Then all we need worry about is getting ye past Gilly and Marach and out of the castle so ye can get down to the village. They're still under orders no' to let ye leave the keep."

"Aye," Annabel said with a grimace. The men had been following her about again ever since Ross had regained consciousness. Not that they'd not followed her about while he was unconscious, but then she'd at least been able to order them to go away when they became too much of a nuisance. Now, they were her shadow.

"I can help you with that," Kate announced and both women turned to peer at the girl now standing in the open bedchamber door.

Annabel nearly snapped at her for entering without knocking, but instead merely scowled and said, "I am surprised Gilly and Marach let you enter without knocking. Fine guards they are."

"They are not out in the hall," Kate said, pushing the door closed.

Annabel's eyebrows rose at this news. "I wonder why. They are always waiting in the hall in the morning."

"Ah . . . well," Seonag said, wincing slightly. "They were on their way up here when ye headed to yer sister's room. But they got one glimpse o' ye rushing naked up the hall, turned on their heels and returned to the trestle tables below." She tilted her head, considering briefly, and then said, "I'm thinking the laird may ha'e had a talk with them about what he did and did no' want them doing after that business when they thought they should accompany ye in here fer yer bath."

Annabel supposed that was possible, but simply turned to Kate in question, willing to listen, but still angry enough that she wasn't expecting much from the girl.

"First off, I should like to say I am sorry, Annabel."

That made Annabel's eyebrows rise. Not the words so much as the solemn tone to Kate's voice. She was not whining or trying on tears; she sounded serious and sincere as she continued, "I am afraid I have been behaving badly out of jealousy."

"Jealousy of what?" Annabel asked with surprise.

Kate rolled her eyes at the question. "What do you think, Bel—" She cut herself off before finishing the old nickname, which had to be a first. Sighing, she took a deep breath and said, "I followed my heart and ran off with Grant, and it all fell apart. I did not think it through, obviously. I thought—" She sighed. "It doesn't matter what I thought. The end result is I am now a ruined woman who ran off with someone who was beneath her socially, and then was tossed aside like so much waste. I am homeless, husbandless, dependant on your charity and a laughingstock or fool to most people."

Kate paused briefly, perhaps hoping Annabel would assure her that wasn't true, but Annabel held her tongue and waited to hear what else she had to say.

"And in the meantime, you married the man I was supposed to and have the life I would have had if I hadn't been so foolish. You who have no training at running a castle, are running this one. You who do not have a clue how to rule servants, are doing it and in such a manner that those servants adore you. You have a home, wealth, and a husband and people who love you." Her mouth tightened and she shook her head. "You have everything I wanted, and the worst part about it is that you only have it because I foolishly threw it all away."

She shook her head. "I am angry and have been acting badly because of it," she admitted. "But I have been taking it out on you when the truth is I am angry with myself for my own foolishness." Kate paused, took another deep breath and said, "I am terribly sorry for it and hope someday you can forgive me."

Annabel was silent for a moment, unsure how she should respond. She wanted to believe her sister had realized the error of her ways and would behave differently now, but it would take some time to trust in that. It would be nice if that were true, however. Then perhaps they could have a real relationship. She would like to have a sister again, but it was hard to believe that the selfishness and nasty streak Kate had displayed was so easily shed.

Finally, she simply said, "I hope so too."

"What's yer idea fer getting m'lady down to the village?" Seonag asked when the two sisters continued to stare at each other.

Kate glanced to the maid, resentment flashing briefly across her face at her daring to ask, and then the expression was gone, and she said, "You shall tell Gilly and Marach they may as well relax at the table because we have a good deal of sewing to do to repair the gowns I cut up, and then you shall send that chest"—Kate pointed to the one in which Annabel's gowns had resided before she'd taken them—"down to Effie in the village claiming it holds the gowns that were in such bad shape you did not think they would do, but now have reconsidered and want her opinion."

"Effie works here in the castle now," Seonag pointed out with a frown.

"She did not come this morning," Kate responded promptly. "The maid who attends me said she was feeling unwell."

"She was under the weather yesterday," Annabel explained when Seonag looked displeased. "I told her if she did not feel better today to stay home and recuperate. I guess she felt no better."

"Oh." Seonag nodded.

Annabel turned to Kate and said, "I do not see how that is going to get me out of the castle."

"Because you will be in the chest," Kate answered simply.

"Oh, nay," Seonag protested.

"Aye," Kate insisted. " 'Tis perfect. You and I shall stay in here and cover for her absence, talking and laughing and saying her name a lot as if she is here. Meanwhile, we shall have servants carry the chest down and put it on a wagon, then deliver it to the village and carry it into Effie's house. Once they leave, Effie will open it and Annabel can walk to the inn to talk to the merchant. 'Tis not far," she pointed out.

"Nothing is far in the village," Seonag said dryly. "But how would she get back to the castle?"

"She can ask that Fingal person or someone else to bring her back," Kate said with unconcern. "I am sure he would be happy to. Then he could get another free meal while here."

Annabel eyed her sister silently. Apparently, her effort to change her ways didn't include not insulting people.

"I do no' ken," Seonag said with a frown.

"You do not have to," Kate responded sharply and glanced to Annabel, eyebrows raised. "What do you think?"

"I think it might work," Annabel admitted quietly. "Certainly, I can think of nothing better."

"Good." Kate smiled, suddenly looking happy, young and relaxed. "Then you had best get in the chest while Seonag goes and gets some servants to take it to the village."

As Seonag headed for the door, Kate added, "Make sure you tell Gilly and Marach that we will be sewing so they may relax if they like, and that you are just fetching some servants to send a chest of gowns that need repairing to Effie to work on while she is home."

"I ken what to say," Seonag assured her grimly as she opened the door.

"Hmmm." Kate walked to the chest and opened it. "In you go, sister. We had best make sure you fit in it before the servants come to take it away."

Annabel almost hoped she wouldn't fit and they would have to come up with something else.

The idea of being squeezed into an airless trunk while bumping along in the back of a wagon was not very appealing. But it was only a short ride to the village, Annabel assured herself a moment later as she curled herself inside the large trunk and Kate closed the lid. God, she hoped it was a short ride. She had never had an issue with small spaces, but this was something else. She was so scrunched up she could barely catch her breath, and was relieved when Kate immediately opened the trunk again and she could sit up.

"I shall watch the door for Seonag's return to be sure we have some warning and the servants do not just barge in and see you in the trunk," Kate said, walking to the door.

"Thank you," Annabel murmured and then got out and hurried over to the small chest in the corner of the room on the far side of the bed. It was where Ross kept jewels and coin, and where the sac of coins her father had handed over on their marriage resided. Her dower, which had been originally intended to be Kate's dower, sat on top. Annabel opened it intending to take just a portion to use to bribe the merchant, but Kate suddenly said, "They are coming. Two big men are with Seonag. Hurry. Back into the trunk."

Taking the bag with her, Annabel closed it as she rushed back to the trunk and curled herself inside again. Kate immediately hurried over to close the lid for her.

Annabel then waited . . . and waited. All she could think was that time passed terribly slowly when you were uncomfortable, because it seemed like forever before she heard the murmur of voices. She heard Seonag's voice first and then Kate's. A moment later male voices joined them and Annabel sucked in a breath as the trunk she was in was suddenly lifted and jarred about.

Annabel knew exactly when they reached the stairs, for she suddenly found her head tilting downward and her body sliding toward it, squishing her head against the panel of the trunk. Damn, that had hurt, she thought when the trunk evened out again. A moment later, she decided that pain had been nothing compared to being tossed onto what she presumed was the back of a wagon. Her entire body was jarred and jolted about at that, and Annabel had to shove the bag of coins into her mouth to keep from crying out.

The ride to the village was a piece of pastry in comparison. It was uncomfortable and seemed to last a long time, but at least she wasn't being tipped onto her head or thrown about. When the wagon stopped, she braced herself for what was to come, but several minutes passed before anything happened at all.

After a moment, Annabel thought she heard a muffled pounding and the sound of male voices, followed by Effie's much higher one. Of course, they'd knocked to be sure she was in and then explained what they had for her, Annabel thought, and then she was tilted toward her head again as the chest was lifted down from the wagon. But it was only for a moment this time and then the chest swayed slightly as she was carried into what she hoped was Effie's cottage.

Annabel shoved the bag of coins into her mouth in preparation and groaned low in her throat as she was set down with a jarring thud. She then took the coins out of her mouth again and strained to hear what was happening. She thought she heard heavy footsteps moving away and a door closing, but then there was silence . . . a long silence.

It was only then that it occurred to Annabel that Effie might not open the chest right away. What if she left her there for hours? The idea was untenable. Annabel bit her lip, but then called out, "Effie?"

The silence continued, but there was a different quality to it this time, a sort of waiting feel.

"Effie, do not be alarmed, 'tis Lady MacKay," she called, making her voice a little louder.

"M'lady?" she heard, muffled through the chest, and then a bewildered, "Where are ye?"

"In the chest, Effie. Could you open it please?"

"In the—what the devil are ye doing in there?" Her voice grew louder as she drew closer.

"I shall explain as soon as you let me out," Annabel promised.

"O' course, just let me . . . do ye ha'e the key?"

"What?" Annabel asked with bewilderment.

"Fer the lock on the trunk. I need a key," Effie explained and Annabel's mouth would have dropped open had she the room to do it.

"There is no lock, Effie. Just flip the hasp up off the latch and open it."

"Nay. 'Tis locked," Effie assured her.

"Kate, you dolt," Annabel muttered with disgust, wondering even as she said it if this was a true accident or another way for her sister to take out her anger on her.

"What was that?" Effie asked.

"Nothing," Annabel muttered.

"Oh." There was a pause and then Effie asked. "What should I do? Should I fetch the blacksmith? Fingal could probably—" She paused mid-word and then said, "Just a minute, me lady, someone is at the door. Wait here, I'll be right back."

Annabel grimaced. There was very little else she could do but wait, she thought with irritation and then listened as Effie shuffled off, her footsteps growing fainter as she moved away. A moment later Annabel heard the murmur of voices and then a thud as something hit the floor. Frowning, she strained to hear what was happening and then gave a start when someone pounded on the chest.

"How are you doing, sister?" a voice sang out.

"Kate?" she said uncertainly.

"Aye."

Annabel sighed with relief. She must have realized she'd accidentally locked her in and had somehow slipped away to let her out. She heard the scrape of metal on metal and as the chest was opened, Annabel said with relief, "Thank goodness you came. I was beginning to think—"

She paused momentarily as the lid suddenly lifted and light rushed in, briefly blinding her. Blinking rapidly, Annabel waited for her eyes to adjust and then released a little sigh and started to smile once she could see again. That smile died abruptly though. Her sister was bent over the chest smiling brightly, but it was the man standing behind her that made Annabel's eyes widen with horror. She recognized him at once as the man who had repeatedly attacked her.

"Belly, meet my husband, Grant," Kate said cheerfully. "Grant, meet my, fat, ugly sister."

"Your husband?" Annabel asked her voice cracking.

"Aye. Is he not handsome?" Kate asked with a grin, and then still smiling, said, "Now, we have to get you out of here without your screaming or otherwise alerting anyone to trouble, so . . . night night, Belly," Kate said sweetly and then hit her over the head with something Annabel didn't get a chance to see, but certainly felt. It was hard enough to knock her out with the one blow.

Chapter 16

"THANK YE FER RETURNING WITH ME," Ross said as he, Bean and Giorsal rode abreast into the bailey. Glancing at his sister, he added, "Annabel likes ye, she'll trust in yer advice."

"Are ye saying she does no' trust you yet?" Bean asked curiously.

"Nay, that's no' what I'm suggesting," he assured him. "Annabel trusts me, but in this instance she might think I am just a heartless male who does no' understand about sisters and such. She will no' think that about Giorsal."

"But I have no sisters and ye do," Giorsal pointed out with a laugh.

"Aye, but yer a lass," Ross said. "And that's what Annabel needs right now to help her sort all this out. Another lass to talk to . . . else she'll let her guilt rule her and make us all miserable for the rest of our days."

"Do ye really think she'd let her sister stay forever?" Bean asked. "From what ye've said she's a nightmare."

"Aye, but she's also her sister," Ross pointed out as they slowed to approach the stables. "And Annabel has the life that was meant for Kate while Kate's life has fallen apart. I suspect Annabel feels terrible guilt about that, and that's why she has no' already sent the lass packing."

"Nay," Giorsal announced with certainty. "This life was ne'er meant for Kate. She never would ha'e fit in here. Ye and Annabel were meant to be together."

"I ken that," Ross assured her. "We just ha'e to convince Annabel."

"Ne'er fear, brother. I shall solve all yer problems ere the nooning," Giorsal said with a cheeky grin.

"I hope so," he muttered, sliding off his horse to lead the beast into the stables and to his stall. Ross was very much afraid that if Giorsal couldn't convince Annabel that she had nothing to feel guilty for, and didn't have to be her sister's keeper . . . well, then he would have to step in and send Kate off against his wife's wishes. He'd prefer to avoid conflict with his wife, but would be damned if he was going to allow the Englishwoman to continue to make his wife miserable. If he didn't send the woman away soon, he would find himself throttling her one fine night when she called his wife "Belly" one too many times, or made her feel bad about her figure.

Shaking his head, Ross closed the stall door and led his sister and her husband to the keep. One way or another, he wanted this matter resolved today. Kate did not have to be gone today, though that would be lovely, but he *did* want to know she would soon be gone and no longer making a nuisance of herself in his home.

God, he had dodged an arrow when the woman had run off with her stable boy, Ross thought, and if she weren't making such a nuisance of herself he'd have thanked her for that. It was most definitely a blessing that he had Annabel and not her.

Gilly and Marach were seated at the trestle table when Ross led Giorsal and Bean into the keep. A bit concerned, he headed straight to the men.

"What are ye doin' sittin' here? Where is me wife?"

"Up in yer bedchamber with Seonag and the English wench, sewing," Gilly answered.

"Nay, Kate went to ha'e a word with the priest," Marach reminded Gilly, and then added for Ross's benefit. "She should be back soon though."

"How lovely," Giorsal said, and when Ross peered to her in question, she grinned and explained, "I am looking forward to meeting Annabel's sister."

"Nay," Gilly assured her. "That's no' something to look forward to. Instead, ye should be thankin' the gods that she is no' up there. The woman is a terror."

"Hmmm. Now I am even more curious to meet her," she said with a laugh and headed for the stairs, adding, "Sit down and ha'e a drink with me husband, brother. I'll take care o' everything."

Ross grunted at that, but simply watched his sister walk upstairs and along the hall, and then turned to Bean and asked, "Ale?"

"Aye. That sounds—" He paused and glanced to the stairs when Giorsal shouted for them from above. Still on his feet, Ross was the first to the stairs. Bean, Gilly and Marach were hard on his heels though, as they hurried to the room he shared with his wife. Rushing inside, he took in the tableau at a glance.

Seonag lay on the floor, blood dripping from her head and staining the rushes. Annabel was nowhere in sight, however, and Ross rounded on his men as Bean rushed past him to help Giorsal with the maid.

"Ye said Annabel was up here with Seonag," he barked accusingly.

"She is, or was," Gilly corrected himself as Marach moved into the room to look about. "Her sister is the only one who left."

"Obviously, that's no' true," Ross snapped and turned to join Bean and Giorsal by Seonag. "How is she?"

"She took a bad blow," Giorsal said quietly. "She seemed to stir a bit when I first knelt next to her though, so I think she'll be all right."

"M'laird?"

Ross glanced to Marach, frowning when he saw that the warrior was examining the chest where he kept their valuables . . . and it was open.

"Should there be anything in here?" Marach asked.

"What?" Ross almost gasped the word he was so shocked by the question. Lunging to his feet, he hurried to Marach's side to peer into the empty chest. For one moment, the world seemed to tilt around him, and then Marach grabbed his arm firmly.

"Are ye all right, me laird?"

"Please tell me that is not what I think it is?" Bean said quietly beside him. "It's not—?"

"Aye, 'tis," Ross growled.

"Damn," Bean breathed.

"There is no sign o' tamperin'," Marach said quietly, examining the small chest and lock. "A key had to have been used."

"My wife has one," Ross said.

"Surely ye do no' suspect her?" Bean asked with a frown.

"Nay. But as chatelaine she has a key, and she is missing."

"And so yer thinkin' she took—"

"Did I no' just say, nay?" Ross interrupted impatiently. "I am worryin' what has happened to her. Seonag is unconscious and obviously the key was taken from me wife, but where is she now?" he asked sharply and then glanced to Gilly and Marach and growled, "Search the room."

They nodded and turned away to do just that, but there was nowhere to look but under the bed. Both of them dropped to their knees, but immediately straightened and shook their heads. Ross turned away with frustration, and then abruptly swung back. "Check the other rooms up here. She may no' have gone below, but she could be in one of the other rooms."

"We'll look," Gilly assured him, and then added, "But I swear we were watching the entire time, m'laird, and she did no' leave this chamber. No' through the door. The only person who came out was Kate."

"And no doubt with your coin and jewels in a sack under her skirts," Bean said dryly and then pointed out, "If she is behind this, she will ken where Annabel is."

"The chest," Marach said suddenly.

"Is empty," Ross snapped. "Go search for Kate while Gilly—"

"Nay, no' that chest," Marach interrupted. "The chest o' gowns."

Ross had no idea what he was talking about, but Gilly apparently did, for he nodded thoughtfully. "Aye. She could ha'e been in that and carried right by us without us even suspecting."

"What are ye talking about?" Ross asked, but even as he asked the question, he noted that the chest Annabel had been keeping her gowns in was gone from the room and said, "The chest at the foot of the bed."

"Aye. Seonag said they were sending gowns down to Effie in the village to look over and see if they were repairable," Marach explained.

"Effie works in the keep now," Ross said with a frown.

"Aye, but she did no' come today. She is ailing," Gilly told him.

"And ye thought yer lady, my sweet Annabel, would care so little fer the woman that she'd send work fer her to do while the woman was ailing?" Ross snapped with disbelief. Both men looked stricken at the question, which was answer enough. They hadn't considered it that way, and now knew they'd made an error. Turning on his heel, Ross headed for the door.

"I'll come with ye," Bean said at once, falling into step with him.

"Do ye still want us to search the rooms up

here and find Kate, m'laird?" Marach asked quietly, following.

Ross paused in the door to consider, but then said, "Aye, but make it quick and then follow us once yer done in case we need help searching."

He suspected the search would be a waste of time, but it was better to have them look just in case. Ross would never forgive himself if he called off the search of the upper rooms and it turned out Annabel was lying unconscious in one of them.

"Do no' mind me. I'll just stay here and tend to Seonag," Giorsal said dryly.

"Good. Thank ye," Ross said as he slipped out of the room with the men following.

"Ye ken she wants to come with us," Bean said as they started down the stairs.

"Aye," Ross agreed. "Ye can order one o' the servants to take her place with Seonag if ye like."

"Nay," Bean said dryly. "Yer sister has no caution when it comes to her well-being. 'Tis better she is here."

Ross nodded. He'd thought as much.

ANNABEL OPENED HER EYES TO DARKNESS, discomfort and difficulty breathing. The discomfort told her that she was still in the chest, but there also didn't seem to be any air, and while she'd thought it was dark in the chest when it had first closed on her, she now realized there must have been light creeping through a crack somewhere, because now she understood what true darkness was. There was a complete lack of light around her, as well as utter silence, and for one moment

Annabel was afraid that she'd been buried alive inside the chest.

Just as she was beginning to hyperventilate at that prospect, sound reached her ears. It was very faint at first, but growing louder as it drew nearer. Footsteps, Annabel thought and hoped to God they were coming to let her out. She would never again willingly get into a chest, or any other small enclosure. She'd had her fill of that, Annabel thought and then stopped thinking and simply waited as she heard sounds suggesting the chest was being unlocked.

This time there was no bright daylight splashing into the chest when it opened and at first Annabel thought it must be nighttime. But then she was caught under the arms and lifted out, and she saw where she was. One of the darker corners of a barn . . . Carney's barn, Annabel realized, recognizing the large building where Ross had made love to her before they'd been attacked.

Her attention swung to the man who had lifted her out: Grant the stable boy. What a misnomer, Annabel thought. The title had drawn an image in her head of a slender youth, not this man. No one this big should be called "boy," she thought, and then cried, "Hey!" when he took away the bag of coins she'd been clutching since grabbing them and hurrying to the chest in her room.

"Hush," Grant warned. "Try to keep quiet and no' make her angry. Kate's no' reasonable when she's angry."

"You are Scottish," Annabel said with surprise, keeping her voice quiet. She had known her attacker was Scottish after hearing him speak in the bluebell field, but was having trouble combining that with the knowledge that he was also the son of her father's stable master in England, and the man Kate had run off with. In her mind, the stable boy had been English until now.

"Aye. Yer father won me father from the Fergusons in a horse race," Grant told her quietly. "That was seven years ago, when I was still a boy."

"How old are you now?" Annabel asked.

"Seventeen," he said quietly.

Annabel's eyes widened. He was younger than she would have thought, but then his size was deceiving, she supposed. But he was also five years younger than her sister.

"We've been at Waverly ever since," Grant said quietly. "Or at least I was until I made the ridiculous mistake o' falling in love with yer sister and thinking she loved me back."

"Does she not love you?" Annabel asked quietly. "She claims she does and that you had abandoned her."

"The tale o' me abandoning her was just to get her into the keep," Grant said, sounding weary. "And yer sister loves no one as much as herself."

"Then leave her," Annabel suggested urgently, adding, "A man who will not steal a horse surely does not wish to be involved with kidnapping. Leave her before she drags you any deeper."

Grant shook his head sadly. "I would no' abandon her . . . no matter what she does. I took her innocence, and gave up too much fer her. I'm stuck with her now . . . like the plague," he added in a mutter and nudged the chest lid closed with the hand holding the sack of coins.

"But—" She let her words die when he started to tug her around the chest and she stumbled on something in her path and fell. Taken by surprise, Grant lost his hold on her and Annabel landed on a pile of furs laid out next to the chest. She was only there a moment before he was grabbing her arm and drawing her to her feet again, but it was long enough.

"You did not follow us to this barn that day, did you?" she asked before he could urge her to move again.

"Nay, we were already here," Grant answered and Annabel nodded. She had just come to that conclusion. First, it had struck her that this was a good place to hide out and take cover. There was no one around, with the owner of the nearby cottage off on some unknown chore for Ross, and it provided a roof over their heads, hay for a bed, and the food stores to feast on. And then she'd recalled Ross's weaving path to get here to prevent anyone following and it had come together in her thoughts.

"I do not suppose you were out foraging or something when we first got here?"

"Nay," Grant said apologetically, urging her out of the shadows and toward the center of the barn. "We were here, but took cover in the oat holder when ye arrived."

"Ah," Annabel murmured and nodded again, but with a wince this time as she recalled everything they must have witnessed. She was beginning to think that perhaps she and Ross shouldn't indulge themselves anywhere but in their chamber from now on, no matter what day of the week it was.

"Embarrassed?" Kate asked, drawing Annabel's attention to the woman sitting in the rectangle of sunlight cast by the open barn door. A pile of jewels and coins were strewn before her on the hard-packed dirt floor.

Kate's question told Annabel that she'd heard at least the last part of her conversation with Grant, but there was little she could do about that. Ignoring her sister's question, Annabel gestured to the small treasure and asked one of her own. "Where did you get that?"

"From the chest in your room," Kate said unapologetically.

Annabel stiffened. "How—?"

"You left it open when I said Seonag was returning with the servants and you rushed to get back into the chest," Kate informed her with satisfaction.

Annabel closed her eyes as dismay, regret and guilt rushed through her. She had beggared her husband and their people with that thoughtless move. Dear God, why did she have to be such a failure at everything?

The jingle of coins caught her ear and she opened her eyes just as Kate caught the small sack Grant tossed to her.

Kate opened and upended the bag on top of all the other coins and jewels and then tossed the bag aside to clap her hands happily. "Is it not lovely, Grant? We can have our happily ever after."

"Aye, on the backs of those who will suffer from this loss," Annabel said grimly when Grant didn't comment.

Kate glanced up sharply at that, but at Grant,

not Annabel. Something in his expression made her own tighten, and then she turned and scowled at Annabel and said, "Grant, go and fetch a bucket of water from the river. I would have a word with Belly."

Grant hesitated, but then left Annabel where she was and headed out of the barn.

The moment he was gone, Kate glared at Annabel. "Do not speak to me of suffering. I need this. I will not live in squalor like a peasant."

Annabel did not point out that Grant was a peasant and that by choosing him she had consigned herself to that life. Why bother? Kate seemed to have difficulty seeing her own contribution to her situation. She just liked to blame others for her troubles and for enjoying a happiness she not only wanted, but felt she was entitled to. Besides, Annabel just wanted to get out of there and see Ross again and she didn't trust that if she angered her sister too much she might not do something foolish in a moment of anger, like kill her. And Annabel really would rather live to see her husband again.

Although once he found out she was the reason he had been robbed, Ross might not want to see her again, she thought glumly.

Kate continued to glare at her briefly, but then lowered her gaze to her treasure and ran her fingers through the coins and jewels as if they were water. After a moment, she said, "Are you not going to ask me how I got away from the keep today?"

Annabel tore her gaze away from the treasure that would no doubt support her sister and Grant for a good many years, perhaps all of the years they had left, and asked dutifully, "How did you get away?"

"I hit Seonag over the head, dumped the contents of the chest into a sack and hung it from inside the waistline of my skirt, then told the men I was going to see the priest and . . ." Kate shrugged and finished simply, "I just walked out to the stables, saddled two horses and rode out on them. No one stopped me."

Annabel wasn't surprised. From what she could tell, Kate had offended every single person she had met at MacKay. The stable master had probably hidden when he saw her coming, and everyone else had most likely turned a blind eye. They had probably been more than happy to see her go and had hoped never to see her again. But Annabel was more concerned with Seonag.

"Oh, I did not kill your precious Seonag," Kate said, apparently reading her expression. "At least I do not think so." She shrugged as if it mattered little one way or the other.

Giving a pleased little sigh, Kate then leaned back and tilted her head as she peered at Annabel. Her voice was pleasant as she said, "I have hated you for such a long time."

"M'LAIRD!"

Ross lowered his hand from knocking at Effie's door and glanced around at that hail from Fingal. Shifting impatiently, he glanced to Bean.

"I'll see what he wants," he said and moved to meet the man.

Ross turned back to the cottage door and knocked again.

"Effie should be home. I saw her receive a delivery no' a half hour ago," Fingal said with concern as he walked past Bean to Ross.

"A chest?" Ross asked.

He nodded. "But she'd barely accepted it when that nasty English bit o' skirt showed up."

"Kate?" Ross asked harshly.

"Aye, and she had a big man on her heels." He scowled. "A great bull o' a man who fit the description ye gave o' the fellow who's been bedeviling ye. So I thought I'd best head up to the castle to tell ye. I was just saddling me old nag when I heard yer horses on the cobblestone and came to investigate."

Ross cursed under his breath and stopped knocking. He opened the door and strode in. Effie lay on the floor not more than half a dozen steps from the entrance. Ross knelt and placed his hand by her mouth, relieved when her breath brushed his fingers. "She's alive."

"The chest is no' here," Bean pointed out, making Ross glance around the small one-room cottage to see that indeed there was no chest.

"They brought it out just minutes after entering," Fingal said, kneeling across from Ross and frowning worriedly over Effie. "The big fella was carrying it."

"Did ye see which way they went?" Ross asked straightening.

"Aye. The road to MacDonald. They were walking at first and I followed at a distance, but they had horses half a mile or so outside the village. I hurried back then to saddle me nag."

Ross nodded, started to turn, but then glanced to Effie and hesitated.

"I'll look after her," Fingal assured him. "Go on with ye. Catch the bastard who has been hounding our sweet Annabel."

Ross did not explain that the "bastard" most likely had their sweet Annabel in the chest he'd been carrying. He merely headed for the door, saying, "Take her up to the castle, Fingal. Seonag was injured as well. Giorsal can tend them both. Then I'd appreciate it if ye'd tell Gilly and Marach to gather the men and follow us. Tell 'em to check Carney's barn first and then follow the road after that if we're no' there."

"Aye," Fingal said. "I will, me laird."

"Yer thinking they're at Carney's barn?" Bean asked.

"I told ye about the day I was attacked," Ross muttered, leading the way out to their waiting horses. "About how I rode fast and weaved about to ensure we were no' followed ere stopping at the barn."

"Aye," Bean said.

"Well, I was sure we were no' followed. I would no' ha'e risked Annabel by stopping had I no' been sure."

"Ye think they were at the barn all along," Bean realized.

Ross nodded, and then admitted, "It only just occurred to me when Fingal said they took the road to MacDonald. It leads right past the barn. Why would they not head further south, or even to the coast? Either direction offers a better chance o' disappearing into a city or escaping on a boat than heading north to MacDonald."

"Aye. And Kate's accent would make her stand

out like a throbbin' thumb there," Bean commented. "I'd have had her stopped until ye could get out to ensure it wasn't her." He was silent for a moment, but then frowned and asked, "But why go to the barn? Why are they no' fleeing as fast as they can?"

"They have Annabel in the chest. I'm sure o' it," Ross said quietly. "I presume there is a reason fer it."

"Well it can no' be fer ransom," Bean said and then pointed out, "The English bitch stole everything from ye. She must ken ye've nothing left to pay a ransom with."

Ross's mouth tightened, but he didn't comment. He was quite sure that Kate was bitterly jealous of Annabel, and because of that, hated her with a white-hot passion that would want some form of torment, or even death to slake it. Ross just hoped he found Annabel in time and he did not learn the hard way which it was that Kate wanted.

Chapter 17

"*Why?*" Annabel asked, eyes wide and incredulous. "Why would you hate *me*? What have I ever done to you?"

"You *exist!*" Kate shrieked furiously, then slapped at the treasure before her, sending some of it flying across the dirt before saying more calmly, "All I heard growing up was, 'Annabel would never do that. Annabel was a good girl. Annabel would have learned that much more quickly. 'Tis a shame you are not as smart as your sister, Annabel.'" She grimaced. "According to our parents, you were a paragon I could never equal."

Annabel realized her mouth was open, and closed it, then took a deep breath. "Kate, they did the same thing to me when they retrieved me from the abbey. Only with me it was, ''Tis too bad you did not get a little of your sister's beauty, and what a shame it is you have none of your sister's training and skills. Unlike Kate, you would surely be a mess as a wife to the Scot.'"

Kate's eyes were dead and lifeless, her voice

cold as she said, "You were there but one day, Annabel. I know. We were still in Waverly woods when mother brought you back. Ross's party arrived on your heels, and we followed you when you left the next day."

"It may have only been one day, but that was pounded into me over and over during that day. I am not comparing my suffering under them to yours," Annabel added quickly as she saw anger building on Kate's face. "I am saying I understand, and that it was them and not either of us that were the problem. Had you been sent away to the abbey and I remained behind I would have had those insults every day of my life, and I know how damaging they can be. I—"

"But you were not there every day, were you?" Kate hissed. "You escaped to the abbey to live. How did you manage that? Why you and not me?"

"I did not *manage* it," Annabel assured her. "I did not even know I was going until we were halfway there and then I wept all through the rest of the journey. I also wept every night for that first year because I missed—"

"Oh, spare me your sad story," Kate interrupted grimly. "No one has suffered as much as I. Look at me," she growled. "I have been living in the woods and sleeping in this barn, eating raw oats like a farm animal while you lived in that lovely castle with its warm fires, soft beds and yummy pastries."

Annabel did not point out that since Kate and her husband had followed them to Scotland, she should know that Annabel too had slept out of doors during that time. As for here in Scotland,

Annabel had only been at MacKay a matter of a few days before Kate had shown up at the gate and she had taken her in. Kate was making it sound as if she had been wandering the wilderness for ages.

"Why have you been attacking me?" Annabel asked finally, uncaring whether Grant thought she should stay quiet or not. She suspected it mattered little what she did. Kate wanted her pound of flesh for what she saw as Annabel's escaping their childhood home, and she would not listen if told just how unpleasant Annabel's own life had been at the abbey. And it *had* been unpleasant. Life at MacKay had taught her that, but it would make no difference to Kate. She was too self-absorbed to care.

"Grant attacked you," she corrected, and cast a scowl toward the barn door before she added, "He was supposed to kidnap you, but he kept mucking it up. And then," Kate added irritably, "after the first two failures to secure you, he started coming back not only without you, but wounded. Had I not helped him away from the barn the last time, you probably would have finished him off."

Annabel did not comment. This explained why Grant had disappeared when she'd checked on him after knocking him out.

"It seems that old saw about doing something yourself if you want it done correctly is true," Kate said unhappily. "For I had no problem getting you away from the castle today."

"Well, you did have a slight advantage," Annabel pointed out, and then had to wonder why she was defending Grant to her sister.

Kate shook her head. "It would not have mattered. His heart was not in it."

Annabel wasn't surprised. Since Grant hadn't even been willing to take a horse from Waverly, she doubted the ransom business had been his idea or even gone over well with him. She just wondered what had convinced him to fall in with Kate's plans over the kidnapping and ransom business, instead of stopping her.

"I think he hates me now for insisting on kidnapping you," she added unhappily, and then burst out, "But I am not like him! I cannot live like this."

"You still have not said why you wanted to kidnap me," Annabel pointed out quietly, deciding a change of topic was in order. She wanted to know what was to be done with her, and what the situation was.

"To hold you for ransom, of course," Kate answered. Her lips twisted briefly and then she admitted, "I did not think this through before running away with Grant. He is so very handsome, and I was caught up in the excitement and passion . . ." She sighed wearily, looking suddenly old, and then shook her head like a horse dislodging a pesky horsefly. When she stopped, her expression was angry again and she said idly, "Of course, now that I have all of MacKay's wealth, asking for a ransom would be a waste of time. But I did want you to know that I was behind all your troubles, and I wanted those coins you had in the chest. I recognized the bag. 'Twas part of my dower. I should have it, not you."

"Well, now you have it," Annabel pointed out.

"Aye," Kate agreed. "And I suppose I might enjoy living as I deserve while knowing you and every last MacKay under you are struggling."

Annabel heard a *but* coming and braced for it.

"Howbeit, that would only be temporary. MacKay would recover after a couple of lean years . . . and I find the idea of your living my life untenable."

"Your life?" Annabel echoed with confusion.

"Ross should have been mine," Kate hissed. "Had I realized how handsome, young and wealthy he was, I never would have run off with Grant."

"But I thought you love Grant," Annabel said with a frown.

"What good is love when you are hungry?" she asked bitterly. "Love does not produce food, or beautiful gowns to wear, and servants to tend you." She ground her teeth and said, "MacKay is bigger even than Waverly and I could be living there with all those servants tending my every need and—" She paused and scowled at Annabel and then growled with frustration, "And with Ross as a lover.

"I know how amazing he is as a lover," she added, getting to her feet and glowering at Annabel. "I saw the two of you, both in the clearing by the river and then here in this very barn. He makes you howl like a bitch in heat, while Grant is clumsy and—" Kate clenched her fingers and growled, "I hate you for that too. Why do you get everything while I am left with nothing? Why do you get the strong man who is not only a caring and skilled lover, but strong enough in will and

mind to do what must be done, while I get a boy
who has not a clue what he is doing in the bedding
and has neither a strong will nor a good mind. It
is not fair," she cried furiously.

A shuffle by the door made them both glance
that way. Grant stood in the opening, silent and
still. Annabel could tell by his wounded expression that he'd heard everything Kate had said, and
she found herself feeling terribly sorry for him.
But after a moment, he took a deep breath, raised
his head and moved to Kate's side, saying quietly,
"We ha'e enough wealth now to live as ye wish.
We can buy a nice estate in the south of France, or
in Spain, hire servants and enjoy all those things
ye wanted. We're well set for life, Kate. Let yer
sister go."

"Aye, we are well set now," Kate agreed and
then muttered, "So why am I not happy? I thought
getting just a portion of this would make everything all right. Instead, I . . ." Shaking her head,
she turned to Annabel and admitted almost with
shame, "I just cannot abide the idea of you enjoying everything that should have been mine. I
cannot bear it."

"Why?" Grant asked, sounding young and
frustrated and angry now himself. "Why can ye
no' just take the money and leave her be? Why
must ye destroy everything?" Turning, he moved
to take Annabel's arm and started to draw her
toward the door, growling, "I'm setting her free."

"Grant!" Kate snapped.

Pausing, he cast Annabel an apologetic look,
and turned back, still holding her arm. "Aye?"

"If we let her go and she tells MacKay that we

are the ones who robbed him, he will hunt us all the days of our lives," Kate said grimly.

"Whether or no' she tells, they'll ken ye took the coin, Kate. And even if they somehow do no' figure that out, we're going to be hunted the rest o' our lives anyway," Grant said wearily. "Ye told me yerself that ye boldly walked into the stables and took two horses and then rode out fer all to see. And ye knocked out the maid, and that Effie woman, and then ye kidnapped yer sister. Ye've ensured we will be hunted. 'Tis as if ye want it. Well I don't," he added. "I love ye, Kate, but ye're never satisfied. Nothing is ever enough, and 'tis as if ye can no' allow yerelf to be happy. And because yer never happy, ye make everyone around ye as miserable as yerself."

Grant shook his head sadly, "I do no' want to spend me life miserable, Kate. I'm done."

Kate stared at him wide-eyed and then whirled on Annabel. "This is all your fault!"

"Mine?" Annabel asked with amazement.

"Aye," she cried. "It was not enough that you had everything else, but you just had to turn Grant against me. God, I hate you," she shrieked.

"Then 'tis good that I love her."

All three of them whirled toward the two men standing in the open barn door at that. Annabel was aware of Bean's presence, but had eyes only for Ross standing tall and proud in the doorway, his hand on his sword, his expression grim. He looked so damned strong and proud, and she loved every inch of him. Better yet, he'd said he loved her.

Did he mean it? Annabel wondered, and hoped

it was so, because she loved him. She might have taken herself by surprise when she'd blurted the words out Sunday morning, but they were true for all that. She loved this man who treated her with nothing but kindness and care. She loved the fairness with which he dealt with her and everyone else. She loved his strength, his intelligence, his lovemaking, and his laugh even when he was laughing at her. She loved this big, handsome, sweet man and was ever so grateful that her life had taken the turn that had placed her with him.

Annabel was so distracted by her thoughts that she didn't at first notice Kate's reaction to Ross's arrival. Had she paid more attention, she would have noticed the way her sister stiffened and then began to vibrate with frustrated rage. And she would have been prepared to get the heck out of the way when Kate suddenly shrieked in fury and flew at her, fists raised. But that shriek was the only warning she had, and it wasn't enough. Annabel stood briefly frozen as her sister charged her, and then Grant was suddenly pushing her to the side and stepping in to take the blows of Kate's flying fists.

Annabel suspected he'd done this before, allowing Kate to take out her rage by beating her fists against him. She also suspected he hadn't expected her to attack so ferociously. Despite the size difference, Grant stumbled back when she crashed against him, and in that move he lost his footing and fell back. They went together, Kate's feet knocked out from under her by his larger ones kicking as he tried to regain his footing.

Annabel cried out in warning, and reached out as she saw that he was about to fall against the two posts and board where she'd laid her gown during her first visit here with Ross. But it was too late. Grant's head bounced off one post as they fell, and then he was lying on the ground, his head up against the post at an odd angle and Kate on his unmoving chest.

"Grant?" Kate said worriedly as she raised her head from his chest. "Grant?"

Annabel bit her lip. She could see that he was dead, his neck broken, but she hesitated a moment before moving forward and bending to place a hand on her shoulder.

"Come, Kate. He is dead," she said gently.

"Nay, he is not," her sister snapped, shaking off her hand. She then began to shake Grant. "Wake up, Grant. Wake up, and show her you are still alive. Grant!"

Annabel bit her lip, and then glanced away as Kate began to shriek hysterically and started hitting the dead man again, pleading and demanding by turn that he wake up.

"Let her be," Ross advised, suddenly at her side and catching her arm to stop her as she bent to touch her sister's shoulder again. Annabel hesitated, but then straightened with a nod.

"Are ye all right?" Ross asked, turning her to face him and running his eyes and hands over her in search of wounds.

"Aye," Annabel assured him, and then smiled shakily and added, "But I am glad to see you."

Ross nodded, and then suddenly covered her mouth with his own for a quick hard kiss. He then held her tight to his chest in a long hug and sighed.

"I'll keep an eye on Kate," Bean said joining them as Ross ended the hug. "Ye'd best collect yer coin."

"Aye. Thank ye," Ross murmured, and then lead Annabel to the pile of jewels and coins on the ground.

When he released her then and knelt to begin replacing them in the sack that Kate had brought, Annabel crouched beside him to help.

She noted that Ross placed a large quantity of coins back in the smaller bag that had held her dower. He then tied it to his sword belt and helped her replace the rest of the coins and jewels in the bigger bag. Annabel did not ask why he did that and they worked quickly and in silence. They were just finishing when Gilly and Marach led a large search party into the barn. They entered, swords drawn, but relaxed when they saw that everything was under control.

Closing the big sack holding the majority of the treasure, Ross pressed it into Annabel's hand and helped her to her feet, then led her to the men.

"Take her back to the keep," Ross ordered, urging her between Gilly and Marach. "And ye can take most o' the rest o' the men with ye. Just leave me two ye can do without fer a bit."

"What about Kate?" Annabel asked worriedly.

"Leave her with me," Ross said quietly. "I shall bring her back after we tend to the boy."

Annabel hesitated, but then nodded and allowed Marach to lead her out of the barn as Gilly moved off to have a word with the men.

"Is Seonag all right?" Annabel asked as the warrior walked her out to where the men had left their horses.

"I am no' sure, m'lady," Marach said quietly. "She was unconscious when we left."

Annabel nodded, and then bit her lip and asked, "What do you think my husband will do to Kate?"

"I am no' sure about that either, m'lady," he admitted apologetically. "But the laird is always fair."

"Aye," Annabel murmured and wondered what would be fair in this instance? Her sister had been nothing but trouble since arriving, but now she had stolen from him, kidnapped her, and attacked Seonag.

Annabel pondered the matter of Kate's pending punishment while they waited for Gilly and the other men to join them, and then during the ride back to the keep. But once there, her concern for Seonag pushed it aside and she rushed inside and upstairs the moment Marach lifted her down off his horse. She could hear feet thudding behind her, and knew Gilly and Marach were hurrying after her, but didn't slow until she reached the upstairs landing. Annabel paused then, only because she had no idea where they had put Seonag.

"The room next to the master bedchamber," Marach said without being asked as he led Gilly off the stairs.

Kate's room, Annabel thought and hurried there. Giorsal was seated by the bedside talking quietly to Seonag when she entered, and the sight was a happy one for Annabel. She had grown quite fond of Seonag during her time at MacKay and was grateful the older woman would recover from her sister's attack.

Rushing forward, Annabel surprised the woman by giving her a careful hug as she said, "I am so glad you are all right."

"Oh, aye, and so am I glad that ye are," Seonag said, blushing slightly. As Annabel straightened, she said, "We ha'e been sitting here fretting over whether the men found ye or not. 'Tis glad I am they did and yer well, m'lady."

Annabel gave her hand a squeeze, then turned to smile at Giorsal as well before turning her attention to the second woman in the bed. Effie. Pale and with a nasty head wound, the embroiderer was not awake.

"She's just sleeping," Giorsal said reassuringly. "She woke up a few minutes ago, but dropped off again shortly afterward."

"Oh, good," Annabel murmured, recalling the thud she'd heard after Effie had said someone was at the door. She supposed Annabel or Grant had knocked the woman out after gaining access to the cottage, and felt horrible that she had not wondered about her well-being at the time.

"Well?" Giorsal said. "Sit down. Tell us what happened. We ken Kate knocked out Seonag, and we presume she stole the family coin and fled?"

"And I see ye've a new lump on yer forehead, so she must ha'e knocked ye out again too," Seonag said dryly.

"Aye," Annabel admitted and quickly explained what had happened.

"So yer sister was behind it all?" Giorsal said slowly. "And she killed her stable boy?"

"Nay," Annabel said at once, and then frowned and said, "Well, aye, but 'twas an accident."

Seonag shook her head. "There is just something wrong with the girl. Her head is no' working right."

"Aye," Giorsal agreed.

Annabel merely nodded. She suspected they were correct. While Kate was selfish and spoiled, her obsession with Annabel's happiness and determination to destroy it was just madness.

The sound of the door opening drew Annabel's attention and she stood up when Ross appeared. When he gestured her over, she moved to the door and then followed when he took her arm to urge her out of the room. He led her to their bedchamber, ushered her inside, closed the door and leaned against it.

When Annabel paused in the center of the room and turned back to peer at him uncertainly, he said, "We need to discuss yer sister."

Annabel's eyes widened and she clasped her hands in front of her and murmured a faint, "Oh."

"We buried the lad and sent word to his father at Waverly," he said quietly.

"Oh," Annabel repeated, and then nodded. "Good."

"And then we brought yer sister back to decide what to do with her. I thought ye should ha'e a say in her punishment," Ross explained.

"Thank you," Annabel murmured, thinking she was lucky to have such a considerate husband. Most men probably would have simply dealt with the matter and informed her of what had been done after the fact. Truthfully, though, Annabel almost would have preferred that in this instance. She had no desire to deal with her sister, or the guilt that would no doubt follow any decision on her punishment.

"We rode in on the heels of a lone rider," Ross continued. "It was the messenger with yer mother's response."

Annabel bit her lip, not sure that made any difference. She suspected that even if her mother agreed to take Kate in, Ross wouldn't allow her to leave and go on her merry way without demanding some form of punishment for what she'd done. In truth, Annabel couldn't disagree with him if he did.

"Your parents want nothing to do with her," Ross said quietly. "They say she has made her bed and may now lie in it. She is dead to them."

Annabel's breath left her on a small sigh. She wasn't surprised, but supposed some part of her had hoped her parents would prove they had some small measure of caring for the daughters they'd given life to. It seemed not, however. "Does she know?"

"I haven't told her, but she may have guessed," Ross said with a shrug. "She asked to go to confession while I read it, and I told a couple of the men to escort her there. But once in the chapel, Kate cried sanctuary."

Annabel stiffened, her head jerking up and back as if under a blow at the news. While the news had caught her off guard, she probably should have seen that coming. Her sister would hardly wish to stand judgment and would hide behind whatever she could. Claiming sanctuary was actually clever.

"Father Gibson felt he had to give it to her, but is no' too pleased to have her there," he added.

Annabel wasn't surprised. Five minutes in Kate's presence was five minutes too long and she didn't doubt her sister was already driving the priest mad.

"So he suggested giving her permanent sanctuary and sending her to Elstow Abbey so long as she agreed to take the veil," Ross said quietly. "And she agreed."

Annabel's eyes widened. Kate would hate Elstow. She would hate the abbess, the chores, the hard physical labor, the shared baths, the plain, tasteless food, the restrictions, the punishments and penances. Annabel had no doubt Kate would refuse to whip herself at the abbess's instructions . . . at least until she heard what the alternative punishments were.

Her sister had no idea what she was agreeing to. Her selfish demanding ways would not serve her there, and certainly would not go over well with the other women. And she would be under constant scrutiny. Kate had no training that would make working in the stables an option, and that was the only place with any freedom at all, and even there it was scant. And she would have to—

Annabel's eyes widened suddenly and when Ross arched an eyebrow in question, she told him what she'd just thought of. "If she is taking the veil, her hair will be shorn for sure."

They stared at each other in silence for a minute and then Ross said, "She will no' like that."

"Nay," Annabel agreed. Kate was too vain to accept that well, but she would have to do it to hang on to the sanctuary she wanted.

It suddenly occurred to Annabel that this would mean they were completely switching lives. Kate would now be living the life that had stretched out before Annabel until she'd been dragged home to marry Ross while she lived the life that had been meant for Kate until she'd run off with Grant.

Only, Annabel suspected Kate's personality would turn the experience from just unpleasant and unhappy to utter misery. Life at the abbey would either reform Kate or kill her . . . or possibly it would kill both Kate and the abbess, Annabel thought. But in a way, it seemed the most fitting place for her sister. Certainly it was better than a beheading, life in a dungeon, or any of the other punishments Annabel had feared would be meted out.

Releasing the breath she'd been holding, Annabel nodded. "Aye. Send her to Elstow."

Ross straightened and crossed the room to take her into his arms. Annabel was still for a moment, but then relaxed into him with a sigh and immediately felt the sack containing the MacKay treasure still hanging from her skirt. She should have put it away first thing, Annabel thought unhappily. Actually, she should not have left the chest unlocked and open for Kate to take it in the first place, she reprimanded herself and then bit her lip and murmured, "I am sorry."

Her husband pulled back enough to peer down into her face with surprise and asked, "For what?"

Annabel had meant to say for leaving the chest open for Kate to nearly get away with the MacKay treasure, but the response that came out was, "Everything."

Ross shook his head and assured her, "Ye've nothing to be sorry fer, Annabel."

"Aye, I do," she countered and pointed out, "You have had nothing but trouble since marrying me."

Ross caught her face in his hands and met her gaze as he said solemnly, "Aye. There has been little else but trouble since our wedding, but none of it was yer fault."

"But if you had not married me—"

"I'd have missed out on the best thing in me life," he interrupted firmly, and then added wryly, "And despite all the troubles, or mayhap because o' them, I have thanked God every day since waking to find yer sister here that it was you I married and no' her."

Annabel laughed shakily and then closed her eyes and leaned her head against his chest with a sigh. "Aye, well . . . still, if you had refused me and married someone else you could have avoided a great deal of difficulty."

Ross kissed the top of her head and assured her, "Yer worth every bit o' trouble yer sister has caused and more. I meant what I said at the barn, I do love ye, Annabel. Ye brighten me days and make me keep a home."

She lifted her head and tilted it back to peer up at him, surprised to find tears rising to mist her eyes. "I love you too, Ross. I thought I would spend my life at Elstow and had resigned myself to it, but I am ever so grateful that Kate's actions placed me here with you instead. I did not know life could be so . . ." She paused, several thoughts coming to mind. She hadn't realized life could be so full of caring, color, happiness and passion. But in the end she simply said, "Wonderful."

Ross smiled and then bent to kiss her. It was a sweet kiss at first, full of love, but then as happened when they were together, passion began to take over.

Moaning, Annabel withdrew her arms from around his waist to slip them up around his shoulders and then rose up on her toes to plaster herself against him. Ross immediately dropped his hands to cup her behind. Raising her off the ground, he then started to carry her to the bed, their bodies rubbing together with each step. But he paused when a knock sounded at the door.

Breaking their kiss, he glanced toward it and barked, "Go away."

"Is that any way to talk to yer sister?" Giorsal called out with a laugh. " 'Sides, I am only knockin' to tell ye Carney is back and he's brought a certain gentleman that I am sure Annabel'll want to see right away."

"Damn," Ross groaned and leaned his forehead on Annabel's.

"What is it?" she asked with concern.

Ross hesitated, but then admitted, "The task I sent Carney on was to fetch the cloth merchant here so ye could buy what ye want. Ye should ha'e gowns of yer own, made just fer ye, not me mother's castoffs."

"Oh," Annabel breathed, tears threatening again, and then she hugged him tightly. "Thank you, husband. You are the most wonderful, considerate husband any girl could ask for."

Ross smiled crookedly, but then sighed. "I suppose I should let ye go talk to the man."

Annabel was tempted, but then shook her head. "Nay. He can wait a bit." Tightening her hold on his shoulders, she raised her legs to wrap them around his waist, managing the task despite her skirts, and said, "I think I should like to thank you properly for such thoughtfulness."

"Oh?" Ross asked with a grin, continuing toward the bed. "Well, while yer in the mood for thanking me, I should mention that I dealt with the spice merchant ere bringing Kate back."

"You did?" Annabel asked, eyes wide. She'd quite forgotten about the man, what with everything that had happened.

"Aye, I did," he assured her. "And after I gave him a couple coins, paid for his stay at the inn, and threatened to hunt him down and geld him if he didn't agree, he promised no' to warn anyone away from MacKay."

That startled a laugh from Annabel, and she shook her head. "You are a wonder."

"Yer happy then?" Ross asked seriously, pausing in front of the bed.

"Oh, aye, husband. I am very happy," she assured him solemnly, then unwrapped her legs from around his hips and kicked them lightly until he turned sideways to the bed to set her down. She immediately took a step toward the door and Ross turned to follow her movement, as she'd expected. It placed him with his back to the bed.

"Where are ye going?" he asked with a frown. "I thought—" The words died on a startled gasp when Annabel suddenly turned and gave him a shove. Caught by surprise, Ross tumbled back onto the bed with his legs hanging off from the knees down.

"Nowhere," Annabel assured him solemnly as she quickly undid her lacings and removed her gown. She then walked up between his knees until her own knees bumped the bed, and added, "You are stuck with me, husband."

"Then I am the luckiest man in Scotland," Ross growled, sitting up to slide his arms around her waist. He squeezed her tight briefly, and sighed, "God, I love you."

"And I love you," Annabel assured him solemnly, and then pushed him back on the bed and bent to crawl on top of him, saying, "Let me show you how much."

Read on for a sneak peek of

Lynsay Sands' next Argeneau novel

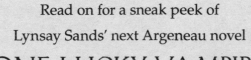

ONE LUCKY VAMPIRE

On sale September 24, 2013

from Avon Books

"*L*AST DAY OF THIS ASSIGNMENT."

Jake nodded silently, but didn't glance to Dan Shephard, the blond man at his side and his partner for this job. Instead, Jake's eyes were busily sliding over the crowd, looking for any possible threat.

"Damn good thing too," Dan added grimly. "One more day of watching out for this arrogant, demanding prick and I might be tempted to kill him myself."

That comment made Jake's mouth twitch with amusement. Their client was definitely an annoying, arrogant and demanding bastard. But then, what else could you expect from a foreign dictator? Besides, working as professional protection in Ottawa meant that a lot of the people they were sent to guard were arrogant, demanding, or annoying. At least on the outside. Some were a different case inside and just acting up out of fear or stress, but not all. This client was as arrogant, demanding and annoying inside as he acted on the outside. But, they were hired to do a job and you couldn't like every client, he thought philosophically.

"He flies out at eight right? Then we're done?" Dan asked.

Jake nodded, but his eyes had narrowed on a man in the crowd. The fellow wore a baseball cap and jean jacket. He was also eyeballing their client. Of course, most people there were since he was answering questions shot at him by the press, but there was just something about ballcap boy that was raising alarms in Jake's head.

"Four more hours then," Dan muttered, glancing at his wristwatch. "Four more hours . . . and counting," he added dryly. "Want to go for a drink afterward? I know I need one after a week with this bast— Where are you going?"

Jake heard the question, but didn't stop to answer. He was hurrying through the crowd toward baseball cap boy, every muscle in his body straining to get there in time as the man pulled a gun from the waistband at the back of his jeans and began to level it at their client.

"That was one hell of a catch," Dan said, slapping Jake on the back six hours later as they headed out of R.A. Protection's swanky offices and approached the elevators. Their four hours of work had turned into six, thanks to Jake's stopping and apprehending the assassin in the baseball cap. First there had been the police and all their questions to deal with and then they'd had to debrief their boss, Hank Latham, on what had taken place.

Now, they were finally leaving work, two hours later than expected.

"I don't know how you did it," Dan continued, shaking his head as the elevator doors opened and they stepped on board. "Hell, I didn't even track the guy as a problem, but I sure as hell couldn't have moved as fast as you did. You flew through that crowd."

"Adrenaline," Jake muttered, glancing at his watch.

"You gotta love adrenaline," Dan commented, slapping him again as Jake pushed the button for the main floor. As the doors closed, he commented, "So we get a couple of play days before the next assignment. Want to go for a drink to celebrate?"

"Can't. I'm meeting someone for dinner and I'm already late," Jake said, leaning back against the elevator wall and crossing his arms. He wasn't really sorry he had to decline. He liked Dan, he was a good guy, but Jake wasn't much of a drinker. Alcohol did little for him.

"Someone? Like a lady?" Dan asked with a grin.

"Someone, like sort of family," Jake said evasively.

"Sort of family?" Dan prodded.

Jake hesitated, and then said, "Yeah. You know, that older lady who isn't really a relation but your parents make you call her aunt."

"Ah," Dan grimaced. "Yeah. I have one of those myself. A lifelong friend of my mom's. She and her hubby hang with my parents all the time and she's been 'Aunt Betty' most of my life. Dotty old bitty now, but good-hearted."

"Yeah, this is the same deal," Jake said, ignoring the twinge of guilt the words caused. The lady in question was old as hell, but "dotty old bitty" didn't exactly fit her.

"Well . . ." Dan eyed him silently, and then

smiled wryly and said, "I'm kind of glad to hear about this aunt who's not an aunt. You never mention family. I was beginning to think you were hatched or something."

"Nah. There just isn't much to talk about," Jake said quietly. "Most of my family lives on the west coast or out of the country. Haven't seen much of them the last half a dozen years or so."

"Ah." Dan nodded. "So . . . ? Siblings? Parents still alive? Kissing cousins around?"

Much to Jake's relief, he was saved from answering the probing questions when they reached the main floor and the doors began to open. Moving forward, he said, "See you in a couple days," over his shoulder.

"Yeah." Dan said, following him off the elevator.

Jake hurried for the building's exit, but his expression was tight. He knew damned right well that wouldn't be the end of the questions. Dan would repeat them at the first opportunity, and have a dozen more to add to them.

Putting away that worry for now, Jake pushed through the front doors and turned right, moving quickly. He was supposed to have been at the restaurant ten minutes ago. Fortunately, the R.A. offices were downtown, just around the corner and down the street from where he was headed. A three or four minute walk if he moved fast.

Of course, it was possible he was rushing for nothing. His dinner companion may already have given up and left. He couldn't say he'd be sorry if she had. He wasn't looking forward to this meeting. He had no doubt his "aunt" was trying to arrange a family reunion, and while it may have been more than half a dozen years since he'd left the bosom of his family, he wasn't ready to return. Not yet anyway.

Worrying about how to politely say as much, Jake reached the restaurant and hurried inside, only to pause abruptly, his gaze searching the patrons.

"Hi. Did you want a table or are you meeting someone?"

Jake glanced to the young woman who had spoken. Dressed all in black, she was blond, beaming, and perky as hell. She waited wide-eyed and head tilted for his answer.

"Meeting someone," he assured her, and then glanced back to the room, his eye caught by the beautiful brunette waving at him from a table in the back corner of the restaurant. She hadn't left. Damn, he thought wearily and headed for the table. She was on her feet by the time he reached her, and immediately stepped forward to hug him.

"Sorry I'm late," Jake apologized as he self-consciously returned the embrace. "I just got out of work."

"No need to apologize, Stephano. I'm just glad you agreed to meet me," Marguerite Argeneau said, leaning back in his arms to smile at him warmly. "It's good to see you."

"You too," Jake said stiffly as he released her. Voice gentle, he added, "I don't go by Stephano anymore."

"Oh, yes, of course, I'm sorry," she said apologetically. "You go by your second name now. Jacob."

"Call me Jake," he suggested, urging her back

to her seat, before settling in the one across from her as another woman all in black approached with menus in hand. This one was a brunette, but she wore a beaming smile as perky as the blonde's at the door as she stopped at the table.

"Good evening!" she said gaily as she set a menu in front of each of them. "Would you like something to drink while you look at the menu?"

"Water," Jake said quietly.

Nodding, the girl then turned to Marguerite. "How is your tea? Would you like fresh tea, or something else to drink?"

"Another tea, please, and a glass of water," Marguerite said, her smile just as wide and beaming as the girl's.

Nodding, their waitress flashed another beaming smile and rushed off.

Marguerite immediately turned to smile at him. "Jake. The name suits you. And I understand you use your father's last name, Colson, now too rather than Notte?"

He shifted uncomfortably as he nodded, and then waited for her to give him hell for being an ungrateful wretch and dropping the name of the man who had been a father to him since he was five.

Instead, Marguerite smiled with understanding and said, "A new name for a new life."

Jake's surprise at her comment must have shown on his face, because she smiled and shrugged.

"I know you didn't want to be immortal, Steph—Jake," She grimaced apologetically for the slip and Jake shrugged it away. No he hadn't wanted to be immortal. His mother had offered to turn him when he'd turned eighteen and the situation had been explained to him, but he'd refused. He was born mortal and had wanted to stay that way. But then some skinny little bitch immortal had stabbed him in the chest while pursuing a vendetta against his boss Vincent Argeneau, Marguerite's nephew. Vincent had found him dying on the office floor and had used his one turn to make Jake, who had been Stephano Jacob Colson Notte at the time. It had been the only way Vincent could save him and Jake understood why he'd done it. He even knew intellectually that he should be grateful for it. But he wasn't. Or maybe he was. He just didn't know it. Mostly he'd spent his time since then trying to ignore it and pretend it hadn't happened, that he was normal and not a freak who had to feed on blood to survive.

"I know you've been struggling with the change," Marguerite continued. "And I respect that. I haven't come here to judge you, or try to get you to see your mother, or guilt you with comments about her loving and worrying about you."

Jake's mouth twitched with amusement at the words. Just saying them was enough to inspire some guilt . . . and Marguerite knew that, but he suspected she just couldn't resist. She was a mother too, after all. But he let her get away with it and simply asked, "So how long has everyone known where I was and what I was doing?"

Jake had responded to waking up to find himself a vampire much like a wounded animal, crawling away to a corner to lick his wounds. Only his corner was Ottawa which was hell and gone from California where he'd lived at the time. And rather than lick his wounds he did his best to pretend there wasn't anything different. Other than sending his mother and brother short notes in birthday and Christmas eCards, he'd broken all contact with the family while he dealt with it. But since he wasn't really dealing with it, this had gone on for more than three years. But then, what the hell? Time was irrelevant now. He could take as long as he wanted to deal with it.

"No one else knows," Marguerite assured him, and when he arched one eyebrow dubiously, she added, "Well, aside from myself and Bastien, of course."

Jake's mouth tightened. He'd had to let Bastien know. He needed blood to survive and while he might now be a fricking vampire, he'd be damned if he was going to go around attacking and biting mortals to survive. Which meant he needed blood delivered, and Argeneau Enterprises had a blood bank that supplied blood to immortals. Jake was sure there were other suppliers with similar setups, but Argeneau was the only one he knew about, and it wasn't like vampire blood banks advertised in the damned yellow pages. So, he'd had to arrange for delivery of a steady supply. But he'd called Bastien personally, asking him to keep his whereabouts and new name a secret. It seemed he'd trusted the wrong person.

"Bastien didn't tell me," Marguerite said solemnly. "He has kept your secret as he promised."

"Then how—?"

"I'm his mother," she said simply. "I can read all my children as easily as reading a book. He can't keep secrets from me. Although he tries," she added with a grin.

Jake smiled wryly and sank back in his seat. He should have suspected as much. His own mother was the same way and had been since she'd met Roberto Conti Notte and turned when Jake was a boy. He had never been able to keep a secret from her after that, which was damned dismaying to a teenage boy full of hormones. Knowing your mother would know what you were doing was pretty inhibiting sexually.

"I've known from the beginning where you were and respected your need for privacy while you adjusted."

"Until now," he said quietly.

"Until now," Marguerite agreed solemnly. "Because now I need you."

That brought him upright in his seat, his eyebrows high. "You need me?"

"Yes." She nodded solemnly, but then sat back and peered past him.

Jake wasn't surprised to glance around to see the waitress returning with their drinks.

"Are you ready to order, or do you need a few more minutes?" the girl asked as she set down their drinks.

Jake glanced to Marguerite as she peered down to her menu. She had opened it, but hadn't really looked at it before this he didn't think. On the other hand, he hadn't even opened his, but didn't need to. He had eaten here many times. The workers were always annoyingly perky, but the food was also always great. It was why he'd suggested it as the meeting spot.

"I know what I want," Jake said now, "But Marguerite might need—"

"Ooh, the quail sounds lovely," Marguerite interrupted.

The waitress chuckled and nodded as she took her menu, and then glanced to Jake in question. "The Grilled hanger steak for you?"

Jake blinked in surprise. "I—Yes," he said slowly, a little concerned that she knew that.

"It's what you've ordered the last three times you've come here," the waitress said gently as she took his menu. "At least the last three times I've been working."

"Right," Jake said, and felt a moment's guilt that he hadn't recognized the girl. Before the turn he'd always made sure to remember details like that, making note of people who served him, showing his appreciation for good service. He'd changed since the turn though. His thoughts now were usually turned inward, and he rarely paid attention to his surroundings or even the people around him unless he was at work where that was a necessary part of the job.

Clearing his throat, he offered her an apologetic smile and nod. "Thank you . . . Melanie," he added, glancing to her name tag. He would make sure to remember her in future.

"My pleasure," she assured him, beaming again before whirling away.

"She likes you and thinks you're attractive," Marguerite said with a grin the moment the girl was out of earshot.

"Yeah, that happens a lot since the turn," he said dryly. "I'm guessing this immortal business includes some kind of chick magnet deal or something?"

"Not exactly," she said solemnly. "Although the scientists at Argeneau Enterprises have noted that we secrete higher levels of certain hormones and pheromones that might affect mortals, both male and female."

"Of course," he said bitterly. "It would make us better hunters."

Marguerite glanced down to her tea and raised it for a sip. As she swallowed and set the cup down, she said carefully, "You must have a lot of questions about how you are different now."

"No," he said gruffly, and then pointed out, "While mother and Roberto made sure I was in the dark as a child, I've known about immortals since I was eighteen. I learned a lot in the forty years before I left California. I know most things I think. I just never realized that my brother, Neil, was such a chick magnet because of what he was, not because of his natural charm and wit."

"Well, see, there's one benefit at least," she said cheerfully. "You're a chick magnet now."

Jake didn't argue the point, but simply said, "You said you need my help?"

Marguerite looked like she wanted to say more on the benefits he'd gained when he'd been turned, but she let it go with a sigh and then asked, "I understand you work as a bodyguard now?"

Jake nodded. Before being turned he'd been a vice president at V.A. Inc. in California, a company with diversified interests. Vincent Argeneau had been the president, but the man had been little more than a figurehead, leaving the actual running of the company to Jake and his brother, Neil. Jake had been the daytime vice president. Neil had taken over at night. But after the turn . . . well, Neil already had the nighttime gig, and most companies didn't need day and night V.P.s. It was only immortal owned companies that did that, catering to both mortals by day and immortals by night. But Jake hadn't wanted to deal with immortals at that point. If anything he'd wanted to get as far away from them as possible, but a similar position in a mortal company was impossible. Vampires didn't work days.

Jake had needed a new career to go with his name change, one he could do at night and one that needed minimal training. He'd always been interested in martial arts and had trained at it since he was six. The bodyguard shtick had seemed a good deal; interesting, exciting even. Boy had he got that wrong. Mostly it was standing around, eyeballing crowds for hours on end. But it was a reason to get up in the morning.

"Well, I have someone who needs guarding."

Jake was pulled from his thoughts by that announcement. He stared at Marguerite with surprise. "Surely Lucian would arrange for Rogue Hunters to protect any immortal who needs—"

"No," Marguerite interrupted. "This situation has nothing to do with immortals. She's mortal and so is the person who is a threat to her."

Jake sat back in his seat, and merely quirked an eyebrow, inviting her to explain. Marguerite was an immortal, and an old one. At least seven hundred or something, he thought, though he wasn't positive. He was pretty sure she'd been born in medieval days. As far as he knew, everyone she knew was immortal. He couldn't think what mortal she would be concerning herself with.

"Her name is Nicole Phillips. Her mother, Zaira, is the sister of my housekeeper, Maria. Maria and Zaira were always close, and their daughters grew up more like sisters than cousins. Zaira was a housewife. She kept little Pierina at home with Nicole for Maria after school and during the summer, but there were days she was sick, or had an appointment and Maria used to bring both Pierina and little Nicole to the house those days with my permission. It was never any trouble," Marguerite added as if she had to explain why she'd allowed it. "They were good girls. They'd play in the yard, or watch movies inside while Maria worked. And it was nice to hear children's laughter in the house."

Jake nodded, encouraging her to continue.

"Well, Nicole was always an amazing artist, and she did very well, growing up to be a very successful portraitist. Her work is well respected and much sought after," she assured him, and then grimaced and said, "And then a couple years back she met a charming Italian while on vacation in Europe. By all accounts, he seemed to adore her. It was all very romantic, a whirlwind affair. He was suave, promising to show her the world and proclaiming his love in the most passionate terms . . . and she was smitten. Then they married."

Jake's mouth quirked at her change of tone on those last three words. They sounded flat and grim. "I gather things changed once they were married?"

"Oh yes," she said on a sigh. "Nicole tried to hide it, but—"

"There is no hiding it from you," Jake suggested quietly.

"It wasn't me who figured it out first," she corrected. "As I mentioned, Nicole was always very close to Pierina, but she moved to Italy briefly to be with Rodolfo—"

"That's the suave Italian?"

"Yes, Rodolfo Rossi. She lived with him in Italy for a bit and then they married and moved back to Canada, but to Ottawa rather than the Toronto area where her family is . . . at his insistence," she added grimly. "He claimed he could better find a job in his field in Ottawa. But I realize now that he wanted to isolate her from her family."

Jake nodded silently. That was usually what happened with an abusive mate, lasso the woman and move her away from family and friends and any kind of support or interference they might offer.

"Fortunately, Pierina came out here to Ottawa to visit Nicole," Marguerite continued, and then told him, "She wasn't happy with what she found. At first, Pierina just thought Nicole was working herself too hard, working her way into the grave in fact. She insisted she come to Toronto for a girl's weekend to relax and I invited the two of them and their mothers for dinner. I wanted to ask Nicole about doing a portrait of Christian and Carolyn for me," she explained.

"And you read her mind and quickly realized work wasn't the problem," Jake suggested.

"I realized it wasn't the *only* problem." Marguerite corrected. "She *was* taking on too many commissions and working too hard . . . at Rodolfo's insistence. She's much sought after with clients from all over the world. She usually has to refuse a good many of them, or book them years in advance she is so busy, but Rodolfo was insisting she could do more and should accept them all. He insisted she should strike while the iron was hot, the commissions might dry up one day and she should make all the money she could before that happened. He had her working around the clock . . . and all the while he wasn't working at all."

"Nice," Jake murmured.

"Yes, well, while that was helping to sap her energy, the real problem that she was trying to hide was that he was terribly controlling and hyper critical. While he was insisting she should do all these commissions, he would then complain that she spent no time with him. He was also tearing at her self-esteem and independence and basically making her miserable. By the time she came to Toronto, he had demoralized her to the point that I don't think she could have left him on her own, so . . ." She paused and glanced down with a sigh and then admitted guiltily, "I gave her a mental nudge to make her leave him."

"Ah," Jake murmured. It was all he could say. He'd never thought much of the way immortals tended to control the minds of mortals and make them do things they might not otherwise have done. The truth was, he didn't like it. But in this instance, Marguerite's heart had been in the right place at least.

"Here we are."

Jake glanced to the side and sat back to get out of the way as their waitress arrived with their meals.

"Thank you," he murmured as she set his plate in front of him.

"You're more than welcome," she said brightly, beamed at him and then slipped away.

They were both silent for a moment as they tasted their food. As Jake had expected, his steak was amazing. But then it always was. It was the first thing he'd tried here and the last. He tended to stick with things when he liked them. Although, glancing at Marguerite's quail, he now wondered if he shouldn't try some of the other dishes here. It looked delicious too.

"It *is* delicious," she assured him, and Jake grimaced, aware that she was reading his mind. While he too was immortal now, it was a new state for him and he knew most older immortals could read him as easily as if he were mortal.

"Sorry," she muttered.

He shrugged with a wry smile. Marguerite was immortal, she could and would read the minds of mortals and the young immortals that she could. It was second nature. Swallowing the steak in his mouth, he asked, "So you prodded this Nicole and she left her Rodolfo?"

Marguerite nodded as she took a sip of her water, and then said, "It all seemed good at first. She left him and started divorce proceedings. She also started to see a counselor to try to undo the damage he'd done." Marguerite smiled. "It's working, Nicole's becoming the happy, strong young woman she was before the marriage again."

"But?" Jake prompted. If everything were going so rosy, Marguerite wouldn't need his help.

"But there have been some incidents," Marguerite said on a sigh, cutting viciously into her quail.

"Incidents?" Jake queried.

"Three gas explosions narrowly avoided."

His eyebrows rose. "You think Rodolfo's trying to kill her?"

Marguerite's mouth tightened and rather than answer outright, she said, "He's going after her money, hard. He's claiming he left his country, friends, family etc. to marry her and move to Canada and she's now abandoning him. No one's buying it," she added grimly. "He was actually let go before the marriage and suggested the move back to Canada himself. Besides, Nicole had arranged interviews for him with companies in his field here before he even landed in Canada. He refused to go, though, claiming he wanted to switch fields. But then he didn't look for work in any field, but lived off of her."

Marguerite shook her head with disgust. "Her lawyer doesn't think he'll get much at all. However, if she dies before the divorce is final . . ."

"He gets it all," Jake finished for her and she nodded solemnly. He was silent for a moment and then guessed, "And you feel guilty because you are the one who nudged her into leaving him."

She nodded again and then said firmly, "I am not sorry I did it. As I say, she's regaining her self-esteem and returning to the cheerful, strong woman she was before the marriage. She's much happier. But—"

"But she's also under threat now, which she

wouldn't have been had you not interfered," he suggested quietly and Marguerite sighed and nodded again.

Jake considered her briefly as she took a bite of her quail and then said, "I'm surprised you haven't just taken care of the husband yourself. Wiped his mind and sent him back to Europe or something."

Marguerite bit her lip and then grimaced and admitted, "That's why I'm in Ottawa. Julius thinks I came to go over photos for the portrait Nicole's doing of Christian and Carolyn, and so does she, but really I intended to take care of Rodolfo and send him back to Europe. Unfortunately, I can't locate him. Nicole moved out and left him the house at first, the understanding being that she pay the bills and he live there and act as caretaker until it sold . . . at which point they would split the proceeds. But he was apparently enjoying the free rent and making sure it wouldn't sell, so she had to buy him out of the house. Nicole has no idea where he moved to after that."

Marguerite scowled and shook her head. "I thought, no problem, I'd get Rodolfo's address from his divorce lawyer. So I got his name from Nicole and then paid him a visit, but even his divorce lawyer doesn't know Rodolfo's actual address. His contact with him is a P.O. Box and a cell phone number that is still registered to the marital house address." She scowled. "It's like he's hiding out. Nicole says when she asked him where he'd moved to, he refused to say, joking that she might send a hitman after him."

Jake's eyebrows rose. He was a firm believer

in that old saying, a skunk smells it's own hole first. In this case, Rodolfo's thinking she might try to bump him off suggested he was thinking that way himself. He probably *was* trying to inherit rather than divorce, but . . . "Why me?"

Marguerite paused with a forkful of rutabaga halfway to her mouth, and cast him an uncertain look. "I don't know what you mean."

"I mean, why me?" he repeated. "Why has Nicole not hired a company for protection? And why are you coming to me? I work for an agency, I don't run it, Marguerite."

"Oh, yes, I see."

She slid the rutabaga into her mouth and chewed, her expression thoughtful and Jake guessed she was gathering her thoughts, so turned his attention to his own meal, surprised to find that he'd eaten half of it while they'd talked. That was a damned shame. The steak was good enough it should be savored, not eaten absently and without really tasting it while you were distracted by conversation. He took a bite of steak now, savoring the delicious flavors.

"Well," Marguerite said finally, "The problem is that Nicole is in total denial and refuses to believe she's under threat."

His eyebrows rose and he swallowed before saying, "This doesn't sound like something easy to deny. You did say there were three narrowly escaped explosions."

"Yes." She set her fork down, obviously preparing for a long explanation, and said, "Nicole bought Rodolfo out of the house last month and moved back in herself. Pierina came up to help her unpack. She says they were sitting talking after the move, exhausted and achy and Pierina suggested a glass of wine and a dip in the hot tub would be nice. So, they went to open the sliding glass doors to check and be sure that the hot tub was on, but couldn't get the door open. Wood was jammed in the door that was keeping it from opening."

"Many people do that to prevent thieves breaking in," Jake commented with a shrug.

"The house is about twenty-five years old, and so are the sliding glass doors. They're a reverse set. The glass door that opens is outside the screen, and the wood was jammed in the track *outside,*" Marguerite said dryly. "A thief could have plucked it out. It was stopping the door from opening from the inside."

"Oh," he said quietly.

Marguerite nodded. "So they went around to her studio to go out that way and it was the same thing. Every sliding glass door on the main floor of the house was blocked shut from the outside."

"Interesting," Jake murmured.

Marguerite nodded. "Pierina says they just thought Rodolfo was an idiot at that point and actually laughed about it."

"But something changed their minds?" Jake guessed.

"The furnace died. No heat, and the house was going cold fast. Nicole called in a heating guy and apparently something had been removed from the furnace. Pierina explained it, but—" Marguerite shrugged. "I can't recall what it was. However, it was preventing the pilot light from relighting.

Well, remembering the doors being blocked shut, Pierina got suspicious and asked if that piece being missing could have caused a buildup of gas in the house and a possible explosion. The man assured her that, no, it couldn't . . . not *anymore*. He also added that older furnaces didn't have the automatic shutoff and it might have been a problem on one of those, but this furnace was newer and had an automatic shutoff that would have prevented it. Still, he was bewildered that someone had removed the piece. He said it had to have been physically removed. It couldn't just fall out, and, even had that been possible, the piece had been taken away. It wasn't lying there anywhere as if it had fallen out."

Jake was silent for a moment, and then said, "I don't see—"

"Someone removed that piece," Marguerite pointed out. "Why? Apparently the furnace in Rodolfo's home back in Europe was old and probably wouldn't have had that new automatic shutoff. An explosion would have been more than possible with his furnace back in Europe had the same thing happened there and Pierina suspects he thought this would act the same way . . . And the doors were blocked," she reminded him. "Nicole would have been trapped in the house had it exploded."

"Surely there are other doors in the house though," Jake said with a frown. "They aren't all sliding glass doors. Her front door for instance—"

"It's a keyed entrance. There are three proper doors on the ground floor and all three are keyed entrances. There is no way to unlock them on the outside or the inside without a key. If the house had blown up in the middle of the night and Nicole had survived that, she wouldn't have crawled out of bed with her keys in hand. She would have stumbled downstairs through the smoke, only to find she couldn't open the doors without keys and then tried the sliding doors to find those were blocked. Then she would have had to find her way back upstairs in the smoke and find her keys, and then make her way back down to use a door."

"I see," Jake murmured, and he did. In that situation, chances were the smoke would have overcome Nicole before she got out. "And the other two near misses?"

"There's an indoor gas grill in the kitchen. Nicole planned to make grilled steak for dinner on the second day of Pierina's visit, but when she turned it on, instead of the grill lighting up, flames exploded out of the base by the dials and shot right up into her face. It took her eyebrows off. Fortunately, she was quick to shut it off, and that was all that happened.

"They called in the gas guy to see what was wrong and he is the one who started asking questions. Apparently there was a layer of foil between where the flames come out and the grill on top that you lay food on. He asked why it was there. Nicole shrugged. She hadn't put it there. When she saw it, she'd thought her ex had done it to catch any drippings so he didn't have to clean the base of the grill. She hadn't thought anything of it."

"But the flames wouldn't have been able to get to the food through the foil," Jake said with a frown.

"Exactly," Marguerite said grimly. "That didn't occur to her though until he pointed it out. Apparently, Rodolfo had always put foil in the oven under the elements, and she hadn't really noticed that the foil would hamper the flames."

Jake nodded. He supposed if she'd been distracted, chatting with Pierina, that wouldn't have occurred to her.

Marguerite took a sip of tea, and then continued, "The gasman removed the foil and right away saw the problem. The gas tubing had been pulled out of its housing, the gas was coming out of the pipe itself, lit up by the pilot and shooting straight up through the dials. He said they were lucky. It could have been much worse than her losing her eyebrows. Pierina says he also then asked Nicole if there was anyone who didn't like her. Pierina told him Nicole was in the middle of a divorce. He apparently nodded slowly, and then said, this was a two minute fix, just put the tubing back where it belonged, but he thought he should check anything else gas in the house."

"And he found something else," Jake said quietly, beginning to agree that Rodolfo wanted his wife dead. He didn't know if the guy was inept, or Nicole was just lucky, but this was two "accidents" that could have been deadly.

"The gas fireplace in the master bedroom," Marguerite said on a sigh. "Pierina didn't know what the issue there was, but he took one look, muttered under his breath, and then started telling Nicole she needed to get a state of the art security system with cameras. He said people went a little crazy in divorce and she needed cameras, lots of security, maybe a couple of guard dogs too, etc., and the whole time he was taking her fireplace apart and then putting it back together so Pierina thinks there was something wrong with it."

"Nicole didn't ask what it was?" Jake asked with a frown.

Marguerite shook her head. "Pierina was the one who was suspicious, but even she was so shocked she didn't ask. Nicole was just dead silent, a troubled look on her face. Besides, Pierina said he was really lecturing the whole time. But Pierina knew he was serious was when he refused to charge Nicole for the visit after being there all day. I mean who does that?" she asked, eyebrows raised. "And she says he kept giving Nicole these worried, pitying looks, and repeating she should get security right away. He actually hugged Nicole on the way out and repeated his warning to get security cameras. Pierina said it was like he thought it would be the last time he saw her alive."

"So the fireplace was probably rigged somehow and was the third narrow escape," Jake murmured thoughtfully.

Marguerite nodded unhappily. "But Nicole laughed it off. She's sure it's all just coincidence or accidents, and the closest she'll come to admitting that Rodolfo might prefer inheriting everything to getting just a little in the divorce, is to say that if he did do any of those things, then he was terribly inept and she isn't worried."

"Major denial," Jake said dryly.

Marguerite grimaced and then sighed and said, "I supposed it's hard enough to have to admit that you made a mistake in your marriage. But it would be positively humiliating to have to acknowledge that not only was your husband not the man you thought, but he's just a gold digging bastard who cares so little he'd kill you for the money he was really after all along."

She was silent for a moment and then added sadly, "But those thoughts are there under the surface in her thoughts. That he never loved her. That's she's so worthless that her only value is money. That he is willing to kill her to get it. But she won't admit it consciously. She can't. Her self-esteem was almost completely demolished by his actions during the marriage. Admitting this now would undo all the work the counselor has done and destroy her."

"And hiring protection would be admitting all of that, which she can't do," Jake said with understanding.

"Exactly," Marguerite nodded firmly. "So, I can't hire a company and send them over there. She'd just send them away, saying she didn't need it."

Jake nodded, but asked, "So what do you expect me to do? She'll do the same with me."

"Not if you didn't tell her you were a bodyguard," she pointed out.

Jake sat back and frowned. "If her husband is trying to kill her, and I will agree that it sounds like he is—"

"I'm sure he is," Marguerite said firmly. "And now that the accidents he set up have failed, he'll have to try something else."

"Then she needs around the clock protection until the divorce is finalized. Once it's done, there should be no reason for him to continue to go after her," Jake pointed out.

"The divorce will be final in two weeks," Marguerite said at once.

"Two weeks, huh?" he muttered, but frowned and shook his head. "Still, if she won't accept a bodyguard, what do you expect me to do?"

"She won't accept a bodyguard, but she does need a cook/housekeeper and yard guy . . . well, snow guy this time of year," she added wryly, and then said, "And I told her I knew just the guy who could do all three jobs for the price of one."

Jake's jaw dropped. He took a moment to absorb that stunning news and then closed his mouth, shook his head and said, "Cook/housekeeper?"

"Your mother brags about you Steph—Jake. I know you're a very good cook."

"I'm her son. My mother is biased," he said dryly. "I can make spaghetti, that's it, and that's just frying up some hamburger, throwing in a can of sauce and boiling noodles. To her that's amazing. But it isn't a cook."

"You're smart, you can read a cookbook, you can wing it, at least enough to get by for two weeks," Marguerite said determinedly and then added, "I'd never forgive myself for interfering if Rodolfo killed her, Jake. She's a very sweet, genuinely nice person. There are few enough of those in the world. And it's only two weeks."

Jake slumped back in his seat again, knowing he'd already lost this argument. Finally, he sighed and said, "I suppose I could take a couple weeks off. They owe me about five weeks' vacation now anyway and have been nagging at me to take it."

"I'll pay you what a company would demand for your time," she said firmly and then added brightly, "It will be a working vacation. You can putter around the kitchen, try new recipes—"

"Shovel snow, clean house and watch out for murder attempts," he added dryly.

"I really appreciate this," Marguerite said solemnly, digging through her purse on the table and retrieving her checkbook.

Jake rolled his eyes and put his hand on hers to stop her. "You don't have to pay me, Marguerite," he said dryly. "I got a hell of a severance package from Vincent when I left, and that's on top of making a lot of money there for a lot of years that I invested successfully. I don't need money. I really don't even need to work anymore, but it's better than staying home and twiddling my thumbs."

"No, I insist on paying," Marguerite said firmly, slipping her hands out from under his and setting the checkbook on the table. "I already did my homework and found out how much companies charge for two weeks of around the clock protection and this is a service I appreciate."

Jake just shrugged and sat back, leaving her to it. She could write it if she wanted. It didn't mean he had to cash it. He accepted the check when she handed it over, slipped it in his pocket, and then crossed his arms and said, "All right, tell me everything you know about Nicole and Rodolfo."

HIGHLAND ROMANCE FROM
NEW YORK TIMES BESTSELLING AUTHOR

Lynsay Sands

Devil of the Highlands

978-0-06-134477-0

Cullen, Laird of Donnachaidh, must find a wife to
bear his sons to ensure the future of the clan. Evelinde
has agreed to marry him despite his reputation, for the
Devil of the Highlands inspires a heat within her
unlike anything she has ever known.

Taming the Highland Bride

978-0-06-134478-7

Alexander d'Aumesbery is desperate to convince the
beautiful and brazen Merry Stewart that he's a well-
mannered gentleman who's nothing like the members
of her roguish clan. But beneath it all beats a heart as
intense and uncontrollable as hers.

The Hellion and the Highlander

978-0-06-134479-4

When the flame-haired Lady Averill Mortagne braves
an unexpected danger at Highland warrior Kade
Stewart's side, she proves that her heart is as fiery
as her hair. And he realizes that submitting to their
scorching passion would be heaven indeed.